GLORIA

by

Ann Chamberlin

The Merlin and The Saint

High Country Publishers

Boone, North Carolina
2005

Other Books by Ann Chamberlin:

Sofia
The Sultan's Daughter
The Reign of the Favored Women
Tamar
Leaving Eden
The Merlin of St. Gilles' Well
The Merlin of the Oak Wood

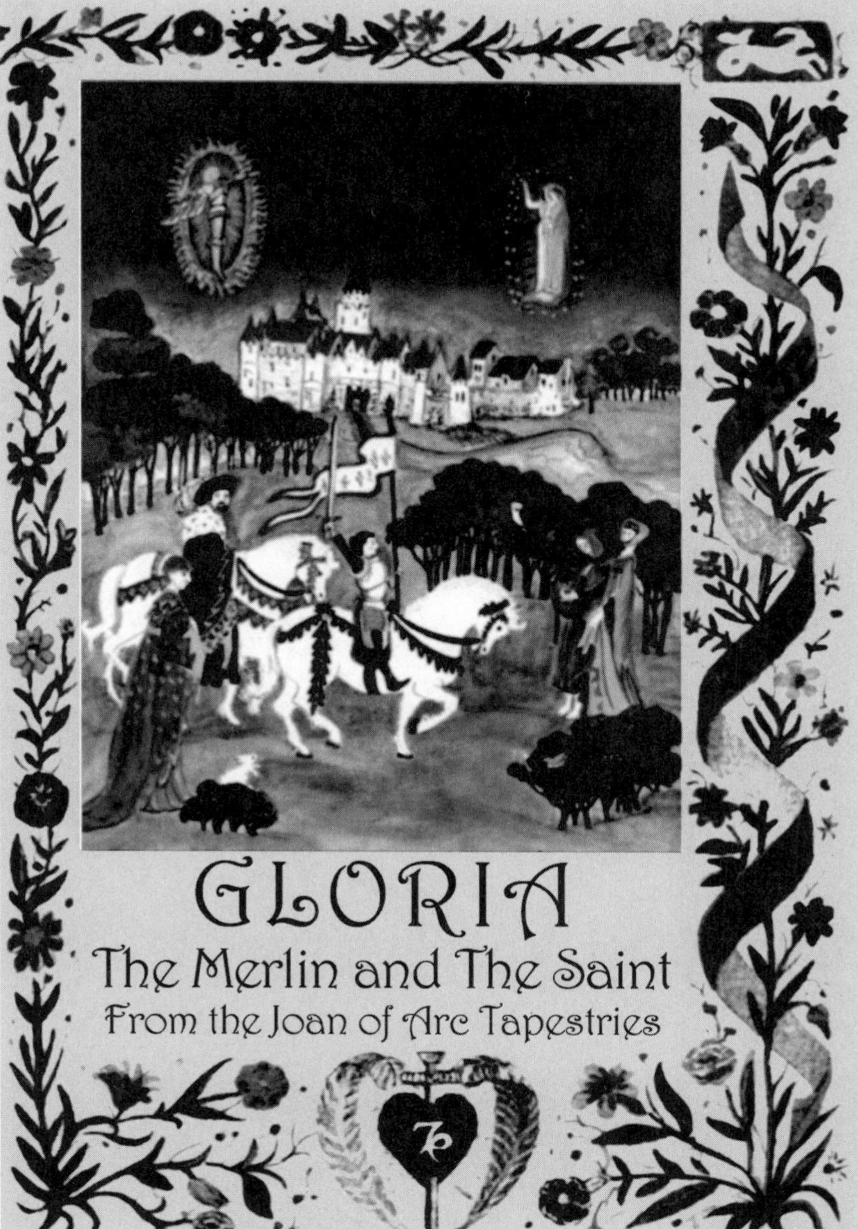
GLORIA
The Merlin and The Saint
From the Joan of Arc Tapestries

Gloria

From the Joan of Arc Tapestries

High Country Publishers
Ingalls Publishing Group, Inc.
197 New Market Center, #135
Boone, North Carolina 28607
http://www.highcountrypublishers.com
editor@highcountrypublishers.com

Cover Painting by Henry Scheffer (1798-1862)
The Entry of Joan of Arc (1412-31) into Orleans, 8th May 1429, 1843
Cover design by James Geary
Interior illumination from a design by Caroline Garrett
Text design by schuyler kaufman.

Library of Congress Cataloging-in-Publication Data

Chamberlin, Ann.
Gloria / by Ann Chamberlin.
p. cm. — (The Joan of Arc tapestries ; bk. 4)
ISBN 1-932158-61-8 (hardcover : alk. paper) — ISBN 1-932158-62-6 (trade pbk. : alk. paper)
1. Joan, of Arc, Saint, 1412-1431—Fiction. 2. France—History—Charles VII, 1422-1461—Fiction. 3. Christian women saints—Fiction. I. Title. II. Series.
PS3553.H2499G58 2004
813'.54—dc22

2004027428

First edition, October 2005

Acknowledgments

Credit goes first, with this volume of The Joan of Arc Tapestries, to Judy Geary, my editor of High Country Publishers, who caught up the fallen banner with a cry of "Excelsior." Her long suffering, her patience, and most important, her constant faith, kept me going through some hard times. Linn Prentis and the others at the Virginia Kidd Agency deserve credit for taking up the other, more practical end, to keep me balanced.

Two critique groups read snatches of this and gave their unflinching opinions: The Wasatch Mountain Fiction Writers and Xenobia. Linda Cook, Jeri Smith and Karen Porcher were all true friends with constant support to shore up the confidence afterward.

The Marriott, Whitmore and Holladay librarians never stinted in their assistance.

And of course, there's my family. My sons in particular were company on my research trips, drew maps and bounced ideas. My husband is (sometimes) patient while my mind is elsewhere. My parents introduced me early to France and her people and my in-laws make it all possible.

En fin, c'est avec plaisir que je remercie en français tous ceux qui m'ont aidée avec cette œuvre en cette langue. Mlle Rachel Hamstead, institutrice de ma jeunesse, m'a introduit au peuple français avec un amour bien sérieux. À Domrémy-la-Pucelle, je m'en souviens de la propriétaire d'Hôtel de la Pucelle; à Orléans, le personnel de la maison de Jeanne d'Arc; à Blois, M. Eric Gault; et partout, Mme Josette Melac et ses filles, Sylvie et Annie. Finalement, je remercie Mme Caroline Donnelly.

None of these supportive people is responsible for the mistakes I've made in these pages; they only kept me from making more.

This is for Judy

Gloria

Bayeux
Brittany
Orleans
Meung
Beaugency
Blois
Loire
Tours
Sauver
Chinon
Poitiers
English-controlled lands
Burgundian lands

France in the Time of La Pucelle

Rheims

Paris

Vaucouleurs

Domrémy

Auxerre

First Antiphon

A Cool Corner in a Room with a Hot Fire

First week of March, 1428.
Lent. Chinon, France

"So, Gilles, how are you?" As I spoke, I caught the hand my milk brother offered me in my good left one. His calluses, hardened by sword play, gripped me with uncommon strength.

At twenty-four, Gilles, the lord of Rais, of Thouars, Blaison and a score of castles in between, was in his prime. His was a beautiful prime, even I had to admit it. Today, in the weak sunshine angling into the narrow street at late afternoon, he was more darkly handsome than he'd ever been, ever since my mother first suckled him. And he had been the sort of child wet nurses loved to fondle and mothers loved to dress in the finest raiment.

Now that he ordered his own clothes, he wore a tight doublet of black, cut velvet pricked with threads of gold cinched by a knight's thick belt. Over this, he carelessly flung back a knee-length cape to reveal the rich sable lining and the magnificent lines of his body. His beauty was that of a cool corner in a room where the fire has grown too hot.

By the flight of a pigeon, a trick of the Craft, I had told Gilles de Rais to meet me here in the city of Chinon this last month of 1428 as the Christians tell time. I was pleased he had been willing to tear himself away from his battlefields to do so. That he met me here in the street by the Saumur Gate, jostled by common folk, instead of waiting for me at the castle, sitting comfortably by the fire that was his due from the Dauphin Charles—that was more than pleasing. It was astonishing.

As a pair of goodwives jostled us for space in the narrow way, Gilles' scrutiny of me was more cursory than mine of him. "An Augustinian now, are you, Yann?" he asked in a dismissive tone, as if men changed their vocations every day. He clearly had other things on his mind.

"Yes, the canon Jean Pasquerel from the monastery in Bayeux, at your service, my lord de Rais."

"Bayeux? Isn't that out of reach, so deep in English-held Normandy?" He wasn't thinking of what he was saying, trying to keep the long points of his shoes out of a pile of donkey droppings.

"Precisely. I hope it is so out of reach that no one here in France will be able to check on my story. The good brethren in Bayeux have no more heard of Père Jean Pasquerel than you had until this moment. I tell people I've been on pilgrimage, visiting the black image of Our Lady in Le-Puy-en-Velay, and got trapped here by the war."

Gilles grunted, but I could hardly take that as a sure confirmation that he thought my disguise would work. Probably merely the effort of getting out of the way of a miller's two-wheeled cart.

We were making some sort of headway, where to I hadn't yet stopped to think. I found myself rattling on, cart-like, of things I hoped he already understood, just to keep his mind centered on me, on the business at hand, if I could. All the while, I counted on the hubbub of the crowds streaming past us, the noise of workshops and the crying of wares, to cover my words from all but his ears. Distracted as he was, did even he hear?

"My garb as a priest of the old religion is more akin to the Dominicans', of course. Those Hounds of God stole our tonsure and our black robes over white in order to fool the unsuspecting into confessing their 'heresy' to the Inquisition. As our old tutor Père Michel used to say, 'I feel no guilt to steal back what was ours to begin with.'

"In the days to come, there may be enemies suspicious enough to look for witchcraft under the habit of Dominique. In my case, they would, of course, find it, and that wouldn't help La Pucelle's cause at all. So—a short-sleeved Augustinian rochet of sheer lawn over all. I feel no guilt in this case, either. And, as you see, my feet are still bare—"

I wagged a toe at Gilles from under my hem, muddied by the roads at this wet and chilly season of the year. It was about to get sloshed by a maid's bucket of dishwater.

Gilles had always taken this as the greatest outward sign of a magician's power, the constant contact with Mother Earth, bare feet always listening; listening to Her whispered will. In early days, when even I didn't accept my calling as heir to Merlin, Gilles had insisted I go without shoes so I, too, would come to know. Now, however, he didn't notice. His mind was definitely elsewhere. Having stopped to wave my toes and avoid the streaming cobbles had made me fall behind him, and I had to scramble to catch up.

Foolishly, I had hoped for a bit of solitude on entering the town. My feet needed time to adjust to the din, the clatter of hooves and cartwheels, the way slick cobblestone swelled such sounds while at the same time muffling Our Lady's voice. My Sight required time to sense whether La Pucelle was here yet, and what my first move towards her should be. Even in the press of people, if I'd been given time alone, I could have accomplished it.

Not, however, when Gilles caught me by the elbow to steer me through the crowds with a direction of his own.

"Oh, God, Yann," he gasped, unable to contain himself any longer.

Any town where the Dauphin was in residence must have its crowds. But he was oblivious to them. For a moment, I thought he was about to take after me and go into a fit. His dark eyes rolled in something like ecstacy.

"I'm in love," he said.

I was obviously not going to be given quiet. Very well. I must hear him out. It was safer than to discuss magic in such a place. Besides, I knew my milk brother and his loves. We'd make no progress until I did.

The brick-and-timber houses of Chinon sprouted turrets above their slate roofs, blue-black like the upside-down pitch of beard on Gilles' chin. But every time I paused to stare up at them, I got jostled. I would have to give up sensing, even sightseeing, and concentrate on that chin of my milk brother instead, riding at just about my eye level.

"In love?" I teased. "So what else is new?"

"No," he insisted. "This time really, truly in love."

How ironic it was that my milk brother who, one would think, had everything in his favor—nobility, wealth, youth, looks—should, in fact, be so needful. He, before whom the world scraped and bowed, whom even the Dauphin owed money, desperately sought something he himself could serve—and love.

I said, "Another boy?"

"Wait 'til you see him, Yann. You will swoon with delight."

I very much doubted that, but I also doubted it would do any good to tell Gilles so.

"I didn't call you here so you could fall in love," I said.

"Oh, yes, what was it you wrote?" Gilles sighed with elaborate boredom. "Something about signs in the skies on the middle Sunday of Lent being 'the cosmic meeting of east and west, war and peace, peasant and king, heaven and earth' we've all been waiting for."

"That's right."

Repeated back to me like that, my words did seem overly dramatic. Who could believe half of it? That this was the season in which, finally, after centuries, the girl foretold would arrive to save the land from a hundred years of war, La Pucelle of Merlin's vision? Even as Merlin's heir, I hardly believed them myself, my own words ringing with prophecy, after the spell of prophecy had faded from me. But at least we were on the right subject again.

Gilles smiled. "You needed hell thrown in besides, didn't you, brother? That's why you invited me."

"I got a message from Père Michel since I wrote to you. Michel? You remember him?"

"Père Michel de Fontenay. How could I forget our dear tutor? How is the old wizard?"

"Père Michel agrees with my interpretation of the signs."

"You always were better at that sort of thing than I was."

Gilles gave a great shove with his powerful shoulder through a throng of apprentices in his haste to get where we were going. Where *he* was going. I was just tagging along.

Then he grinned back at me. "Master's pet."

"Not only that, Père Michel told me that he'd just seen someone off to Chinon. You'll never guess who—"

Gilles didn't guess. Instead, he dragged me sharply left. "Just let me show you this," he said.

Important as it was, I lost my train of thought. "Where are you taking me?"

"This way. There's something you've got to see."

"What is this place?"

"The Golden Stag Inn."

"I've never heard of it."

"There's one in every town."

I knew this evocation of the deity of the woodlands over an establishment's door was often a declaration of the religion of the owner—or at least of the original owner. But I doubted very much that worship of the Stag was Gilles' purpose this day.

"Gilles," I told him, "I will not join you on a soaker ... "

"Keeping a good Christian Lent, are you?"

"The Old Ways, too, recommend a time of reflection and purification at this season."

"Nobody said anything about getting soaked but you. Although it would be quite delightful if I could coax this gorgeous boy into something ... Well, this is where I first saw him—Dear God, tell me I haven't lost him—he hasn't gone ... ?"

As my eyes adjusted to the Golden Stag's dark interior, I was able to see Gilles beside me, standing tiptoe in his thigh-high riding boots, searching the crowded, noise- and smoke-filled room. In spite of myself, I felt my attention drawn along with his to the shadowy rear of the place. As if there were a light there, when there clearly wasn't.

I saw how the back of this main hall, pushed up against the castle mountain by the River Vienne, was let into live rock, as many houses in Chinon were. Within the limestone at the back, no doubt, the host had his wine cave. Yes, it was the prophesied Sunday in Lent, but you'd never know it at the Golden Stag. Not when court was in town.

So this was the sort of place Gilles came on his prowls, a forest to the panther. Where he blew his fragrant breath, mesmerizing his prey.

"There."

Gilles suddenly lost the indignity of tiptoes and dropped his head close to my ear. His voice dropped, too, though it hardly seemed possible that the lord of Rais should care who overheard him. The room was far too noisy in any case. Like a panther, I thought, he simply didn't want to frighten off his prey with any noise.

But could it be—? I looked quickly from trying to see over heads to where he pointed and back into his own face. Yes, it just might be. My milk brother, whom I'd thought nothing could impress, had lowered his voice—in awe.

So again I looked where he'd gestured, where now his gaze lingered, as unswerving as any pointing finger—or flying arrow.

There was, indeed, something different about that corner of the room. A calm in the midst of general rowdiness. What was it? I couldn't tell. I hadn't been allowed the quiet to sense aright, but if I hadn't known better, I would have felt myself on the very rim of a visionary spell.

Six or seven men sat huddled—earnestly, soberly—around a table. They had the remains of a spartan meal before them and a jug of wine, but the drinking was for thirst and health, no more.

I focused my skills of attention on what they might be saying to one another, as a Master can do and hear words, sometimes even thoughts, over the rudest brawl.

"But what are we to do?" one of the men was saying. "The Dauphin simply must see us soon. The duke's four francs are gone and old Metz here, though we all know he'll gladly give the shirt off his back to further the cause—"

There were some light chuckles at this, and one of the men—not "old", but the youngest, it seemed—fingered his shirt as if judging its worth.

"—The fact of the matter remains," the speaker went on, "even his money will run out in the next day or two; and then how will we manage?"

About all I gleaned out of this was that they were in financial difficulty—who wasn't, these days? But that might make them easy prey for a great lord like my milk brother, flaunting himself now—for love's benefit, no doubt—in his doublet and cape.

And that they called one of their number "Metz". For his town of origin, no doubt. Metz, far to the east, in Lorraine. Was this man the one Gilles eyed so keenly? I couldn't tell.

"Can't you see him?" Gilles hissed in my ear like someone whispering in church, fully aware that he should not.

So which of the men was it? The great, red-faced one who had spoken, who took up half the bench facing me? Surely not. There was the young one, the one called Metz, not unpleasing but nothing remarkable. A pair of servants, knowing their place and huddled at the end. Never. A man with his back to me, a back broad with an archer's muscles but still, nothing to turn Gilles' head, I thought.

The last figure at the table—well, yes, here was the smallest of them, surely the most likely to find my milk brother calling him "boy". But this young man was nothing like the usual angelic, blond-haired, blue-eyed creatures Gilles couldn't keep mind—or hands—off. Who had always disappointed or betrayed him.

The figure was thin, yet somehow solid, built like a peasant's ill-fed yet necessarily strong ox. Small, dark eyes pierced the room before them, a mole marred the lower lip. No angel. He kept dragging his fingers through the worst-cut head of black hair I'd ever seen short of the mange. How could my fastidious Gilles possibly—?

And yet: "Isn't he *wonderful*?" Gilles whispered. There was nothing short of worship in his voice.

"Come with me, Yann," Gilles was pleading, tugging at my elbow. "Come with me while I go and introduce myself. I'm so in love, I'm afraid I'll make a total ass of myself if you're not along."

Gilles? Shy? I couldn't fathom it.

We were close enough still to the room's entrance that I could hear the bells of St. Maurice then, sounding the end of mass, that Lenten mass called in the Latin *Laetare*, if I remembered correctly: "Rejoice".

"Rejoice. Arise. Shine. For thy Light is come."

Then, at last, the light behind those common features struck me, too. I knew. I refused to budge to the tug of his arm.

"That's no boy." When finally I could speak, I was not at all surprised to find myself forced to whisper, too, my heart panting with awe. "It's *she*."

"What the hell do you mean, 'she'?"

The word was a prayer, pulled from the very white-hot core of my Vision.

"La Pucelle," I said.

Chapter One

Night Hunting

Dark came early this Lenten time of year. Gilles, lord of Rais, pacing back and forth along the quay of the Vienne, could hear the quiet slip of the water. He couldn't see it, even with the help of the torch boy, shivering and stumbling at his erratic heels.

A girl. Yann assured him this boy, his new love, was—a girl.

It hardly seemed possible. He, Gilles de Rais, should feel this way about a girl? Even one dressed in a doublet and hose?

Gilles was married, of course. Any nobleman must be. He had doubled his lands by his marriage. He'd had, for a month or two, hopes of getting an heir. But when his attempt to do so without coming near the lady failed, he'd given up on that project. Personally, at twenty-four, he intended to live a good long while. And there was always his younger if lack-luster brother, René.

For all other purposes, Gilles had been happy enough, if a little bored, with Roger de Bricqueville, his companion-at-arms—and at other things. Gilles hadn't even seen his wife, Catherine de Thouars, for over seven years. And now he'd left Roger holding the line for him on the English front. For what?

For this—this divine creature.

Yann said the creature—yes, he, too, used the word "divine"—was a girl. The Girl, in fact, La Pucelle, the one for whom generations of witches, ever since Merlin, had waited.

Well, maybe Yann was wrong.

Gilles didn't hold much by prophecy. If he wanted something to happen, he was too used to making it so by his own efforts. He'd order his lackeys to it, he'd buy it with his limitless wealth, he'd fight for it.

Not that Yann didn't have power. Gilles knew that well, ever since they were boys together. But Yann's power, unnerving even to those familiar with him, was different from Gilles'.

Then again, Gilles at least had to consider that his milk brother, against all appearances, might be right. If so, seeing the girl up close might do away with these unnatural feelings altogether.

And yet again, if seeing her closer than across a crowded, smoke-filled inn did not turn this feeling into nausea instead, if then ... Well, that would be a miracle, wouldn't it? Gilles de Rais in love with a woman. A thousand everyday, run-of-the-mill prophets could never have foreseen such a thing.

Ushering him quickly from the inn, Yann had not allowed Gilles to approach the object of this strange attraction. In fact, he had made Gilles promise not to try to meet with the girl any closer until after she could be introduced at court.

"She must be allowed to prove herself from the beginning to the many who will doubt," the hermit-priest had said cryptically. "You must make things well on the royal side for her entry, Gilles, with your cousin the high chamberlain and the rest. I will see to things here among the common folk."

Gilles had given Yann his word. And because, half crazy as he was, there was just that much chance Yann knew what he was doing, Gilles had so far kept it. This, even when keeping his word was not something the great Lord of Rais did on a regular basis, certainly not when it suited him as ill as staying away from this girl-boy did tonight.

He felt himself drawn, chin first, through the darkening streets, like a moth to flame.

And yet, something about the whole business did unnerve even the brave lord of Rais just enough that he didn't resent having given Yann his word. Much as this attraction had struck him instantly in the way he'd always given the name "love" before, something was different about it this time.

Was it because this was in fact a girl? Was this tumble of heart and whirl of brain what every other man felt when he said the word "love", something Gilles de Rais in spite of all riches and power, had been missing?

Somehow he didn't think so. This—this was akin to—could he think it without laughing out loud? Why not?—to religion. The awe of a silent chapel, the shudder of an angelus bell over misty hills, the physical creep of reverence over his skin. Nay, it was more. It was the meeting of his warm breath with the night's cold air, creating ghostlike wraiths in the golden torchlight. The reel of stars, light with dark, in sharp clarity overhead. The purl of water on stone in the heart of the forest, the source of all life.

Even the place in his heart reserved for his uncle Amaury, dead long ago on Agincourt's field, even that was being invaded, like some old shrine by tendrils of living vine. And after only two brief glimpses.

God was afoot in this. Whether the Christian's God or the Stag King of the forest, the lord of Rais couldn't tell. What Christians called the Devil, Yann's God, was more awe-full in Gilles' experience if only because He was less easily bought and sold. But God was here, and Gilles, the great lord of Rais, was a mere feather on divine breath.

Gilles had given his word. He meant to keep it. And yet—and yet, here he was, wafting down by the Vienne, among common houses. He might have been up in the castle with other lords and their ladies, taking such courtly amusement as the bitter Lenten season and a nervously pious prince allowed. Here, where the stench of kitchen slops and wood smoke poured out of hovel doors along with the sounds of domestic squabbles and fussy brats.

And for this he'd worn his best black velvet, had the beard trimmed and combed neatly over the permanent streaks of blue on his chin, like the kick of a stag, the mark of the God. He'd debated long over whether or not to wear the red garter. He knew how well it looked, rich crimson against the black. But he also knew it frightened people, those who understood it as an emblem of one who'd sold his soul to the devil—or given it freely, rather, to the God in the womb of Mother Earth.

Usually he didn't care who knew or guessed at his allegiance. He was too powerful to care for either prince or prelate. And a twinge of terror in the onlooker was a conscious part of his costume, his cultivated attractions.

But perhaps it wasn't what he wanted—not with this new love.

He wasn't going to meet him—her—remember? And yet, if he should ... In the end, he'd worn the crimson band of silk. If she were who Yann said she was, this would be all the greater attraction. If she were what the itching of the mark of the God on his chin told Gilles de Rais.

All the preening was for naught, of course. He'd promised to avoid her. Just for a day or two, until he'd seen her introduced at court.

He would keep his promise.

He pivoted and gestured for his page to turn, too, to go ahead with the light. Before the boy got there, an open door of a fisherman's hovel against the surrounding dark blinded Gilles for an instant. A child stood framed in the golden rectangle, a little boy of six or seven, angelic with a halo of curly blond hair. The boy carried an animal, a long, wriggling ferret, in his arms. Probably going rat-hunting, to earn a sou or two for the family.

Wild instincts, those of a beast, a hunter, washed over Gilles de Rais in waves of blood heat. Was it the animal? Or the boy? He tried desperately to think if he had any rats that needed catching. Hirelings usually saw to such things for him. For one brief moment, however, Gilles de Rais felt himself overwhelmed.

Then he remembered La Pucelle.

Quickly his eyes adjusted. Deep gulps of air cleared his head. He saw the grime on the loose hempen smock, on the pallid face in the greasy, odiferous light in the doorway. He lost his appetite.

For one more moment, Gilles stood still, remembering the angelic image, thinking of La Pucelle. And the struggle between the two left him breathless.

Chapter Two

Blue in the Gold of Torchlight

The only thing that broke Gilles' gaze into the fisherman's hovel was a new sight. He saw him. Not the girl-boy, but one of the men from her party. Thinking she must be with him, and remembering his promise to Yann, Gilles turned and began to move in the other direction, feeling something close to panic. He nearly tripped over the tag-along page and his curling flame.

Within two steps, Gilles' ears caught up with his brain. He realized there was only one pair of footsteps behind him. The man was alone, probably out—as Gilles could always say he was himself—for a walk along the quay. Out for some of this sharp night air, a relief after the close, crowded inn.

So Gilles turned back again. He bowed slightly. "God give you good evening, monsieur."

The greeting from a stranger in a strange town took the fellow a moment to digest. Gilles rested his left hand casually on the sword at his hip, making sure it caught the torchlight. The fellow paused another moment. Gilles saw the sheen of his own silk and gold glint in the fellow's eyes, saw him make appraisal.

And he saw something more, a look of hope, as if the fellow imagined that he, Gilles de Rais, could be the answer to some private drama. Gilles disliked any suggestions, infrequent though they were, that the story of the world did not have himself as its hero. People who knew the sire de Rais knew better than to ask favors. This fellow did not know him, and Gilles' guard went up.

Meanwhile, he made his own appraisal—something he hadn't been able to do in the presence of the girl in the inn. A certain elegance to the cut and fabric, which heavy use could not conceal, told him the man was noble, after all. Lesser nobility, of course. Every other sort was. But noble nonetheless.

Still, what right has *he* to that girl, the greatest of prizes? Gilles felt a flush of anger rise with the thought. The hand on his hilt flexed spontaneously.

The fellow came to his senses then, bared a head of brown curls to the dark and chill. "The same to you, monseigneur."

The title of deference did not make Gilles relax. Quite the contrary. The fellow was more convinced than ever he could get something out of this new acquaintance—that God, indeed, had thrown the lord of Rais in his path.

"Allow me to introduce myself," Gilles said. A lofty tone might give the fellow pause. "I am Gilles, sire de Laval, baron de Rais."

"Indeed, monseigneur, I have heard of you." If the fellow had a second hat, he would have removed that. Instead, he bowed a second time, even more deeply, hope making his face fairly glow. "You are a close confidant to His Majesty Charles, the Dauphin."

Keep the fellow under scrutiny, Gilles told himself. That would put off the inevitable. And lead most quickly to the girl. "Not from around here, by your speech."

Gilles wondered if the girl had that same tightness to her vowels, heaviness to her consonants, that habit of adding *i* to the ends of her words. He supposed he'd like it on her tongue.

"Indeed, monseigneur is very astute. Forgive my slowness to return the introduction. I am from Metz, though my family estate is at Nouillonpont."

A second son, no doubt.

"I am called Jean, your servant, monseigneur," he concluded.

"From beyond France. From Lorraine." That part was right, then. Lorraine was in the prophecy. That was where the girl should arise.

"Monseigneur is correct. I wonder if I might—"

Gilles spoke quickly, stopping that direction of discussion. "And not long at Chinon, I think."

"Again monseigneur is correct. We arrived two days ago."

"How do you find it?"

"Very—very expensive, monseigneur. And we have been wondering—"

Gilles laughed. Was it this easy? Reaching two fingers into his purse, he tossed the fellow a coin. "See if this doesn't help you out," he said.

In his surprise, Metz missed. There was the unmistakable ring of gold on the cobbles. Metz retrieved the coin and, holding it to the light, stared in wonder.

"I cannot take this, monseigneur. Not so much."

"Of course you can. You bent for it. It's yours."

"But—but why? I've done nothing for you."

I toss money like that at Charles, Gilles thought. The Dauphin himself is just as desperate. It's not for you, fool.

But Gilles heard more than wonder in the fellow's voice. Suspicion. That wouldn't do.

"You can tell me of the way you came, the lands you passed through. That's worth something to me."

Metz continued to study him warily.

"I am a commander of men, don't you know?" Gilles added.

"Yes, yes, even in Lorraine, we've heard of the baron de Rais' exploits against the English."

"Well, I'm glad of that. The information you can give may help in our struggle." And I may finally get to the girl, he thought.

The fellow's continued hesitation pleased Gilles to some degree. Good to have such a man—cautious of spies, of spilling vital information—close to the girl. On the other hand, such caution, turned against *him*, stretched Gilles' patience.

Fortunately, Metz decided to talk before that taut wire snapped. He gave up looking from coin to donor, coin to donor, as if weighing one against the other, and said, "Eleven days. For eleven days, we were alone in enemy territory. Just the seven of us. With God and His holy saints."

"Eleven days?" Gilles repeated.

It was astounding. Yes, let the fellow thank heaven. It was miraculous. Gilles would not have dared such a thing himself, even with Roger and five more handpicked men. Of course, blazoned and on fine steeds, they would be very easy targets, even for the least watchful of *goddams*.

"We traveled mostly at night," Metz went on, "camping away from settlements, in secluded places mostly by day. Most of the time we didn't dare have a fire, for fear of the enemy."

Gilles nodded at the wisdom of this. Still he couldn't help but wonder, "No fire? In Lent? And such a wet, cold Lent as we've been having?"

Yann had to be wrong. No girl could endure such a journey. Few men could. And yet, Metz shrugged and the torchlight caught something of a grin playing at the corners of his mouth. Certainly there had to have been something more than your usual *chevauchée* about this journey.

Gilles wanted to challenge the fellow, to ask outright just what that grin was all about. You weren't even saddle sore? he wanted to say. *She* was not? Impossible.

That was what he really wanted to ask. And about the girl. But as the words formed on his lips, Metz began to say something, too, so Gilles let him speak. It was always better to let the lesser man risk himself, offer the most clues to his position, before jeopardizing one's own dignity.

"I have to say, with all of our precautions, the trip was so uneventful that at one point, we made our own trouble. Two of the others and I wandered off and then circled back. But we circled back through the bare woods and blasted bracken, pretending to be *goddams* on the attack. Ho, you should have seen the others take to their heels and run. All but—"

He almost said "she". Gilles was certain he almost said "she".

"All but one of our number," he said instead, "who stood firm and shouted, 'Stay. Our mission cannot fail. We will beat them all, if only you'll stand.'"

Metz laughed aloud, remembering. "By St. Michel—by my martinet, I mean."

Gilles wondered at such a strong oath. Was it the girl?

He let Metz finish his thought: "We'd have run them all the way to Chinon. If it hadn't been for—for that."

The man could have been naturally pious, of course. War did that to some. Still, most went the other way, having seen too much that made one doubt any greater Power gave a damn. Gilles couldn't escape the impression that in this fellow, the average man-at-arms' nature had gone through some major transformation.

"What of Auxerre?" Gilles tried on him.

Among a dozen other honors, the Dauphin had named Gilles' cousin, Georges de La Trémoïlle, governor of Auxerre. Of course, the title, like many others handed out these days, meant nothing. Charles raised money and faithfulness on the fiefs, though what sort of faith it could be, Gilles was skeptical. As long as the English and their Burgundian allies held these lands and raised their defending armies on the proceeds, it was like handing out lukewarm air. Still, he could always say there was personal interest here.

"Auxerre?" Metz repeated.

"The great Burgundian garrison there? How far did you have to go out of the direct route to go around Auxerre? It can't have been too far, to still have made such good time."

"Indeed, we didn't skirt Auxerre at all. We went right in."

"You went—?"

"We did. In, past the Burgundians on the great stone walls. You see—"

Gilles thought Metz began to say "she" again. Of course, that was the word for which the lord of Rais was listening.

"We—" Metz said instead, with just enough emphasis that Gilles could tell this was not the first word on his tongue. "We wanted to go to mass. We hadn't dared all the previous days, but then—well, it is Lent, after all and—"

Almost said "she" again, Gilles thought.

"*We* thought, with God's help, we'd come to no harm. And we didn't."

"A miracle," Gilles suggested.

"Yes," Metz agreed. "We strode in right under their noses, heard mass to our heart's content, then strode right out again."

"But what of the girl?" It burst from Gilles' lungs before he could stop himself.

Metz' eyes narrowed. The frankness that had engaged Gilles pulled back, like the men-at-arms of a sortie party retaking defensive positions behind castle walls.

Gilles waved the torch higher. It shook in the boy's shivering hand, but by its dancing yellow, he saw Metz clearer. He was young, nervous—not at all unhandsome. And very, very male, something women might find interesting and he, Gilles, not at all. The tremor of light seemed to enter Gilles and attack his knees.

The fellow was in love with her himself. He'd had her all these eleven days and God knew how long before.

Seeing the enemy pull back and take a stand, Gilles pressed the attack with a warrior's instinct.

"You came all this way with a girl. Everyone knows you came with a girl. You've been hammering for an audience for days—for this girl."

Metz gulped. Gilles watched the bob of the knot in his neck with a butcher's interest.

"That's so, monseigneur," Metz admitted when his voice recovered from that gulp.

"But they call her The Maid."

"That's so, monseigneur." Metz swallowed again and seemed to make a decision. "She is a sainted virgin. She is La Pucelle."

Gilles pretended the name did not send chills down his back. "How can she be, having crossed eleven days of *goddam* territory?"

"It's as I told you, monseigneur. We passed without harm."

"Into Auxerre for a pleasant mass and then out again? You expect me to believe that? My lord of Bedford's men are not known for leaving many virgins in their wake."

"How we passed, I can hardly tell you more than I have. Except to repeat it must be a miracle, the hand of God on us."

"I am not thinking so much of *goddams*, either."

"Burgundians, sir?"

"I'm thinking of you. And the rest of your party. You expect me to believe you all kept your cocks in your braies with this maiden, lying there in the open between you?"

Metz shifted his dark, worn boots nervously on the frost-slick cobbles of the quay beneath their feet. "It is a wonder, I agree, monseigneur."

"Speak to me no more of wonders." Gilles dropped his voice, like a cat on the kill.

But far from quailing, Metz seemed to get a spur of inner strength. "My lord de Rais, you could get us to the Dauphin, more than any man we've met. She must see the Dauphin."

Gilles ignored him. "This girl is young, not poxed or in any way unattractive."

"She is."

"And you seek to cloy me with child's tales of miracles and saints?"

"You have to believe me, monseigneur, since first I laid eyes on her, I've never felt that way towards her for a moment."

"What sort of man are you, Jean de Metz? A eunuch?"

"I ... I am like any other, sir, full of lust and vice, may God amend me."

"You confess then?"

"But if you knew her, sir, if you'd see her for yourself, you'd understand. All the court would understand."

I have seen her, fool, Gilles wanted to say. But a sudden thought began in the back of his mind that made him dumb as it crept forward.

"With the other men, it's the same." Metz spilled words into the void he left him. "Ask them, my lord. We don't feel towards her as ... as men feel towards other women. All I can think is, it's something about her. It's the hand of God, a miracle again, like our whole passage to Chinon."

Gilles had always known himself to be different from other men in his appetites. Was this yet one more proof? It must be so. He closed his lips firmly on the thought.

A further moment of such silence between them gave Metz the courage to go on. "You know, monseigneur, this afternoon when we went up to the castle to try to see His Majesty again, one of the guards said lewd things to her. He hadn't really come close to her yet, so he—"

"What things?" Gilles managed, just to keep a presence in the conversation. His mind raced over these discoveries. Should he keep his attraction a secret, then? It could well prove more dangerous than all his buggery with Roger de Bricqueville.

But could he keep his attraction—strong as it was overwhelming—a secret? For how long?

"Oh, you know, monseigneur, the things soldiers like to say. She announced herself, 'I am Jehanne the Maid come with good news and relief for my Dauphin.'

"'The Maid, did she say?' the fellow asks. 'The Maid, ho ho. Well, she's come to the right place. Leave her half an hour with me, and I'll see that she goes away in a different state. I'll send her off well satisfied.'"

"And what did she say to that?" To his horror, Gilles heard his own voice crack, like an untried youth's.

"'I wouldn't speak that way, fellow, if I were you,' she said. 'Not with death so near your door.'"

"Did she indeed?" Gilles smiled in spite of himself. Unfortunately, such spunk did not mar the maid's attraction in Metz' eyes. Quite the opposite. "He didn't try anything, did he?"

"No, monseigneur. I think she did take him aback a little. He still didn't let us in, but he didn't say anything more. Rest assured, we wouldn't have let him touch her."

You six against the Dauphin's guard? Gilles wanted to laugh.

Metz must have seen some of the foolhardiness, too, after the fact. But, "We went eleven days through *goddam* territory," he said. "I don't doubt God would have helped us here as well."

A sudden splashing and gurgling and screaming countered his words. Gilles turned to the sound, upstream near the bridge, unseen in the dark save for a line of torches. Metz turned, too, then glanced at Gilles with a deep look, something akin to horror at their shared mortality. Gilles found himself trying to return the gaze, but he couldn't be certain if he succeeded. Few folk thought they shared humanity with Gilles de Rais.

The crying and splashing continued, growing more desperate. Metz turned and ran in that direction. With only slightly less good will, Gilles gestured to his page and followed.

"It's a man, fallen into the river." Metz had stripped off his boots and cloak in the chill air and was working on his doublet.

Others answered the cries. Soon a few, then more, organized a chain, following Metz down the bank of dead reed and bare willow into the dark water, flowing sluggishly close to ice.

Gilles himself was caught up in the frenzy and took his own boots off. The mud stood rigid with cold beneath his feet. The water bit like sharp hunger, as high as he let it, up to his knees. The flesh went numb, then stupid, as if gnawed clean away to the bone. Gilles snatched the torch from his page's hands and raised it while others pulled a dark and inert form, sluicing water, up the slippery embankment.

Gilles continued to hold the torch while others worked, thumping, kneading, rolling, trying to revive the man. Gilles looked into the face, round and bewhiskered though nearly blue, even in the gold of torchlight. More than that he couldn't say about the man except that he wore the red and green *cotte* of the Dauphin's guard. And, to Gilles' battle-trained eye, that there was little hope.

"Do you know him?" Unknown voices panted, shivered, as they worked desperately.

"Aye, it's old—"

The name spoken next meant nothing to Gilles.

"What cause had he to be in the river on a night like this?" asked another.

"God and His blessed saints know," said a third. "I left him not a quarter of an hour ago. He was hale, singing, as full of mirth as could be."

"You'd been drinking, I suppose."

"Not much," the fellow protested, turning his head aside from some who tried to smell his breath.

Gilles smelled nothing out of the ordinary where he stood. The cold air, however, seemed to freeze even the stench of the river and hovels away from his nose.

"No more than usual," the one who claimed to be the victim's companion amended, "when our shift at guard duty's over."

The others grunted in reply, neither disbelieving nor condemning, but busy about their desperate work.

"It is he."

These words, in a different voice, hissed right in Gilles' ear and came with a fierce grip on his elbow that made him jump. It came between wildly chattering teeth, and the Lord of Rais took a moment to realize he did in fact know the speaker. It was Jean de Metz, his cap gone altogether and the dark hair flattened to his head, still dripping with ice water. Gilles suspected Metz had been the one to actually go in at the deep point and haul the victim up.

Metz had recovered his boots and clothes, but was still shivering violently in the air that frosted about his head with each breath like haloes. If he didn't get to a fire soon, he'd catch his own death.

"It's he," Metz said again, oblivious to his own plight. "The guard who said those things to La Pucelle this afternoon. It's he. She said he was close to death and look—"

Metz' voice faded away and Gilles turned his gaze in the same direction, suddenly very interested in the stricken stranger. The lord of Rais trembled, with more than just the cold.

A large man who, though wet, wore the dusty look of a miller, worked harder and longer than the rest. Finally, he too ceased his efforts and rocked back slowly on his haunches with a deep sigh. "It's no use." The miller crossed himself. Others followed his example. "God rest him. He's dead."

This is what happens, Gilles thought. This is what happens to a man who dares make unwelcome advances to the girl-boy who calls herself The Maid. Whose life purpose is to be La Pucelle.

Gilles looked at the dead man's face again, whiter than a mirror's surface in moonlight. The lord of Rais shivered.

Second Antiphon

A Dark God in King's Clothing

That very next evening, Gilles grabbed my arm yet again. This time, however, it was an attempt to keep himself from pacing, not dragging me after him.

"But will he—*she*. Damn me if I don't still think of her as a he. Will she come?"

"Of course she'll come," I assured him. "Didn't I report all that was said when I went to the inn and introduced myself?"

He twitched the fur tumbling off his shoulder impatiently, as if seeking cover. How, even in that rich throng in the Great Hall of Château Chinon, anyone could miss a move made by Gilles de Rais was beyond me. Especially dressed as he was, the borrowed royal robe over the same black velvet doublet—better, in fact, than anything the Dauphin owned. Gilles' black hair curled to perfection under the simple gold crown. His freshly trimmed beard glistened with fragrant pomade. The tell-tale red garter rode high up one calf in brilliant contrast to the pure white silk of his hose.

But Gilles was not thinking of the impression he made on the court. "She seemed glad to know you?"

"I didn't go as the Augustinian," I assured him, catching him and speaking close in his ear. "Not like tonight. I wore the ancient Craftsman's robes, same as her Père Michel. And the tonsure, of course. She recognized them and said, 'I was told you'd be here, Père Yann.'"

"She knew your name before you gave it?"

"Of course. Père Michel must have told her. It was no magic."

"She didn't know my name? I don't suppose Père Michel gave her the name of Gilles de Rais?"

"Perhaps he did. It didn't come up. It's very important that it didn't come up, Gilles. For the sake of tonight's magic."

He nodded, then said, "But was she glad?"

"Yes, I'd say she was glad."

"That's not what you said before."

"What did I say before?"

"'Her face brightened like a lamp just kindled,'" Gilles breathed.

"Very well, 'like a lamp just kindled'."

"And then?"

"And then I said: 'A very great lord has heard of your plight and is even at this moment making arrangements with the host of the inn to cover all your expenses.'"

"And she said?"

"And La Pucelle said, 'Thanks be to my Lord.'"

Gilles sighed and smiled contentment.

"She didn't mean you," I told him impatiently. "Monseigneur—'My Lord'—that's how she always refers to the God. After the fashion of the Craft."

My milk brother accepted that with a shrug of ermine before he pressed me further: "And then?"

"Then I said I knew of her desire to win audience with the Dauphin."

"And?"

"And, if she and her companions would ride up to the castle this very night, this same great lord—I meant you, this time—would see that they received admittance."

"And what did she say?"

"Pretty much the same. 'Thanks be to my Lord.'"

"And?"

"And that was it. I came away and found you huddling in the closest archway like some urchin. I told you, Gilles, keep away."

"And so I did. You didn't tell her my name?"

"No, I did not."

"Nor point me out to her?"

"I told you this plan came to me all at once the moment I saw and recognized her. She must not know you, not yet."

"I wonder if I should have had you give my name at least?"

"This way is best," I assured him. "She's not much of a figure to impress the court as she is, small, poorly dressed."

I looked around the glittering room yet again, weighing my magic against its own. This constrained me to add, "There are going to be some, right from the start, who find her, well, a little mad. Not all the world accepts Merlin and his prophecies, you know."

"I know."

"But this masquerade—this little bit of Craft—I hope will make them—most of them—sit up and take notice."

With a swish of ermine cape about his heels, Gilles turned from me. He had nowhere to go. He was pacing again.

He did look very Kingly, infinitely more when I weighed him against Charles. Charles the Dauphin—heir to the throne of France, but still uncrowned, unannointed six and a half years after his father's death—stood off to one side of the company. He had on the plain, even dowdy, grey-green doublet and hose I'd advised him to wear while Gilles borrowed his trappings. Charles was wringing his hands and cracking the knuckles, as nervous in his own quiet way as Gilles was in his brashness.

I caught Charles' eye and assured him with a nod. I even sent a stroke of mind power from the initiate's mark on my back to the mark I'd placed on his with my own hand. One St. Stephen's Day long ago, in a cold wood, when I'd been eight years old and he even younger, I'd first met this prince. Monsieur le Vert was all the name I'd had for him then, Sir Green. But with the power of my Sight, I'd known that same day, in spite of two older brothers, some day Charles would be King.

I'd held that faith through the invasion of England's Henry V, the betrayal of the Dauphin's Burgundian kinsmen. I knew it now, knew that it was my task, the great calling of my life, to get him to that throne against all odds. This evening in the great hall of Chinon—with Charles cowering in a corner while Gilles strode about in his royal gear of black-tipped fur and a coronet—the accomplishment had never seemed further away. And yet, bring in the spark, La Pucelle, to this carefully laid kindling, and all I would have to do is stand back and watch the place ignite.

That is, if I were any sort of magician. The sort of magician I would have to be.

I gave Charles another nod of encouragement. "Well, things can't get worse than they are now," I read words into his shrug. "I'm already the laughing stock of all Europe, driven to this small outpost in my own country."

In spite of my intentions to be evenhanded with every witch I might add to my company, Gilles pulled my gaze back to himself as his pacing brought him past me again.

"This pack of courtly fools will not be impressed," he tossed at me, not caring who overheard. "They'll think we have a trick arranged, that we've given her plenty of clues beforehand, like a sleight-of-hand man who has planted his assistant in the crowd."

"But you know we have not," I said. "And Charles knows we have not."

"But she *is* coming because I spoke to the right people."

I turned and scurried to keep up with him. If the two of us paced, perhaps his nervousness would not be so blatant to the curious courtly eyes around us.

"You were careful to let your friends know the girl has no idea—"

"*Yet*—" he insisted.

"Yet," I nodded, "who her benefactor is. They know. They will have told others."

"But this business with the Dauphin's crown and robe? Will it work?"

"Of course it will work. Every eye in court will pop when she rejects you—sitting crowned on the throne—for the real Dauphin."

"I don't mean, will they be impressed? They're all such damned fools, pulling a rabbit out of a hat would impress them. What I mean is—will she get it right?"

"You can ask that, Gilles? Having been in her presence?"

"Of course. Of course," he said with distraction.

"She will reject you," I assured him. "And if I'm not mistaken, she will even be able to pick Charles in his common clothes out of all the crowd afterwards. The blood royal can be sensed, by those with the gift."

"Oh," Gilles cried. "That's exactly what bothers me."

"It bothers you to have La Pucelle among us? At last? After all these generations of Earth's suffering?"

Gilles stopped so suddenly, I nearly tripped over his heels. He turned on me and grabbed me by the shoulders with such violence that it was only by a rapid retreat into the skills of the Craft that I managed to keep from crying out.

"It bothers me," he spat, "that she must reject me. That I must deceive her. I—don't—want—her—to—reject—me."

Each of those last words got one hot breath of its own, as if they had to push past a heart swollen to bursting.

"I see," I said.

"Me? For another?"

He let me drop to my own support while I was still considering. When he did, I had to raise an eyebrow to tease in the way of brothers. "Gilles de Rais. In love. With a woman. Fantastic."

He gave me half a smile, but truly it had little mirth. He was in deadly earnest. Earnest, too, was his pain. "Fantastic, yes. Perhaps—perhaps at last, the evil spell is broken."

Once having recovered from the shock of discovering that his new love was not the sex he'd first imagined, my milk brother had allowed himself to fall headlong into loving her anyway.

I could see it: It was the first time in his life he'd felt anything for any woman. He'd come to think normalcy quite beyond his grasp, so much that he ignored it as irrelevant. Now, here it was, tantalizingly close and definitely not irrelevant.

She's not only the salvation of all France in general, I thought. She is the salvation of Gilles de Rais in particular. She's going to make him feel like a man, a man among men.

And yet the normalcy he hoped for was as otherworldly as the boy-girl creature he longed for.

Consider, Gilles, I wanted to say then. How is this to be? La Pucelle is hardly a normal woman herself. That is part of her power for salvation. I wanted to make that plain to him.

It is part of your own power, Gilles. But I held my tongue on the most of this, merely saying, "You know, she is La Pucelle."

"At least you don't remind me—God, don't I know it?—that I am already married."

"You know I wouldn't do that."

"No. Not the man who presides over orgies on Midsummer's Eve. And participates in them, too."

"I only worship the God and Goddess—wherever they find themselves."

"What a pleasant way you have of phrasing it—Holy Father." Sarcasm shot through his voice now like the gold thread through the black velvet of his doublet. "Only La Pucelle. Only La Pucelle—the only woman I'll ever love. And she must be out of bounds."

"Virginity is a piece of her power. The virgin-whore."

"I don't like the whore part, either. Suddenly, I am—I am very, very possessive." His teeth clenched rather than allow too much passion into his voice. "I don't like her choosing that fool Charles—anyone—over me."

"In some ways, this is very, very good," I said, nodding in scrutiny.

"Here we go again." He rolled his dark eyes. "The good all mixed up with the evil again."

"That's how the world is meant to be, Gilles. That's what she comes to reestablish, the divine balance. And neither your will, nor anybody else's, must come in the way of that."

"Yes?" Now his eyes were keen with threat.

"I intend to see to it, Gilles."

He backed down first, but without words. Only the fight seemed to go from him in a wash of despair; and he turned from me so I could no longer read his face.

I let my words back down, to make peace. "It may be, Gilles—after her mission is done—it may be that she can relinquish her calling—for another."

"Is it possible?" He was trying so hard to throttle any hope from his voice, but not with much success.

"I'm not sure."

"You and your Sight. Can't you tell?"

"Not for certain. But there is an inkling there. Of something else besides warrior maid."

Now I saw his pupils widen with the hope and the expansiveness spread quickly to the rest of his form.

"Possible—?" he whispered.

I nodded into a shrug of helplessness. "I simply cannot say."

"Well. So. So." He took the words like stairs, up to greater hope. "So." He swept before me in a grand gesture. "How do I look?"

"You look splendid," I assured him, not for the first time that evening.

"Like a King?"

"Even if you must be rejected tonight?"

"Even if I must be rejected."

Did he look like a King? "By heaven, Gilles. You look like a God."

The announcement of the herald at the door broke suddenly into our conversation. "By the will of His Highness, Charles of France: Jehanne, called La Pucelle."

The Swirl of Four Witches in a Room

Gilles vanished from my side as if he knew more Craft than I usually gave him credit for. When next I saw him, he had appeared in his place, on Charles' throne on the little raised dais at one end of the room. I tried to catch his eye with one last look of reassurance, but his gaze was fixed towards the doorway. He tried to sit as relaxed and regal as a cat, but I could feel his tension: like the same animal just before the spring.

The room fell amazingly silent for such a crowd. Somebody said three hundred people were gathered in that room, besides men-at-arms. I found that very difficult to believe, for though this was Charles' Great Hall, the great hall our impoverished Dauphin had managed to build was not so very large. And it rested on the foundation of his ancestors—most prominent among them, ironically, half-English Plantagenets.

When you consider that each man must have had his pike or sword, room to sweep his great plumed hat in courtly bows or move his shoes with their stylish points; when you consider the women with their long, dragging trains both forward and aft, the astonishing henins, some half again as high as their wearers, perched precariously on severely plucked brows and afloat with sails of frothy white; when you consider the effect of so many dazzling colors colliding together on the eye, the richness of fabric and fur, precious metal and jewels— Include the great fire blazing under the white carved plaster of the mantel, fifty candelabra with all-beeswax candles sweating the walls. Every breath pulled through the thick velvet draperies choked, every sip of wine had to include a mopping of the brow. Obviously, there were practical limits to the press. There simply wasn't space to pack three hundred people in that room.

Nonetheless, there were many of them. And these were the highest, most brilliant lords and ladies in the land—lords to whom Charles the Dauphin bowed his head—with the worn old grey-green doublet on his back.

Into this crowd, La Pucelle strode, a simple, plain girl in mud-splattered men's clothes.

And she out-dazzled them all.

Even though I had set up the paraphernalia for this bit of cunning myself, I had to step back and draw in breath sharply as it actually played before me. There is no other word for what happened. It was magic.

The girl in boy's clothes strode down the red carpet runner towards the dais on which my milk brother sat, scepter in his hand and crown on his head. She'd hardly reached the halfway point when she stopped short. She saw past Gilles in one glance and didn't even begin a bend of obeisance. She wasn't afraid, but I did sense a moment's confusion.

She found me in the crowd next. I wanted desperately to reassure her, to look towards Charles, if only to read his reaction. But I also wanted to give her not the slightest hint, let her show them, show them all the stuff of which she was made, centuries worth of prophecy. So I tried to wipe the slate of my mind clear, so she'd read no hint, even there.

Of course, even such measures could not suppress her. She was La Pucelle.

Not to mention that, if you put four witches in a room, power will whirl. She felt it the moment I did. She guessed the game and almost laughed aloud with delight at the sport. I could see power tingle in her limbs, as it did in mine. I could smell it in her.

And the royal blood, even in such unpresuming veins as Charles', began to thrum. Gilles' power and mine only served to pump it louder—in him. The girl sensed it. She turned, a bloodhound on a scent. The moment her eyes found Charles, she knew.

The crowd parted dumbly before her as she stepped off the carpet and walked to him. Then I lost sight of her as she fell to her knees before the true blood royal she'd been sent to serve.

La Pucelle had arrived.

The single aspect of the event I had failed to fully calculate was the effect of the meeting on my milk brother.

"That look," Gilles exclaimed, stepping, stumbling off the dais to join me while she won Charles' shyness to her beyond our sight and hearing.

"Listen to them," he continued. "Everybody is saying the great miracle was her picking the Dauphin out of the crowd. Or what she's telling him in secret now—letting him hear her Voices or whatever she's doing."

His tone rang with jealousy, but he went on: "No, once she saw past the throne and the scepter and all the trappings—and, by God, she'd done that halfway down the carpet on her march towards me—after that, all she had to do was to look around the room to see who was blushing the deepest.

"No, the miracle was in that look, when our eyes first met. She looked at me as the infinite sky looks into an infinite pool and is reflected. I knew at once and at last: here is someone who knows me. Who knows me and is not afraid. Someone who will neither overlook my evils nor overpraise my virtues. Someone for whom my inherited wealth means nothing. The first person on earth who isn't trying to sell me anything.

"The only person I can ever truly love."

And I could only shake my head sadly because La Pucelle seemed the only person whose love Gilles could not have.

Fourth Antiphon

Pheasants in a Withy Cage

"Bless me, Father," the girl said. I smiled down at the dark head bowing before me over her clasped hands. I saw the mark on her neck, the purple-red mark of who she was, which she could never erase. I made the sign and placed her under the protection of the Stag.

Some effort had been made to clean up the wild, hacked look of the hair first revealed when she'd removed her black woolen cap in the Dauphin's presence. Someone must have clapped a bowl on her head and straightened the fringe up into a regular soldier's helmet cut: shaved close up the back of the neck and high over the ears.

They had taken her under their wing; indeed, I might have said, taken her into custody.

But vagrant tufts of hair still stood to a startled attention over her widow's peak, especially after she'd dragged her fingers through it, as she did often. Like a magic talisman.

I continued to find Gilles' acclamations of "beautiful", "angelic", "exquisite" on the verge of madness. But La Pucelle's simplicity, her guilelessness, the almost visible radiance of her mission, even before she opened her mouth, must be plain to everyone. It must make both men and women, all but the most dead to things of the spirit, feel an irresistible attraction to her.

I saw it clearly in the men who had accompanied her from Lorraine. They'd caught some of her glow and not a one of them would think twice to die for her. They had been pushed aside somewhat, relegated among the lowest of the common soldiers, by the press of others to catch some of that glow. That saddened me.

Some people couldn't tell the difference between power of the spirit and power of the world. And some, like Gilles, confused the difference between physical love of the body and the higher love of souls activated by the divine.

Truth to tell, I was halfway to being in love with her myself.

But over the past few days, I'd begun to feel it was the people without any soul at all who'd clamped hold of her. She'd come upon us, bursting with purpose and energy—and she'd run into their stone wall.

I knew our partnership was meant to be, had been ordained since the ancient days of Merlin, if not before. Still, I was flattered that she had sought me out here, under the ash trees in their Lenten austerity, in the castle gardens. Flattered—and relieved. It was much better than me trying to think of a way to reach her.

For, since her success in the great hall, I hadn't seen her, not even momentarily. The head chamberlain, La Trémoïlle, and his people kept her turreted in the royal Tower of Coudray. It was supposed to be an honor. It seemed more like a trap. The single entrance to the tower was over a drawbridge that dropped scores of feet into a gorge all around.

Was it for her safety? Or for their own? In either case, it had kept me from her, from the union that was meant to be.

I'd been able to think of nothing else to do but to walk here in the garden, as close as Gilles' influence could bring me, all day, every day, waiting. Sometimes I'd felt her appraisal—or maybe it was her spirit crying for assistance that I didn't know how to bring her. She was with the Dauphin, at least under his roof now. Maybe there was nothing more for me to do, and I was wanting to be more important for the unfolding of these events than I was meant to be.

But she was here now, and we were alone. I gestured for her to rise up off the damp ground, wondering if I shouldn't be kneeling before her. She stayed down.

"Now you're supposed to shrive me."

She looked back towards the tower whence she'd come, expecting, probably, that someone was watching. I looked, too, but saw no one.

Then she remembered the ritual and added hastily, "Bless me, Father, for I have sinned."

I couldn't keep a note of surprise from my voice as I replied, not quite to ritual: "Have you sinned, daughter?" And I felt awkward calling her daughter. I already knew hers was a soul much, much older than mine. Older than I ever hoped to be.

"Everyone's a sinner." She sounded as if she were still in ritual, but I didn't argue the point. Not yet.

"How long has it been since your last confession?" I asked instead.

"I confessed and heard mass in Auxerre on our way here to Chinon."

"So I heard. The Burgundian city. Wasn't that a bit dangerous, for six strange men-at-arms to walk into mass like that?"

"That's what my companions told me. I assured them my Lord would allow nothing to happen, but they didn't quite believe me. Nothing did happen."

She had Seen truly and here she was, kneeling safely before me. Still, I had to gulp at the danger in retrospect.

But the girl wasn't finished. "We stopped at Sainte-Catherine-de-Fierbois once we got safely into France. I confessed there. I confessed last Sunday and took communion here at Saint Maurice. I've been to mass every day—until I came to the castle and here they seem determined to stop me."

"Why?"

"They want me to confess."

"Why?"

The girl shrugged, their ways unfathomable—and unimportant—to her. "Oh, yes, and before I left Vaucouleurs, Père Frontey exorcized me."

"Exorcism?" I was really astonished and shivered involuntarily. I remembered the touch of bones and the smell of death at my own exorcism as a child, at the hands of Père de Boszac. People always try to drive out what they don't understand.

She shrugged again. "Robert de Baudricourt wanted to be careful."

"That's a lot of churching, my dear."

She shrugged a third time.

"Confession once a year, during Lent, is usually recommended as sufficient for the average mortal who, I suspect, is a lot more sinful than you are, my child. Do you really need so much?"

She turned up her face and met my eyes, studying me for a moment. I recalled Gilles' words about the reflection of an infinite pool and almost flinched from such fierce scrutiny. Fortunately, she quickly turned that gaze from side to side to make certain nobody else was near us in the winter garden.

Then she said, very low: "Following forms doesn't annoy me. If I follow the forms—flood them with forms, people don't bother to look any closer."

"To?"

"To things I cannot tell them. Things I See—and Hear —behind the forms."

I nodded. So she had come to me—they had let her come to me—because in my outward form they saw what I meant them to see. And she saw through to the core, as she had from the first. "Why don't you get up off the ground, daughter, and we'll talk about it."

She scrambled up and strode away. I followed the stride of her riding boots as they crunched along the gravel path. At the end of the path, backed into a corner where two great stone walls of the castle met, half a dozen pheasants were kept in a large cage made of bunches of withies banded together.

When I caught up with her, she was clinging to the cage with both hands, her feisty little widow's peak pressed hard against a crossbar. The pheasant cock was threatening her with ruffled feathers, a quick, nervous, back-and-forth pace and his call like rusty hinges.

After a moment, when she didn't speak, I folded my hands up in the sleeves of my habit and asked, "Are you feeling caged, too, La Pucelle?"

Her laugh was as bright as little bells when she pushed herself away from the cage, made a quick spin on one heel and then landed with her buttocks against the withies this time. A red mark remained across her forehead, and I saw she'd been crying. Tears came to her as quickly as smiles, I was to learn. That, too, was part of her power.

"You remind me so much of someone ... ," she said.

"Who?"

"Someone. Just another priest. At home."

"Is his name Michel?"

Her brightness paled a little with wonder. "How did you know?"

"He was my tutor when I was a boy. Didn't he tell you? You knew my name when first we met. He must have told you something."

"That is so."

"He introduced me—to the Craft."

"Did he make you a priest as well?"

"No, that was left to another—his old Master. By that time, you see, Michel had to leave me."

"Why?"

"Because you'd been born."

"You're lying."

"I'm not."

"You knew that?" Thoughtfully, she touched a small wooden box on a cord around her neck. "You Saw that?"

"Even before."

"Just as Père Michel said. And you are really his Yann?"

"Yann. Father Jean ... I'm going by Pasquerel at the moment."

"Pasquerel?"

"So not too many people connect me with the lord of Rais. My milk brother. So not too many understand what is at work."

She nodded, understanding it all in a blink, as I knew she would, given but the chance.

"We thought it best."

"I see, I see." She stomped her feet in impatience. "One deception after another."

"The Craft must work in secret—if it is to work at all."

"So you didn't just happen to walk into that inn three days ago, just happen to walk up to our table—?"

I shook my head. "Every sign known to the Craft is focused on Chinon at this time. We've all waited so long, La Pucelle. The whole world has been waiting."

"Oh, why did you have to tell me that? Why?"

She bounced off of the cage with such fury that she sent the pheasant flapping with a squawk.

"La Pucelle? Daughter? What's wrong?"

"What's wrong? In there," she flung an arm towards the Tower of Coudray, "they try to put me in a dress. And then you tell me everything I do is known to you and all the rest of the world before I do it. You wonder that I feel caged?"

I had nothing to answer to that. It was true.

"How ... how is dear old Père Michel?" I asked instead. I missed his wisdom. This task was already proving too much for me.

"His knee bothers him. I begged him to come with me, but he couldn't."

One man short of the coven I needed. This was going to take a coven, all thirteen witches. I couldn't do it on my own, that was clear. And I didn't have a man to spare.

"I hope—I hope he heals soon," I said.

But she was crying again. She fought it back, tossed her head once more—having little hair to toss—and turned to face me, swallowing hard.

"So? Will you shrive me or not?"

"Do you need to be shriven again? So soon?"

"Madame ... Madame ... Madame what's-her-name says I do. The Dauphin's mother-in-law."

"Ah, Madame Yolande of Aragon. Yes, I know the woman."

"Madame says I may not attend mass with the Dauphin until I am shriven. She worries I might damage his relationship with the divine. His relationship—? What is that supposed to mean? Anyway, I don't know how else I'm to come to him again. He's the one I need to be talking to, not his mother-in-law. He has the soldiers, right? I am to deliver Orléans. I need soldiers."

"And Madame Yolande is in charge?"

"In charge 'of my virtue'." La Pucelle's voice swam with sarcasm. "They've put me in the room at the top of the tower. 'Best view,' they tell me. What they don't say is that I have to pass by her room to go anywhere. In truth, it's like a dungeon."

"I see. Well, I think you're very important to her son-in-law's cause."

"I can do nothing for her son-in-law's cause if I have to sit up in that room over three floors of dainty ladies pricking at their embroidery hoops."

"No, you can't."

"And the first thing they had to do—the very first thing—was to check me out."

"Check you out?"

"You know. Down there." Her eyes made a quick drop to the general region. "You know, like I'm a cow in calf or something."

"I see. To make certain you are—"

She didn't let me finish my sentence. "Female, first of all. They didn't believe I was female." She ran her hand with distraction through her short hair.

"Well, you do give people doubts," I suggested.

"Then, of course, they had to check out the intact part."

"And are you?"

"They're satisfied, though with all that poking and prodding, I don't know how I still can be."

"'This is a perverse generation, seeking for proofs'," I said. Then, when she didn't catch my biblical reference, I went on. "They need to be careful, make certain you are what you say you are. That's all."

"I say I'm La Pucelle. Does La Pucelle lie? Can she? Another thing I'm prevented from doing." She kicked miserably at the gravel.

"So lying is not what you must confess to me."

"No," she said. "Murder."

"Murder?"

"There was this fellow."

"You killed him?"

"Of course not. Though I wish I had."

"Tell me."

"We were riding up to the castle—what? Three days ago? Four? One of the guards at the gate yells out, 'Who goes there?'

"And I answered, 'It's I, La Pucelle, come to see the Dauphin.'

"Well, he didn't seem to know what La Pucelle meant, the knucklehead, so I said, 'The Maid, Jehanne, from Lorraine.'

"'Oh-ho, the Maid, is it?' says he."

I had to hide a chuckle at her mimicry of the guard's deep and jaunty voice. "Ah, yes, I heard this. And the fellow ended up dead in the river."

She scowled.

"Gilles told me," I said. "Gilles, the lord of Rais."

"Oh, the one with the blue beard."

"That's right." Few souls but hers would have seen through to the God's mark tattooed in blue on my milk brother's chin.

"The one who tried to deceive me."

Poor Gilles, if he were to hear her! "He knew you wouldn't be deceived. He's one of the coven, daughter. The group of witches I am hoping to gather to help you in your mission—and he is my milk brother. We were raised together. Gilles has a great—a great interest in you."

She sniffed at the residue from her crying. I heard skepticism there.

"Gilles was at the river. He helped pull the fellow out. I don't think many in Chinon have not heard the tale, in one version or another, by now. I suppose court has its version, too. Is this the murder you think you have to confess?"

"I knew before it happened. The words just came to me, so I said them. 'I wouldn't be thinking such thoughts, man, if my death were as close to me as yours is to you.'"

"You warned him. The rest—that was an accident."

"That's not what they think," she said with another glance towards the tower.

"So they accuse you of murder? Or of witchcraft?" I felt a finger of ice on my heart. "Or both?"

"I only said what I saw. They think I put a spell on him. Not that I didn't wish it, after how he made me feel. Like he scraped up scum from the very moat he was guarding and flung it all over me."

"These are soldiers you're hoping to lead. You may have to get used to this."

"I won't. They won't dare. Not when they know who I am."

Her virginity was not something she took lightly, then. Neither, for the good of her work, for the good of the Land, should I. "It may indeed take some magic to teach them."

"Did my words kill him?"

"Of course not. No more than my Seeing your prophesied birth should make you feel trapped."

"Is that how it is? Truly?" She turned to me with such sudden hope, it hurt in the pit of my stomach.

"It only means you are much more sensitive to the waves of being all around you."

"And you are, too?"

"It's not so difficult. Not for you, who were born with it."

"And you?"

"I was born with it, too. And received the best training."

She nodded, as if things were settled within her now.

"Such skills," I said, "used to be much more common. A long time ago. In the Old Ways. But now that they grow more and more rare, people come to fear them only because they are rare—and misunderstood."

"I know you speak the truth."

She came and clasped my hand for joy. It was the right one she clasped, that scarred and twisted claw that hangs all but useless from my wrist. Her first reaction was the common one, to draw back in horror.

Then, she understood. Without my having to say a word, she knew that this was the touch of the God, a mark of the time when, at three years old, I'd first heard the voice of the King Stag in the wood. She understood that this was another thing she needn't fear just because it was uncommon. She smiled and pressed the hand again.

"So, La Pucelle," I said. "If I grant you absolution, will the ladies of the court believe the soldier's death was an accident? An accident you foresaw, but could do nothing to prevent—for one who wouldn't listen, who must go drinking anyway?"

"Madame wanted me to go to her confessor."

"And?"

"And I wouldn't. I don't trust the man. He's so—so—he's like a new-plowed field before the seed's been sown. Nothing there."

"I'm flattered by the comparison."

"And the Archbishop has his candidate for confessor, too. I'm certain every word I said to him would be reported."

"You feel the world's waves aright, La Pucelle."

"I didn't like the fellow at Saint Maurice, either."

"It sounds to me as if you don't like priests in general."

"Whenever I tell them of my Voices, they ask, 'Was a priest nearby when you heard them?' When I say, 'No,' they say, 'Then they were of the devil.'"

"Your Voices are not of the devil, child. If they are, so am I."

She squeezed my hand again, hard. "You're the only one I knew who would tell me what I know, as deep as I know that I live. When people who have control of you, control of your body, when they try to tame your mind, too—"

Tears threatened the corners of her eyes again. "I knew from the first you were not like other priests."

"You understand the reason, of course."

"I'm not sure."

"La Pucelle, there are many who, if they looked closely into my priesthood, would not accept it. I am a Master of the Craft rather than a doctor of divinity."

"What can be the difference? Power is power and spirit is spirit, no matter where it is found."

"I agree with you. But there are many who would separate the difference into black and white, condemn one and embrace the other, never thinking that the world is made of light and shadow all the while."

"It is the very thing I dislike in the others."

"Of course."

"Is it a bad difference?"

"What do you think?" I reached up and touched the wild, short hair with one fatherly hand. "What do your Voices say?"

"They say La Pucelle must have no confessor but Jean Pasquerel."

"Then La Pucelle does Jean Pasquerel great honor."

"Am I absolved?"

"La Pucelle, you had no sin when you came to me. The Craft knows no sin. That is, if you are true to your Voices, you cannot sin. The land and the people have become separated from each other in this new religion. That is the sin. That is the evil we fight. There is no evil but what comes from that, what comes from seeking too much good for oneself, and hence removes itself from the land, which works in balance."

"Ah, you sound like Père Michel. Père Michel and his martinets. And his mosquitoes."

I bowed slightly. "Again, La Pucelle honors me."

"So I can go to mass?"

"You can. Some people's faith in you may depend on your observation of such forms, and you must be La Pucelle to all."

She was skipping now, up the path and then back down again, incongruously in her heavy men's riding boots. It was a wonder, how she went from ancient soul to child in a heartbeat. But, of course, the most ancient have learned to have a child's delight in everything. And how should she not rejoice, when legs freed by hose were so new to her—so new and yet, so original, such a part of her nature. She had never doubted that nature, of course. Only how she must present it to the world had confused her.

"I can see the Dauphin again?" she asked.

"That is the least of things you can do. Things you must do. Yolande of Aragon doesn't keep you from the news, does she? I suppose you've heard?"

"The latest from Orléans?"

I nodded. "Another shameful, shameful defeat for the Dauphin's forces. Any army outnumbering their foes as those

Dauphinists did the Burgundians should have been able to win. Overrun by a few ill-guarded carts full of salt herring, the *goddams'* Lenten fare. The French had the lay of the land with them, too."

"Ah, Father, you sound like a man of arms instead of the cloth." Her eyes glistened.

"Not so, my Pucelle. I am a man who believes even a soldier should sense the ground beneath his feet before he fights, to understand Her will. That is what you've come to teach this land of France, is it not?"

She considered for a moment. She'd obviously never put it into words like this. But then she nodded in serious acceptance.

"If they'd just listened to the lay of the land under their feet," I went on, "they would have had all those barrels of food for poor, besieged Orléans. Instead they got beaten like dogs and must go whining back to the safety of the walls with their tails between their legs. That is why you have come. You must teach them."

"The siege of Orléans must be raised," she said tentatively, like someone trying out a tooth that has pained every other time she'd tried it in the last few days.

"Of course."

"I knew that—but they tried to confuse me, to divert me."

"You are the one who must raise it."

I knew this by the feel of my bare feet on the gravel. She knew it—well, she called her means her Voices, her Council. Perhaps it was the wind blowing past the liberated hollow of her ears, prickling the purple mark on her neck. Whatever it was, I knew it was as true and solid as my own senses. I knew because the vibrations I felt grew stronger every step I took towards her.

"So the Dauphin will finally listen to me?"

"Charles is not only of the royal blood, La Pucelle. He is one of us."

"What do you mean?"

"He's been initiated. I initiated him myself. He knows the Old Ways. He knows the Sacrifice and I think—I hope—he accepts it.

There is no greater understanding a King can have, besides the understanding that he is King."

"Truly?"

"Truly."

"I hadn't been sure. There are some things about him that—"

"Yes?"

She shook her head and tried the tooth again, with more daring. "I will get my army?"

"What do your Voices say?" I urged.

She strode all the way back to the pheasant's cage and set the birds into a frenzy by pounding her hand from one withy to the next. Suddenly it seemed a very flimsy cage indeed.

Then, "Yes." She flung her head back and yelled it to the accompaniment of pheasant's cries like a whole army marching in armor, glittering with color. Their squeaking joints only needed a good oiling.

"Yes, I shall."

Chapter Three

In the Dungeon of Decay

Gilles, sire de Rais, found his milk brother at last. Père Yann was in, of all places, the dungeon beneath the Tour de Coudray of Chinon at the top of which La Pucelle had her room.

Unlike La Pucelle, Gilles thought bitterly, Yann wasn't a prisoner. The dungeon was abandoned, no longer used for the refuse of humanity, but for lesser sorts of garbage. Scraps and bones and broken crockery cluttered the floor. Drunkards losing their way to the latrine must have used it as well, to judge by the stench.

Gilles hesitated to go too much further down the curve of steps towards such a floor. And hesitation quieted the sound of his boots on the last tread or two. His milk brother, he saw, was down there, barefoot in the mess. Little concerned where he set his feet, Yann was closely scrutinizing the walls of the place. A tear-drop of flame dancing at the end of his left forefinger served as a taper, that old sorcerer's trick Gilles himself had never managed to learn. So intense was Yann's concentration that—very unlike himself—he seemed unaware that he had company.

Gilles' next step scraped some rubble between stone and boot leather. Now Yann heard—and quickly extinguished his finger, plunging them both into blackness.

He still doesn't know who I am, Gilles thought. He is absorbed in this place. He'll pretend to have dropped his candle with the start. He'll work a spell to make me forget the little magic I saw. Maybe even pass by me in the dark like a bat and be gone.

"Never mind all that," he called out into the smothering blackness before him. "It's only me—Gilles. You can flick on your finger again."

Presently, warm yellow light pooled over the rough subterranean surfaces of the enclosure once more. Gilles hadn't realized how unnerved he'd been, standing at the edge of this eerie place in impenetrable darkness, until the light washed the tension out of his limbs in a flood of relief. Certainly it had seemed—when he had no vision to go by, to delude him—that the place was not only dank and filthy but peopled, *spirited*, as well.

"I've found you at last," he said, trying to shake off the feelings with a little cheer. "After searching this whole accursed castle. I own I'd never have thought of looking for you here if I hadn't—"

"If you hadn't?" Yann studied his face keenly.

"If I hadn't used that old searching spell Père Michel tried to teach us."

"Ah. And it worked for you? Finally?"

"I suppose. Maybe. A little."

"There. See? You never really tried before."

Gilles changed the subject. "You've got to come. A fat lot of good you do as a protecting confessor. She's in real trouble."

"Who's that?"

"Who? La Pucelle, of course." Truly, Yann could be dense at times.

"Whatever is the matter?" But he didn't make any move towards the stairs.

"They've called her into the King's cabinet."

"Yes. I was here when they came for her and I heard her go, overhead."

"But—but she may need your help. In the confines of the cabinet—"

"You don't think La Pucelle can handle Charles' ministers? If she's going to handle the English, she must be able to take on a few old men."

"My cousin Georges—"

"Sworn to give her a bad time, has he, old La Trémoïlle?"

"He will brook no one to come between himself and the power of the throne. Why, you know what he did to Comte Arthur de Richemont."

"Still hiding out at Parthenay, didn't you say the count was? Ran there like a whipped cur."

"Richemont is the best soldier in Christendom." Gilles didn't truly believe this. In truth, he thought he himself should own that title. But as long as Richemont was, in theory, his commander ...

"La Pucelle is not the comte de Richemont," Yann said.

"Of course she's not. La Trémoïlle will eat her alive."

"He seemed genial enough that first evening in the great hall."

"He couldn't very well put on a scene with the whole court in attendance. But in cabinet—Yann, you cannot imagine. He can wrap ... well, wrap is too gentle a word. Beat is more like it. As a cooper might beat hoops around a barrel. He beats Charles into submission. And Charles is such a milksop, he'll go where La Trémoïlle leads every time."

"What dreadful weapon does your cousin threaten her with?" Yann seemed more amused than worried.

Gilles said, almost desperately, "He's going to demand that she give them a sign."

"And what sign does anyone need more than her picking Charles out of the crowd over you, my dear Gilles?"

Gilles still hadn't overcome the jealousy of that. He tried to press it down, however. "That is sign enough for Charles. But Charles has so little substance, he's blown by whatever wind howls the strongest. And, trust me, for I have been there—in the cabinet, my cousin Georges is that wind."

Yann sighed deeply and shook his bush of mouse-colored hair and beard. "Doesn't your cousin know scripture? 'An evil and adulterous generation seeks for a sign.'"

"You, Yann, quote Christian scripture?"

"Why not? When it suits the occasion. I am supposed to be Père Jean Pasquerel of the Augustinian order, after all."

"But what of La Pucelle?" Gilles felt himself quite frantic now.

"Can you not trust her yourself, brother mine? Do you require signs and portents? Before you will believe?"

"No. No, I do not," Gilles confessed. "But I need ... I need to know that she'll be safe."

"That is your need, then, and not hers."

Gilles scrubbed at his goatee but managed to keep his mouth shut.

"For your sake, then, let me assure you, this girl has signs enough. Until she has completed her work, as old Merlin said, there is nothing that can stand in her way. Not even your old boar of a cousin."

Gilles grated his foot on the rubble again, but said nothing.

After a pause, Yann went on. "Of course, I was going to do what I could for her."

In one quick pull, the Augustinian robes were off, revealing the druid's pure white linen below.

"You were?" Gilles felt himself light up. As if he could do the finger trick, but with his whole face.

"I figured this was the only place within Chinon castle walls that I could draw my circle and not be interrupted. Did I misjudge?"

Yann finished folding his habit and moved to a sack of magical utensils which, until that moment, Gilles had not noticed as any different from the rubbish on the floor. The Master's hands, one good, one twisted and weak, hovered over the mouth of the bag, teasing.

"Is somebody else going to come barreling down those stairs after you the minute I've called the powers?" he asked.

"No, no, of course not. An excellent place." Gilles found himself taking a comfortable seat on the rubbly step.

"And so? Will you join me? Or do you intend to go back to the cabinet? Run an extra quill or two in for your cousin? Serve as his secretary, as you've been known to do?"

"I'll join you."

Gilles looked dubiously at the floor of the place again, but didn't stop unlacing his boots. Surely he could wash his feet of anything down there. If La Pucelle should see him in any close connection with La Trémoïlle—well, that was a pollution he didn't think he could wash off so easily.

"So? What do you make of this place?" Yann seemed in a mood to make conversation while he waited for Gilles to get himself ready to spell.

"Frankly?"

"I always expect frankness from you, Gilles."

"Frankly, I've never seen—or smelled—any place more vile."

Yann wrinkled his nose and nodded. "But what else?"

"La Pucelle sleeps here. Four floors above."

"That makes it all right?"

Gilles wriggled out of his doublet. "Purifies it in a way, I'd say."

"Balances, Gilles. Purification only leads to more evil unless it is balanced. Heaven with earth. Life with ... with death."

"As you say."

"Go on. What else?"

"The place ... " Gilles laughed to make nothing of it. "The place seems haunted."

"Exactly what I thought." Yann was serious. "What do you make of that?"

Gilles busied himself with more laces. Then he stopped short. "Somebody once told me ... " He looked around, wonderingly, seeing the dungeon for the first time. "Yes, this must be it."

"What?"

"Somebody told me Philippe IV kept the Knights Templar imprisoned in this castle for a time."

"Of course." Yann let out his breath in a gasp of discovery and turned quickly back to his intense study of the walls. "The warrior-monks. The murdered magicians."

Yann muttering such things into his beard told Gilles nothing he didn't already know. "Yes? He kept them here. While he tried them. Before they burned. So?"

"Of course. I certainly sensed something, but not these details. This explains everything. Gilles, look at this."

Yann raised his finger to the far wall. Gilles had nothing left either to take off or untie. He stood up and felt the cold breath of the dungeon air creep up from the stones under the fine linen of his shirt, which is all he still wore. He might as well brave the floor, now or never.

The uncanny light from Yann's finger danced across the uneven ashlar. Then Gilles saw them, engravings cut into the wall, not by any mason with decorative fancies, but shallowly. As if by a prisoner armed with no more than a rusty nail. Or the sharp edge of his own manacle.

Gilles picked out a cross, simple enough. The instruments of passion. A few blazons he couldn't identify. Rough signatures. What looked like a grid for some game. And in the center, an oval impression that might be a heart. Indeed, it must be a heart, for as he looked closer at the impression and the numerous etched lines radiating out of it, the thing seemed to pulse.

Within the rays, by Yann's flickering finger, Gilles then picked out a single phrase. The hand, or hands, that had scratched the grey stone away to white had been by no means illiterate, but in such suffering that the pain shook through the ages.

"'A curse ...'" Gilles stopped. That was enough for him.

"'A curse upon the King of France,'" Yann read it all. "No wonder France has been in such grief."

Images of the war-ruined land he knew only too well crossed Gilles' mind: Fields abandoned and knee-high in thorn, burned out shells of houses, dead and dying beasts, men, women and children. Some of this destruction, he knew, was his responsibility, the forward charge of a man who feels the earth thrown out of kilter beneath him. And can do nothing about it.

As if his thoughts were heard, Yann said, "The Templars laid this curse long before your brother René stole his uneasy life. This is the very room where they were kept, Gilles. Jacques de Molay and his companions. Before being led out to their horrific tortures. Then to their deaths on the pyre. It, like La Pucelle, was prophesied by Merlin. He said a great war would begin between Ou and Pu—the magician's names for England and France—because of the misjudgement of a cleric. And see, those words were fulfilled in this war that has cursed our land for over a hundred years."

Now that the thing was said, Gilles felt it in his soul, as if past, present and, yes, even future met upon his head in this place all at once. Thousands of men of the ancient order of the Temple suffered similar fates, all over France, that Friday the thirteenth of October over a hundred years before. Molay, he heard, had died as the high, holy Sacrifice in that ancient time.

"They were sorcerers, the Templars, weren't they, Yann? That is what they died for."

"Very great men of Craft," his milk brother assured him. "The last time there was hope. The last time there was an attempt to renew the Old Ways. Fourteen cycles of Sacrifice ago, Jacques de Molay took the royal blood upon himself and died in the place of the King. He died in Paris. They tossed his ashes into the Seine and the people, even the monks, scrambled into the waters after them, and carried them away to holy places."

Gilles could almost see the event reflected in his milk brother's eyes. After all, Yann had sacrificed a King himself and poured the blood out upon the ground on the selfsame holy island where Molay had died.

"I thought it was the King who imprisoned the Knights," Gilles said, remembering other details as if they pulsed off the wall and into his mind. "Philippe the Fair. He wanted the Templars' money, the same way he chased out the Jews and the Lombards before them."

"No doubt there was some of that. But earlier, Philippe had wanted to join the order, after his first wife died."

"If they refused him, that might have made him angry enough to hound them all to oblivion."

"The Templars tried to cover their Craft with Christianity."

Gilles saw his sorcerer milk brother, his Augustinian robes cast off but a moment, and wanted to make some remark about Craft covered in Christianity. Wolves in sheep's clothing, the proverb never was more apt. But he saw his milk brother as the priest instead, the ancient Man in Black, heir to Merlin of old.

"Notice the cross?" Yann certainly had no doubts. He raised his finger up to that image again. "Molay and the Masters before him thought that following the church in cutting women from Craft might help. Then that fighting under the cross might cover their secret necessary rites. They sought papal protection for what can have nothing, safely, to do with the pope at all. In the end, they regretted their mistakes, and we must learn from them."

A vision flashed across Gilles' brain, of the secret rite in the crypt below Angers' chapel. As a child, and very impressionable, he'd witnessed it, how Charles, also very young, not even Dauphin yet, had given the blood of his arm to the harper. Then the old, blind man had instantly turned around and died with the cycle. Saved the Land. And become a God.

"So when Philippe the Fair came, asking to join them," Gilles asked, "Jacques de Molay had the foresight to take the royal blood on himself instead?"

"Molay understood, as Philippe cared only for the order's wealth, the King was not likely to die when the ninth year came. Molay played with Craft this way and that, hoping for acceptance in a growingly Christian world. But in the end, the Master realized he would have to be the one to die. He held them off for years, suffering imprisonment and repeated tortures, making confession after confession, retracting them, playing for time. Until, at last, May came, one of the proper months for Sacrifice, in the proper year. Then, he went. So bravely that Philippe, who meant to rid himself of a thorn in his side, made Molay a martyr—and a God—instead."

"I would not have died for such a King as that, whether I had the blood or no."

"But that's the point. The King who will not die his own Sacrifice loses, not the man who takes his place. Surely you remember Charles VI, our own Dauphin's father. Raving mad for thirty of his forty-year reign because he would not shed his blood when the Man in Black came to him. Worse than that madness is the madness into which such a refusal plunges the land. The Sacrifice is not for the King as a man, after all, is it?"

"No."

"It's not like going into battle, dying perhaps, so the men in power may stay there."

"No."

"What is the Sacrifice for, Gilles?"

Gilles found himself, against his will, like a student at his own milk brother's feet. And yet the place, and the lesson, were of such weight that he didn't mind. He couldn't mind.

"The land."

"The land? The land named France?"

"No. The Earth."

What Gilles saw in his mind's eye was very much closer to the stench in this close, dank room than what thoughts of "the land of France" had first set there. The word "Earth" conjured a picture of rich, brown loam, not the wind-stiffened pennants and battle cries that usually filled his head when he thought of dying for King and country.

"The Earth," he repeated. "Whatever name is shoved upon Her. The Earth, as death and decay renew her, so the Sacrifice—"

Yann smiled and nodded that it was enough. As long as Gilles remembered that catechism—before any other. His milk brother turned to the dungeon room once more.

"Ah, but this is wonderful, wonderful." The collision of times and powers seemed to dizzy him. "Gilles," he said, "do you realize that the last time a full coven met on French soil, it was in this very room? In the person of the Grand Master de Molay and his twelve companions. And now ... now you and I are about to draw the circle in the selfsame place again."

With a solemn flourish, Yann withdrew the sword from his sack and after it, the cauldron. He withdrew some herbs then, finally, a small, simple hoop of lead.

Gilles shivered in spite of himself. But he remembered the purpose of this present magic and managed to push from his mind how the last drawing of the circle in the Tower of Coudray had ended. What had the death of Jacques de Molay fourteen cycles ago to do with Jehanne la Pucelle, after all?

Chapter Four

Lead to a Golden Crown

Yann drew the circle with the point of his sword. He drew the powers from each cardinal point to that place. He set the cauldron in the middle and filled it from a skin of rainwater. The odor of burning herbs smudged the worst of the fetid dungeon air.

It wasn't long before the smoke parted and Gilles saw the figure of La Pucelle dancing lightly on the surface of the empowered water. She stood before the great lords in the King's cabinet.

Charles slouched, cowering in his throne. He was a year older than Gilles himself, almost two, but seemed much younger than his twenty-six years. The old archbishop of Rheims, Regnault of Chartres, was there. Young duc d'Alençon, the fop. La Trémoïlle, of course, hogging attention. Comte Charles de Bourbon. One or two others.

Golden light streamed in through the high, narrow windows. The day was fair enough to make one think April was already come and Easter past and gone. The girl kept looking in that direction, as if what happened in the room with her was of little concern. Certainly things were grim enough within the chamber, along the full length of the great, somber, beeswaxed table.

"The problem is, my dear," La Trémoïlle was saying in a greasy voice, "people cannot believe you on your word alone."

"Why not? I speak the perfect truth."

La Trémoïlle probably would have laughed out loud but that Charles whimpered, "I believe her."

The chamberlain's amusement was therefore kept to a crackling smile before he went on. "Yes, we'd all like to share in his majesty's simple faith, of course—but it is difficult. Every madman in France comes to the King claiming to have heard God. Not only does no one believe *you*, very few people believe Charles has any right to the throne, either. His own mother has confessed to a bit of—er, feminine frailty—where this fellow is concerned."

La Trémoïlle narrowed his eyes with a gleam, as if he suspected La Pucelle to be all too familiar with feminine frailty—or he thought he might teach her. Gilles was sorely tempted to break the magic circle that instant and dash up to give his cousin a blow between those eyes that might change his mind. He restrained himself.

Charles only shrank deeper into his throne. He seemed used enough to hearing his mother called a whore. He probably believed it himself.

"Then my Lord knows more than you," the girl replied calmly, quietly. "For He knows that the Dauphin is the blood royal of France and that I am to see him crowned and anointed at Rheims."

"There, my lord archbishop," the comte de Bourbon said aside, rather unpleasantly. "And you thought never to see your cathedral again."

La Trémoïlle continued: "We here all support Monseigneur Charles for our various reasons, few of which, I'll confess, have anything like your faith behind them."

Charles squirmed, but seemed used enough to having his sovereignty, too, called into question. La Trémoïlle did it every day; it kept the Dauphin malleable.

"Mostly," the chamberlain went on, "we have no choice if we wish to ever see lands or fortune again. So you see why we must be skeptical of you—of turning these hopes over to you, Jehanne, as you call yourself."

La Pucelle stood as ever, straight, her legs apart, a slight smile playing with the mole below her lip and her eyes fixed on the motes dancing in the sunlight.

"My faith is in my Lord," she said patiently, as if to a child who hasn't been listening. "And my only will is to do His."

La Trémoïlle chuckled. "But you cannot expect *us*, with the firm hand of Mother Church behind us, to ... "

The greasy voice faded out. For in the Templars' dungeon, Père Yann had lifted up the ring of dull lead. He moved it slowly over the cauldron. As he did, the tips of his fingers began to glow with flame, first the left and then even the twisted digits on his right hand. The fire struck at the heart of the hoop until it glowed.

Within the water, the reflection of this phenomenon appeared in the motes of sunlight towards which La Pucelle steadfastly gazed. Suddenly, the motes fused together and took on a spiked, round, golden form. A crown floated in the midst of the cabinet.

Gilles couldn't tell just how real the image must appear to Charles and his ministers. The scrying water sent a very unclear image to him in which separate specks of dust could still be seen floating. But Yann always Saw much clearer than he did and every man in the room had become suddenly rooted to the spot. Their eyes were round and golden and some were unable to shove their jaws back up into place. More than one or two must have seen the crown not wafting through midair but borne by a heavenly messenger—in druid white.

The apparition made reverence to the cringing Dauphin, saying, "Blessed art thou Charles, the son of Charles, the son of Charles, of the blood royal of France, born to be King. And blessed art thou for the beautiful patience you have shown in the face of the great tribulations you have suffered."

A rare fragrance filled the dungeon. It probably filled the cabinet as well. La Pucelle stepped to the angel's side and then, slowly, the two of them moved across the room until the crown stopped, hovering in front of Regnault of Chartres. The old archbishop shrank back, suddenly no more self-possessed than Charles in his throne. The angel must have gestured for the prelate to take the emblem. In the dungeon, Yann made the gesture and urged the crown forward. At last, the old man's liver-spotted hands shook as if palsied up from the arms of the chair he'd been gripping. He reached out, took the golden circle. In the dungeon, the hoop of lead floated in midair.

In the cabinet, the illusion must have been tangible enough, for Regnault's hands did not meet one another through it. As if carrying live coals, Regnault rose and brought the crown around the corner of the table until he stood before the young King. Then, raising the image on high, never taking his eyes from the wonder, he set it on Charles' head.

La Pucelle's voice rang out, "Sire, this is your sign. Take it."

Charles seemed to shrink under the weight. To Gilles' eyes, La Pucelle, standing in the streaming light, remained the most regal sight in the room. If not divine.

Yann held the crown yet a moment more in midair with the power of his spell alone, long enough to let the vision burn into every mind. Then he caught the emblem out of the air and set it back down on the dungeon floor. It returned to dull and common lead. In the cauldron, Charles sat bareheaded once more.

"So, my lords." La Pucelle was the first in the cabinet to find voice again. Indeed, she spoke as if such visions were everyday occurrences to her. "How soon do we leave for Orléans?"

Chapter Five

A Fresh-Baked Roll

"Ah, cousin. Come in, come in."

Gilles, lord of Rais, stepped past the silent liveried servant into La Trémoïlle's chambers at Chinon.

"My lord." Gilles bowed low. Nobody was summoned lightly to these rooms—more luxurious than the Dauphin's under the Dauphin's own roof. But Gilles had even more reason to be cautious. Among the high and mighty, he never felt threat, for he was as rich and powerful as any in France. This man shared his blood, however. And, by what alchemy Gilles didn't quite understand, blood had the ability to taint where nothing else could.

Once upon a time, Gilles had paid out 14,000 *écus* to ransom his cousin from Burgundian captivity. He had done it then for family honor. In return, and lacking sons, La Trémoïlle had made Gilles his heir, of rich Bordeaux besides a dozen lesser fiefs. Gilles held lands enough in his own right. Such promises should not matter, especially since these lands had yet to be wrested from the English, and nothing that had happened in the last five years had brought them any closer.

Nothing but the arrival of La Pucelle, Gilles reminded himself.

Yet in some perverse way, the promise of more land did matter—when Georges de La Trémoïlle gave it.

There was another matter, something that bit even deeper at the lord of Rais' soul. When first Gilles had met his cousin, the man had only hopes of power. He'd been living in borrowed rooms, with a borrowed whore. Even his feasts had been on loan.

Now, as lieutenant-general of France and chamberlain to

the Dauphin, La Trémoïlle was arguably the most powerful man in France, English-circumscribed though the country was. Somehow—he couldn't see, looking back, how it happened—Gilles knew himself responsible for the handing of these powers over to the man.

Gilles had been there, leading the force that had first arrested, then tortured and tried Pierre de Giac, the former holder of these offices, finally throwing him in Dun le Roi's river. At the time, it had all seemed perfectly justified, a necessary move to get someone into these positions who was more willing to help fund the war effort. And La Trémoïlle had seemed the perfect candidate, unsuited as he was to actual campaigning. Owing Gilles for his very freedom as he did.

His former justifications were something Gilles didn't like to look at too closely any more, not now, after two years of life under this cousin of his.

And certainly not with the future of La Pucelle at stake.

The lieutenant-general had been in the room when the signs had been given, both of them. When the girl picked the Dauphin over ... well, over Gilles de Rais. And when the golden crown had floated to the Dauphin's head. But Gilles was far from convinced there was anything like a soul beneath the great bulk of the man's chest to be touched, even by such things.

"Sit down." Georges de La Trémoïlle waved Gilles into an armchair. The lieutenant-general's personal coat-of-arms—three eagles separated by a chevron worked in blue, gold and red—pressed its elegance into Gilles' back as he sat.

"Join me in a little something to eat?"

The older man waved again, making certain the rings on his huge fingers caught the candlelight. The table between them, as usual, was loaded with food and drink, all of the best.

"Thank you, no," Gilles said. "I just ate."

He fixed his eyes on his cousin, hoping to send the message, So did you. We both were there, with everybody else in the great hall, eating our Lenten fare of eels and boiled greens not an hour ago. What would our pious Dauphin think, to find you misusing the holy season so?

More to the point, what would La Pucelle think? Gilles had watched her eating across the great hall, picking at her food, like one too impatient to eat. Or even, too unhappy.

The memory made him angry, angry at himself for being part of the slowness and especially angry at his cousin. The message didn't carry across the burdened table, however.

The bulk of flesh facing Gilles was imposing enough, and La Trémoïlle certainly liked to throw it around, putting pressure on everyone to gain his own way. The man must eat like this to keep up his weight.

La Trémoïlle took up a goose leg and seemed more interested in that than in anything else in the world.

Gilles took a breath and decided he would have to broach his subject first. He didn't like to, because that would give his cousin's play the power of finality. But, the younger man thought, he might not get another chance.

"Cousin, are you behind this keeping La Pucelle up in that tower like some enchanted princess?"

Georges de La Trémoïlle tossed the denuded bone aside. "Now, yes. It is of the girl I wanted to speak. How on earth did you guess?"

"Nobody speaks of anything else, in case you haven't noticed."

It was so. A frisson of jealousy crept up Gilles' back, from the spot where rich tapestry pressed into his hose to the base of his neck. He knew he mustn't betray the feeling. He mustn't give his cousin anything more to work with than the old devil already had.

"You—or Madame Yolande or whoever keeps her up there where nobody can get at her—" Gilles took a breath, startled at the pain those words "can get at her" gave him.

La Trémoïlle moved into the gap as he moved into any room, filling it instantly. "That's exactly the point. This girl has proved herself a virgin; we would like to keep it that way."

Gilles looked away from his cousin's keen eyes. He must give the old pork no chance to guess any more.

"La Pucelle can take care of herself." Gilles was sorry to say it. He would rather have spoken to the warm protectiveness swamping his chest.

La Trémoïlle chuckled into his many chins. Did he guess, and that was what made him playful, like a cat with a cornered mouse? "But of course, that is not the only reason we keep the girl safe."

"What is the reason, pray?" Gilles spoke deliberately, keeping his temper and with it, he hoped, the secret of his feelings.

"It's not the girl who is in danger. She herself is the danger."

"I ... I don't understand." He really didn't, and he turned, open to his cousin for explanation.

La Trémoïlle narrowed his little pig's eyes in scrutiny and Gilles at once felt a touch of panic, that he'd been too transparent. The old man's words increased his fear.

"Ah, Gilles, Gilles, don't tell me you've come under her spell as well as every other idiot in this place."

"I have not." Gilles wondered if his denial had come just a little too fast, a little too forcefully. He knew he lied and, if he weren't careful, so would everyone else.

"Then certainly you must see just how dangerous this girl is."

It gave him a thrill to think that others thought it as well as himself. But all he said was, "Why?"

"You said it yourself: everyone is talking about her. Nobody talks about anything else. Nobody cares a fig for the deliberations of councils, the wisdom of older men."

Gilles slapped his hands on the table where he could find a bit of space between the viands and leaned far into the lieutenant-general. "Well, maybe it's about time the older men stepped aside and let some action take place. All she asks is a small army—"

"Oh? All?"

"Nobody else is leading them, certainly not you, not the lieutenant-general who ought to be. God forbid, he might miss a meal on campaign. The men just sit around and get into trouble fighting each other. Just a small army, just to try her out—and Charles has promised it to her. What is going on? What is holding things up?"

"You, Gilles? You would hire out your sword? To a girl?"

"Yes, I would. I give it to her freely."

A glint in his cousin's glance made him wary of double-entendre.

Hastily he added, "Just—just to see some action around here." He worked now to rein his enthusiasm in. "Charles has said she may have the men—so it must be you holding things up. Cousin, what the hell are you waiting for?"

La Trémoïlle laughed out loud. "Gilles, Gilles. Surely you don't want to risk your own bets on this chit of a girl?"

"I don't know what you're talking about." Gilles kept his peace with difficulty, but after the last outburst he knew he must give the old man nothing else to play on.

As if he'd won a point, La Trémoïlle released Gilles from his gaze. He toyed idly with the sauce left in the bottom of a platter, drawing circles in it with the tail of the goose.

"I do believe Jehanne of Lorraine," La Trémoïlle said, "should be given her chance."

His cousin exhaled these words along with a great deal of garlic. Nevertheless, they were sweet, making Gilles light as a feather. Blessed girl, to work magic that penetrated even to this overstuffed and deeply buried heart.

"If she succeeds—very well," La Trémoïlle went on. "If not, it'll be a diversion. Give me plenty of time to lay other plans—cut her loose when it serves."

The lightness left the lord of Rais. "You are a bastard."

"Yes, this is where you come in, Gilles."

Gilles only just managed to keep from speaking his thoughts aloud: Now you're going to twist the dagger, aren't you?

"The fact of the matter is," La Trémoïlle confessed, "holy people like this girl are the hardest of all to manipulate."

"Nothing in common with them, have you, coz?"

"You never know which way they'll jump. Holiness has the damnedest habit of turning to the sulphur of hellfire when you least expect it. We must send her to Poitiers, certainly, to be examined by the university men before we do anything."

"Poitiers? Why that's a week there and a week back." And for some reason Gilles remembered the body of Pierre de Giac, floating handless in Dun-le-Roi's river.

"Oh, at least."

"Why do you waste time like this?" My time. *Her* time.

"As I've said, these holy people are just too difficult to handle. You simply can't be too careful with them. Reason, logic, money, none of the usual currency works with them. Even threats fail. They'd love nothing better than for you to make them a martyr."

"That's not true—not in La Pucelle's case."

La Trémoïlle seemed to read right through him, so Gilles shut his mouth and tried to shut his mind.

"The worst of it is," his cousin went on, "such people can drag the whole damn populace with them wherever they go—to the stake, even, if that's where they choose to end up."

Your exploitative little soul is in a fix, isn't it? Unfortunately, Gilles couldn't enjoy speaking the observation aloud.

"So we've considered ..."

Gilles wondered who this "we" was. Probably just his cousin, talking like the King he was in all but name.

"... what is it this girl needs?" La Trémoïlle mused. "What does a holy virgin need?"

Certainly not someone like me, Gilles thought. His cousin had at last finished his meal, wiping his hands on the tablecloth and motioning for a servant to clear the platters. At the last moment, just to do something, Gilles flung back the napkin covering a basket to reveal a heap of fresh-baked rolls. He took one. It was still warm.

"A holy virgin needs a confessor," La Trémoïlle answered his own rhetorical question. "So we tried that first. The Archbishop of Rheims put forward a candidate, Madame Yolande put forth another, both men we could trust."

Maybe those names took care of the "we"? "You would have used the confessional to learn La Pucelle's secrets?"

"That might not have been necessary. A spiritual advisor sometimes just has to give a nudge one way or the other at the right time to get his charge to do what's required. So actually breaking the seal might not have been necessary. But still possible, you understand."

"You are vile."

Gilles continued to hold the roll in his hand, having no appetite. It was as warm as a little bird.

La Trémoïlle continued: "The girl would have none of it."

"Your scum may have met its match in purity, La Trémoïlle." Gilles fervently hoped so.

"She chose some complete stranger, a sort of wild man with a twisted hand."

Yann, of course. It was good that people were beginning to associate La Pucelle with Père Jean Pasquerel, as he called himself. If they knew the Old Ways, they would begin to see just what her power was. If they did not, Yann gave the glamor of Christianity to her. Better still, the girl's confessor was his, Gilles de Rais', milk brother, and not even his own cousin knew it.

Nonetheless, the sounding of their two names in such close proximity, and on such a tongue, made Gilles uneasy. He wished it were his name there. He would join any priesthood to earn such honor. And he had to make an effort to hide from himself just how jealous the thought of his milk brother sharing La Pucelle's every confidence made him.

"We can't even reach this fellow's mother house in Bayeux so we could have him recalled or at least swayed our way," La Trémoïlle complained.

How surprised his cousin would be, Gilles thought, to learn that Yann's "mother house" wasn't in Bayeux at all. It was a heap of rocks in a possessed forest in ancient Amorica. In another manner of speaking, Yann's "mother house" was the same as Gilles' Château Blaison. He decided Yann was right to keep their milk brotherhood a secret in Chinon. But that didn't ease his jealousy.

"So the next thing we thought she might need—" La Trémoïlle paused for effect. "—is a bodyguard."

Gilles sank his teeth into the little roll-bird and bit off its head. The warm life of it filled his mouth like blood and he had to force himself to keep chewing, not to gag.

"A chit of a girl who proposes to rush out into the heat of battle—well, she needs some protection, wouldn't you say? So she doesn't get herself killed in the first instant."

Gilles nodded, chewing vigorously. He could feel the action send a quiver through the blue stain on his chin to the very end of the beard he grew to cover it.

"I thought you, sire de Rais, might want to be her bodyguard."

Gilles felt the little pig eyes in the jowly face studying him closely. He stopped chewing. He could feel his heart racing with the thought: bodyguard to La Pucelle. To be with the young woman day and night, watching her, caring for her ...

But he knew his cousin too well to trust the thrill of it. Finally Gilles found spit enough to swallow the wad he held between his teeth. He swallowed again, to be certain his mouth was clear and would work.

Then he said, "There's a catch here, isn't there?"

"You know how these things work."

"No, coz, I don't. Tell me how these things work."

Chapter Six

The Pen Impales the Ink Well to its Black Heart

Gilles, seigneur de Rais, does solemnly swear to serve Georges, seigneur de La Trémoïlle, with all his might, during his life until his death, toward all and against all, lords and others ..."

Gilles read the paper his cousin had shoved the apple tart aside to make room for. Gilles knew who "others" meant. "Others" meant La Pucelle. He must vow to break every confidence, to spy on the girl's activities for his cousin. Yes, even to arrange an "accident" for her, if she got too much in the way.

Pah! he thought. A man can sign as easily as he moves his tongue to swear. It is no more difficult to break one oath than another.

"And if you're thinking of breaking this oath," his cousin said to him now, with a squint of his little eyes, "just consider that I have this paper. If I go down ... you go down with me."

"Suppose I refuse to sign?" Gilles knew he didn't have that option. But he liked to make his cousin think he did.

"The post can always go to another," La Trémoïlle suggested. "I was also considering that young, handsome duc d'Alençon."

"Alençon's a pretty poppycock."

"Nevertheless, he has left his lovely young wife and come all this way to see this Pucelle of whom everyone speaks. I'm certain he'd be very devoted."

Too easy. You're giving it to him too easily, Gilles told himself. "Add a clause that I do so swear, excepting only my allegiance to the properly anointed King." Then he tried to make a joke of it. "I'd hate this slip of calf's skin to make an ass of me, to send me to the block for treason."

"Willingly," La Trémoïlle said, taking up the pen at once. "Considering that Charles is not properly anointed nor is he likely to be, with Rheims as far away as it is and solidly in Burgundian hands." La Trémoïlle turned what he had written in his round, heavy script for Gilles to read. "... in the King's good grace and love ..."

Silently, Gilles replaced the words "La Pucelle" for "the King" as he took the pen out of the sausage-fat fingers to sign.

Then, in the midst of the lavish flourishes he liked so well over the double "ll" of his simple 'Gilles', he stopped to brush the red garter on his calf with the vane of the feather.

"Do you know what this garter means, coz?" he asked.

The big man shrugged. "It means you're a popinjay in my book. As indiscreet a fop as God makes them."

"In Brittany, it is a symbol of someone who has made a pact with the devil."

La Trémoïlle raised his brows, only languidly interested. "Is that so?"

"I think, after this night, there may be nothing vain in my wearing it at all." Gilles let the pen impale the ink well to the center of its black heart.

La Trémoïlle chuckled while he set the fat lump of red sealing wax to the flame of a candle.

Gilles fumbled in his wallet for his own seal. He had only a small one with him, the head no bigger than a sou, engraved with the ancient symbol of a horseshoe.

All fifty candelabra were alight in the great hall at Chinon again. In Gilles' eyes, the greatest light came not from them but from her. This was the first time he'd been in La Pucelle's presence since the last audience, and he didn't dare meet her eyes.

The Dauphin's voice whined. "Yes, La Pucelle will lead my army to go and raise the siege of Orléans. I have decreed it. I believe in her. She believes in me. You are all to believe in her. And obey her orders."

Gilles was conscious of a quick little shift of La Pucelle's feet. He wanted to dance with her.

"What else?" the Dauphin asked.

Georges de La Trémoïlle bent and whispered discreetly in the young prince's ear.

"Ah, yes." Charles remembered what Gilles could not forget, the word pounding in his brain. "A bodyguard."

Beside him and a little to his left, Gilles heard the voice that sang to his very soul, even when it spoke with a little petulance, as now. "God is my guard," La Pucelle insisted.

La Trémoïlle offered more advice into the Dauphin's ear.

Charles said, "La Pucelle, I should never forgive myself if I didn't give you a bodyguard. Maid, I give you Gilles de Rais for your personal escort. I have no braver man, no man more careless of his own life, for reasons he alone understands. No better soldier."

True, Gilles thought. But such praise still made him shift anxiously in her presence.

"Maid," asked the prince, "will you take him to be yours?"

Now Gilles could avoid the move no longer. He turned and took the brunt of her scrutiny full on him. That look! Again that look that seemed able to kill.

By God, there had been that foul-mouthed soldier. Saying things no worse than a thousand other men said in the same day. But he'd said them to *her*. He'd been fool enough to cross *her*. Two hours later, the river itself reached up and took him.

By God, if she reads so into my soul, she must know. And if she knows, she must reject me. Then I might as well end up in the Vienne, too.

He wanted to look away. But he could not.

With a grunt, La Trémoïlle urged the Dauphin to haste.

"Maid," Charles repeated, "will you take this man?"

La Pucelle turned to set the same uncompromising eyes on her prince. Gilles felt the release of that turn. It made his head light.

Then he heard that sweet, sweet voice: "My Dauphin, I will."

Gilles found himself on one knee in front of all the court. He didn't care, so long as it was also before those ragged, baggy hose on women's legs. He took her hand—his nearly doubled it, but he felt it like some powerful talisman—and kissed it.

"Arise, sire de Rais."

Yes, she'd said his name. But not Gilles. Not yet.

"Truly, I have no need of your knees to the ground," La Pucelle said. "I have heard of your deeds. I have need of your strong arm."

She turned from him to the company, raising one fist high to the shout. "I have need of all strong arms here. To the *goddams*! To Orléans!"

No man in the room could refuse to mirror the salute, or to raise the echo of her shout, "To the *goddams*! To Orléans! For God and for the Maid!"

But Gilles only gave her that one hand to gesture with. He kept the other to his lips and whispered, though he doubted she could hear over the shouts that filled the room: "La Pucelle, you ask from me only that which I would beg you, prostrate at your feet, to take."

The shifting of Georges de La Trémoïlle's bulk distracted Gilles' attention from where he wished it could stay forever. He saw the huge man eyeing him, the smile on those thick lips, the patting of the chest as if at just a bit of indigestion. But it wasn't the pepper sauce at all, only a touch to his cousin's bosom where, Gilles knew, the paper with his seal was waiting for him.

Chapter Seven

Budding Foliage like Clouds of Gnats

"So, Lady." Gilles felt his tongue heavy and stupid as the stalwart little figure turned from the tower window to face him with a flip of short doublet skirts about her hips. He bowed again to cover his awkwardness at being alone with her in her room like this.

"Where would you like to go?"

"I am free to leave the tower, then?"

"Yes, Lady."

"As long as I have you to nursemaid me?"

Gilles felt his face grow hot, then decided making light of it would be the best policy. He gave his brightest smile. "That's right."

"Good. Let's go to Orléans, then."

"Orléans?"

"I'm to have a bodyguard who's hard of hearing," she said in exasperation. "Yes, Orléans. My Voices say I must go to Orléans. I must raise the siege there."

She'd begun pacing like a horse feeling its oats. The room was not large, but it was very nearly empty. Of material things. Of invisible energy, it felt full to bursting. The sense of it set his heart racing with awe. He was even a little afraid. But fear, he'd always known, attracted him.

"It's days to Orléans," he said.

"I don't mind a bit of a ride. Do you?"

"Not—not at all."

"If you do, you'd better stay behind and put somebody else in charge of me, because I'm going."

Gilles spoke even more carefully now. "Relief of Orléans will require a lot of men and supplies."

"So what has my lord the Dauphin been doing all this time I've been here if not collecting men and supplies?"

"Lady, these things take time."

"I see." She stopped her pacing for a moment and looked at him hard. "My lord de La Trémoïlle has the getting of the army."

Gilles bowed his admission that this was so.

"And he wants you to bring me safe to this tower every night."

Gilles bowed again. Love opened him like a flower before her.

"Yes. It would be better to go with men-at-arms than alone." She said this finally, with a toss of her stubble-haired head.

Had she heard her Voices, then? Right here, while he'd been watching? He strained his ears, trying to share more than just the space with her. He heard nothing but the resumed step of her firm little boots.

"And La Trémoïlle is working on it? In his own slow fashion?"

"Yes, Lady."

"Then I must be content."

"Where would you like to go?"

She returned to the window and said, her back to him, "Where the men are."

Gilles felt himself hot again, envy riding like coals at the base of his neck.

"Where men-at-arms are practicing," she elaborated.

"You mean the lists?"

"Lists? Is that what you call such a place?"

So Gilles took his charge to the practice yard. It was laid out beyond the fort of St. Georges alongside the river towards the east and the Azay-Tours road. The palest green haze floated above the chestnut and scrubby elder trees that lined the Vienne. The first budding of this year's foliage was little more than clouds of gnats as yet: if you brushed at it, or so it seemed, it would be gone.

Vineyards terraced up the far slope to catch the warm southern sun. The vines were bare still, grey and pruned tight to their posts as if knotted there by some skilled seamstress. Under normal circumstances, Gilles never would have bothered to notice such things, nor the arching green blades of daffodils that shot out from the nearest bank. Now, every weapon-like thing made him look twice.

He eased the threat in his mind. In a fortnight or less, the flowers would bloom and the bank become a treasury of golden goblets.

I will bring her back then, he told himself.

In the meantime, there were snowdrops in shadowed, protected places, and shy violets. He stooped to pick a fairy's bouquet of tiny flowers and offered them to her, held between thumb and two fingers. The tenderness compressed in the gesture, the intimacy he wanted to convey, sent tremors through his hand he had a hard time controlling.

At first she ignored him and that shook him more. She let her eyes fill with the grand sweep of territory about them, looking back to the chain of three bone-colored castles along the spine of the hill, then forward to the vineyards and the tilt-yard beyond.

He was about to toss the flowers away, his heart black with curses, when she did notice. She laughed carelessly, as if it were a childish joke. She took them, the touch of her fingers swift and light on his. Then she stuck the bouquet carelessly in the band of her black wool cap and scrunched it back on her head.

Intermittent clouds scudded across the sky, frequently blocking the sun and chilling the air. But there had been no rain for several days and the winter's mud in the yard was dry, though not yet pounded to dust.

Just that fast, he could tell, the flowers were gone, pushed from her mind by the cheers and clash of arms rising up from the lists. They drew her to them like clover drawing a bee.

La Pucelle turned her face to catch the stiff, cool breeze that came out of the west and funneled down the valley. Then she turned back to fill her lungs with the sharp smells of the yard: horses, their feed and their dung, sawdust and the bodies of fighting men. A full view of the lists spread below them for a moment, over the painted roof of the spectator's gallery. Then, as she hastened her step on the steep, downward slope, they appeared nearer but only in patches. Groups of men clustered at each discipline: its open arena for hand-to-hand practice, its wooden lanes for jousts, its mounted, swinging quintains for the practice charge and, beyond, the butts and straw targets for archery. The combination of wind, sounds and smells that were second nature to Gilles seemed to light up her face like a torch in a dark night.

Gilles felt a pang of guilt for his complicity in keeping her cooped up in the tower most of the past week. But he had to think that even La Trémoïlle meant it for her own good. Her talk of weapons and raising sieges—which Yann, curse him, tended to encourage—was madness. Divine, but madness nonetheless. In the tower she might prick her finger on a spindle, put the finger to her mouth for a moment and be done with hurt.

Here, behind St. Georges, were no women armed with darning needles. Here were men clamped in steel, swords, lances, maces. A thousand ways to die.

A thousand worries for the bodyguard.

"The men look very well practiced," she commented over the sounds of that practice.

Overhead, banners cracked in the stiff wind. Highest of all was the gold and red of Chinon: three fortresses interspersed with the royal fleur-de-lis. And, of course, every man at practice had set up standards of his own.

"Since your coming, they're being more pious," Gilles teased, taking the opportunity to bend close to her ear. "They've thrown away their dice and drink. They have nothing else to do."

Having said it, and seen her nod as if to say, "Yes, that's as it should be. Very good," he led the way up to the stands. Here, tucked up in the shadow of the fort of St. Georges and somewhat out of the wind, noncombatants could watch when tournaments were staged. The stands were empty, this early in the year. There were no noncombatants now but La Pucelle and himself.

No one but himself.

He suddenly realized that his charge had not followed him up the wooden risers. Turning quickly, he found her, still down at the rail, close to the dangers of combat. Splinters of lance could fly, daggers be knocked from soldier's hands.

Worse than that, she had found the rack where spare swords were kept, in case some warrior needed one. An arc of silver rose out of its bracket and over her head with a dangerous hiss.

Gilles leapt off the benches like a mother going after her toddler who's found the cutlery.

"Oh, Bluebeard, you startled me," La Pucelle gasped as he bounded to her side and laid a protecting hand on her shoulder.

Gilles took a deep breath and tried to calm himself. With waves of panic tumbling over shoals of self-loathing, he realized that, holding a sword as she was, she was much more likely to hurt herself if he startled her at the wrong moment. Or hurt him as she turned and raised the blade in a reflex of self-defense, though that was of little matter.

He took another deep breath, and when he could do so without frightening her more, he said, "Be careful with those things. They're sharp."

She had gone from one blade to the next throughout the rack, then returned to the second from the left, the quicksilver steel with the pommel that curved at the hilt like royal fleurs-de-lis. She stretched her arm out, weighted by the weapon and waved it.

"I think this one's best," she said.

Gilles felt a fool for having said the obvious, *They're sharp*. In a moment's time, she'd picked out the sword he knew from personal experience handled best. Handled best of the rejects in this common pool. Of course, any man worth his salt had swords made to his own specifications, much better than these. Still, she knew, just as if she'd been swinging swords all her life.

By now, the men in the yard had recognized the new arrival. They stopped their practice, stepped closer in adoration and began to shout her name. "La Pucelle! God bless you, La Pucelle! La Pucelle, hail!"

"Hail, men of France!"

She shouted back, waving the sword above her head. Her face was wonderfully unguarded, open and so transported with joy that Gilles ached with the beauty of it.

Ached that she never turned that face to him, certainly never when they had been alone. When it was just the two of them, she had seemed more watchful and guarded, less at ease. Less happy. That was too painful, when all he wanted in the world was her happiness.

Or perhaps, it might be better to admit, her happiness in him.

The entire field was chanting now, “La Pucelle, La Pucelle!”

The young duc d’Alençon, that popinjay, broke out of the general circle of admirers and strode up to the rail. He tore the expensive beaver chaperon off his head and swept it before him in a deep bow.

“La Pucelle,” he said, intimately, under the chanting.

La Pucelle returned the bow. “My handsome duke.”

Handsome? Well, perhaps, in a pale-blond, artificial, mama’s-boy sort of way. She’d never called him, Gilles, that. Gilles glared at the young duke and bristled.

“That sword looks good in your hand,” Alençon said.

Gilles would have taken insult if anyone had said the same thing to him in the presence of such a miserable blade. But La Pucelle seemed flattered.

“Thank you, my handsome duke,” she said.

She made a couple of joyful passes over the duke’s head. Gilles lunged out and caught her hand at the wrist. She turned and gave him a look that could only be called a scowl.

“I didn’t want anybody to get hurt,” he said.

She actually rolled her eyes at him. He let her arm go and she turned back to the duke.

Alençon swept his hand in a courtly gesture towards the field. “La Pucelle, would you do me the honor of trying a few passes with me?”

Gilles nearly jumped out of his skin.

Chapter Eight

To Slow the Charge of a Destrier

"Good God, Alençon, are you out of your mind?" Gilles exploded. Gilles was close enough to hear his charge's heavy sigh. That was meant for him.

To Alençon she said, "My handsome duke, it would give me the greatest pleasure."

Gilles grabbed her arm again. "Lady, I don't think that's such a good idea."

"Why not?" she demanded, her eyes attacking him again.

"As your bodyguard, I must insist—"

Her eyes shifted from him to a spot beyond his head and to the left. He turned ever so slightly in that direction, following her gaze, but he knew nothing was there. He heard only the furious beat of his heart, as he did when Yann stopped to See something.

"My Voices insist that I do," she said, returning to face him.

God, that excuse—that power. No man on earth could refuse it.

"Very well. Very well," Gilles muttered.

She'd already slipped around the rail and into the tramped earth of the arena. The entire field of men began to back up and circle around to watch the fight.

Gilles followed her, but Alençon was his goal. He caught the young duke by the arm as he shifted out of the crushed velvet of his doublet. Gilles could feel the other man's muscles and he didn't like it. Alençon might be a fop, but he was a fighter, too. He'd been three years a hostage with the English and only recently ransomed. The experience would have hardened anybody.

"Take it easy, Alençon," Gilles hissed in his ear.

He didn't mean her to hear, but La Pucelle had just wriggled her head out of the neck of a protective vest of padded leather and did. "No, don't go easy on me, my handsome duke."

Somebody with his head in the right place was helping her to arm. Somebody else was strapping a helmet under her chin. Damn. That was his job, her protection, the lacing up under her arm, the smoothing around her neck.

"If she comes to any harm at your hands, by God, Alençon, you'll have me to answer for it," Gilles threatened the fellow again.

Alençon shrugged Gilles' arm off at the same time as he got rid of his doublet. His bright blue eyes gave a sideways look that said, "What kind of ass do you take me for, Rais?"

"Don't go easy on me," La Pucelle insisted. How had she overheard? "Will the *goddams* go easy on me?"

"No, no!" Men shouted in answer to her shouted question, and then began to chant again, "La Pucelle, La Pucelle." The noise was drawing others down from the castle, and the watch along the turrets of St. Georges.

"That sword stinks, La Pucelle," somebody called. "Here, take mine."

"Take mine!"

"Take mine!"

A dozen offers pressed her. Damn, why hadn't he been the first to think of that, too?

"Mine, lady?"

She came to his after many others. But she quickly by-passed it, too, and finally settled on La Hire's. Well, the old dog had an eye for steel, that was well known.

Gilles tried to press shields on them, but nobody listened. He resigned himself to swords alone, realizing his charge must have difficulty enough swinging the heavy blade with both hands, without having to juggle an extra object in her left.

In no time at all, they were ready. No time for Gilles to consider any way out. The arena cleared again. He went to the rail with the others, but he stayed on the near side, his rejected sword still unsheathed.

"La Pucelle! La Pucelle!" His head buzzed with the chanting.

"Alençon."

The girl's clear voice raised above all others as the two combatants made the preliminary circles about the ring. By God, she was actually taunting her foe, her arms up and open in the gesture of invitation.

"My handsome duke. Come."

Alençon closed.

Gilles took a quick, relieved breath. The duke headed in to strike the girl's sword. That would give her the impression of contact—not least of which was the satisfying ring of steel on steel—but not expose her to any real danger. That, Gilles, decided, was just what he would have done. He'd keep aiming for her safe zone until she wearied of the game and La Hire had to pay a visit to the smith to take the dull nicks out of his edge.

What happened next came so fast that Gilles had to piece it together after the fact. La Pucelle caught her opponent's blade on her own. But instead of simply clashing, or perhaps letting her sword be pushed back towards her shoulder by the blow, the girl met force with force—and beat it.

She caught the duke's sword. Then, with an arc that carried two lengths of metal as well as her opponent's muscle, she brought both blades down. Alençon found himself in danger of being pinned to the ground.

In fact, the young duke barely saved himself from falling flat on his face. He did it by taking ten or twelve skittering steps with most of his body heaving forward before his feet.

La Pucelle helped him along by a nudge to the nape of his neck with her elbow as he passed. Her one movement was the natural outgrowth of the other, like the sway of a tree in wind.

The field of grown men gasped. Then, once recovered from surprise, they cheered wildly. None of them had ever seen—or not seen, if they chanced to blink—anything quite like it.

Most of the men supposed the duke to be clowning, and laughed and cheered accordingly. But Gilles was directly in front of the man and not four paces away when his skitter came to an end.

Alençon raised his face. There was no clowning in it.

The man had been taken completely by surprise, his overture of care and playful gentleness met with dead and powerful earnestness. Before Alençon whipped around to the ring, his face had the look of one struck by lightning on a cloudless day.

Gilles did not like that look.

He liked the sudden fire kindled in those eyes even less. A man with that look felt his honor touched to the quick. A man with that look had stopped playing. A man with that look would forget himself in a moment. Forget whom he was fighting.

Perhaps Alençon had already forgotten.

Gilles shifted his hands on his own hilt, exactly as Alençon shifted his. Gilles raised his unsheathed sword to the same guard position with the consciousness of a novice: pommel at the groin, point high, before the face and a little to the right-hand side. Feet apart, solidly planted, the left a little behind.

Nobody tried to stop him. They were all watching the fight.

Eye on the target.

The target. Where Alençon's leathers gaped a little to give movement to his waist.

"Come, my handsome duke." La Pucelle's voice sang high and sweet.

The circle of men chanted like the drumbeat to the charge.

Gilles would run that "handsome duke" through his very handsome kidneys.

Eye on target, so ...

Gilles found the basic instruction—he'd considered it second nature—as difficult to stick to as an easily distracted boy at his first lesson. He couldn't keep his eyes from the girl and on the spot for which he was aiming.

There was no doubt she was fast. Sometimes her feet seemed a blur. They hardly touched the ground as she drew her opponent first this way, then that. Alençon might have been a baby in his nurse's arms, swung here and there at her will, not his.

Gilles could feel the man's ire rising, growing more and

more out of control, more and more deadly. But that clear pocket to the kidney kept whirling in and out of sight as the duke tried in vain to keep his eye on his own target.

She's fast, Gilles thought, but still tiny. Alençon was not a big man, but she only came to his chest. Often Gilles couldn't see her at all behind her opponent's nervous, twitching mass of well-trained muscle.

She must tire. In swordplay, it's muscle and endurance that win. Tiny, ill-trained *and* female. That first pass had been only beginner's luck. She couldn't keep it up, certainly not against a cock with battle madness swelling his wattles.

Easy. Eye on target ...

Before Gilles had finished the thought, something like a stinging wasp had flown through the circle and out again. Alençon clutched his sword arm. Between his fingers, the bleached linen was sliced, wicking bright red blood.

Eye on ...

Before Gilles could think it again, La Pucelle had taken quick advantage of the weakness. She fished the man's sword out of his hand, one cross-guard on the tip of her own weapon, and flung it from him. Alençon scrambled, but she was there before him, her boot hard on the loose blade.

In yet another swift, sure movement, her pommel came down sharply on the still-bent back, hitting straight in the ribs. The breath shot from him in an "oof".

Alençon sprawled, his own blade useless under him. La Pucelle had him straddled in a flash. Her weight effectively kept much air from returning to his lungs. She held the tip of her sword pointed at the jugular. The handsome duke was a pig about to be stuck.

La Pucelle's laughter rang suddenly from vineyard to the turrets of St. Georges.

"Get up, my handsome duke." She swung off him, tore off her helmet and reached down a hand.

At first, Alençon managed only sitting, even with his victor's aid. From that position, he fixed her with a look that Gilles found himself hating more than the rising fury of mid-fight. It was beaten, it was wonder, it was honor replaced. The look was abject, a willingness to die. It was lust.

"Get up," La Pucelle repeated. "I promised your wife I'd bring you home as handsome as you left her. La Pucelle keeps her word."

Gilles remembered that the duke had invited the girl home to meet his wife and she had gone, before he'd been declared bodyguard. Her words now evoked scenes of domestic intimacy Gilles could neither share nor offer. He transferred those scenes into the dance with swords he had just witnessed. A red haze of jealousy filled the edge of his vision.

He fixed his eyes on Alençon's throat and raised his sword—

But the crowd, that had gone wild with the victory, now broke the ring and swarmed onto the field. Each man had to be near her, to call her name, to win her magic for himself for the day when he faced impossible odds in battle. Each man had something of the same lust Alençon had showed. La Pucelle had to be shared.

The fight tension flooded out of Gilles de Rais. The tip of his sword crashed to the ground of its own weight. The only thing that gave him the strength to pick it up again was the thought that his being on the outside of this press of adoring—and armed—men was just the chance an enemy might be waiting for.

For lust can move to death as well as life.

And every man was the enemy of sire de Rais today.

He fought his way toward the girl's side, pommel foremost.

He came upon Alençon, sifted from the throng like chaff by a passionate wind. The young man was on his feet now, but still holding his side, bent into the pain and coughing for breath.

"Nice of you to let her win, *mon gallant*," Gilles snapped.

"I swear to—I mean, I didn't let her win." There was something in the young man's words that demanded belief.

Gilles left him to recover on his own and elbowed and kneed and pommeled and flat-bladed his way forward until he was able at last to see the dark little head. It was shorter than any other, the tufts of hair ecstatic with sweat and exercise and victory. To be the one to produce such ecstacy—

The old dog La Hire was in the center of the press with her, reclaiming his sword.

"La Hire?" she asked him.

"At your service, mademoiselle."

"Are you next?"

"Mademoiselle?"

"I saw you with the horses when I first arrived. I'd like to try a tilt against you."

"God's blood, mademoiselle—!"

Gilles said the same thing, but La Hire's bellow, at closer range, drowned him out.

"Now, La Hire, I know you've won your name for your tongue like the anger of barking dogs. But I forbid my army to swear."

"You'd as soon stop the roar of the ocean as try to stop La Hire's mouth," someone nearby said.

"Anyone who can't take the force of my oaths had better not ride against me, mademoiselle." The twinkle pressed into the old warrior's eyes by the grin in his massive cheeks was teasing her.

La Pucelle met the tease evenly. "As a special case, La Hire, you may swear."

"Thank you, mademoiselle." The big man gave a little bow.

"I will allow you to swear—but only by either the little martinets in the sky or by your own staff."

"My staff, mademoiselle?"

Gilles was not sure if the girl understood the double-entendre of her last word. But the old warrior clearly did and betrayed it by a nervous shifting around the broad patch of cloth that served him as a codpiece. God's blood was something he could take or leave, but not his own "staff". He would not swear casually by that. What man would?

"And you may swear by these things only if you prove them."

"Prove them?"

Perhaps she did understand. She was a peasant girl, after all, used to watching the copulation of all sorts of beasts.

"Otherwise I may come to believe you win your battles by dreadful oaths alone, no force of arms. And, you understand,

French oaths mean nothing to the *goddams*. So, you must prove it. You must ride against me."

"Now?" There was an sudden effeminate squeak in the old dog's growl.

The crowd had taken up La Pucelle's challenge and there was very little La Hire—or Gilles—could do about it. The girl and the old warrior were carted off to armor, lances and steeds, far out of any help of the sire de Rais. He knew too well that, although quickness could perhaps save a sword fight, in the lists, weight was all. And La Hire probably outweighed the girl threefold.

After several attempts to get close enough to stop the arming, Gilles turned in desperation. He hated to lose sight of his charge even for a moment, but there seemed only one thing to do.

He ran from the lists. He ran up the slope that brought him soon to the butts and the lanes where archery practice was held. The place was deserted: Everyone was down watching the joust. He snatched up the first bow he came to and a quiver of arrows.

Gilles was not much of a bowman, and this was not an English bow or even a crossbow, to pierce a horse's bardings and hit a vital spot. He was quite certain, however, he could at least slow the charge of a destrier.

Chapter Nine

Teaching Her Other Half

A great roar swept up the hill behind him. Gilles turned as if snapped with a whip. Too slow, he was too slow. They'd already run and only one combatant—the green-plumed helmet—remained in the saddle.

Then he saw that the white-plumed rider was being helped up again. She wouldn't learn. She must keep at it until she broke her neck. He swung the quiver over his shoulder and started to run back, the hard-won air tearing at his lungs.

Here, he decided. Here he must stop and make the shot. Quickly, quickly—but not so quickly as to fail.

He pulled the bowstring to sight—and stopped. He had thought the green plume must be La Hire, because that was the color that had remained seated after the first ride. But now that he took aim, he couldn't imagine how that great hulk of a man could make such a tiny mass on any horse. This rider's legs were so short, they stuck out from the barrel of the war horse's back like a child's. It must be the devil to try and cling and keep one's seat with legs like that.

And he remembered that La Hire's colors were black and blue, peacocks and grapes on a silver and gold ground.

It couldn't be—but it was. In the first bout, La Pucelle unseated the great La Hire. He was the one to struggle, dazed, out of the dust and insist on another match. And now, even as Gilles watched, La Hire's lance went wild—as if a sudden clearing of the sun had blinded him. But she did not flinch. Her weapon held steady as statue stone—until it splintered like kindling against the peacocks and grapes of her opponent's shield.

La Pucelle dug her heels into her mount and continued around the yard in a triumphant gallop, her whoops sounding high and strange above all the rest of the celebrating, worshiping, delirious crowd.

"God's balls," Gilles murmured as he lowered the bow and stumbled in a haze down the hill.

La Hire must have begun to grunt a similar oath, but La Pucelle stopped him as she pulled up before the defeated man and allowed a dozen pairs of hands help her down. She undoubtedly reminded him of their bargain, for when Gilles got close enough to hear, the big man was swearing, yes, by his own staff.

"Remember that, La Hire," La Pucelle told him, laughing merrily. "I promised *your* wife nothing. She might thank me for making her a widow. But I want you to win reprieve for your soul by fighting the *goddams,* so let us try to work together."

"I am your servant, mademoiselle," the old warrior promised. A squire under each arm supported him as he executed a dignified bow. Then they helped him from the field.

Still carrying the bow, Gilles managed to get close enough to her now to speak for the first time since they'd arrived at the lists. Men were vying with one another to put away anything she had touched, and others were scrambling for the splinters of her lance as if they were bits of the True Cross. As he came behind her, he saw her shove the sleeve up on her jerkin. Thinking she was unobserved for a moment, she was examining a scrape on her elbow. A network of shallow red-brown lines etched the nut-brown flesh.

"Ah, so arms practice is dangerous after all," he said. "You should have listened to your bodyguard and stayed out of harm's way."

"Nonsense. It's nothing," she assured him, hurriedly dropping the sleeve.

"Come on." He laughed as at a wayward child and took her other arm gently. "I've got some excellent salve. I'll send my man to fetch it."

Purposely she lifted her arm out of his grasp, refusing to move a step. "No. I've one more fight to fight today."

"I doubt you'll get any takers. You've scared them all off, see?"

"One more."

"Who?"

"You, Bluebeard."

Gilles tried to laugh it off. "Maybe another day."

"You, Bluebeard. Now."

"Oh, no, Lady. Not I." Again he tried for joviality, but La Pucelle's voice, with the slightest rise of frustration to it, was quickly drawing a crowd of adorers. They would do anything to remove that frustration from her.

"What are you?" she asked, her fists taunting on her hips, her tiny body leaning forward so it was tinier still. "Afraid?"

"I am your bodyguard. I ... I can't hurt you."

"No. You can't hurt me. My Voices have declared it. For one year, nothing can be stronger than their goodness in me. You don't believe in me—Gilles?"

Gilles worked his tongue over the dryness in his mouth at the sound of his given name—the name of the saint of the dark wood—on her tongue.

"I will follow you, Lady, to heaven or to hell." He only wished there weren't forty ears to hear this declaration and so weaken it.

"Then pluck out your sword."

"Yes, pluck out your sword, monseigneur." The gathering crowd cat-called. He could tell they enjoyed the experience of taunting Gilles de Rais, something they wouldn't dare under usual circumstances.

Gilles turned to walk away. His nature struggled against the move. He knew it was, in some measure, a retreat.

He hadn't gone a step, however, before he felt his hand—the hand with the bow—snatched back. Quick little fingers worked the weapon out of his grasp and into hers. She brought the bow up, then, and urged him round to face her by catching him under the chin with the tip.

"You've been spoiling for a fight this whole day, Bluebeard. I've seen you."

The bow's tip played teasingly with his beard. She could see the blue stain underneath, if, in fact, that was what she was looking for.

"I was trying to keep you from breaking your neck." He couldn't decide which hurt him more, the fact that she had seen—or that she didn't appreciate what she had seen.

"And you feel cheated." The croon of a mother to her wounded child invaded her voice and wounded him even deeper.

"Someday somebody's going to teach you that this is a dangerous business." He kept his voice very low—with difficulty.

"Why don't you teach me? Now?"

"Someday you're going to get hurt."

"Why don't you try to hurt me? Now," she said.

The surrounding voices crowed. "Yes, try."

"Come on, coward."

"Dung hill cock."

"Lady," Gilles protested, "I am supposed to watch your back."

"How can you expect to do that if you don't know what it's like to come at me head on? Come, Bluebeard—Gilles, I must teach you."

"There's nothing you can teach me about war that I don't already know—Lady." He gave her the title dripping with sarcasm. Let her call him "Gilles" all she cared to. "I've been fighting—and killing—*goddams* since before you wore your first pair of hose."

"That was less than a month ago. I'm not surprised."

"I've fought them all, in ambush, on the walls, in the open field."

"But you've never fought La Pucelle."

"I mean to fight beside you, not against you."

"You need to fight La Pucelle. In order to support me, you must learn what it means."

For a moment, she seemed to have finished there. But she had not. And though what she said next seemed little more than repetition on the surface, Gilles felt the flesh on his back creep under his leathers. He knew it as revelation, clear and hard as a diamond.

"If you are to be her other half, she must teach you what it means to be La Pucelle," La Pucelle said.

As if it had a life of its own—or as if it answered to some dark summons that could make stones dance in a ring—he heard the whisper of his own sword as it left its sheath. It twitched in his hand.

"La Hire! Your sword. La Pucelle needs your sword again!" the crowd announced.

La Hire was in no shape to bring the weapon himself, but there were plenty to run the errand for him, to lace her into leather again, to helmet her.

Yet again, the ring was cleared and the many-throated chant began.

Chapter Ten

Corps à Corps

Gilles opened and closed his grip on the sword. He'd had the hilt wrapped in snakeskin, and the skin on his sweat-soaked palms pulled off the binding with difficulty. Snakeskin was an excellent grip. When new, it took the imprint of his palms and fingers in dull black. After a few heavy fights, soft leather indentations cradled each swell of his flesh.

He momentarily set the weapon on the guard rail before him and pushed aside his desire for hesitation with a grunt of will. He snapped on his heavy-plated gauntlets. They swallowed the immediacy of sensation, numbed his doubts, so he could regrasp the hilt and turn center.

She was there, waiting for him.

He began to circle. It was hard to believe his eyes. He had just seen two fine warriors bested by this same opponent. Whether by shame or prowess, at this point it hardly mattered. What mattered was what he would—or would not—let defeat him. But what sight showed him now was so small, small and feminine.

Part of him still wanted to back down, but he'd run out of ways to do it. Another part of him wanted to beat her at once, quickly, just to teach her—since nothing gentler had done it—that war was not child's play. This part was winning inside him. To defeat it, he would have to fight not only her but the tendency of years and years of training and experience. He could feel mind and body gliding into the blade he held *en garde* before him. He always fought best that way, mind gone to the point of the steel, limbs following with their reflexes along the edge.

Some men told him their minds went blank during battle. That was the only way they could deal with the horror. Afterwards, they couldn't remember a thing, either heroics or cowardice.

Gilles had always found himself just the opposite. Not only his mind remembered. Every limb did as well, remembered the jar of steel on steel, the more giving feel—the burst of surprise, the sigh, the scream—when steel met flesh. Every particle of him recalled every battle as it recalled the nourishment of food—and craved repetition of the same movements with a similar hunger.

As he and La Pucelle circled, however, he felt the old ritual fail him. What flowed through the grip was not hate. He couldn't force it to be so. He called it love, and knew it puffy, unused as the flesh of an infant's foot. He wore no protecting calluses anywhere on such skin.

Perhaps this was what slowed down the others, Alençon and La Hire. It had frozen them into inactivity.

Gilles, however, did not feel frozen. He felt very, very quick, life's blood very near the surface. The skin keeping it in seemed thin and jumped with pulse.

He looked across the short stretch of pounded dust at his opponent—*Eye on the target.* She was brown and tiny, moving in quick hops like a sparrow, her hose bagging around sparrow-thin legs. Yes, that was the trick. He dehumanized her, made her a bird or a man-woman monster and saw her as no more than the bound straw of a target in the butts. Now, now he could do it.

He let her come to him, catching her cut to his head smartly on the forte of his blade. Then, while she recovered the extra energy required for an attack, he struck her steel in return. The satisfying rings jarred down his arms and throughout the trunk to his hip sockets. They came in tempo with the chanting crowd, but Gilles no longer heard the chanting. He heard only the throb of steel on steel and the protest of blood in his own joints.

They continued thus, exchanging whack for whack, until nobody could have kept a tally of hits. As close as anyone could come would be to say, "We are on an even count" or "an odd", and that was easily known by whether Gilles took the parry or La Pucelle. And even that tally must change as fast as it took to say so.

Now, Gilles thought, now I will take the advantage. I can do it, of course, whenever I want to.

He put forth the effort. The advantage didn't come. He strained again. She met him, blow for blow, and he had to work harder just to meet what she sent him.

At least, he thought—and even his thoughts came separated by heavy panting—at least she doesn't take quick advantage of me, as she did of the others.

Gasping for air, he managed to speak aloud between teeth clenched with strain. "Will you confess it first, Lady?"

Her low attack to the inside leg he parried with a one-handed swing. "Or shall I?"

Letting the sword's weight do the work, he took a swing at her own inside leg.

"What?" Easily, she beat that off.

"That your sword is equal to mine?"

Cutting high, she retook the attack. "Never."

The onlooker might forget that there was any purpose to the sport other than to clang swords. The talk was the give-and-take of dancers on the floor and, to lulled eyes, the two figures in the ring might seem a pair of dancers accompanying themselves with the music of strange tabors. In fact, Gilles had to keep reminding himself they were antagonists, one of whom might be done to death in the next instant.

And then that instant came.

He expected her blade to come outside. It came inside instead, and so quickly he barely had time to move his guard. He caught her full force near the very end of his steel. Even applying all the strength of both hands 'til his biceps screamed with the effort, still the edge of her sword fulcrumed close enough that he could feel it pass along his neck. He thought a curl or two of his hair must have dropped free, but he couldn't stop to make sure.

Just a friendly reminder, the move said, you are fighting for your life. It seemed this was a move she had been capable of at any time before then. Even, that she had come up short, just to taunt and unnerve him. Next time, she would not be so generous.

He had the feeling this was true, but there was no time to consider the matter fully.

The girl followed her thrust as if dragged by a horse she couldn't control. He got his hilt up further on her blade and they locked, hilt to hilt, *corps à corps*. They stood straining together until Gilles became aware, not only of the strain, but of other things as well.

He realized that every time his panted breath came, hers went. What he breathed in was her expiration, warm, and full of the sweet smell of her he was trying to cut open to the air. The mingled air moved between their close-pressed bodies like breezes between heaven and earth on a summer's day.

He was exquisitely conscious, too, of the placement of her every limb. He wondered, not just what his opponent might move next, as he would in any fight, but at the perfection of each form.

Her right leg measured up the inside of his. The fork of her body vised him just above where he wore the red garter. There was a center of heat here, and snugness against which he shifted. His sex, always aroused when he fought, clashed against the buckler of her belly, her small breast jabbed into the base of his sternum. At the level of his armpit, even as he bent into the struggle, he wondered about the spikes of her hair, if they stood to rigid attention under her helmet or if the leather and sweat had slicked them down in a cast of the scalp beneath. The limbs were wiry and thin—almost too thin—and hardly able to support her own body, it seemed, let alone the pressure exerted by his.

This was a woman's body, he entertained no doubt, and in the ordinary way, he should feel only revulsion for it. He should not be suffering this drive, this attraction. But in the ordinary way, no woman should have exchanged blow for blow with him until his arms rang like iron on the anvil. He should not be straining so to break a simple lock. He should not hesitate so to crush her—if this was hesitation and not physical inability.

Then La Pucelle lifted the point of her little chin and opened her eyes. Only then did Gilles realize he'd been avoiding her gaze throughout the engagement, concentrating on the flash of her blade, avoiding the deadly contact with the windows to her soul.

And she'd kept her eyes closed with the strain of the first few instants of their locked intimacy. Now, the dark lashes parted to reveal pupils entirely given over to the engorged black of the irises. Such happens to other women when they see their infants. Or their lovers. Was La Pucelle's arousal in the midst of battle a parallel to his own? Or was, perhaps, he himself a lover in whose presence she suffered this reaction?

No, he couldn't believe that. She wouldn't let him believe that. Alençon and even La Hire in the fury of his ride must have met those same eyes—and that had been their undoing.

Yet Gilles wondered how anything short of a mirror could be a closer reflection of his own soul. Perhaps that was what was so heart-stopping about those eyes. He saw the swallowing black of the night sky's sphere twice, moonless, starless, even cloudless if that were possible, and he knew it for himself.

No wonder his predecessors had lost their nerve so quickly. They'd been mesmerized, like rats by the serpent's stare. But Gilles was already well acquainted with the depths of his own being. He knew it too well to let the reflection startle him.

It wouldn't startle him, but he could startle her in the same way. He could return her reflection in his own eyes. He did so, feeling the escape of a blinding light.

He was not a moment too soon. He only realized, as he felt her draw back in reaction, that she had been taking advantage of his momentary bemusement. She had hooked her left toe around his ankle and pulled his foot completely out from under him.

Reflexively, he reversed the move on her, pulling out of the lock at the same time, sending her sprawling. The audience roared in protest, but she rescued herself in a three-point landing so gracefully executed that it seemed on purpose. When he thought to close on his advantage, Gilles found her sword tip a breath away from gelding him. He beat the threat left, then right, taking a step back with each hit.

She moved like a sparrow after his grub.

He knew what he must do to that. He turned cat and stalked.

She turned hound.

His ox tried to gore her hound.

Her parasite attacked small and to the heart. The great beast died, wriggled with flies, then turned to rich black earth once more.

The opponents circled. She moved like summer's heat towards him.

"My winter is the equal of your heat." He wasn't certain if he spoke aloud, or if the moves spoke for him.

"Match the glory of my day," said her attack.

"My night comes and pushes your day over the western hills."

"East bursts forth my sun again."

"Blocked by my cloud. And my mountain."

"Washed away to my flat plain."

"Swamped by my river."

"Shoaled on my sand bar."

"Life."

"To death."

"To life again."

"Will you confess, La Pucelle?"

"Confess what?"

"That life and death hang in perfect balance?"

"That is what our Masters say."

"But you fight against it."

Her answer was a grunt of attack.

He parried, "So do I."

Gilles knew he spoke aloud now, panting heavily as he took another attack. More from exhaustion than aggression the swords slipped together again and locked. He was close enough that he could have bitten her on the nose or neck—ears, too, if they hadn't been covered. She could have done the same.

Instead, he hissed his taunt, yet so low that only she could hear it above the drumming chant. "Confess that evil and good hang in a perfect balance."

She might as well have been bitten. Her reply was an elbow to the stomach, trying for lower, and a leap away.

"Never!" she gasped, her once-quick foot dragging with exhaustion.

"It is the way of the Craft. My magic balanced against yours."

"Never!" she repeated, but it came out a sob.

"Nay, Lady. Don't weep. I shall have to pretend to lose if you weep."

Her lunge was more a stumble. "Then I am—I am stronger than you."

He caught her blade, but lacked the strength to hold it properly so she almost did fall. "No, by God. No woman's tears ever stopped me before."

They fought on, but his limbs were so tired and aching they could only meet her stupidity with stupidity of their own. He knew the audience must find the spectacle ridiculous, for their chanting had died. He, too, would have laughed if he'd had the energy. But he did not.

"Where shall you and I meet, my angel? Where come to some peaceful agreement?" Perhaps the dialogue was only in cut and parry again.

"In ... in no man's land, you ... you devil."

"Now, now, no swearing. 'Tis your own rule. Where ... Lady ... where?"

She gasped, "In no man's land."

"In no man's land? Yes? You swear it? Some deadly ... neutral place ... between the camps."

"Where common mortals ... would perish."

"Some place ... between heaven and hell?"

"Yes!"

"You swear? It is possible?"

"I swear."

Gilles suddenly dropped his sword to the dust and caught her under the arm as she threatened to follow it. "Very well. You win." The strength to stay upright was his. He held her, their breath mingling.

The crowd began to swarm the field now.

"Remember—Jehannette," he said in an undertone and quickly, while there was time. "You have promised. We shall meet."

"I do not forget. But Bluebeard, you must call me La Pucelle."

"Very well—La Pucelle."

Satisfied, La Pucelle found the strength to stand on her own and turn to the thronging men. "So now—" she shouted, only a slight cracking hoarseness in her voice. "—Now we take on the English!"

"To the English!" came the wild reply. "Hooray!"

Jostled from one pair of arms to another, La Pucelle found herself in the presence of her previous victory. La Hire came for his sword and clearly gave her more pleasure than another confrontation with the lord of Rais did.

"I thank you, La Hire."

"Mademoiselle, it is I who thank you," the old warrior bowed stiffly. "Old La Hire's sword will never win more glory than this, to say it once fought in La Pucelle's hand."

"You speak true, old dog," she said. "La Pucelle needs a sword of her own. One more fitting than this. My Voices. Yes, my Voices will lead me to such. In time. My Voices—"

Gilles heard no more, La Pucelle's prophecies drowned from his ears by the crowd. They were chanting the Noël now, the ancient hymn of a crowd who has discovered a God.

"*Noël, Noël to La Pucelle. Noël, Noël to the Maid!*"

Gilles found himself standing alone as Alençon had after his defeat, staring after the surge of the crowd and the little brown figure he was meant to guard.

But I am not like the "handsome duke", he thought. That man was defeated because she took what was good in him and made it her own. La Hire's case is the same. Even that old dog with the sins of twenty years of battle on him has enough good in him to serve her end. But I—

Gilles stooped to pick his sword up out of the dust though his hands rebelled a moment at trying to curl around the snakeskin again. He realized too clearly that he had, in fact, been fighting for his life. La Pucelle had promised to teach him exactly what he would be guarding, what it meant to be La Pucelle.

The next idea made him even more uneasy. She might teach him what it meant to be Gilles, sire de Rais.

Chapter Eleven

On the Road to Poitiers

The company of forty horses climbed the rise that finally brought the sleepy town of Rivière into view. As they did, the featureless grey that had leadened the sky all day broke for a moment. A watery sun appeared to the right. La Pucelle pulled up her horse, yanked at the brim of her boy's woolen cap and scowled at the heavenly sign.

"We're going south. We're not going east to Orléans at all. You're taking me south. You lied to me."

Gilles felt the accusation in her voice as sharp as if she'd jabbed him in the ribs with a sword. He knew the hoax was up.

"I did not lie to you," he protested weakly.

He glanced over to Yann for assistance. Yann, taking advantage of the halt to look back the way they'd come over the rump of his dull old palfrey, refused to meet his eye. Yann had warned him he ought to explain the situation straightforwardly to her before ever starting on the road. And he hadn't. He'd wanted to protect her, even from this.

"I simply told you," Gilles went on, stammering, "I finally had permission to take you away from Chinon."

"Whose permission?"

"Monseigneur le Dauphin's."

"And?"

"And my lord de La Trémoïlle's."

"La Trémoïlle. Ah, I knew it." She yanked the reins around and began to force her gelding to retrace his steps.

Gilles made a clumsy attempt to go after her, all twisted

reins and stumbling hooves beneath him. He knew the eyes of the rest of the party watched his discomfiture in silent amusement.

"Lady, please, listen a moment."

"You listen to me," she snapped back. "How many times do I have to say it? I am sent by my Lord to raise the siege of Orléans. I need to go to Orléans." She flung a determined arm eastward. "That way."

"The Dauphin has yet to give you the armor you need."

"Maybe I don't need armor."

"You said there was a sword to find. Your Voices haven't said where yet. And what of all the men you require?"

"Maybe I don't require any men."

"You can't relieve Orléans with only these few men, half of them priests."

"Perhaps you could not, Bluebeard. But La Pucelle can."

He wasn't quite certain when she'd started calling him Bluebeard instead of sire de Rais. Certainly she must know what his trim beard concealed on his chin. It hinted at the magical ties between them, but was hardly an endearment. It was nothing close to the "Gilles" he hoped for. It was even further from the "my handsome duke" Alençon got.

Struggling over his disappointment, Gilles said, "Believe me, I would take you to Orléans if I could."

"I don't know that I need you at all. I think I will simply go."

Gilles sighed helplessly. Then to his surprise, she pulled up on the reins and halted. Why, he couldn't comprehend. She seemed to be waiting for something, looking the direction Yann did. It was enough that, for the instant, she had halted and rode no closer to Chinon.

"So where are you ordered to take me, Bluebeard?"

"Poitiers," Gilles mumbled. It wasn't something of which he could be proud. "Where you're to be examined by the religious college of the University of Paris in exile there."

"Examined? Again? What for?"

"For possible heresy. For witchcraft."

"But I've been examined for all of that. And everything else."

"The Dauphin fears that in such an undertaking, he cannot be too careful."

Gilles got no answer to this. His reticent charge kept her eyes fixed on the way they'd come, but at least she wasn't following the downward slope any more.

Presently, as he heard the accompanying horsemen behind him shift, creaking their leather and rattling their bridles in their boredom, he attempted further: "Won't you let me take you on to Poitiers, Lady? I swear to you I'll hasten the silly business in every way I can."

"I think you ought to wait for this messenger first," she said. "The message, Bluebeard, is for you."

Only then, riding through a smoky haze of still-bare trees, did he pick out the man. She could not possibly have seen him before that instant, for every other portion of the road was invisible. Yet she had known.

"Why don't you just tell me what this is all about," he snapped at her. "I'll toss the man a coin when he gets here, and we can be on our way without wasting any more time."

"I think you'd better wait for him." The "I-know-and-you-don't" in her eyes boiled fury into hot bands all around his chest.

They waited. In no undue haste, the rider came up. He was a huge, loose-limbed, almost spastic young man. Gilles had the feeling he knew the fellow, and it was not a comfortable knowledge. Yann was looking with outright cheer on the approach. Something to do with witchcraft, no doubt. A member of the coven.

But it was Gilles and not Yann the fellow addressed. Gilles could hardly resist the urge to throttle the creature in his haste to get the words out of him. They ought to have given the fool a less lofty speech to memorize.

"Your lady wife, Madame Catherine de Thouars, hearing you had left the battlefields and joined the court, has followed you thither, monseigneur de Rais. She rests this night in Chinon. She hopes she may soon have the honor of your company, as the years have been long since you've paid her any husbandly attention."

By the end of the stammered, halting delivery, the lord of Rais found himself reduced to an almost inarticulate groan: "Oh, my God!"

La Pucelle, on the other hand, had plenty of words. "Your wife, Bluebeard? I must confess I always thought you single. But, of course, every lord must have a wife. I should love to meet her. I hope you will soon introduce us. I did so enjoy meeting my handsome duke's lady duchess."

"You will not enjoy meeting Madame Catherine de Thouars, Lady. Of that I assure you."

She looked at him still in sideways amusement. "Nay, Bluebeard. I rather think I shall. Since she is such a torment to you, we shall get along famously. You will not turn back to Chinon for her this night?"

"Not for my life." Gilles turned his horse. At the moment, he didn't care if that monstrous woman-in-men's-clothes followed him or not. "If you're not careful, Lady, I may see to it that we stay in Poitiers forever."

La Pucelle laughed out loud, that wonderful peal of hers, like high church bells. He didn't think what he'd said was so humorous.

She cocked her head, listening to something that wasn't there again. Then, to his astonishment, she turned in her saddle towards the south, towards Poitiers. She hadn't turned the horse, but she was nonetheless considering ...

"Poitiers?" she said. "That's where Charles Martel turned back the heathen, is it not? It would be good to see the site of such wonders."

Poitiers is also the site of the battle where England's Black Prince defeated France's King Jean. That's more recent history, Gilles thought, but didn't say, stifling his own voice of doom.

"And then there are these tedious clerics who can do no better even for themselves than exile from Paris," she went on, turning to look at the priest on the palfrey. "I trust Père Yann will see that they do not waste too much of my time."

For one instant, Gilles went blind with jealousy that she should express such confidence in his crippled milk brother.

One among the other riders, Yann lingered behind now, pressing his mount closer to the simple-minded messenger who'd brought such ill news. How could that be a threat? Yet Gilles hated her confidence in anyone but himself.

La Pucelle still wasn't ready to let up. "Poitiers may be difficult, but my Voices will counsel me so it shall not last forever. Orléans shall come soon enough. And who knows? Lady de Rais may find it convenient to join us there in the meantime. Certainly, it's likely, if she found no difficulty at Chinon. And it's quite clear she could never join us later at Orléans, in enemy territory."

The girl was trying to annoy him, and she succeeded. In a fury, Gilles set his mind to something else, anything else that might distract him.

"Tell me, sire de Sillé," Yann, the sorcerer in Augustinian robes, was saying to the messenger, adding a second coin for information of his own. "Did your lady mother accompany her granddaughter to Chinon?"

"She did, Père Yann."

Sillé. Now Gilles recalled why the messenger was so familiar. He'd been thinking him just one of Catherine's servants seen briefly in passing. Now his milk brother's words recalled to him the child his stepgrandmother had had in old age, the one her previous husband had refused to legitimize. One could hardly blame the old lord. Few men claimed idiots with relish. Then the lord of Rais remembered that the creature and he shared the name of the dark forest saint. Gilles. This was Gilles de Sillé. As if their origins were somehow connected. Fortunately, the baby name Bibu clung to the child-man except when tricksters like Yann weren't trying to flatter him by calling him "sire de Sillé".

Then Yann, always up to some unfathomable hocus-pocus, said, "You'll forgive me, daughter Jehannette, Gilles. I think I'd better return with this man to Chinon."

"Oh, Father, please not."

Gilles was quite certain La Pucelle would never have expressed such disappointment if he'd said the same thing, and it made him raise his whip. He only just managed to resist bringing it down, which would have made his mount leap forward in a very undignified frenzy.

"How shall I escape the snares of these devious scholars without you?" her plea continued.

Yann reached out a hand and patted hers where they rested on the reins. "Don't worry. Trust to Gilles and your Council. The God willing, I won't be long. I'll catch up with you as soon as ever I can."

With that, Yann urged his palfrey up beside the idiot and the two rode off together. Then, to Gilles' amazement, La Pucelle, without another word of protest, turned her horse. Her back plumb, her head high in the lowering sun, her short legs aligning contrary to the horse's broad back, she rode off in the other direction, towards Poitiers and the examiners.

He followed her.

A Handful of Dried Red Rowan Berries

"Ah, look, Bluebeard. A magpie's nest."

I was still close enough to hear La Pucelle's comment as they rode to Poitiers, and I followed Gilles de Sillé, called Bibu, back to Chinon, to his powerful witch of a mother. Looking back, I saw the large, untidy clump of twigs, too. A bit of a breeze out of the west tossed it in the arms of an oak, tall, but yellow yet with the first cloud of budding. I knew not how it had stuck there, to the uppermost branches, through winter gale and storm, unless it was magic, bird magic.

La Pucelle's wonder seemed just that, a child's delight at a conjurer's trick. But, I pondered, is there more? Does she do this by instinct? Or does she know that taking a man to the woods and showing him a magpie's nest can cure him of impotence? Would she try to feed him cat's brain next, or a raven's head? Such potions I would have used to treat his "problem", had he asked me.

He never had, of course. He didn't see it as a problem, this specter raised by Bibu's news. Neither, actually, did I. Gilles wasn't really impotent, only with women. No matter what the old witch, Anne de Sillé, had done on his wedding night, this avoidance of his wife was a spell, rather, of Gilles' own setting. Or the God's, from Gilles' birth, stronger than my magic, and able, like the dark of the moon surrounding a candle flame, to work magic of its own.

This didn't seem La Pucelle's sort of magic, however, to consciously work as an old wise woman might, to counteract his aversion to females. As for having Gilles de Rais piss through his wedding ring—well, my milk brother didn't wear such a thing now, if he ever had.

And yet, maybe La Pucelle worked as the magpie did, without reason. And maybe, if this were a spell that needed to be broken, she could, by feel alone, wisdom coming to her in impulsive gurgles of delight, break it.

Leave her to it then, I told myself, and set my attention to following Bibu de Sillé.

Yet another kind of magic had given this child's mind in a great man's body the ability to carry such a message. The magic was short-lived, no doubt because of its difficulty. I wouldn't have attempted such a spell myself, and it had worn off before we'd ridden out of sight of those heading for Poitiers.

"What does your lady mother want?" I tried to prod my new traveling companion. "She didn't send you after monseigneur de Rais just for her granddaughter's sake. Any messenger would have done for that. But you, her son, the God's son—"

Bibu could only grin and drool in reply. Madame de Sillé had known I would answer such a messenger, even if my milk brother did not, even if the message consisted of no word. Here was part of my coven, a very powerful part, powerful in the way of old crones.

Madame Anne de Sillé was related to Gilles de Rais twice, as his grandfather's second wife, as his own wife's grandmother. I was more interested in her personal power. I'd seen it often, on the gallows in the city of Nantes, ridding her granddaughter of an unwanted child. If we were to have a coven circling to the light of La Pucelle, Madame Anne would be essential. If she had half the power I credited her with, this was the reason she'd come to Chinon.

I tried to put thoughts of disenchanting my milk brother behind me, as I put him behind me as well. Sweep the thoughts away, as a bridal chamber should be swept of anything that might impede the newlyweds at their conjugal union. Traces of witchcraft: two halves of an acorn, perhaps, or granulated beans.

And yet, I thought, if a cure were sought for Gilles de Rais, one might do no better than to carry bread and salt to Madame Anne, without her knowledge. If Gilles were then to eat of such fare, it would go far to heal his impotence, of that I was certain.

Such musing so distracted me, I neglected my own magic, the chant with a hackney's lope that would keep my mount from throwing a shoe. In the last half league to Chinon, off it came, the horse went lame, and I had to climb down at once.

Bibu de Sillé offered me his fine steed, or even to take me up on the pillion. But I knew he'd driven his beast just as far as mine had come, and much faster, so I made do with my feet, bare on Mother Earth whose exposed bones cooled quickly those early spring evenings.

I arrived in Madame Anne's rooms, alone and out of breath. My calves ached from the climb, first up to the castle and then to the chamber they'd given her at the top of the tower. They'd given her the room La Pucelle had just vacated.

I knew the old witch at once, her red-rimmed eyes and owl-like face, though she wore her grey hair braided and properly coifed for a noblewoman. She was not alone. Indeed, the crowding at the door prevented its closure, spilled out onto the landing and almost to the turn of the stairs. Women's smells, heavy, cloying clove-lavender fragrance of pomander incongruously mixed with the natural milk-and-swaddling smell of infants in the close space. Some minutes passed before I could discover the reason for all of this: madame la dauphine, Marie d'Anjou, Charles' wife, was before me in consultation with Madame Anne.

Madame la dauphine had brought her two children for the old woman's blessing as well as the new one rumor was just beginning to set in her belly. That royalty came to wait on one of lower station instead of calling Madame Anne to her was honor indeed. But of course this entailed nurses and pages as well as maidservants and ladies, hardly room for breath at all.

Exhausted as I was, I decided to watch and wait my turn. By concentration, by making myself small and, yes, by a little magic, I at last worked my way into a corner. Here, I wasn't intruding on anyone, but I could see all.

I'd seen very little of the woman who would be queen since she was a child, since at four or five years old she'd been betrothed to the Dauphin. He, although twice her age at the time, had been young, too, and wanted nothing to do with girls then, in her father's hall at Angers. This was before anyone suspected he had a chance at the throne, although her mother had always had an ambitious imagination.

Gone was the lively little girl I remembered. The years had done this, decades now with Charles. Charles liked women well enough, but not this woman he'd been handed for ambition's sake. His sense of duty had grown somewhat, enough to get these two children and many between. But those between had miscarried, no doubt because duty only had been at their getting. The God, as we of the Craft like to say, had not been present.

The lives of two children had been unable to make madame la dauphine shake all the effects of previous deaths. The wimple with which she wrapped her chin like an old woman, was, like the rest of her garb, royalty's mourning white.

Beneath the white, Marie d'Anjou's soul floundered as if in the mire beneath the shallow water of a peat bog, staining all her days. Something must be done now to prevent her life from being sucked into an unending procession of gloomy pilgrimages. Madame Anne was trying to take such steps.

For the pregnancy, Madame Anne provided a kerchief full of grey tablets made of licorice root, recommending a feverfew infusion as well. To that regimen, she added an acorn—"to carry about madame's royal person." I knew that was a charm against aging rather more than a strengthener of the womb and thought it just. I might have added an infusion of valerian myself.

The younger of the royal children, the princess Catherine, was hardly sitting on her own yet. Her long, thin, flaccid limbs had been unswaddled for inspection. They and her old man's face and pallor gave her the Valois' usual air of languidness, if not to say stupidity. A delicate linen cap failed to conceal the prominence of her ears. The image of the little girl using them to fly away presented itself to my mind: She was certainly miserable enough at having to be the center of so much of madame's poking and prodding. She twisted and squawked in a most unladylike fashion.

Still, the baby girl seemed healthy enough, unlike the other royal children, in numbers I'd lost track of, lost before birth or shortly after, in the past five years. Madame Anne prescribed only a handful of dried, red rowan berries to be sewn into the seams of the princess's garments to preserve that health.

The older child, the son and heir Louis, was a different story. There could be no doubt, as there had been in his father's case, that he was his father's son. His features were so close to those of the young Monsieur Le Vert as I remembered them, crowned in the forest of the wren hunt, that I might have been suffering the Sight again.

But Louis was a spider-like child, weaker, paler, thinner than even his weak, pale, thin father had been. I realized I'd seen very little of him at court. I'd been assuming that was because he was young still, and in the care of women. Now I saw there might be other, health reasons for the withdrawal.

Even before the dauphine and her ladies began a recital of the lad's ills, a frisson of terror took hold of me. This was the body through which the royal blood must pass to future France? The line was weak, had been with the old, mad King, and grew weaker with each generation. I had no doubt this was because they hesitated to take on the full burden of their callings, these men of the fleurs-de-lis. As they grew weaker, their devotion to the Craft grew weaker. Or vice versa, one weakness playing upon the other in a vicious, mirror image of the eternal cycle of life.

But what could I do to urge them towards this duty, more than I'd already done? What was I, as priest of the Sacrifice, going to do in two years' time when the Sacrifice came again? And nine years after that?

I suppressed such thoughts. Time enough for them in days to come. Now I must concentrate on the immediate tales of woe rehearsed by Louis' caretakers.

The boy, not quite six yet, had been slow to walk on those spindly Valois knock knees. For this, Madame Anne exerted her healing touch. She had the boy hold his unhosed limbs out and stroked them lightly, but for a long time. Then she prescribed rubbing the legs with a warming salve and having the child wear his shoes to bed, only shoes made a bit too large and on the wrong feet. The long, pointed toes would bend the legs in the proper direction all night long.

Louis was also slow to speak, a very worrisome thing in a prince. Even now, his own mother couldn't understand him and had to turn for translation to the boy's dearest nanny. For this, Madame Anne took out a small but very sharp knife, cleansed it in a free flow of wine while she whispered a spell, then had a pair of women hold the boy as she cut a nick out of the fiber at the root of his tongue.

Prince Louis wailed at the pain and got soothed by nannies and honeyed chestnuts—which made the pain worse. I would have instructed, "No food until after prime in the morning."

But Madame Anne was speaking to the dauphine: "I will make an amulet for monseigneur the prince to wear. I require some time in the making of it, but I will send it to you when it is done. You are to see that he wears it around his throat, next to the skin. We'll see if that doesn't untie his tongue."

That was how the old witch dismissed her court. Ladies who hoped to linger with complaints of their own she shooed off, saying surely they must understand that the health of their prince came first.

I made a move to push among the trains and veils and make an exit, too. A glance from Madame Anne made me stay, however, crushed against the wall.

Good, I thought. The press of my thoughts has magicked her mind.

But then it occurred to me: Perhaps her thoughts—the thoughts of such a powerful witch—might have the sway over mine.

Feathers in the Direction their Life Grows

Still the patients dawdled outside the room of Madame Anne de Sillé. When next I caught the old woman's eye, I spelled the message to her: "You will need a jackdaw for this amulet you propose to make, madame. Let me go fetch you one from the dovecote and the birdkeeper. When I return, we may have the room to ourselves."

She gave a nod of agreement, so I went. And when I returned, the jackdaw squawking miserably in his wooden cage at being disturbed at this time of night, we were alone. Madame Anne closed the door behind me, threw the bolt, then took the cage from me by its bent wood handle.

She raised the bird's small, grey-black head to the level of her large pale one, equally beaked, and began to make bird sounds to him.

After a while, in an attempt to bring human speech back into the room, I cleared my throat and mentioned how well I thought she handled the royal cases.

Madame Anne seemed to find squawks and chirps more compelling for a moment. But finally she said, "What? You would have done otherwise?"

"No. That's just the point. I've been here at Chinon for weeks, but nobody approached me. I would have handled these ills in just the same manner."

"Ah, well," she said, between chirps. "Does not the Craft teach us that the world is balance between, among things, male and female? You may know what I know, but there are things women are more comfortable bringing to another woman. And that is part of how the balance is maintained."

I nodded. She was winning similar concessions from the bird, whose voice no longer registered terror. I found this quite remarkable in light of the fact that her speech to him, as far as I had ears to understand it, told him quite bluntly what the next few minutes had in store for his little life.

"You understand, of course," she told him, "this is for a prince, for the blood royal. As your sacrifice now may help him, his Sacrifice, at some future cycle year, may in turn help all the world in which you will be living then in some other form."

The bird gave a sound very close to a coo for one so gravel-throated.

Madame Anne opened the cage, then, and reached in. The bird didn't struggle, but fit his breast to her palms. With a finger, she stroked the feathers of his head in the direction their vibrant life grew. My ears, having grown accustomed to sound at bird-pitch, could hear the little heart resting in that breast, no bigger than a fraise-des-bois nestled in the litter of a forest floor. At that moment, the pulse seemed to fill the tower room.

Madame Anne took up the little knife with which she'd cut the prince's tongue. She considered it, still beaded with the royal blood. Then, as quick as a flash, with a final pair of bird sounds, she used it to cut the feathered throat. She had to take what blood she could before the little heart stopped pumping, before the unconscious protest of flapping wings could stop. I caught it for her in a plain iron goblet that she'd stood ready.

I commented: "All I could think of, watching the prince earlier, was, 'this is the vessel in which the blood royal must be carried to the next generation? A very poor vessel indeed.' I am glad, madame, that you are doing what may be done to repair it, though I have doubts that one jackdaw's life may be enough."

Madame Anne shrugged, but that may have been no more than a shouldering into her work. She couldn't spare concentration for words at the moment. Using the same knife again, she cut out the bird's tongue, the forejoint of his right wing, and then strung them together on the tiny ligament of his right leg. This bundle she suspended over the fire, which she stoked with bunches of herbs to work through the smoke, among them sage and carrot seed. She swung the jackdaw parts on their hook to just the right level over the flames and then turned, straightening her back to face the room.

"They tell me," were the first words she had for me, "that they just cleared La Pucelle out of this room before they moved my granddaughter and me in."

"That's indeed so."

I joined her in a silent survey of the room, the yellow stone walls rounded, matching the curves of the tower, with a great fireplace as the focal point. Often as I had visited La Pucelle as her spiritual advisor, I hardly recognized the place now. Though the foundation was the same, countless trunks of women's gowns and accessories, several devoted just to Madame Anne's herbs and magic paraphernalia, now crammed it full.

"You've seen the girl then?" she asked me.

"I have."

"She's all the prophecy foretold?"

"I think so, yes." I hesitated a little in my statement. The skepticism I read in the old woman's eyes, set like gems in a filigree of wrinkles, was so virulent it passed contagion to me.

"Yes." She nodded.

And then I decided what I read was not skepticism at all but—jealousy, perhaps? Or an old person's compensation for what, through life, had been too many disappointments.

She spoke again: "Yes. When we arrived, it surprised me. 'This must have been a man's room before us,' I said. That was what I sensed, a man. 'Yet, what man would they put at the top of a tower devoted to women?' The answer can only be La Pucelle, the Virgin-Whore, the Woman-Who-is-a-Man. Yes, I sense her power. I hope to see her in the flesh myself, very soon."

"They've sent her to Poitiers."

"So they say. Idiots, who can't tell the truth of such power, just by being in this room."

"They are only folk who want good power but not the bad and are not content to work with both."

"Exactly."

Now, I thought, is the time to turn the conversation round again. "Your grandson, monseigneur de Rais, has gone with her."

"So they say." Madame Anne sighed audibly and sank upon a stool, the day's ride along with its other activities finally catching up with her.

Perhaps I shouldn't bother her, but some things I had to know. "I'm surprised your granddaughter, Gilles' wife Catherine, isn't here. She too must have wearied on the journey."

"She fled when the dauphine and all her ladies arrived. She'll be back soon enough, I imagine."

I nodded. Madame Anne rested one arm full across the table where the jackdaw's dismembered carcass rested. She stroked it idly, as if conversing with the process causing it to slowly stiffen and grow cold. She made no effort to get up and unbolt the door so Madame Catherine could return when she was ready, however.

"Being childless herself, Catherine cannot bear to be among other women when they parade their offspring," Madame Anne explained presently. "Even pale, bandy-legged creatures cause her grief."

"That's understandable."

Madame Anne gave a little snort of skepticism.

"My lord Gilles got her message, that she wants to see him," I said.

Madame Anne answered the note of doubt that had crept into my voice. "That's right."

She got up now, limped over to her herb chest and withdrew a small, thin box from its depths. She lifted the lid, inlaid with mother-of-pearl, and considered its contents: a single length of black and embroidered lacing, knotted in seven places. That may not seem like much, but the lace had once belonged to Gilles de Rais, and the knots had been tied just as the vows of his wedding to Madame Catherine were being pronounced. It was my milk brother's virility Madame Anne kept with her in that box, his own ability to consummate his marriage.

"Has she come to demand an annulment?" I asked. "Gilles

will not gladly part with Thouars, Tiffauges, the rest of the lands he gained by the union."

Madame Anne shook her head. "My granddaughter has come to the conclusion during these past eight and a half lonely years that all men are pretty much the same and that romances are a pap given to girls to lure them into the evils of their lives—'for the sins of our mother Eve. Better the devil I know,' she tells me. So—she wants to prevail upon Gilles to give her the child she so longs for—that their fiefdom requires."

I let my breath out in something close to a whistle. "I think Gilles would rather lose the lands than grant Madame Catherine's wish."

"That's only because of the spell I cast on him eight and a half years ago." Madame Anne gestured to the lace in the box again. "I cast it when that rash young lord of Rais kidnapped my granddaughter and forced her to the altar for her lands. Catherine has begged me, weeping, to undo the knots so she may no longer be barren—and so I shall, as soon as we are close enough to her lord for my magic to be sure of working."

The back fringe of my hair scratched my neck as I tried to deny her hopes. "Madame, the nature of my milk brother is such that I think more than your knots are to blame. It is a magic nature," I went on, stumbling, trying to explain. "Almost the mirror of La Pucelle, if I may put it thus. He's kept his distance from you and your granddaughter, else you'd know it's true."

Madame Anne took my words under consideration, looking around the room as she did so, sensing the magical girl whose powerful spirit still pervaded it.

She nodded. "I told Catherine if she would not undergo the shame and trouble of appealing to the Holy Father for annulment, she might get a child as I got my own Gilles—by the God at Midsummer. She would not. I didn't have the raising of her, alas. She's too much the Christian: sin, pollution, all that."

"I see." It would have been the simplest solution, surely. How often the new religion, I thought, limits a person's options with its labels of good and evil.

"Well," Madame Anne said, packing the lace in its box and

setting it carefully in the trunk. "I can only do what I can do."

"And you do much, madame."

The smell of the singeing feathers and flesh along with their burning herbs filled my throat for a moment. When it cleared, I tried another of my concerns on her.

"Your mention of sacred Midsummer puts it in my mind. My heart holds no greater wish than to celebrate it this year with La Pucelle and a full coven. You and your son will join me, I hope?"

"But of course."

"That leaves me still one initiate short of a coven. I find that Tanneguy du Châtel is not to be trusted, initiate in the Craft though he is."

"Whom do you have?"

I listed them: "La Pucelle, Gilles, you and your son, Charles the Dauphin, Roger de Briqueville, Hamish Power the Scottish merchant, Gwencalon son of the God and the old harper. My Pieronne and her mistress, the witch of the Mont-Saint-Michel. I must send for them soon. Père Michel, if he can come. Myself. The list is short on women. Can you, madame, eke it out?"

"Certainly." She named her maid, La Meffraye, a Welshwoman. "I left her behind in Champtocé, to have a care of the old man, and to look after the place in general. But I can send for her at any time."

"Madame Catherine cannot be prepared for this? It might be something if Gilles knew she was with him in the Old Ways."

"No. I've told you. She's too much the Christian."

"As are so many—far too many—these days. I certainly hope that such a convocation—under La Pucelle—may do much to change this."

"And so it may," said Madame Anne. But she didn't sound over hopeful.

I couldn't let her pessimism darken my prospect. We had a coven! I had what no Master for many years had. I had La Pucelle and twelve other adepts of the Craft to gather on the year's shortest night, perhaps even before. What power might we not raise then? I must send for those not close here. I must plan.

Madame Anne decided the pieces of her amulet had cured long enough. She got up off her stool and went to the fire. She pulled back the hook with a corner of her full sleeves and as soon as the blackened bits of jackdaw were cool enough to handle, she wrapped them in a bit of new linen and tied them with a blue ribbon for the young prince's neck.

Then she turned to the goblet of blood, trickling drops from a vial into it as the fluid thickened and darkened, working to keep it thin enough to pour. What she added looked like plain water, but I knew enough to tell it was sanctified, scooped from a chapel font when some priest wasn't looking.

She didn't leave me alone in my glowing thoughts for long.

"There's another problem as much or more your concern, Master, than Midsummer covens or the lacing of your milk brother's groin." She turned the white linen brilliant red now by dipping it into her goblet.

"And that is?"

"The Sacrifice. Only a Master can provide that, and it must be provided or else—"

"Or else?"

"Or the world will end."

"So they say."

"Certainly the world as we know it will end. The world where the Old Ways are kept."

"Of course I know that. But there's time. There's time yet."

I remembered the last Sacrifice, how uncertain I'd been until the final minute that I could manage a willing victim. And it didn't seem nearly enough time had passed since Charles VI had become the God in my hands to be discussing finding another with the necessary royal blood—and willingness.

"Two years to make the Sacrifice willing," she mused, speaking my thoughts aloud. "Who is it going to be?"

"I am—deliberating," I confessed.

"You don't know him yet? Then how will two years suffice to persuade him to lay down his life to keep the cycle going?"

"Charles isn't yet anointed King. Let us get that accomplished—with the help of La Pucelle—and then—we shall see."

She considered the stain on her amulet, gave it one more dip and then said, "I don't think you can have Charles."

"Certainly not in two year's time," I agreed, and nodded towards her artefact. "Prince Louis will hardly be ready to rule, no matter how you weight his neck with dead jackdaws. And can Charles the son of Charles the son of Charles do all the prophecy requires of him in two more short years? It seems impossible. Taking Charles, then, is out of the question."

"I have to agree with you."

"His uncles and cousins are a lost cause."

"The handsome young duc d'Alençon is a prince of the blood," she suggested.

I liked the idea. "But the duke's not initiated."

"He might yet be. He was among the first to greet Catherine and me when we arrived. He seems to be very taken with La Pucelle."

"So he is," I agreed, keeping the second half of my thought to myself: more, perhaps, than anyone save my own milk brother.

"That's half the conversion, I should think."

"So it is."

"Otherwise, I can't think where this royal blood is to be found."

"Charles could always give his blood into the veins of another willing to die in his place. He did so once before, when we were children. When the old harper turned the wheel with the throb of his blood."

"That's possible."

"Madame," I said, "You sound as if you doubt our Dauphin—for anything."

"Well, you have been at court—and around His Majesty—longer than I have. But I don't like what I've seen of him, even in so short a time."

Perhaps she was right. Perhaps I had been so thrilled by La Pucelle's coming, I'd failed to see danger signs in that other person so vital to the prophecy's fulfillment, Charles the son of Charles the son of Charles.

Was Lady Anne's power strong enough to overhear my thoughts? She answered them, in any case. "I think you'd better have some plain talk with the Dauphin, Master of this coven. Before you join us on the road to Poitiers—heading after this recalcitrant grandson of mine."

"I initiated Charles myself."

"His counselors— Well, talk to him, that's all I ask."

She moved to hang up the amulet to dry, and as she did, something seemed to catch in the muscles across her shoulders. I ran to assist her. She waved me off, but the words she used next did not inspire me to leave her.

"Here is another who will not be able to give you the Sacrifice," she said, not of Prince Louis. "I feel it in my bones."

The amulet dangled in an inconspicuous place to dry thoroughly before Madame Anne sent it down to the prince. She crossed the room and lifted the bolt just as her granddaughter arrived, out of breath at the top of the stairs, flanked by her maids.

"Père Jean," Catherine de Thouars greeted me upon our introduction.

She had forgotten any previous acquaintance, saw only the surface of my disguise. She knelt and kissed my left hand while I blessed her with the God-touched fingers on my right, twisted so that she could not tell if they made the cross or the sign of the Stag.

Catherine de Thouars was as pink and blonde as ever. Though perhaps grown a little plump with inactivity, it was not unpleasant. Childbearing had not worn her yet like many another woman, madame la dauphine, for example. She was beautiful—too beautiful for me, I couldn't help thinking with bitterness. And also, I thought, too beautiful for her husband, Gilles de Rais, who had a dark beauty of his own.

"I come from your lord and husband," I told her. "He sends his best greetings."

"Is he here in Chinon?" she asked. "Will he come to me?"

"His duty to the Dauphin sent him to Poitiers with La Pucelle."

"Duty. Always duty. What of his duty to me, his wife?"

"He asks that you join him in Poitiers." I knew I lied, but I stole a glance towards Madame Anne's chest of spells. Magic just might change falsehood to truth.

I made my excuses as soon after that as I could and prepared to leave the ladies.

"Don't forget," the old woman's final words to me were. "You must visit with Charles before we set off."

And so, the next morning, I did.

Seventh Antiphon

Bets Set Upon a Fence

Over Château Chinon, Nature flew her late March pennants, barred blue and grey. On the castle grounds, within earshot of the pheasant cage, gardeners gave the season her due honor by setting out young cabbages. The men wore vestments that included rims of bare flesh around their buttocks where they'd left their hose unlaced for easy bending. So with flashes of winter-whited skin they moved within the tight confines of their triangular plots, edged in shin-high boxwood or tightly trimmed rosemary. They bent, rose, bent again in a dance of prayer. And the pyx in which they delivered the Host was the dibble.

Earth Herself provided the incense, the sweet fragrance of newly turned soil enriched with manure that smoked in the cool, moist air. The passage of the faithful over bare clods left bursts of life in their wake, bursts of blue-grey, Mother's own livery that day: life conjured from the potential of earth by the magic signs they worked with their hands.

I knew as I watched the rite that here was a true sacrament. Manure set between teeth of clods and pebbles was the appeasement of a great hunger I'd been feeling in my own flesh—sympathetic to the Earth under me—to the core of my bones. The divine was fed and would continue yet another year.

My own knees bent, my hips buckled slightly in their desire for communion in this worship. But I stayed to the gravel walk. The breeze that shivered the new-standing clumps of cabbage leaf and blew their watery scent to me also caught the hem of my robes about my ankles. There was a sound over the breathing of the gardeners—heavy, like lovers'. A sound of growing.

But I had to answer that other sound, that thunk, thunk, thunk—cheers, thunk, thunk—cheers, coming from the cloister across the garden instead.

Tennis, I thought, is a thoroughly Christian game, with its emphasis on individual salvation.

The cloistered court reminded me at once of the origins of tennis. This game was not the product of groups of men fighting out in the fields on winter nights for the next year's crops. Tennis had originated among young Christian clerics and monks, men cloistered away from the earth. The even lines of flagstones and its walls and overhangs—which scored, declared fair or foul—were the archways of a monastery garden.

Four men were playing in the doubles configuration preferred whenever there were players enough. I recognized one of the lords as the duc d'Alençon. Not many spectators peered out on the sport through the open arches of the *dedans:* the hour was too early and the breeze still too fresh to call out much gentle blood.

Those spectators who braved the chill were, however, betting warmly. The wagers—purses, gems, a fine dagger—lay in a heap to the edge of the low wooden wall at center court over which the ball had to be hit. At the end of play, the lot would go to the winners. Somebody had added a doublet of purple velvet worked with gold threads to the pile, somebody short of coin. The Dauphin himself, perhaps? Betting his raiment for the funds to raise an army to the relief of Orléans?

Monseigneur de La Trémoïlle was present, up betimes and keeping an eye on his prince. If he had placed a bet, it was something he did not mind to lose, for he did not attend to the game. He sat off on a bench to one side, speaking lowly to this courtier and that as they came and went. I thought I should stand still, perhaps. If I stood still enough and concentrated, my Sight might be able to sense the topic of their conversation.

But Charles was present, too, of course, and he was the man I had come to see. It was Louis, the sickly young prince, I remembered at once when I saw the father, not the King of my vision, crowned the glory of the wren wood. Charles had yet to outgrow the awkwardness of his youth. Knock-kneed, thin and chalky of skin, nothing of him suggested strength, stamina or determination. Rather than a King, he gave me the impression of a rabbit, skinned and hung up to ripen, but with still a fevered, frightened life in his eyes. Not hale enough to provide interesting competition himself, he came exclusively for the betting—and would sit out almost any weather to do so.

Charles' chair at the center of the *dedans* had been made throne-like by a dais and drapery overhead. Gold fleurs-de-lis had been sowed across the blue silk canopy like young cabbage plants. I suspected the cloth had originally been cut for a horse, emblematic of the second-hand nature of the court of this "King of Bourges". Nonetheless, the gold fringe shivered in the breeze, lending frail dignity to the otherwise straitened surroundings.

"Ah, Père Jean Pasquerel."

While I'd been preoccupied taking in the scene, there'd been a pause in play. Charles had seen me and called my name, my present name, in a way that said he was still trying to learn it.

I replied, "Your Majesty," and drew closer.

He seemed surprised to see me, though not unpleasantly. In either case, he did not give me the reverence due a Master of the Craft as he had always done before. To anyone watching, I might have been just another cleric.

Well, I thought, this is a very public place. Best to keep up the disguise, even between witches. Indeed, how are we to talk here?

I gave him what's due to a Dauphin, then, an unchrismed King. I bowed. He had a courtier vacate the stool at his feet, and gestured towards it. So. Let them think I hear his confession, nothing more.

Play began again with a shout as courtiers turned to spectators again. I crept forward, avoiding their flailing arms and the absurdly long toes on their shoes as they leapt with excitement until I made it safely to the proffered seat.

No one envied me this sign of favor. They all preferred to be up at the rail. The Dauphin himself disliked being chained to the dignity of his chair and rose with a shout twice by the time I'd settled at his feet.

"I thought you'd gone to Poitiers," he said, accusingly. The ball had dropped out of play, but he watched it still, for signs of life. "To see our Maid through the learned doctors' scrutiny."

I ventured a glance towards La Trémoïlle. He had no interest in the game. He was watching Charles and me with the same scrutiny the rest set on the ball court. I didn't think he was close enough to overhear us, however. Certainly not once the whack, crack, thunk and then cheers began again.

"Certain business forced me to return," I told him, "for a day or two only. I mean to catch up with La Pucelle's party again before they reach Poitiers. I may even set off today, if all goes well."

Charles nodded vaguely; I knew he hadn't heard half of what I said. A servant set the ball into play for another set, "served" it, as the terminology was. Until the ball "died", mourned by a groan from all sides, the Dauphin of France had nothing more to say.

At the pause, he asked me how I liked the play and, when I had nothing to say on that subject, he asked instead, "How do you like our little Pucelle? Quite the thing, isn't she?"

I had come hoping to see the best in this man, hoping to learn that Madame Anne was wrong in her estimation of him. But this first speech set my teeth on edge.

"What? Did you create her?" I asked. "La Pucelle, the hope of centuries' prophecy?"

"In a way, yes, she is my creature. Had I not chosen to see her that first evening, what would she be? A peasant girl. Nothing."

"And if she chooses not to help you, what will you be?" I exploded. That, I think, La Trémoïlle heard. He grinned, and there was nothing happening on the court at the moment to please anyone.

"Still Charles the son of Charles the son of Charles, as in your prophecy. I will always be that."

Determined to keep my voice down, I struggled with the passion to say, "An uncrowned King, Charles, with hardly a castle to your name."

"There are other ways to win a throne."

"Other—" My fury left me speechless for a moment now.

"The girl speaks such fiery words of death and destruction."

"That is the task she is called to."

"But what profit is there in a city burned out? In people dead so we can no longer ask ransom for them?"

In a flash I remembered children I had seen, starving to death in cages no bigger than hampers as their captors waited for this ransom Charles so blithely named. But I said nothing. I could say nothing. They were playing again.

"Père Jean, there are other ways. There is the way of treaty and compromise." Charles remained remarkably calm. His man had scored. He cast a glance over at the bench where La Trémoïlle plotted. I didn't like the hope in Charles' eyes at that moment.

"There is no other way," I insisted.

But the ball was in play and Charles heard nothing until the *marqueur* who stood beside the center fence called out, "Chase two and three."

"That's deuce," Charles cried, triumphant. "Now Alençon will have his turn to receive. Terrific player. And he doesn't use those hickory rackets as some of the other players prefer. Just wraps his hands in strips of leather and takes the smack of the ball at full force."

Thus instructed, I watched the wild to-and-fro of the hard ball wrapped in triangles of dark felted wool until the next point was gained. During this play, I had time to collect my patience and consider what to say next. "You know the price of this throne, Charles," was what I came up with. "You learned it when you married this land, at your initiation."

I had been the one to initiate at that sacred marriage. My love Pieronne had taken on the part of Mother Earth there in the precincts of sacred Chartres. Charles remembered, too. I could tell he remembered, play or no play.

"But I have learned other things about being a King since that time," he said. Another look went, like a ball with a sharp cut to its flight, across to the old schemer. "There are other costs to keeping a throne."

"If you put your faith in La Pucelle, I assure you, all creditors will soon be satisfied."

Charles laughed—as if I were a simpleton he had to humor. "Do you have any idea how expensive it is to raise an army? To feed it? Clothe it? I confess I had no idea. I was a child. A babe in the woods."

"But La Trémoïlle—who lends you money—he, I suppose, does know?"

"He does. And he knows how to charge interest."

"If you put your faith in La Pucelle, soldiers will come from the peasantry to her banner. They will fight for free. And the Earth herself will yield up everything needful for their maintenance. That is 'this girl's' power, if you only knew it."

"I do have faith in her. Even La Trémoïlle thinks she may prove very useful."

"I'm not talking about using her like—like some racket to bat around your ball. I'm talking about giving her your undivided confidence. She's very ready to give hers to you."

"She is a simple peasant girl—unused to the realities of court."

"And I?"

"You, Jean, are simple in many ways, too."

"It's true I find the rules of your game too complicated for me." I said this only because the game had recommenced and it didn't matter what I said to the Dauphin; he wouldn't hear it.

"The hard thing is, Jean—" The Dauphin gasped a curse. Alençon had missed the play. "—Your religion asks me to put the Land above myself."

"That is asked of every man. Especially of those who come to the mysteries."

"Above all of humankind, even."

"Most of all, that excise is asked of a King."

"And perhaps I shall pay it. Perhaps, in time, I shall."

"Your Grace," I said, trying to contain my frustration. "I saw your children last night. Your son, he who is to follow you, he's so sickly. He can hardly walk. He hardly talks."

"I understand an old witch is working to remedy that."

"What Madame Anne de Sillé can and cannot do with her skill is beside the point. Such weakness in the blood line is an indication that all is not well with the Sacrifice."

Another thunk, thunk, *thunk* on the court followed by cheers and groans drowned out the last of my words. Under Charles' "Did you see that? What a play!" I told him, "I have a coven, Charles. The first in France in a hundred years."

Did he hear me? Maybe not those first words but the next I made sure he could not mistake: "I need you to make the thirteenth, Your Highness, to support the work of La Pucelle. Her work that will support you. Can we count on you? Will you come and work the old Craft?"

He heard me, but I could not make him meet my eyes.

"Sire, remember the madness of your father. Can't you feel it hanging over you?"

Staring straight onto the court, he said, "That is a gamble I am—for the present—ready to take."

"To gamble with your sanity, not to mention the future of the Land?"

"The odds are actually in my favor. I am only in danger if I set my belief on the Old Ways—and then refuse to play by their rules. I could, of course, stick to new rules when the play falls out."

"What? Change rules in the middle of the game?"

"The man who can do so—to his favor—is certain to win."

I stared in disbelief at the sport being played out before me, a sort of game jumped and run and hit over the flagstone lines. The ball careened wildly off the sloped eaves of the galleries.

"Worse than second gallery," the *marqueur* called out to a battery of groans to which I included my own, but for a very different reason.

"I'm not a saint, Père Jean," Charles started up again when play stopped. "I never can be."

"But La Pucelle is. She is the culmination of ancient prophecy."

"I'm not the stuff of which sacrifices are made."

"Once you are anointed, you will be."

"I don't think so, Jean."

"Look, even now you sit under a canopy. What other thing in the world receives that honor, save only you, the King, and the Sacrifice of the Eucharist? When the flesh and blood of Sacrifice is borne through the streets to the dying, it goes under a canopy. So does no man on earth but yourself—or you will do when you are King. Sitting under this canopy makes you the Sacrifice, whether you would or not."

"Only in your view of the world." He stole another glance, from me to La Trémoïlle and back again, like following the rapid flight of a ball. "Sometimes I think it will be better if I cling more closely to our Catholic faith. Better for my long life at least. That faith teaches that the world required but a single Sacrifice, once in all its history. Christ Jesus shed the Blood, once and for all."

"And nothing more is required of any man who comes after but to believe?"

"Even so. How else shall things get along?"

"Things, as you say, 'should not get along'. They are meant to turn."

"The straight path is easier, as the Gospel says."

"And narrow, my prince, so confiningly narrow for all the living things of this earth."

"My life, however, seems to be straitened. And the life of a King, extended, can do much to extend the rule—and benefit—of his people. Are we never to have Kings who grow old in the wisdom? Surely there must be benefit there."

"Once you set foot on this path," I warned him, "you cannot turn back. And alas, as King, you take the world along with you."

"You misunderstand me. I have said nothing against La Pucelle. I hope she may do a half of the things she says she can do."

"She never will if you don't let her loose of all your scrutiny and ministers and bureaucracy."

"'Let her loose.' Well put. That is a frightening thing. An aberration such as she is. Male-female. Virgin-whore."

"La Pucelle is the true value in this world. And would you put her on the fence with your other bets? Along with your paltry coins and velvet doublet? To go to whoever wins?"

"I want to be a good man, Père Jean. You know I do. But the fact is, heavenly voices don't talk to me. They never have."

"But they talk to La Pucelle. Listen to her."

"If only I could be sure."

"Will the word of the doctors of Poitiers assure you?"

"Sometimes I think so. I hope so."

"But why should you believe them over her?"

"Exactly. I don't. A bunch of dusty old men." Another glance at the chamberlain. "The only thing that seems a solid truth is that six coins will always, always be more than five."

"And so you are willing to set all coins on the fence to ride on the outcome of a bet."

"If only there were a *marqueur* for scoring of life like there is for tennis," said our most Christian prince at his most Christian sport. "Ah, hush now, Jean. They must lay this chase. They simply must!"

And then a great cry went up because the game was won and lost. And the Dauphin's purple doublet and the rest that he had bet went to those who'd laid their wagers against him.

It was time, I decided in that instant, to lay my own great wager. It was time to call the coven.

Chapter Twelve

Borage and Thyme in the Breathless Vigor of Spring

Inside, behind Gilles, was his wife, now a guest of Poitiers' solicitor general. For such a dull creature, Catherine could be very determined.

Outside, in the night, was La Pucelle.

They expected him not only to guard La Pucelle. They expected him to sleep with his wife.

Outside was glory, triumph, victory, the purpose of his life. His love. Inside lay only the humility of defeat.

Gilles de Rais shoved himself off the doorjamb when he heard La Pucelle's familiar quick, light steps coming up the garden path. He scuffed the long toe of his shoe on the doorstep and coughed. He didn't want to scare the girl on this dark night.

He couldn't see her. The sky was still clouded over from the afternoon's rain and, against the absence of starlight, even the sloping roof of the narrow privy hut remained invisible.

Rain enlivened smells. Far off in the dark, below where Poitier's Clain River grew vicious, there were smells of flood and mud and dank.

Closer to hand, here at the kitchen door, the solicitor general's wife kept a herb garden. There were the smells of feverfew and sage, of borage and thyme in the delicate, incautious, almost breathless vigor of spring. Gilles thought he could smell the girl, too. Her fragrance was one with the garden.

She wasn't aware of him. Not yet. In other-worldly conversation again, no doubt. When her Voices spoke to her, his own voice might have been nothing at all.

Gilles reached a hand to the shelf inside the door and brought out the candle he'd left burning there to light her way. How ungenerous she remained towards herself, even in this richest house in Poitiers. She steadfastly refused anything that smacked of "waste", even to the lighting of a strange path in pitch darkness.

Was that a peasant's manner? Gilles wondered. He'd never known a peasant so closely before. It might well be. Peasants must be conscious of where everything came from, how much time and effort it would cost to replace the finger or two of beeswax he held up carelessly now to burn quicker in the fresh night air.

Gilles himself had never considered anything like that before. He considered it now, but only for an instant. Then she noticed him. Him and the light.

He had hoped not to frighten her. He saw at once that instead, he'd ignited her tinder-dry temper—her wonderful, wonderful temper. He could just see her, stopped short in her tracks between the spring shoots of thyme and sage. The flame of his candle barely etched the deep black of her figure in gold, caught the bristling spikes of her hair like a curry brush. Her arms akimbo, her legs wide: her favorite stance.

His favorite stance in her.

No one on earth who didn't know her could think of her as anything but a boy, like this. He himself would suffer tortures before he'd admit what three midwives had already told him he must: That flat chest didn't belong to one of his own sex. Those tight little buttocks ...

How glad he was that he hadn't answered his impulse and put out the light.

"Please, Bluebeard," La Pucelle said, keeping her voice low for the sake of the rest of the house, trying to sleep. "Can't you even let me go to the privy on my own?"

"I don't want anything to happen to you, that's all." He sounded like a simpleton on purpose: to keep that anger boiling in her. It warmed his belly, lightened his head like strong drink.

"I have told you. Nothing can happen to me 'til my calling is fulfilled."

"We have you for one year. You said that today at the inquest."

"Or maybe a little more."

"A year. That's all."

She shrugged. The words didn't come from her own mind but from her Voices. She couldn't explain them any more than that.

"Come on." She sighed and the extra air in her lungs seemed to propel her. She strode towards him. "Put me to bed—Nanny—if you must. I am exhausted."

"Are you? I am surprised."

"The second watch was set ages ago."

"I mean, it surprises me that you can tire like normal mortals. Just the same as it surprises me to see you use the privy. There are so many things normal mortals do that you do not."

"Such as?"

She was level with him now. He let her stand still on the step above him and, with a silent arm, refused for the moment to let her pass. They rested eye to eye. The candlelight between them sleekened the round lines of her childish face.

"Such as eating. Doubting. Swearing." He took a breath and made the flame dance when he let it out again. "Loving."

"I love," she insisted without a flinch, without a blink. "I love the whole world."

"But no man."

"No man more than another, no. That is not La Pucelle's way."

He held her gaze, long enough to let her know he didn't need to flinch, either. The candle's yellow teardrop burned double in her dark, wide-irised eyes. Then he moved his arm aside to let her pass.

"I was all day with the university men." She returned to an earlier topic, explaining her momentary lack of divinity—if indeed there'd been one.

She spent every day with the university men in the main hall of the solicitor general.

Well, one evening, Gilles had taken her on a walk through a light rain on the city's cobbled streets. Their steps had brought them to what remained of the Temple of Poitiers, from which the Templars had once controlled their important holdings in Poitou and Aquitaine. The roofless, crumbling walls had matched the mood of the rain. La Pucelle's face had run with rain and pity for the fated brothers, held in this fortress as they'd waited to plead their case—fruitlessly, as it turned out—before the pope.

A lighter experience had been the single real break they'd been allowed in two weeks, for Palm Sunday. Gilles hoped he had earned her devotion that day by taking her out of the city on a crisp, clear day. They'd gone to the nearby lake and shrine of St. Hilaire, still sacred, Yann had told him, to the Mother. The faithful continued to toss tokens of their devotion into the lake's waters, and Gilles and La Pucelle had done the same with a pair of silver medals.

Except for those brief times, which he hoped she remembered as he did, she'd been in the possession of the university men. Or the burgher women. But he intended not to reproach her with that. Not tonight. She was anxious to get on with her work. She was just as glad as he that these sessions were drawing to a happy conclusion.

So he congratulated her instead. "And did very well. Had an *alter* to their every *primo*."

He followed her steps through the kitchen and the lower hall, speaking softly so the scullery lads on their pallets wouldn't waken.

"I'll tell you, as I told them, I don't know *A* from *B*," she said a little huffishly.

What had he been thinking? To try to impress her with his Virgil? "Yet when they asked for a sign, like the Gospel's scribes and Pharisees—"

The Gospel meant little more to her than Virgil. "Sign? What sign can I give them here in Poitiers? Send me to Orléans. There I'll give you a sign."

He smiled. She'd said the same words to the present-day Pharisees. "Who love the uppermost seats in the synagogues and greetings in the market," he recited to himself. "These ye ought to do and not leave the other undone."

Aloud, he chuckled. "And when you told that fellow from Limoges that your Voices spoke better than he did ... "

"Well, they do. I could hardly understand his '*testa*' for '*tête*' and '*tchantar*' for '*chanter*', his '*oc, oc, oc*' like some sort of bird."

Gilles had to laugh again, but at her own Lorraine peasant's flattened vowels and harsh *r*'s—speech he would have credited to the brain-damaged four weeks ago—he had come to love in her.

"And then, after you've answered the men, there are the women," Gilles said.

They stopped talking now, for they'd made their way up the well-waxed stairwell to floors where more of the household was asleep, including the solicitor's feverish daughter. But Gilles' thoughts kept a quick pace, anyway.

He had to admit that one woman in La Pucelle's presence could make him more jealous than all those university men taken together. The women waited in long, gossipy lines at the solicitor-general's door all the time La Pucelle faced her interrogators in the great hall of Richard Cœur-de-Lion. Then, when the provosts and advocates and deans and chancellors and canons and bachelors of theology got tired, and recessed in order to go home to their dinners, then there were the women.

The men were taking weeks to be convinced. The women were converts at the first word of the coming of the wonderful Maid. They brought her their napkins, their medals, their ailing children and ailing goats to touch.

"Men-at-arms, that's what I like," she'd told her examiners impatiently, not caring that on the wrong ears, such words made her sound like a whore. "Give me men-at-arms."

But she hadn't done badly with babes-in-arms, either, or their mothers. When the dusty books, musty pens and inks and stiff, somber robes of menfolk got to rest, the hugging, crying, laughing of the women had only begun. Gilles was exhausted just trying to follow her through her day.

Women he found particularly exhausting, always had.

And one woman, his wife, more than all the rest.

They'd climbed to the third floor now. La Pucelle's room was at the end of the hall, a tiny room, hardly more than an alcove, with space only for the bed. Until last night, she'd been sharing that bed with the solicitor's daughter. But the child had taken a fever and the mother brought her downstairs for easier nursing.

"We wouldn't want it said," the solicitor's spouse had added, "that La Pucelle took sick under our roof."

"Don't worry yourself, madame," La Pucelle had insisted, repeating herself as she did, as liturgy did. "No harm can come to me, not yet. I should like the nursing of her. Perhaps sleeping next to me might cool her fever, do her some good."

But the mother had insisted and tonight, La Pucelle lay in her room alone.

Before they reached it, however, she paused in front of his door, expecting to bid good night to him here, as she had done every other night since their arrival in Poitiers. This was the room he'd shared with four of his men, just a thin plaster wall away from her, listening for the slightest sound.

This morning, however, the men had moved to billets in a nearby inn.

And Catherine de Thouars and her grandmother had arrived and taken their places. Now La Pucelle, like everybody else, expected him to sleep there still.

But he would not. He almost thought he could hear Catherine, blubbering herself to sleep again—in his bed. No, he *could* not. Catherine was ... Catherine was *his wife.*

As if she half read his thoughts, La Pucelle said, "It gave me great pleasure to meet your lady wife this afternoon."

Gilles' heart sank. He'd had to leave the room when Catherine had joined the rest of the whining women in line. He'd stayed just outside the door, close enough for any emergency, close enough to act as a sieve to all who came to see the saint. Even if Catherine should decide to murder her rival—unlikely, since she couldn't possibly guess she had a rival. A female rival, at any rate. The rival herself didn't know.

Yet, more than disheartened, he felt surprise at La Pucelle's avowal. This was a young woman who stood in doublet and hose before the exiled theologians of Paris and declared without blinking that she "loved men-at-arms above anything". To hear her find something attractive in his fragile rose of a wife was remarkable.

"You liked her?" he had to repeat for confirmation, wondering if, low as they were speaking, the women in the room beyond the door could hear them.

"Yes. I had a sister named Catherine. Who died." As if that, even with the abrupt halts for emotion, explained everything.

"Lady Catherine tells me," La Pucelle continued, "you have no heir. After almost nine years of marriage."

"So far she didn't lie to you."

"Bluebeard, I cannot take men into battle with me who leave no heir behind them."

"By the Stag God, Lady, what does it matter?"

"But it matters very much. It is my purpose to turn the Earth, to recycle it. I will not see it sunk at my passing unreplenished as if into some sterile monastery."

"Aren't there unloved brats enough in this world already?"

"The child would not be unloved. The mother will love it if you cannot."

"That isn't the problem."

"What is the problem?"

Gilles looked to that blank door now, the mocking whorls of its grain. He didn't imagine sobbing behind it now. Instead, there was a breathless sort of straining—straining for every word.

"It's the mother I cannot love." There, he'd blurted it. And loud enough that they might have heard him on the next floor down, never mind just within the chamber door.

"I cannot," he repeated almost with a sob, which he quickly fought back. "My God, do we have to discuss this here, of all places? Please, Lady, let's go to your room."

La Pucelle studied him, a scrutiny like burning the dross out of iron. Twin ghosts of himself wavered within the unblinking dark eyes, as before their fight in the lists.

She looked at the door to her room, then back at him. Finally, she shrugged and nodded at the same time and led the way down the hall.

Chapter Thirteen

Trying to Cast a Shadow to Slip Through

More than once during the past weeks since he'd first seen this creature at the table in the cavernous back of the inn, Gilles had wondered how people really ever told male from female. They saw the clothes, but that meant nothing. Hadn't he himself played female parts on the stage? Off the stage, for that matter.

And in this case, the clothes had lied to him from the start.

Or, not lied to him exactly, because La Pucelle couldn't lie. Doublet and hose were a perfect reflection of what existed at the core of her being. Never mind that more than one midwife had declared under oath that this creature was female in every way she could tell.

Probably capable of replenishing the earth, if it came to that. Getting him the heir she said he needed. Making him the man he'd always doubted he really was. Certainly capable of receiving his love. Although he'd never found male genitalia a hindrance to that before.

Quite the opposite.

Gilles was certain the body standing in the candlelight before him now would not sicken him as the same body parts in his wife did. They could not. They were not having anything like that effect on him now, in the close quarters to which the cramped room and spread of bed—serge and grey linsey-woolsey—pressed them.

Her parts would make him whole. Of that he was almost certain. He wanted—oh, how he wanted!—to see.

Gilles considered all the tales he's ever heard of tricksters or wise men revealing men from women, no matter what the outward dress. There was no lack of such examples. They began with the tests Sheba set for Solomon, the girls pushing up their sleeves to wash arms as well as hands, the boys content with a cursory dipping.

There was the tale of the distaff set in the room which the true woman found of such deep interest, she couldn't keep from picking it up. The man ignored it. To pass the time as they rode south to Poitiers, La Pucelle had told him her misadventures with a distaff. He doubted that test would enlighten him in this case.

Another story had the test of the tossed ball. Yet another, spilled peas. In these, too, La Pucelle would come out on the male side, her throwing and catching superb and her steadiness unsurpassed no matter what was underfoot.

No, there was only one test that would satisfy him. And he wanted, oh, how he wanted, to perform it now.

La Pucelle watched him steadily through his every turn of thought, sensing he knew not how much of it. "I am sure, Bluebeard, you're a masterful wooer." She had understood something, surely, to be able to say that, and to have such a teasing sparkle in her eyes as she said it.

He set the candle down on its little bracket, watching in amazement how his hand shook ever so slightly with anticipation as he did so.

"Not much wooing. No," he found himself confessing instead. "Catherine de Thouars was out for her morning ride. With fifteen men-at-arms. I abducted her and had the nearest friar sanction the abduction at knife point."

"You forced the clergy?"

"That shocks you more than that I forced the lady?"

"But you didn't force the lady."

Gilles hardly heard her, so keen was he to make a full confession. "Her patrimony doubled the size of mine. And we couldn't have married in the normal way. We are cousins."

"Incest? That might well make a man squeamish."

"His Holiness has declared us legitimate."

"That's all right, then. Or—is it not?"

Gilles shook his head, helplessly.

"I suppose you like women, Bluebeard—in that way—no more than I like men. I've no time for them."

He turned, unable to face her keen gaze another moment. There was nothing to see but the door. Withdrawing there would bring him that much closer to his own door. To Catherine.

He turned back. "See, Jehannette?" Dared he use that name? Well, he'd done it now. "I have made another deep dark confession to you. You bring it out in me. The desire to come clean. To be pure and honest ... "

"Catherine de Thouars must be very happy," she said.

Gilles laughed darkly.

"To have won a love so fervent as yours," she added.

Surely La Pucelle was not jealous of Catherine? But there was that in her voice. She must be teasing him again. "For an avowed virgin, you are hopelessly romantic, sweet Jehannette." She had not flinched the first time he'd said it. He said it again. "She was not so happy when she came to ask your blessing this evening."

"No. She was not. She wants a child. And you, Bluebeard. You will give her one. Tonight."

She was teasing him again. It made the blood course wildly through him. He ought to raise his hands to her face. Now, he ought to do it. But they refused to obey him, as if weighted by some heavy spell. Only his tongue still worked.

So, he confessed. "My only love does not escape beyond the light of this small candle, Jehannette. My Jehannette."

Perhaps his tongue did not work, after all. She certainly seemed not to have heard him. With a great sigh of mixed exhaustion and delight, she flopped backwards onto the bed.

"Ho, what a day!" she exclaimed. "I'm certain fighting the English won't be half so exhausting. I declare, I'll have to sleep with my boots on. I'm too tired to take them off."

Gilles found he could move now. He could kneel at the foot of her bed and begin unlacing the boots for her. They began above the knee, far onto the sturdy little thighs where the grey hose spread.

La Pucelle gave a grunt of delight at such service. Then, dreamily, she said, "I, too, will marry."

"You will?"

Jealousy battered his heart. Of course, he could be the man. Not chained to Catherine as he was, of course. But possibly— Or did she not speak with prophecy? It did seem her drowsy mind only played with the images created by the leaping of their single flame.

"Yes. Some day. When France is won."

"Then we will win France in a hurry," he promised her, promised himself, and worked his fingers with the same haste to loosen the laces down as far as her neat little ankle.

"At least—at least my Voices say I will have three sons, and it would be a sin, would it not—to—I mean—"

"I know of only one other Immaculate Conception in the history of the world."

"Three sons."

"Thrice immaculate."

"No daughters to drag around in skirts after me."

"You do everything right."

He let the left boot drop to the ground, then took the pleasure of holding the warm little foot for a moment, counting the toes through the wool, wondering that there should be exactly five, just as in other mortals.

She counted, too, but only got to three. "One will be a King, one an emperor, and one a pope."

He brought the foot to his face and mingled his breath with its little warmth. It smelled wonderfully of old leather, damp wool, the sharpness of sage and thyme. "I hope I might have the honor to father one of them," he breathed.

"Bluebeard!" The foot jerked out of his hand. She had raised up on her elbows, looking at him.

"That was a stupid thing to say," he apologized.

"I thought so."

"I'm sorry."

"I am La Pucelle. I am not meant to have children."

"But you said—"

"Only wishful thinking."

"And I only meant, La Pucelle, if they are to be such great men, think what renown—I mean, for their father."

"You, sire de Rais, will earn your best renown for having fought at my side at Orléans."

"Your voices tell you this?"

"My heart tells me this."

With another sigh, she sank back into the mattress with a fresh crackle of straw. She offered her other boot, and Gilles took it.

"There is a difference between your voices and your heart?" he asked.

"Yes. I think so."

"Tell me about your heart."

"That's not important."

"You are La Pucelle."

"That's right."

"And not allowed a heart."

"That's right."

The fit of his finger between boot and hose was wonderfully, achingly snug and warm. "Tell me about your Voices," he said.

"That—that's a divine pleasure. There's blessed Ste. Catherine. She always comes with a wheel, the symbol of her martyrdom."

He drew off the second boot and languidly let it fall. "She speaks to you?"

He feared he might just be making conversation. He knew only too well how relaxed the girl became whenever she was allowed to return to this subject again. Slowly he moved up onto the bed beside her. She didn't notice, her eyes fixed steadfastly up at the yellow loops of candlelight where the uneven plaster of the ceiling spread between waving beams. She appeared intent on finding recognizable shapes in the irregular, meaning in the abstract, like someone pointing out faces in the clouds. Gilles remembered how he and his milk brother Yann had lain side by side in their closet bed, doing the same thing.

"You can't hear her?" she asked him.

He stared up at the same place. “I can see her. I think. Like statuary in an old church.”

“Yes.”

“But, no, I can’t hear her. Teach me.”

Gilles moved a hand and touched his true love’s thigh. When she made no complaint, he set to work to undo the laces holding up one hose.

“Teach me to hear her.”

“‘Most dear, beloved daughter-God,’ she says. ‘Be pure and chaste.’” A saint’s smile flooded La Pucelle’s face, beatific, reflecting what only she could see.

“‘Pure and chaste’.” Gilles sighed, trying to avoid a groan, and started on the other hose. This required that he roll just that much closer to her.

“And here, here comes Ste. Marguérite, with the dragon chained.”

“She speaks, too?”

“‘Go, speak, do, fearlessly, for God is with you.’ God sent men’s clothing to Marguérite,” La Pucelle mused, “when she prayed to escape the lechery of a man she hated.”

Gilles drew off one shaft of grey wool, down the smooth length of leg. “And who is this?” he urged, forcing his attention back to the ceiling once more. “With the flaming sword?”

“St. Michel.”

“Marguérite chains the dragon,” Gilles considered.

“St. Michel slays him.”

“So there is no dragon left at all.” The other hose came off and joined its fellow on the boots on the floor.

“No. Of course not.”

“He is a mythical creature?”

“No. But quite dead.”

“I have voices, too,” Gilles admitted.

Her own Voices enraptured her. She didn’t hear him. Nor did she notice that he had begun on the first of the bone buttons running down the front of her doublet.

“I know you’re not interested in anyone’s voices but your own.” He hardly expected to be heard. “Your perfect, white-light Voices.”

"This may be heresy, but I sometimes—nay, often—doubt the existence of the devil and his minions."

"I do not doubt it." Gilles had to laugh. It was deep, and began with a quiver in the blue on his chin.

"Especially when I hear my Voices."

"That is not heresy. Certainly not according to the wise old Masters of the Craft."

"Everything that at first blush seems evil in the end works to God's will. If we embrace the evil—with faith, hope, charity—it becomes as innocent as a child."

The doublet opened now, like the thorny hull of some soft and smooth fruit. The slow, sleepy rise and fall of her breath was just visible, as was the pink glow of her skin, through the crumpled linen.

He leaned, poised to smooth that crumple with the press of his own body. It seemed he could not resist the pull of her any more than a man tumbling from the height of a castle wall could resist the pull of the earth. And yet he did. Somehow, the yellow glow of the single light formed a cocoon, a buffer around her. He could not breach it. He understood, hard as he fought the idea, that this was magic. He shifted his body here, there, trying to cast a shadow through which to slip. But his own magic was too weak to counterspell such things.

"Embrace me, Jehannette." Gilles suddenly begged, whimpered, his voice too hoarse to amount to much.

"In no man's land, Bluebeard," she whispered, soothing a child. "I've promised. In no man's land."

"Where I stand already. Waiting. How to bring you here, Jehannette? Here, where the power of evil is at least as real as the good."

And now it seemed all he had left of strength and vigor was in his voice. He used it, wildly, like a sorcerer, chanting spells. "Certainly. I often feel the imps of hell as they brush past me, hastening on some dark business. A cold breath makes the candles flicker low on a winter's night. Then, their hot, sulphur breath breathes upon my face, and they whisper. My ears hear the sound, but the words I cannot quite make out, as I cannot make out your heavenly Voices, although I sense their presence, too. I am afraid, Jehannette. The baron de Rais confesses to you that he is afraid. I am afraid that some day I will catch actual words from the pit. Orders. Without your help to hear heaven, I fear—"

La Pucelle stopped him with a magic sign that amounted to no more than the light settling of her fingers on his lips, on the place where blue marked the skin beneath his beard.

"I am La Pucelle," she said, as if that were Alpha and Omega all at once.

"You said the purpose of La Pucelle was to turn the cycle of the world once more."

"And so it is."

"You urge me, to this end, to have an heir."

"So I do. Now. Tonight."

"Does this not include—a copy of yourself? For the next generation? So they must not dwell in darkness as did those who came before?"

"Go to her, Gilles," she whispered. "This very moment. I go with you. I will be there. Helping you, against your nature, to turn the earth."

She leaned forward and, very, very lightly, touched her lips to his. It was a part of the spell, he knew, and not a gesture of love.

Gilles got up. Every muscle cracked as if they were shot through with ice he had to break in order to move. He didn't want to go. He thought he'd be unable to. But he did. He found himself next door, the door flinging open, it seemed, of its own volition before him.

The two women within—awake, listening, as he'd known they'd be—were not a little surprised to see him there. The older, his stepgrandmother Anne de Sillé, was busy over a bit of fire she'd coaxed to life after drawing aside the night's metal cover. She was burning something, slowly, deliberately, knot by knot. Odd, but it looked like the sort of black hose lace he preferred.

Seeing him, Madame Anne tossed the remnant of the lace in quickly, whole, and shoved the cover back over the flames.

She shot a glance to the other woman as she got to her feet in her long, loose shift and hair.

"I think—I think I may go beg half a bed from La Pucelle tonight," Anne de Sillé said, and snuffed the candle as she closed the door behind her.

Gilles' heart lifted somewhat that he had not had to look Catherine full in the face before the light went out. The image fixed still to the back of his mind was that of La Pucelle, lying back lazily on her grey serge coverlet, arms draped over the hedgehog bristles of her hair.

He found his wife, certainly. He could hardly help himself, even when he found her soft and flaccid like raw oysters. He hated raw oysters. The thought of them slipping down made his throat close on itself in a stranglehold. Oysters had made him sick once, and the nausea was more real than memory. It shifted through his intestines like ground glass from top to bottom and then back again.

But he managed it. Roughly, there was no doubt. And it was "Jehannette," he cried out at the climax. "Jehannette" shattered the house's night quiet as the vessel of his own being shattered and spilled like thick warm wine in pulsing gurgles from a bottle's narrow neck.

Beneath the press of his cheek, he could feel Catherine biting her lips to keep from crying out. But she'd got what she wanted.

La Pucelle, too.

Heat Worse than the Sands of the Holy Land at Midday

The time had come. At last. For no other purpose had I been born, called by the Stag as a child and grown to know the ways of the Craft, but for this. It was time to call the coven to support La Pucelle in her work to save the Land.

So one morning early, before the first greying of a wet spring dawn, I retreated once more to the foul-smelling dungeon beneath Chinon's Tour de Coudray. With me was Hamish Power, the some-time merchant who had been initiated among the remnant of the secret order of the Templars in his native Scotland. He could see death around those fated to it and had moved his family to a shop in Tours where he worked his other skills on cloth.

Besides Hamish, I had the assistance of Anne de Sillé, returned from Poitiers, and of her great, simple son, the other Gilles called Bibu, the child of the Midsummer God in His horns.

With us we brought four wicker cages carrying nine pigeons in all, one marked for each of the witches to be called. The birds cooed and rustled sleepily in the dark archway where we set them.

I outlined the circle, the pentangle like the apple's sacred core. I invoked the spirits at the tip of my Master's sword, placed the cauldron beneath the very point where the six ribs of the dungeon's roof intersected. From that point, between the sky beyond and the Earth below, I drew down the cone of power.

On the dungeon's wall throbbed the Templars' carved heart, in time to my chants, to Madame Anne's and to Hamish's. I could feel the spell building, just as it ought. And yet, just before it burst the bounds to release into the world, the power backed off. It happened a second time.

I'd had men come to me who could not perform in the marriage bed. It seemed as frustrating as that, pent up desire falling back on itself in pain. Something like my milk brother Gilles must have felt, under his stepgrandmother's spell. I knew what to do when a man suffered thus. But an invocation? The entire world?

Hamish, madame and I exchanged glances, then did the only thing we could think of: threw our efforts to chanting, to mind control, to visualizing more than ever. After a third time, I began to understand what the obstacle was. I shot a glance in Bibu de Sillé's direction.

Certainly he was distracting, that large body, the largest body in the dungeon, and powerfully built. He had the features, the pudgy, unfurrowed face of a very young child, however. Drool ran constantly from a mouth he seemed unable to close, lips cracked, chapped and twitching from time to time into some nonsense word or other.

His mother hissed at me for suggesting such a thing of her son, even if with but a glance. But how could I help it? How could a spell rise when not every witch in the room set his mind to the work? If he could ride messages for his mother, why couldn't Bibu concentrate on such an important rite of Craft?

"Monseigneur de Sillé," I urged him. I felt the falling sickness coming over me as a result of the frustrated effort.

His mother hissed at me again. "He's a child of the God."

Fine, he's a child of the God, I wanted to snap back. Let the God come and tend him for a bit, then.

Feeling bitterness rankling the magic, I resisted, and threw myself with fervor, perhaps even desperation, again into the spell. If I lost consciousness before we were complete, wouldn't that be disruptive? Every bit as disruptive as the presence of a full-grown man who was wandering about the chamber with his loose-limbed, lumbering gait like a child bored with his elders' business?

Then, Bibu de Sillé plopped down on the rubble of the floor and sat, his large legs straight out in front of him as very little, very flexible children sit. Out of the corner of my eye, I couldn't help watching him. From previous visits and from walking over the room barefoot I had a better notion than I wanted of just how foul the debris was, detritus of untold lives left here to rot. The God's son, like his Father in the dank and moldering nooks of swamp and forest, was stacking the rubble, as a child might play with blocks. Then I saw that he had found something under the debris. The very notion made my stomach lurch and my head reel more violently.

It seemed to be a rag. No, a small cloth bag, dirty grey, crumbling with age. Through one moldering corner, the contents slipped out. They were two or three, uneven, fire-blackened lumps about the size and shape of sheep's knucklebones. As if a great feast had been held, but the boy set to watch the joint turning over the fire had been distracted by the merriment and let the meat burn right to the bone on one side.

I looked away, feeling such disgust at the plaything that I couldn't tell falling sickness from the queasiness it induced.

And then, I looked right back again, thinking of Bibu de Sillé no more. For a strange, lucid voice intoned:

Ah, ah, the fire.
The heat worse
than the sands of the Holy Land
at midday.

All I could imagine was that someone, a stranger, had come down upon us through the twisting staircase at the God-son's back. There was no one. No one but Bibu de Sillé, sitting in his childlike posture, gazing at his new toys—and speaking in a voice coherent, mature, wise even, and totally other than his own.

"What's that? What have you found, my love?" His mother had left off her chanting and was at his side in a moment, bending as low as her age allowed.

And suddenly, the blackness faded from before my eyes like bubbles off a pool. I knew I would neither fall nor See, not this time. Unless the Sight were a sudden, sharp memory of Bibu de Sillé in a deserted hut on the jousting ground on a foggy night in Nantes. For, God's fool though he was, I did number him among my coven, and not merely for the great lot of space he took up.

In that damp fog years ago, edged by firelight set up under a cauldron, I had seen him touch a hanged man's skull—and speak in a voice suddenly sensible. Not merely sensible. He'd spoken in the voice of the departed spirit and told what it saw on its haunting rounds.

"What? Are those bones? Human bones?" I exchanged a glance with Hamish who, as the realization hit him, forgot his own incapacity. He didn't twitch all the time I looked at him.

"Hush," insisted Madame Anne. "He speaks."

And he did.

"Mother?"

"I'm here, love."

"Mother?"

But he looked, not at his mother, but to something beyond. Even his eyes, usually a placid, simple sort of blue, had changed. It was as if, by looking at the two odd lumps in his hand, the blue had gained an edge, a brown edge. They were another's, a dead man's eyes.

"Ah, you were so proud of me."

"I am. I will always be proud of you." Madame Anne knew how to feed her son the lines when his gift had hold of him.

"When you first saw me in my white robe with the sign of Our Lord in blood red splayed over the heart."

"A crusader?" After a glance at Hamish and me, Madame Anne forgot her surprise and pressed on. "Ah, but you were handsome."

And she reached out to give the dull, fair hair a motherly caress.

But her son, or the man he was now, would have none of it. He shoved the hand away so violently that it jarred the blackened lumps in his other palm. He clutched for them desperately, as if for life itself.

"We must not," he exclaimed in horror. "We must not kiss women."

"Not even a mother?"

"Not even a mother. We must not touch one, even as we lie dying. We must not enter a house where a woman lies in childbirth, nor stand godfather to a newborn. This is the law of our order."

The magicians of long ago who had been prisoners in this tower. I remembered them. They had been so desperate for acceptance from the power of Christianity that they had cut out half of magic. The feminine half.

Bibu de Sillé is a Templar indeed, I thought.

Ninth Antiphon

The Templars' Curse

Madame Anne sat back carefully on her heels, allowing her son and the spirit that animated him their own invisible magic circle. But she kept the motherly tone—bordering on awe at what her creative power had wrought in her son—and fed him her feminine from outside.

"So you went with the Knights on Crusade?"

"I walked on the very ground where Our Lord walked, the greatest of the dying Kings. I walked on those burning sands. I fought at the fall of Acre, the choking smoke and the death, and always I was willing, if the Master should command it, to stand and die though the Saracens scrambled over the walls at us in their thousands.

"They fight with their mouths and noses muffled against sand and smoke, only their black eyes gleaming over the top. Their scarves, I always thought, concealed the features of the imps of hell ... And yet ... and yet ...

"I have seen eyes more like infernal pits here, in Christendom. Fair eyes, keen as flints, in the slits of a headsman's hood ... ah ... "

The stranger's emotion so overcame the great child seated on the floor that he seemed to have reverted into himself again. Tears and drool and mucous mingled on his broad face. He scrubbed at it with the fist clenched around the two black bones.

"I never would have thought," his mother urged gently, struggling against her instinct to take the poor soul in her arms, "to see my great, bold knight weep so."

"Ah, Mother. You cannot know ..." The spirit fought the child and presently, with effort, won.

"We lost Acre, with the death of most of our men. That was our last stronghold in the Holy Land. Those of us left among the living retreated to Cyprus and afterwards, some of us were reassigned to our houses in Europe, with orders to raise the men and funds for a new campaign. But do you know what happened? Do you know what I discovered upon my return?"

"Tell me, dear."

"Those people who'd stayed behind, comfortable in their homes. Those *Christians*. They blamed us. They blamed us for the loss of Jerusalem. We who had bled and suffered in the distant land. We, who suffered still, old wounds in body. And in mind. The dreams of death and dying. The bodiless screams and unknown terrors that continued to come upon us, even in the gentlest night. Or even, sometimes, while waking. In broad daylight.

"They blamed us, those who hadn't shifted from their homes. They envied us, they hated us. I found other Knights of the order were the only people among whom I was comfortable. And even Templars who'd never been east were strangers to us. Sometimes I thought I'd rather see those black eyes coming over the wall at me. Those men were at least not traitors in their hearts.

"To compensate, I began to turn from the active life I had known to the inner secrets of the Temple, of the Craft. And then I began to learn that the true Holy Land was not what we'd been sent across the seas and hot sands to defend. That land is holy to those who are born there, whose Mother She is. Our Mother is the forest and green fields, the running rivers of France. We had done that fighting only to delude pope and King into thinking we were Christian when we were ... something greater and older than Christianity, encompassing the newer faith within its broad bosom.

"That had been a mistake, those nearly two hundred years of dressing as Christians. As foolish as wearing tight, heavy European woolens in the heat of the desert. Yes, at heart we really were more like the Muslims, whom we'd set upon and killed. Those sons of Allah would call off the fighting at harvest time so the men could return to their villages. They knew where the water was and so they never fought in desperate, blinded thirst as we did at the Horns of Hattin under misguided orders—orders that came from the heart of Europe without proper translation.

"I don't know how magicians in Palestine work magic. But as I practiced, as I studied the ancient wisdom, I came to understand how it works here. All of the brothers did, above a certain rank. We understood that this land we call France lives only with the spilling of royal blood. Every nine years demands the death of a King, whether he be the man on the throne or not, an echo of Christ's God-making.

"Jacques de Molay—our Grand Master—I am locked up with him in this cell. Seventy other men are crammed into this narrow tower with ..."

Bibu de Sillé looked around him with a hint of love, as if the spirit, watering in his eyes, actually peopled the dark confines of this dungeon with so many beaten, tortured men. Their wounds smelled, their rags sloughed off their backs, their wrists and ankles dragged in chains, their bowels coughed in protest at bad food and water. Such was the power of this spirit that I could almost see them, too. Or smell them. Hear them, the air never freed of the oppressive chink of chains. I could feel them, the press of so much heavy, pained, betrayed humanity.

Bibu de Sillé went on. "Master de Molay took it upon himself to be Master of the Craft as well as of the order. He went to the King, Philippe the Fair, and warned him of his responsibility. Philippe came after his wife died, asking for initiation. Our Master gave it to him. But when he heard the whole of our requirements for one of royal blood—beyond chastity, poverty and obedience—Philippe balked. Either he, or one of his three royal sons, must die at the next turn of the Sacrifice.

"Now, no one had ever warned Philippe that this was the price of his crown. That balance in the Land despises great power swayed without great payment in return.

"Philippe balked, like a Saracen camel under a load too heavy. First, he gave the demand the service of his lips. Then he told the Master: 'Very well. If I must die, the order must lend me money out of their great wealth beforehand, that my few remaining years may be as lavish as I like.'

"So we turned our possessions from the service of a distant Holy Land to the renewal of this closer holiness.

"As the time drew near, King Philippe began to love his life more than the land that gave it to him. 'If it weren't for these Templars,' he thought, 'mighty men that they are, I would defy the ancient gods of this land. What are they but dirt and rocks, water and weather? I would desert them for Jesus, who only died once and for all instead of every nine years as the Templars say. These dark magicians are mighty, with chapter houses more fortress than cloister. Didn't I myself flee to the Temple in Paris when my uncouth people rebelled, demanding my blood and the ancient ways instead of following the necessary law of the marketplace? Now the Templars require my blood as well.'

"But the King went on to consider that many of his subjects—among the nobility, mostly, and the town-dwellers—were not so opposed to him. The peasantry has always understood our Craft, but the nobility and the town-dwellers mistrusted us. If he moved by stealth, the King thought, he could play upon that—and, with the element of surprise, win.

"We suspected nothing. The Thursday after the feast of the martyrs Sergius, Bacchus and Marcellus, the King gave our Grand Master place of honor in a procession. Before dawn the very next morning, the King's men-at-arms were pounding on the Temple gates. We on watch suspected nothing. What should we think? We let them in.

"I've been in shackles ever since. I will die in these shackles. If I do not die sooner, in fire. I don't shame to tell you, Mother, I do fear the stake. The slow, choking flame. I, who stood on the walls of Acre and feared nothing, I fear the fire. For I have been tortured and the torture ... "

Once more the spirit lost his ability to speak, leaving his medium a frightened, blubbering child. After a moment, Madame

Anne reached out a hand to comfort him, but again he pushed it away, staring wildly at the small bones as if they were live coals, yet he was unable to drop them.

"Do you know the fire torture, *maman*?" he asked at last.

"No, my son. I cannot imagine this horror. Tell me. If you can."

Between each of her phrases, he made an attempt to begin until he managed to blurt out all at once, "They tie your naked feet out straight, so. They slather them with oil, like a duck for the spit. Then, they stoke up the brazier and bring it close. Close? They stick your feet right in it.

"When they think you're ready for questioning, they shove a board between your smoking feet and the flame, remove it again if they don't like your answers."

"Alas, my baby," madame cried, her hands at her mouth in horror.

"I never flinched at Acre," her son went on. "But I told them anything and everything they wanted to hear as the soles of my feet first blistered, then blackened. Then smoked. Whatever they say I said—I myself do not know. I did not hear it for my own screams, choking on the stench of my own burning flesh. And the cleric calmly writes everything you say as it's blasted from your lips. Whatever they say, do not believe it. Or don't believe it came from my heart or my mind. Only from my smoking feet."

"Never fear, my darling, my son," madame crooned. "I'll believe nothing about you but the bravest and best. And every false witness I'll turn upon its head."

The spirit hastened now to finish his tale. "I don't know how long it was, four or five days perhaps, of a black fog of pain, before I slowly grew aware of the dungeon surrounding me again: the other men, my comrades. The quiet murmur of last rites as torture took one, then another. One man hearing his fellow and all saying the same: 'I did nothing wrong, as the God is my witness. I did nothing against the God of this land, once I came to know him.'

"In my delusion, I thought I still smelled fire, though the cell was too dark and too cold for that to be possible. Then I understood it was my own feet I still smelled. Sinew and flesh both burned away, right to the bone. And soon, these bones, from my heels, worked their way free and, with nothing to hold them, fell out. I will never walk again without the aid of crutches."

"Ah," madame exclaimed, dashing away tears. "My brave young lad, to whom I held out my arms when first he learned to walk!" She hummed on like that, in lullaby fashion, until the spirit could take up the tale again.

"I keep these bones with me," her son said, more to the bones themselves than to himself. "To remind me always of the cost of truth and faith in these days when the King forgets the price of Kingship.

"Some of the men here with me in Chinon's Tower of Coudray hope appeal to the pope will save us. 'The pope?' say I. 'What good is a pope when he works by the same rules as the King who will not die?'

"The only comfort I have is that our Master de Molay has the blood royal in him. He has it since Philippe came to us and they performed the rite together, the exchange of blood, gashed arm to gashed arm. No matter how they rack Master de Molay, they cannot press it all from him, and he is determined to die as the Sacrifice. The Sacrifice that all the people will recognize.

"Not only that, but now, while there are still thirteen of us left in our right minds, now we will curse this King and his land with the blackest of our combined power. A curse upon this King and his land! Master de Molay, with his gift of Sight, sees that neither Philippe nor the pope will outlive him by as much as six months for their violence against our order and our Land. As their own scriptures say, 'He who seeks to gain his life shall lose it.' The King will die, gored by the boar, as is always the sign of one cursed by the ancient Goddess, not taken to the Earth as a God."

I knew this was so, for I myself had cursed a man to die on the tusks for sacrilege: the former sire de Rais, Gilles' father.

"And all those three young princes," the spirit went on, heedless of my memories. "One after the other, they will die cursed deaths, too, without issue. And the throne of France will pass to a cadet line, a more faithful line, that the blood may be renewed and continue and cause the Land to flourish once more.

"For this spell we have cast against Philippe and his line, I have granted a counter-spell. In time to come, in a hundred years or more, men of Craft may find the key to break our enchantment, to set the wheel turning once again. They will know the time is ripe when what was done by men alone may be undone by a woman. This counter-spell, it is contained, as is only just, within a hymn to Our Lady.

"For it was in neglecting women that this last coven of ours shall fall. For, as any magician knows, every 'Our Lady' on Christian tongues, even all unknowing, sings praises to the Goddess. Praise Her, cloaked in blue seamed with stars, tripping barefoot on the crescent moon. Every Notre Dame is a house unto Her glory. We will chant the hymn once before the curse is cast, then secret the words away, scratching them into the wall of our prison."

Bibu's words ceased. When their echoes died, I expected almost to hear those immured voices, intoning the words we had to know to raise our thwarted power.

But I did not.

Tenth Antiphon

Eight Birds Loosed from the Tower of Coudray

I looked on the walls of grim Coudray Tower around me. The only words etched there were names and blazons I'd noted with my milk brother. "Galube" or "Juan"? Was one of them the man long dead whose voice we heard? I was sure we would have heard a Spanish lilt in the voice of "Juan".

Was the counter-spell to be found in the words *Je requier à dieu pardon,* "I beg God for pardon," scratched in archaic Gothic letters and spelling? Had this spirit dug them into the stone with some nail he'd found? Was it for the lies he'd spouted under torture that he asked forgiveness? Or for the order's denial of the feminine half of magic? None of this seemed to be the hymn of which the spirit spoke.

Then Bibu de Sillé said, "Look for the words in an alcove in this tower. There they will stay hidden until such time as it is safe for the curse to be lifted. A Master to come, by the prophecy of Merlin, he will know this time."

I was that Master. I knew the time. But the words—?

Bibu de Sillé began to chant in a frenzy of pain and fear:

Our Lady Mother,
Queen of Heaven,
Wide bosom of the land ...

I listened intently. But his words became garbled after that, choked with drool and clogged in the grey of a malformed brain.

The moment he would let her, madame de Sillé caught up her son into her arms.

"Wait. He must chant the song again," I said.

But he collapsed, sobbing, into her arms. Gently, she worked the bones out of the clench of his fist, even as the spirit must once have worked them out of his own charred flesh. She passed them quietly to me, never ceasing her croon. I secreted them in the bosom of my robe, vowing to have a new bag made for them as soon as I could. A bag of fine velvet. Or perhaps a casket of gold, as the relics of any martyr. But the chant ...

"Look here," Hamish said behind me. "Here must be the alcove of which he spoke."

The Scotsman uttered the truth. Now that he knew what we were looking for, he had found it easily, tucked away within the thickness of the wall, beside an archer's narrow slit and beneath the twist of stairs. I lit my finger to it, and we soon conned the rest of the words.

"But such a lifting of a spell will require blood," Hamish said, and twitched. "Blood for blood."

Madame continued to cradle her great child. Then, a different cooing drew my gaze beyond this pietà. The pigeons. We had brought them down in their cages to be blessed before we loosed them to fly to the nine other witches we needed to be powerfully whole.

"It'll have to be one of the pigeons," I said.

"Which one?"

"Gilles de Rais and La Pucelle are together in Poitiers," I suggested. "One bird could serve to bear the message to them both."

"It will not do to slight La Pucelle by not sending her own pigeon." Hamish twitched again. "Not when all this magic pivots on her."

I had to agree. That left Pieronne, who lived together with her teacher in the Craft, Tiphaine, on the Mont-Saint-Michel.

"Pieronne will not mind, I'm certain." I hoped this was true. The wish to see the woman I loved above all others—ill done for a Master though such affection was—she wouldn't mind. In spirit, I suspected we were close enough that a mental message could bring her as quickly as flight.

So we wrung the neck of one of the birds that had been brought from the sacred mountain in the midst of the bay, and sprinkled its blood in the cauldron as we added the Templar's chant to our work.

When we were done and had released our circle, we carried the eight birds up through the tower rooms stacked one upon another. Through madame's private chambers at the top, which had been La Pucelle's, we reached the roof.

Coudray Tower perched like a woodpecker at the edge of the rock outcrop. Fog was lifting off the Vienne. I could see as far as the abbey of Fontevraud, where the Angevins, two Kings of England, Henry and Richard—with Eleanor of Aquitaine, the queen they shared as husband and son, between them—lay buried. Shifting slightly further north, the view opened up over the Île Bouchard as far as the roofs of Saumur. And all along both banks of the river, the trees were a haze of pale, new green.

With the distraction of pigeons to let loose, Bibu de Sillé was his own, foolish, happy self again. Indeed, I'm not certain he remembered what his tongue revealed when under his gift's enchantment. In the same way, sometimes the falling sickness came to me with Sight I could not recall, even after years of practice and training. The man-child's great hands fumbled with the loop-of-willow latch on the cage, and he laughed out loud as the birds soared off into the sky of perfect blue.

As they flew, Marie Javelle, as the bell in the castle tower was called, began to ring out. The ringing has a song, they say:

Marie Javelle	*Marie Javelle*
Je m'appelle	*I am called*
Qui m'a mis	*Who placed me here*
M'a bien mis.	*Placed me well.*
Celui qui m'ôtera	*Whoever removes me*
S'en repentira.	*Will repent of it.*

The sweet tones might have counteracted our good work, Christian as they were. But the perfect alloy of bronze and silver recalled the Mother whence they were mined. The tune worked with the Templars' repentant hymn of praise and carried rather than hindered our birds. They flapped off in their nine different directions:

For La Pucelle and Gilles de Rais.

For Père Michel in Lorraine and for Roger de Bricqueville on the front lines fighting the English.

For Charles the Dauphin, who was actually here in Chinon, necessary to our plan, but who had gone out riding early that morning and hadn't come to work the magic with us.

For La Meffraye, madame's maidservant left behind in Champtocé, to help bring up the numbers of women counteracting the ancient Templars' neglect in this age of La Pucelle.

For the son of the old bard who'd died and become the God in the crypt below Angers chapel almost sixteen years before. Gwencalon, who'd inherited his father's name and his harp.

And for Tiphaine and my—I couldn't suppress the thought—*my* Pieronne.

But no. There were only eight birds. I had forgotten the little heap of bloodied grey feathers we'd left in the reeking rubble of the dungeon. My nostrils caught another whiff of that decay as the thought crossed my mind: feathers to replace the long-buried bones concealed now in the bosom of my robe.

The fragrances of spring soon blew my lungs clear again. It was going to be a gorgeous day.

Chapter Fourteen

A Globe Set to Roll on a Smooth Surface

Through most of April the Dauphin's entire court made its lumbering way on to the city of Tours. Here, La Pucelle's Voices spoke. La Pucelle must have a banner, like any battle lord. They told her what it must be: white silk, with a forked tail—"like a white martinet," she said—and gold fringe a hand wide around the edges.

Her confessor, Père Yann, saw to it that Hamish Power had the making of the ensign, of acquiring the fabric, of finding the sage women to do the needlework. Gilles de Rais knew Power of old, a Scotsman who'd made his living, for a while, until the English came, trading dry goods in Picardy. Now he'd opened a shop in Tours profiting, Gilles thought skeptically, like everyone else from the war.

War excitement caught hold of them all, from banneret to page, as news of the Maid spread across once-disheartened France. Men who thought they'd hung up their shields for good came out of retirement and descended on Tours where the army of France was regrouping. Their dusty gear, like their renewed spirits, needed refurbishing. Under striped awnings, Power provided tabards and surcoats in the colors of any livery, from fabrics stacked to the ceiling. Around the walls of a back room, shields and bucklers stacked three deep, new ones and old ones receiving fresh colors, for he also painted blazons on fabric, wood or metal.

Hamish Power had his hands full to overflowing, although the state of his purse was more doubtful. Most of this trade was done on credit, the hope that English treasure or hostages or perhaps simply the opening of heaven's golden gates would soon make up the lack. How Power, a late comer to Tours, should fare so well had something to do with rumors of the protective magic with which Gilles had heard he imbued his work.

None of this alone would have been enough to attract the attention of Yann, even though the Merlin was a draper's son. Hamish Power, great, burly man that he was, red hair and red, whiskered face, might have served well swinging battleaxes against the English beside his compatriots. But the powerful build of the man was marred by a nervous tic that would have sent any blow or shot he attempted dangerously awry. And, fiery as his outer shell appeared, a very different humor was Hamish Power's at the core. Gilles knew it well, a moist and misty humor, a breath of chill up the spine.

For the Scotsman had the "gift"—such was Yann's word for it—of being able to foretell death, to See it as a grey shadow behind the doomed. Gilles had firm evidence of the truth of this Sight at the fated siege of Saint-James-de-Beuvron—and had been saved from a shifting shadow of his own only by Yann's and Hamish's quick magic. Naturally, such a man stood high on the Craftmaster's coven list. Naturally, a lot of strange herbs and muttered chants went into transforming the image La Pucelle's Voices gave her into the fabric of her banner.

Gilles was happy enough to take La Pucelle to see how the work was progressing. But naturally again, he held back from the cluster of women, enclosed in the small back garden. On this fine day, they'd moved hoops and needles out to the sun. A hedge of quince, pleached along a southern wall and already covered with delicate rosy thimbles, served as backdrop.

He noticed how the gilt-wound threads were laid upon the white silk like the smooth grey branches of the hedge against the wall. He saw how the gold was then couched down with silks of every different color, not just the quince's pink. The threads had been dyed in Hamish's own workshop, in small, special lots. Gilles suspected that more than dying herbs had gone into the work. Every color must have its meaning, its spell. Every stitch circled with magic.

That was all he needed to see. Hamish knew his business, the women knew theirs, and Gilles knew enough to keep a respectful, uneasy distance.

La Pucelle took a keener interest. What she saw delighted her, made her linger, talking and talking to the women. Her delight delighted him, but Gilles remained, watching the scene from the doorway.

Suddenly he felt a dagger slip lightly across the hairs at the back of his neck. In a moment, his lungs refound breath. The touch of cold steel was imagined, the fear a prickle of the former cloth merchant's sudden presence at his shoulder. The large, constantly jerking man managed to move up to him with the stealth of the very death he could See. Now he stood, filling the other half of the doorway, looking out in the same sunny direction.

As soon as his heart settled back in his chest, Gilles turned to his host and tried to catch the blue eyes, tried to read them. Not for himself this time, no. He hardly cared about himself. What did Power read when he looked at La Pucelle?

The blue eyes, so vacuous, so blind-seeming in any case, ticked away and Gilles couldn't guess. He let his gaze wander back in the same direction the Scotsman's went, back to La Pucelle, toward the needles plying over hoops. It seemed the women couched the open spring air and light in among the threads, magic itself.

In the center of the banner, the figure of a man neared completion. Bearded and haloed, he could have been Christ. Nevertheless, even at these few paces, Gilles could see a pair of horns cunningly worked into the light around his head. Christ He might have been. But He was also, and more originally, the Horned One of the Old People, the Stag of the Forest, the God Who Must Die.

In His hands He bore a globe. It was not merely a circle. Something about the colors of the threads made the rim seem to curve and recede away from the viewer, and the center to advance. This was some dark magic that Gilles hesitated to delve into.

"What is that globe meant to be?" Gilles asked when, for an instant, La Pucelle looked up from the work and met his eyes.

"The world," she replied.

He hated her tone, as if he were a simpleton. Worse, the words made his blood run cold as he remembered the fury that had come into their tutor's eye when they were children, and Yann had suggested the roundness of the earth. "Heresy! St. Boniface wrote clearly against the heresy of Vergilius when he told us a spherical earth is contrary to scripture." And he had given Yann the lash for speaking "such a damnable error."

"The world isn't a globe," Gilles said, partly in self-defense, partly to defend her from the fury of such attitudes as he knew to be rampant among the powerful. "All the wisest scholars say it's flat. And the Bible speaks of the earth's four corners."

"I admit the physical part seems flat, the part you and I are standing on now."

Yes, Gilles was very aware that he was standing on the same stretch of smooth-worn stone as this wonderful girl. He was certain that, if he took his boots off, his feet would be flooded with sensations as keen as those Yann reported through his well-thickened soles. But the sensations were difficult enough to control without losing a man-at-arms' demeanor.

"Still, it cycles," La Pucelle went on. "That's the part I needed to portray, how the seasons make their rounds in the ancient way. And a ball suggests much more the way the cycles must be balanced. A ball is harder to keep stable than a slab of wood. It is much easier to stop a slab of wood from rolling on and on. That is the hopeful thing I wish to show the soldiers: They fight so that the world may turn and continue. That is what my struggle is for."

He loved to hear her talk, especially as she went on and on about her Voices. When she did, her speech became his own divine Voice, and it was like breathing air for him. It didn't matter what nonsense she babbled. He was fool enough to believe it—because he had to keep breathing.

At this point, she must have looked into his face and read bemusement there. She circled around to the other side of the work, giving a playful tug at the red garter on his calf—close, too close to his vitals—as she did. "Surely a man who wears that must understand," she said.

He promised her he did.

She went back to her circle. Sewing in a circle, that is magic, Gilles thought. As magicians circle, drawing down power. This sorcery ringed him out.

And, among the women sewing, on the side to which she now circled, sat one quite young, almost of an age with La Pucelle. La Pucelle seemed to find this lively redhead's work—or the girl herself—quite attractive. A quick look was enough to tell Gilles that, in spite of many freckles, the girl was pretty enough, but buxom and comely after the way of women. She held no interest for him.

His charge, however, stood speaking with her for a long time. When La Pucelle bent over the work, she steadied herself, as if by chance, with an arm about the redhead's shoulders. And once, after having fingered a skein of brilliant silk, she reached up and fingered a strand of kinky hair escaped from its simple maiden's linen.

"Like the gold thread you work." He overheard that murmur as La Pucelle smoothed the lock back behind an ear.

Gilles found such gestures odd, then disconcerting. They were exactly the sorts of tendernesses he would have liked to lavish on La Pucelle. But women were always very demonstrative among themselves, walking arm in arm, embracing for no cause that he could ever see. He tried to set it, and the feelings it aroused in him, aside.

"My daughter, Héliote." This was Hamish Power, speaking with a certain pride at his elbow.

Gilles should have noticed the family resemblance, the exotic import among the darker bending heads. He nodded, dismissively. What did he care for men's daughters? Then, for a brief moment, he remembered that, through La Pucelle's magic, he might soon be a father himself. He had certainly taken the first step in that direction. No, the thought was too unnerving, too unstabilizing, like a globe set to roll on a smooth surface. He hadn't seen Catherine since that night and had no word. Well, that was how he liked it. His escape didn't make the event any less real, however, nor any less binding in ways he did not like.

He brought his attention back to the present, to the more stable flagstone of the workshop yard. Hamish Power interested him in ways other than the fact that he had a seamstress daughter. He could see danger, death. Gilles was willing to turn to the gifted Scotsman for this faculty while the girls talked. The man's blue eyes still refused to tell anything of what they Saw, so Gilles tried a more open tactic.

"I recently heard La Pucelle speak to the Dauphin. 'Use me wisely,' she told him. 'You'll have me for a year only. Or maybe a little more.'"

Power nodded—or perhaps it was only a tic. There was no commitment in the gesture in either case.

La Pucelle must have overheard them. She looked up; it was Power's eyes she met, not Gilles'.

Now jealousy roared in Gilles' ears so wildly that if his charge and Power had exchanged words, he certainly couldn't have heard them. Gilles knew, however, that something passed between them. La Pucelle gave a little nod, of acquiescence, of submission, then turned back to the redhead and the banner.

Power knew something. He'd Seen something, some threat. The girl's safety was on Gilles' shoulders. He felt the surge of blood to every nerve, ready to jump, a readiness that only part of him knew was madness in the quiet of this yard.

Sunlight caught a flash of metal, and Gilles leaped forward. He realized at once it was only the redhead's needle, not the sword he'd first imagined.

"Would you like to work a stitch or two, La Pucelle?" the redhead asked.

Gilles' heart still raced, however, and it relieved him to no end to see La Pucelle refuse the offer.

"No, I thank you," she said. He saw her shift, then color a little. These were the moves of a person about to tell a lie. "I once had no rival for my seams," she said.

What made her have to embroider so, with words if she couldn't do it with needle and thread? She'd told him herself she'd never had any woman's skills. He'd believed her and thought it added to her perfections. Did she actually feel the need to try to fit into this circle? Here, the fact that she unseated La Hire at the first pass might not mean as much as it did in the lists. Was it apology for the life she'd left behind that still lingered? Or was she trying, just a little, to impress the redhead?

"But that was before, as a child," La Pucelle continued, returning to her normal stance and color, "now I ply the sword."

Gilles felt certain he would have had to snatch the needle before she touched it if she hadn't refused on her own. There was that old folk tale, about the princess who pricked her finger and fell under a spell. Certainly, there was enough magic buzzing over the white silk to make such a thing possible. But whether his fear was part of his calling as bodyguard, or part of the jealousy that she should bring herself any closer to Power's daughter, he couldn't tell. One thing was certain: the look that had passed between the elder Power and La Pucelle had done nothing to ease his nerves.

Gilles' defensive movement against a woman's tiny needle had brought him close enough to study the banner more than he would otherwise have done. The "angels" to either side of the Stag were not as close to being finished as their Lord. Still, Gilles saw that they would be garlanded with many-colored flowers and standing in dancing poses, maidens worshiping their God at Midsummer.

The last time they'd visited Power, when the silk had just been cut but still blank, the Scotsman had suggested, "Perhaps you'd better write something on it, Lady."

"Write something?" La Pucelle had laughed at him, her voice like peals of bells. "I can't read. And most of the men can't either. What would be the point?"

"The point would be for the men who can read. The men whose world is flat as a book and might think you a witch for suggesting heaven tells you otherwise."

"Very well, write something. Sketch something out with charcoal on the silk for the women here to stitch. And make it plain, for they can't read, either."

"What shall it be? And be careful, Lady. Consider the sorts of men who will read it."

"I don't care. I can't read, so it doesn't matter at all to me. Write for those people who think it does matter."

Then Gilles had suggested, "How about 'Jhesu-Marie'?"

He'd read it on her ring. She'd touched that ring as he'd said it. Then she'd grunted and shrugged. It still didn't matter to her.

Now the *J*, the *H* and the *E* of the 'Jhesu' had been worked up in black and gold threads. Gilles pointed them out when he saw a chance to say something before the redhead could.

"That looks all right," La Pucelle said without commitment.

"It could almost be spelling your name," Gilles suggested, "the way it is now."

"My name?" She looked up at him, her eyes glittering.

"Jehanne. *J E H* ... "

Now she ran her fingers over the needlework with new interest, as if she might some day be called upon to trace the shapes from memory. With a pen, perhaps.

"Could you teach me to write, Bluebeard?"

"But, of course. I'd be delighted, Lady."

Infinitely better than that she take up the needle with Power's daughter.

He imagined long days in a sunny scriptorium, his head bent close to hers over a single slate, his hand holding hers as he helped her to form every letter, over and over. In some far-off time, when the wars were done, there might even be the hours to teach her to illuminate, as he loved to do. And poetry ...

"Just my name." She interrupted his daydreaming with a new decision. "Now that I have started sending and receiving letters from so many people, I can see how it might be nice not to always have to make an *X* whenever I must sign something. The rest is not important, if I have scribes to write down what I say."

"You might want to be sure they've written the words aright," he said. "That they haven't written what you don't want to say."

"They wouldn't do that, would they?"

"Alas, dear Lady, in this wicked world, they might."

"I hadn't thought of that," she said. "Ah, I always knew speech was better than paper any day. You can read in a man's eyes when he tells the truth."

Gilles found himself looking away, afraid of her reading his eyes, afraid of what she might find there. Wondering what she'd read in Power's eyes.

"Well," she went on, not thinking of him, "if I ever have doubts of my scribe, I will mark an *X* and an *O*, like the round world together with my mark, so you at least will know I doubt the truth of what I've signed."

"Very good, Lady. That way I'll know. But suppose—just suppose you should want to write a secret letter, a private letter for the eyes of only the person you were sending it to. No scribes at all."

Like a love letter, Gilles was thinking. He'd spent many long, idle moments trying to compose something he might write to her to explain all he felt, for he'd found himself totally incapable of speaking his feelings aloud. He'd always condemn himself quickly for a fool when he did so, knowing she would have to ask someone to read it for her. But if she could read ...

"No, it's not necessary." She broke into his thoughts with perfect assurance. "All the acts of my life shall be very public."

He thought his heart would break to hear it.

"When I look at this," she went on, "I won't think of Jhesu so much. I'll think of me, Jehanne. This is my banner, and my magic is in it. It is good not to be able to read."

It is good, Gilles thought, that the people for whom we write "Jhesu - Marie" can't hear you now.

After that, he shadowed her to the armorer's.

Chapter Fifteen

At the Armorer's

The man who had taken the French name of Colin de Montbazon, armorer to the Dauphin, had his shop in the Rue Colbert. A stream rushing down to the Loire turned his polishing mills and heavy hammers, and filled the workroom with a constant roar, even when the anvil, bellows and forge were quiet.

Anvils and stakes of various sizes and shapes cluttered the master's workbench; hammers in similar variety arrayed the wall above. Man-sized barrels of quenching water and oil stood by the furnace, which breathed like a live thing. The stone floor crunched with litter, the air smelled of hot charcoal, pig grease, singed goat skins and, over all, iron turning slowly, magically, to steel.

The armorer was a dark gnome of a fellow with a forked beard and round cap, and shoulders so powerful he seemed as wide as he was tall. Of Milanese extraction and training, Gilles decided, before the man even opened his mouth. A glance at the pieces of his workmanship hung up for display on pegs like so many dismembered limbs was enough to tell. His was the school famous for their full white armor, smoother than the heavy fluting favored by the Germans. From the hauberks' polished faces, Gilles saw La Pucelle, who had entered with him, reflected back a dozen times.

So the Maid's armor was to be white, silvery steel plate to stand out on a battlefield like the sun at noon. Gilles thought of the contrast to his own favorite field suit, blue-black steel trimmed in gold.

Yet in this switch from the women's domain of Hamish Power's shop to this of men, a new pall came over Gilles' soul.

He quickly gave it the name of threat. He felt a mortal threat to his charge from every one of the four or five men crammed into that space. They were no more than the usual group gathered to talk and watch the leather-skinned smith in his leather apron raise the sparks and the smell of hot metal and hot men on his anvil. Gilles even mistrusted the look in the young apprentice's eye as he gazed up from his bellows to La Pucelle. The lad, hardly more than ten, seemed a threat for no other reason than that his little awe-struck face was blackened with soot.

The longer his hand danced on his hilt, the more ridiculous Gilles found his tension to be. None of these men meant her any harm. On the contrary. He was certain they would lay down their lives for La Pucelle in an instant if she required it. Just as he would.

And there, precisely, was the threat.

"What is taking you so long?" he demanded of Montbazon.

Gilles couldn't wait to see the effect of the two of them, La Pucelle and Gilles de Rais, striding across the field together, silver-white and gold-black. He couldn't wait to find fault with the armorer, whose great shoulders and upper arms might be very attractive to a woman.

The armorer drew him aside a little and, with telling gestures and an Italian lilt, explained: "I've never had to make a breastplate with—you know—before."

In spite of his care, La Pucelle had overheard him. "Don't worry about the breasts," she told him merrily. "I haven't got much to speak of."

And at that moment, when every eye in the shop was on her, she quickly wriggled out of nearly every stitch she had on. She wanted to try on the new pourpoint she must wear as padding under the metal, over the shirt next to her skin.

"If I lace it tight enough, I'll be flat as a boy," she declared, her voice muffled as the quilted linen went over her head.

Over the roar of the stream, Gilles heard the click of swinging laces and points as she worked the garment on. The points were waxed well enough then; they must not stretch under the weight of the sheets of metal they would be asked to bear.

One desperate part of him had hoped that, confronted by the naked womanness of her, the old disgust that had always come to him in the presence of any female—including and especially his wife—would return. He had hoped, hope against hope, that he would be able to leave this mad infatuation for the old, comfortable life that had suited him so well—up until the instant he'd seen La Pucelle sitting in the Golden Stag Inn.

But Gilles saw those breasts as the unlaced hose dropped to her ankles, as she bent forward to tug them up again and the still-loose shirt and pourpoint fell open. There was no escape.

No, her breasts weren't large. But they were definitely not male. And they were beautiful. He'd never seen anything so beautiful in his life. He closed his eyes against the ache of longing to touch them. It might very well kill him.

All the while, La Pucelle was as innocent of her effect, and as carefree, as a newborn colt frisking in a pasture. Was it being raised with brothers? Or having embraced her life among soldiers so closely she never considered how different she was?

The men in the shop, the normal men, didn't seem to notice. No more than they would watching an altar uncovered and re-draped with a fresh, white cloth. Of that, Gilles was glad.

"The breastplate," Montbazon announced.

"Allow me," Gilles said, and snatched the piece out of its creator's hands. He could give no one else the honor, the intimacy, of arming her.

The muscles in Gilles' arms had prepared themselves for some resistance from the burly man. There was none. More to the point, the breastplate weighed much less than he had expected, much less than his own, and it nearly flew from his hands.

La Pucelle was as pleased as a child with a new toy. "Made just for me—" she murmured, and reached out to touch the armor.

But Gilles snatched it back from her. "It's very light," he accused Montbazon. He thought he could feel the steel give as he torqued it between his hands. It might as well be boiled leather.

"Of course it's light," the man said. "You think I would put something as heavy as monseigneur can carry on those small shoulders?"

"It must protect her, all the same," Gilles insisted. "What do you mean, to have her shine on the field like a full moon in the night sky, so everyone can see her, and give her no protection from the first ax blow?"

"It will stand up to axes—"

Gilles ran his hands hungrily over the shape, her shape. The metal was flesh-warm from sitting beside the forge, and smooth. Smooth was how the flesh would be, under his hands, but for a breastplate, it was too smooth.

"There's not a proof mark on it," he exclaimed.

"Well—"

"Did you proof it?"

The armorer seemed to have forgotten every word of French he ever knew.

"You didn't even proof it?"

"What does it mean, to proof it?" La Pucelle asked, hovering nearby as if to save her armor from being torn apart by the passions of two very like the mothers of Solomon's wisdom.

She didn't need to know details. He meant to take care of them for her, without her being aware that he was doing so. His frustration that this time the care was not invisible pervaded his answer, even though she wasn't the person at whom he was angry. "Armor, properly made, should prove itself before purchase."

"You mean, someone should try to whack it with a sword or a lance?" she asked, a gleam of excitement in her eyes.

"Someone should also try a crossbow quarrel at it. At twenty paces, no more." Gilles saw the armorer blanch behind his black beard when he said this. He took pleasure in pressing the matter, just to watch the man squirm. "A cuirass that's proven itself will have a dent where the bolt hit—but didn't go through. This piece has no such mark."

Gilles meant to toss the breastplate at the armorer's feet in contempt. La Pucelle caught it from him instead and he let her have it, while he pursued his complaint against Montbazon.

"It's not the custom of our craft to try our armor after it's already been faced and filed," the artisan dodged.

"Well, then you must break with custom or start all over again with a new, heavier piece of iron," Gilles told him.

"Oh, don't start over again," La Pucelle protested. "We'll be stuck here in Tours for ever and never get to Orléans at all."

Gilles gave her a glance. With the help of the young apprentice, who'd given up his bellows altogether, and one or two of the other bystanders, she was putting the cuirass on with obvious delight. There, the flesh was shut away from him. Well, let her play where she would. He, who understood the seriousness of war, would see to the important matters.

"All care that can be taken has been taken," Montbazon urged.

Gilles turned back to the argument, and got a demonstration of how the helmet deflected a strong dagger blow without a nick.

"Note how all the rivets have been filed flat, all buckles and joints carefully worked on the inside. There's nothing for a weapon to catch on. See how the lames of the arm pieces overlap downwards. Again, the blow slips off like water."

Gilles found fault where he could. "But the pauldrons that will cap her shoulders—they're huge, nearly overlapping like wings in the back—especially the right one. Couldn't you take some weight out there and put the rest into thicker plate?"

"But see, when she raises her arm, what good protection this will give to the vulnerable underarm. You, monseigneur, might not need so much when you fight, your sword running parallel from your arm with its thrusts most of the time. But, as St. Dunstan loves me, La Pucelle will ride into battle with her banner held high in this hand, thus. And to reach to any man's vitals, even with a sword, it's an upward reach for her."

Gilles saw the man's argument, saw that careful thought had gone into this piece of artistry. He wouldn't admit it, but before he thought of a way to avoid having to do so, he heard something that made his blood run cold.

La Pucelle's voice, high and clear, shouted: "Yes, go ahead, Marco. Shoot. Straight at me. Prove the armor."

Gilles wheeled around. She was no longer in the shop.

Chapter Sixteen

The Armor Proved

Pushing past the onlookers, Gilles found the girl out in the street, near where the shops of artisans ended and turned to those of bankers and merchants. He saw her one instant before the armorer's apprentice, at twenty ten-year-old paces, pulled the trigger on the crossbow and let the quarrel fly.

Gilles made a dive for the boy's legs, knowing even as he did that he was too late, might only make a good aim a bad one. A scream filled his head. He thought it was his own, feared it was hers, then realized it was the boy's, who had landed hard.

Gilles let him lie. Spitting street muck from his mouth and wiping it from his eyes, Gilles got to his knees, then, more slowly, to his feet.

At the end of the street, La Pucelle still stood. Sunlight on white metal transformed her into something that swelled the heart, as otherworldly as the icon of a saint. Gilles had to look away, even as he stumbled towards her. He looked above, around, for some place else the quarrel might have flown: into the side of this house, into this goodwife's laundry hung to dry.

Then—there, on the ground at her feet. He saw it, a glint of the copper fletching that gave the bolt its deadly, whirling, steel-puncturing path through the air. He looked up a little higher, saw a little dimple in her metallic breast where there had been none before, just above where her heart must beat. He found he couldn't raise his eyes any higher. He reached out and touched the proof mark instead.

On all sides of him, grown men from the shop, burghers who'd stopped to watch in the street, all fell to their knees.

"Bless me, Lady," they murmured.

And she did, but with distraction.

Then Gilles looked up, into her face, and lost his temper. "What, for the love of God, were you thinking?" he demanded. "Getting that boy to crank up a crossbow and shoot it at you?"

"We proofed the armor, see?" She bent down and picked up the quarrel. "We don't need to wait for new to be made."

"You didn't even have the helmet on, or the arm pieces or anything but the breastplate."

"That's right."

"Usually the armorer sets his work up on a pole, not with anybody in it."

"Oh. I didn't know."

"You could have been killed."

"No, I could not, Bluebeard, not here, not now. Not before my work is done. But you couldn't accept that. Even after our fight in the lists, you couldn't accept it. You wanted the armor proofed. I proofed it."

He met her eyes then and saw something trying to give itself to him. He didn't want to be her beneficiary. He wanted only to give.

"Though maybe," she concluded, looking away, "it was myself I proofed for you instead."

How could he ever give anything to her—or take it from her, even—if she got herself killed? The full force of just how close he'd come to losing her hadn't hit him before, when there was no time for logic. Now it made his knees weak.

Had the apprentice gone at her with a sword or knife, his young arms couldn't have put force enough behind the blows to do damage. But a crossbow, with its winding mechanism, made even the weakest hand deadly, so long as it had the patience for a complete winding. No wonder the pope—one of them—had condemned this weapon as a tool of the devil. It leveled the battlefield too much, setting all a man's work and training and God-given gifts at naught.

That must be it. The boy had only cranked the windlass back so far. But far enough to make that dent, Gilles had to admit, his gaze dropping to the fatal spot again.

"By God," he told her, "that blasted boy's aim had every chance of being bad, of sending the bolt into your arm or leg—or, God help me, into your brain."

"But see, Bluebeard, it didn't."

How could she stand there, so calmly staring back up at him? The dark eyes, the gift still there, left him speechless.

"You wanted to see me wounded?" she teased.

"Of course not."

"Well, never mind. You will."

"God forbid it."

"God will allow it. My Voices have told me. Armor or no armor, my blood must flow at Orléans."

Ah, is this what Hamish Power had Seen? "No. I won't let it. We won't go to Orléans then."

"Yes. I'm afraid, too. A little. But it must be."

"It's my job to prevent it."

"You can't, Bluebeard, so stop trying."

Gilles made a decision and decided to tell her: "My ancestor Bertrand Du Guesclin, the Sword of the King, refused to hear the warnings of his wife about what she read in the stars. Thus unheeding, he rode to his death at Châteauneuf-de-Randon."

"Truly?"

"Yes. It's a well known tale in my family, passed down these fifty years or so."

"No, I mean, you are truly related to the great Du Guesclin?"

"Yes." Finally, something about him that impressed her.

Before he'd thought of a way to bring his relative's fame circling back to his own, she said, "Do you know anything of a ring?"

"A ring? No."

Just as quickly, the interest—in him—was gone. "My Voices tell me I must have a ring," she said. "A ring—and somehow connected to that last hero who rose to save France two generations ago. But if you don't know—"

A ring. Required of someone related to Du Guesclin. Well, here, at last, was a need he could fulfill. In fact, he'd acquired a ruby recently; he'd just been looking for a way to give it to her so she would accept it. If he took it at once to be set with the best local goldsmith ...

They'd arrived back at the workshop door now. Parrying the comments and exclamations of the men and seeing to the rest of her harness consumed all her attention. That and young Marco's scrapes. She made the boy hoist up his shirt. She examined the blood beading in several long grazes with sympathy and certain oblique suggestions that there'd been no need for such roughness on the part of a certain lord.

Seeing the same red on white belly forced Gilles to look away. The urge to deepen those wounds, exaggerate the pain in the young fool, made the lord of Rais lightheaded for a moment.

When he returned to his senses, he saw that nobody was competing with him for her attention. Nobody—but something beyond.

Her Voices—? Then suddenly she was back in the armory in full consciousness, too. She said hastily, "Now a sword. Now all I need is a sword."

"Here, Lady," said the smith. "My brother is a swordsmith, and I have some of his here. Take a look at these I have. This one is the best—"

La Pucelle hardly gave the shaft of silver a second glance but followed some unheard sound out of the dark and heat of the shop into the light of the street beyond once more.

"No, no," she said. "Another sword. One set for me, hidden, that must be found."

And so, the armor proofed, Gilles found himself on another quest—a pair of them, one for a sword and one for the perfect ring.

Eleventh Antiphon

Pilgrims to Fierbois

At the shrine of Ste. Catherine de Fierbois, La Pucelle had said. "That's where my sword lies. You will find it there, Yann, behind the altar."

A secret sword, revealed by Voices, hidden behind an altar. Echoes of King Arthur, wonders of the Grail.

Georges de La Trémoïlle didn't like that. He didn't like that at all. He would have been very happy to hand the girl the best sword in the kingdom, acquired in the usual way, rather than that. But she had given her proclamation too publicly. Somebody had to go to Fierbois to look.

La Trémoïlle determined he had to ride to the shrine himself for the discovery. The bother put him into a foul mood, but it had to be done. He would put his own meaning on anything we found, of that I was certain. And his meaning would devalue anything of the miraculous.

He required La Pucelle to stay in Tours, much to her own frustration. The lieutenant-general knew her powers too well. She'd make a miracle of anything, and at least half the army was ready to believe without question. She had to stay behind.

It was only by dint of great effort that even I was allowed to come along upon this quest. Gilles had worked hard, diplomatically, with his powerful cousin. The other witches, too, had worked their own magic, until one means or the other, or both, had met, at the last moment, with success.

I had to go, I had never doubted that. I had little to do as we waited for the rest of the coven to make its way to us, but my presence at Fierbois was necessary for more than for my own diversion. Had La Trémoïlle forbidden it, I would have had to go under some disguise, something other than Père Jean Pasquerel of the Augustinians, confessor to the Maid.

Since every accompanying man-at-arms, every lackey, would be carefully chosen for the lieutenant-general's purposes, I had considered taking animal form. I'd thought of replacing the soul of La Trémoïlle's own great stallion—poor, laboring beast—and went to the stables to make friends with him, just in case. But such a form would limit my ability to work magic once we got there, and heavy magic was going to be needed, of that I was certain.

La Trémoïlle's permission, when it came to Jean Pasquerel, was a relief on that count. I was even ordered to ride on ahead with Père Ambrose, to prepare every comfort for the arrival of monseigneur le chambellan. Père Ambrose was the archbishop's man, the priest intended by old Regnault and La Trémoïlle to replace me as La Pucelle's confessor. That he would break the seal of confession sooner than he'd break wind was written all over the slick sink holes of his cheeks.

Riding ahead gave me a blessed chance to at least reconnoiter the ground of this miracle. But on many other counts, the whole business still made me terribly uneasy.

A lot of the problem was with La Pucelle herself. Not that I didn't believe in her, of course. Not that I didn't know this tiny, strutting girl was the very one we'd been waiting for, but rather just because she was. It was her power, her great power. Power, misused, misunderstood, employed too soon, is always dangerous.

She was so young in magic, our Pucelle, and far too unused to curbing her speech, treading lightly when her observers might take her words amiss—or too near the point. Fearless as she was to do battle, she didn't understand that there were other things to fear besides arrows and spears, and on her own side, too.

Then, again, she didn't understand that magical Voices often speak in metaphor. She took everything as plainly as she spoke herself. Gilles had told me how her Voices had told her she would bear three glorious sons. My magic doubted very much these were literal offspring, of her literal body, this pope, this emperor, this King. Virginity was far too much wrapped up in what this maiden was, as far as I could sense. I never chose to discourage my milk brother by telling him so, of course.

Ancient Merlin would have known to take such statements as clouded prophecy, in need of careful interpretation. I knew the same myself of my own Sight, having learned it after many difficult years.

But La Pucelle, she did not know. Not yet.

So what to make of this sword? There might be no sword at all behind Ste. Catherine's altar, but some other symbol. I would have to forge meaning from it, and forge it fast, even if there proved to be nothing at all. Too much magic would either detract from La Pucelle herself or reveal the Craft so blatantly that everyone from the Dauphin down would know her for a witch. Too little, and there'd be no miracle at all, especially if La Trémoïlle had anything to say about the matter.

As my little donkey stepped wearily into the clearing before the shrine and its outbuildings, all I knew for certain was the tension riding hard upon my own shoulders.

Fierbois is on the Great Pilgrim's Route which flows westward from all lands towards the holy house of St. Jacques de Compostela, at the end of land, in Spain. At some little remove from the road and from the village itself, in the wood, Ste. Catherine, patron of captives of war, keeps her shrine. Bracken and creepers overrun its grounds and walls.

I didn't enter the shrine at once upon handing my mount over to a lay brother. Perhaps I felt a little afraid of what I might find. I went to the nearby hostelry instead, thinking to study the sort of congregation our miracle might draw, thinking, perhaps, to win them to our side.

The first week in March was usually the time of the *mouette*, the time of departure for forced pilgrimages, and it was past. It was, however, too early in the year still for the great flood of pilgrims. A group of only five huddled around the hearth that late afternoon, nursing their feet which had trudged pilgrim-naked—as naked as mine—through the deep mud of rain and thaw. Although they probably didn't realize it, they all wore the Goddess's emblems, too—strings of cockleshells about their necks. The shells were not real, not yet, on the road to Compostela rather than home again. The emblems had been carved of wood in the pilgrim's native land—Germany, by the clumsiness of their attempts to greet me.

I returned the traditional greeting as I joined them for a moment to take the donkey's cramps out of my back side. "Pray for me, brothers, at St. Jacques'."

I found in this salutation no conflict of loyalties. Compostela had been a holy place long before that lately come St. Jacques, just as this shrine at Fierbois had been. I knew the earthly feeling the pilgrim's naked feet knew; they followed the same route that had been used since time was mist.

Let these Germans once actually see the great churning, fecunding crash of sea on land. That ancient awe could not, I knew, help but convert them to a sense of something older. Even if they used the new, Christian names still, they would say them differently, after that.

I certainly had no difficulty understanding the reverence given Ste. Catherine at this way-station on the greater route. In the midst of a rather bleak and featureless plain, one miserable day's ride out of Chinon, here was the sheltering mystery of an ancient, inviolate woodland grove. There was also no question why the place should have made a deep impression on La Pucelle. Even the saint was her own Voice, Ste. Catherine. The statue of the loose-haired maiden before the wheel of her martyrdom in this shrine was almost identical to the one where the sacred ashes were kept in Maxey near La Pucelle's home. The girl herself had told me so.

The attraction was too easy to see. I wished it were not so. When she was so transparent, La Pucelle's detractors found her easy to doubt.

Discovering the hostelry so empty added to my fears: There was little chance the brothers who kept the place would have forgotten the girl-dressed-like-a-boy who'd passed here three weeks before, fresh from the marches of Lorraine. La Pucelle stood out in any crowd. How much more so when there was no crowd at all. That she had been here before, had time to scout, to lay the materials of her conjuring, perhaps—that would be all too easy for La Trémoïlle to prove.

I bade the German pilgrims such farewells as I could and rose to quit the hostelry for the shrine. At the threshold, Père Ambrose came bustling up to me with the local prior in tow. Of course, the archbishop's priest had insisted on being the one who would seek out our host and phrase the first questions in his own manner.

"Yes, Père Jean," he declared, a triumphant smile cracking the hollows of his cheeks like drying mud. "Père Eustace—" He gestured to the priest behind him who stood with hands carefully hidden within his sleeves. "Père Eustace remembers her well. Three masses a days she heard. Excessive, don't you think, brother? Even for a pilgrim?"

I had to nod and smile, though my heart was sinking. Whenever she tried to fit her piety in with the prevailing sensibilities, she only stood out that much more. She couldn't deny the ancient holiness of the place, but knew only how to worship it openly, in current forms. La Pucelle's innocence made things so difficult.

"Can the good father provide tonight for monseigneur de La Trémoïlle and his men?" That was my attempt to change the subject.

Of course, the major reason Père Ambrose and I had set off early on our stubborn donkeys in miserable weather was not to prepare miracles. We had to prepare the way for the lieutenant-general and his men-at-arms, to spare them some of our misery. The priesthood should be more Christlike than the laity, after all. But it should have been obvious, even to a fool, that with pilgrims so scarce, no great lord with his purses full would be skimped on lodging. And even if he were, La Trémoïlle would suffer hardship gladly—anything—if he could prove the maiden-soldier a fraud.

“But of course.” Père Eustace answered my question, his hands shifting about in his sleeves like some unseen creature thrashing in the undergrowth. “If you would be so kind as to follow me, brother, you may come and inspect the chamber for yourself.”

I did. And I made a great show of shifting mattresses and sniffing at the mildew patches on the walls, plain enough to the nose the moment we walked into the unaired noble suites. Still, there was the one great luxury none of the rest of us would enjoy that night: privacy, escape from the snoring, coughing, diseased, lice-ridden community of wayfarers who had forsworn all ties to this world. I could always get my own solitude, of course, as well as fresh smells and bedding, by sleeping in the open, as a Craftmaster ought to do. But where I decided to sleep depended heavily on what happened between now and the fall of dark.

Our inspection had not yet concluded when the priory bell rang three heavy times announcing the arrival of the great lord himself. His war horse had made so much better time than our clerics’ donkeys. La Trémoïlle merely grunted at his accommodation, though I was certain the rat’s nest in the straw of his mattress would give him something to roar about later on. He didn’t even care that his great bulk had brought in enough mud from the road to keep a peasant family in radishes for the year.

“Let’s see this shrine of Ste. Catherine,” he demanded. “Let’s see if heaven has indeed provided this Maid with some miraculous weapon in this place. Now.”

“But of course.” The twitch under Père Eustace’s sleeves betrayed a frantic wringing of hands. “This way, my lord.”

We all followed the man, then, out of the hostelry and across the muddy yard. La Trémoïlle’s dozen men-at-arms left their horses half-unsaddled and came along, too. The squeak of armor joints threatening to rust up in the damp accompanied our every sloshing step.

“Messieurs.” Père Eustace bowed over his nervous hands and stood aside to let us enter.

"Give us some light here," La Trémoïlle ordered.

Père Eustace, Père Ambrose and I scurried around lighting candles. I did it the mundane way, of course, snatching up the closest still-flickering taper left by some pilgrim instead of my finger. But even when only heaven and the low-burning pilgrims' devotions had been present, there had been enough light to make the state of the chapel plain.

My heart sank to my bare feet.

"Pah!" La Trémoïlle exploded. "This is that tart's idea of a miracle? I can do better myself."

I was tempted to agree. For every candle I kindled, a hundred other flames leapt into being. The walls of Ste. Catherine de Fierbois—both bays of the chancel, and the nave, separated by the narrow transept—were covered clear up to the lean moldings with swords in every design imaginable. There were plenty of other sorts of arms with them: bucklers, shields, helmets, breastplates, axes, maces ... hundreds of years' and thousands of battles' worth, under that dust and rust. Any man whose prayers the saint had heard in the midst of battle or in captivity had left a token of his safe delivery from the valley of the shadow of death in this place. I recognized it at once as an extension into Christianity of the ancient pagan practice of hanging up the spoils of war to the Gods.

The thought of such waste of human youth weighted my heart. But I could readily imagine what La Pucelle's reaction had been, hearing her three masses a day in this place. Her head must have spun with the thrill of it. Her head had spun—and I had somehow to salvage a miracle out of this.

La Trémoïlle's grumbles were growing close to bellows. "'Go to Ste.-Catherine-de-Fierbois,' she says. 'Ste. Catherine, she holds the sword for me.' The tart rejects the finest swordsmiths in the land, rejects even old La Hire's steel, and sends us here on this fool's errand. 'She has seen the sword of victory in a vision,' all these gullible fools cry. 'We must fetch the proper sword for La Pucelle, revealed by a miracle.' Miracle, my ass." La Trémoïlle's anger boomed around the sanctuary, reverberating off the accumulated weaponry.

Père Ambrose was at his lord's side now. He gestured towards Père Eustace. "This good father confirms it, my lord. He remembers the girl's presence here."

The sarcasm of La Trémoïlle's conflagration roared. "'A sword in a church,' those damned fools said, fawning on her. 'Wonderful, wonderful.' There's not a scrap of wonder in it. She was here, and she saw. It would be more wonderful if she'd suggested a trip down to the armory. We'd be less likely to stumble over a sword there."

By all my magic, I was afraid I had to agree.

Twelfth Antiphon

Under Dust and Rust

Père Eustace, the prior of Fierbois, had little comprehension of the matter. All he could fathom was that his noble guest was very angry and that somehow it was the fault of his shrine. "My good lord," he said, his sleeves twisting apologetically. "I pray you will understand that gallant knights have been dedicating their arms here to Ste. Catherine for centuries. Each weapon or piece of armor represents the answer to some vow or thanks for deliverance on the battlefield."

I noticed at least one of the men-at-arms with us crossing himself with a silent vow of his own. That was something to go on, anyway. Somebody felt something for the power of the place. At least, he didn't want the accumulated centuries of valiance and divine grace to stand against him the next time he found himself in the thick of a fray.

"They say the tradition began as long ago as Charles Martel," our host continued, taking on the tones, no doubt familiar to him, of pilgrims' guide.

I could have told him it was older than that, but I held my tongue. Charles Martel, the Hammer of the Infidel, the grandsire of Charlemagne, was good enough for at least one of the men-at-arms.

"Is Charles Martel's weaponry here?" asked the fellow in stumbling awe. He was clearly looking for something to worship.

Charles Martel, I thought. Not bad, my girl. If you intend to rid the land of its present-day invaders, you could do worse than to ally yourself with one who has the same name as your gentle Dauphin. One who also worked miracles seven hundred years ago by stopping the Muslim hordes from Spain not far from here at the Battle of Poitiers. Had she known this connection, having heard the set tour of the place as we were now doing? Or had she merely sensed it? I hoped the latter, but there was no way I could prove it to present company.

"So, pick a sword for your doxy, priest." La Trémoïlle threw all his anger at me now, in particular. "Any sword. A common sword for a common whore. Then let's get out of this insufferable place."

The lieutenant-general turned his great bulk at the door. I tried to sympathize with the discomfort of the ride he'd endured. He was wet and caked with mud. He was probably hungrier than I, there being twice as much of him to get hungry.

"My lord," I attempted against such impatient discomfort. "You forget just what La Pucelle said." When I did not find my head immediately snapped off, I continued, "She said we were to dig behind the altar, about three spans down. And she said we would know it by the five crosses on the blade."

"There is no such sword here," Père Eustace assured us, beginning to sense which way the wind blew between us. "I've been prior here for twenty years and I've never seen or heard of such a thing."

"Still, Père Jean is right," said the soldier who'd crossed himself, the same who'd asked after Charles Martel. My best ally, I thought. "I myself heard her," he went on. "'The best is to be found behind the altar of Ste. Catherine, whom I love.'"

"No doubt the little witch planted it here herself on her visit last month." La Trémoïlle grinned at his own brilliance.

Where would she come by such a thing? I wanted to demand. A poor girl from Lorraine in borrowed armor?

I had no need to. Thinking only that he helped the cause of his noble guest, Père Eustace said, "I assure you, my lord, there's been no digging around behind my altar."

La Trémoïlle was pleased, as pleased as he could be under physical discomfort. If there'd been no digging, I would find nothing. He grinned some more, humorlessly, like a man devising tortures for his enemies.

"Go ahead, priest," he said, fixing the nasty, small piggishness of his eyes on me. "Dig for your sword."

"But my altar—" Père Eustace protested weakly.

"Dig yourself to hell if you've a mind to. Anybody with any sense will join me for supper."

And La Trémoïlle rolled his bulk out of the shrine followed by a lot of creaking armor and swishing black robes.

With a heavy sigh, I began to walk slowly back to the chancel. My fellow priests and I had come nowhere near this point in our scurry to light the place, and what we had lit seemed to have blown out of its own accord at the great lord's departure. The likes of me were not worth illuminating. I felt chilled to the bone, very dark and deserted. Was this, indeed, a fool's errand La Pucelle had sent me on? She could have sent me alone, at least, and spared me public humiliation. Before the lieutenant-general, no less, who was already only too reticent to give up even a tiny corner of his command.

I kindled the stump of a taper for my solitary use, by magic and a smell of sulphur at the tip of my finger. I stepped up on the dais as priests had done every day, all the centuries of this shrine's existence. Doves and crosses decorated the front of the altar. I went further, stepping to the narrow space behind.

I could always fetch the best-looking sword down from the wall, I thought, and pretend, by the same sort of sleight-of-hand I used to kindle flame, that I'd found it. I went so far down this path as to turn for a moment before the snowy, gold-fringed altar cloth and consider the walls once more. I doubted I knew enough about weaponry to pick the best with confidence. I ought first to consider the place where this blade was supposed to be found, I thought. There might be some little niche convenient for a magician's props.

To my surprise, I got a tingle of the sensation I'd felt when I'd known just where to dig at St. Gilles to claim the implements of my own calling almost a decade ago. I raised my candle to a better angle. The space behind the altar was not so frequently visited as the rest of the shrine. The dust and grit lay so thick, in fact, that it crunched under my foot and left my bare prints behind.

It ought to be good for the skeptics to see that, I thought, too late. If La Pucelle were here less than a month ago, her small prints ought to have been here, too. Unless some would suggest she flew as she went about hiding the sword. But I didn't think there was much point in calling for witnesses. Not when the sensation in my feet left as quickly as it had come, and I wasn't at all convinced myself there'd be more than dust to find back there.

Like the rest of the church's floor, the rear of the altar, under the dust, was laid in flagstone. There was, however, a single square missing, dead center. That made my heart thump with hope—or dismay. I bent closer to investigate. I made a tentative scratch at the place with my nails. It might as well have been stone, for all the impression I made.

"Here, try this."

I jumped. I'd fancied myself alone. But here was the pious man-at-arms handing me—of all things—a shovel.

He chuckled at the wide-eyed stare I fixed on the incongruous object. "I suppose sappers have their victories, too," he suggested as he dusted the shovel off.

"Excellent." I found the word at last and took the tool from him. "But look," I said before I put it to use. I pointed out the dust, only just becoming cluttered with our prints, and the soil packed so hard, it could not have seen pick or shovel—perhaps since the beginning of time.

"You don't need to convince me, Father," the soldier said. "La Pucelle didn't plant any sword here. And we will find one. Engraved with five crosses, just as she said. I'll make sure no man in the army doesn't know it."

This last was addressed particularly to my own doubt, which must have shown vividly in my face. I had to steal a glance down at the man's feet, to see if he wasn't barefoot and more sensitive than I, to have come up with such perfect faith. He wore a soldier's usual riding boots.

"I am surprised the sire de La Trémoïlle brought such a man as you along on this excursion," I commented wryly as I made the first weak shave of hard grey soil off the top.

"He could hardly help himself if he wanted a full contingent to accompany him. The whole army is ready to die for La Pucelle already."

Thus encouraged, I began to dig in earnest. As soon as the soldier had taken off enough of his armor to move with ease, he came in and took over from me and my twisted hand. He dug quickly. The heap spilled around the doves and crosses on the forward side of the altar.

Then, about three spans down, we both heard the distinctive ring of metal on metal. The soldier's face lifted to me, dirt and sweat streaked, glowing with excitement in the light of my low-burning taper.

"I think you'd better go for the witnesses now," he said, grinning.

I did. La Trémoïlle came grumbling, whether more at the interruption of his supper or at the pilgrim fare that comprised that supper, it was hard to tell. The rest of the party, priests and pilgrims, came, too.

My ally stood waiting for the piggy eyes set in the florid face, waiting for all of us to stumble into the nave on one another's heels. As soon as we had all crowded around the altar—candles held high in several hands and the flame whipping eerily on every face—he crouched down and scraped away the last of the dirt. Then he stood tall in all his griminess like a priest beside the white of his altar. We stepped back. Like a priest, he elevated the sword over our heads.

The thing seemed hopelessly rusty, on the verge of returning to the soil whence it had come. But as we pressed silently closer to see, the soldier took the sleeve of his pourpoint to the rust and it sheeted off like water, revealing a perfectly clean and polished blade beneath. The workmanship was ancient, the metal perhaps not of the latest strength. And it was unusually small, one might almost say lady-sized. But there was no mistaking the five crosses etched along its runnel. By their arrangement, an equal-armed cross made of equal-armed crosses, I recognized their significance as the Craft's five elements. But I let the others interpret it as they would.

"And look. Look here," exclaimed the sword's discoverer.

Worked into the hilt in twisted coils of metal was a figure that seemed very like a hammer. It might have been the hammer of the ancient God of Thunder. Or it might have been as the imagination of those crowding around instantly interpreted.

"The Hammer! Charles Martel. It is indeed the sword of the Hammer of the Infidel. Brought forth when once again the Land needs liberating from cruel invaders."

Some of them crossed themselves. Some of them even fell to their knees. Only La Trémoïlle seemed not impressed. He was annoyed.

Père Eustace tried to placate him. "I swear, my lord. I swear the girl never brought that sword into my church. I told her it was here? No, impossible. I had no idea myself."

Everything the priest tried to swear only distressed the lieutenant-general more. The glare in his eyes as he turned back towards the door seemed very dangerous indeed. I pitied the man's supper. How he would tear into it!

Hawthorne Dawn-Pink in the Brakes

Leaving Blois, where the men and provisions had gathered, we crossed the Sologne, the flat, marshy, tree-shrouded land caught within a great, sweeping arc of the Loire. The land was wild, filled with boar and deer that had never learned to fear men.

Through such holy land, the march on Orléans was heaven come to earth.

La Pucelle rode on her new white charger. Her legs stuck out from the barrel of his belly. I imagined the toes inside her *sollerets* curling and uncurling in excitement. Charles the Hammer's sword swung at her side in a red leather sheath the good folk of Fierbois had presented to her. Her other side flaunted a sporty little battle-ax, to which she had taken a child's liking the moment she had it in her hand. "Ah, what hearty blows this can give!" she had declared, as if at something as good for life as a peasant's oatmeal. Of course, the ax's owner had given it to her on the spot.

They'd give her anything, these men, these suddenly holy, newly shriven men. Their lives—oh, those were the most ready of the gifts they wanted to give, if she'd but point them in the right direction, today rather than tomorrow.

The spring sun glinted off her silver-white armor so brilliantly, she was difficult to look at, like some divine creature taken from the very heart of a fire.

More conjuring than anything was the banner, the white silk and golden threads Hamish the Scot had imbued with the power to throw sparks whenever it fluttered. The sparks spewed off onto hillside and dale wherever she rode. The sparks turned to silken petals on the orchards in bloom, golden light on the leaves and shoots, an aching green in all their youthful vigor.

So it was not just in the divine creature, the centuries of prophecy made flesh among us, that I saw heaven. It sprang everywhere I looked, brought the prickle of tears to my eyes. We rode through clouds come to earth, hawthorn touched with dawn-pink in the brakes, apple and pear trees, the plowman's promise of a perfect day overhead. Bluebells were the sky itself at our feet. We felt blown along effortlessly by fragrant breezes, the taste of a future turned to good ran rich in our mouths. I felt heaven everywhere with my heart thrust into my throat.

Before they were given the chance to die for her, the soldiers brought great armfuls of the bloom she inspired to La Pucelle. She could not have taken every gift of this sort; the charger, accustomed as he was to carrying an armored man three times her size, would have been swamped. She took only enough to crown the stiff little spikes of her hair like the Queen of the May, and tied a great bunch, thick with vervain and hawthorn, to the top of her banner.

The men took the rest to themselves, stuck posies in their hats and in the place of plumes in their helmets. Whole branches showed, snug against the swords in their sheaths. Sprigs sat jauntily in the hardware of horses' bridles, wound within the large-beaded rosaries they carried at their saddles.

A great number of cattle, sheep and goats trailed between the forward and rearguard, and carts of provisions for the people of Orléans. No steer was without a posy between his horns, no cart without tendrils woven in its tailgate. Not only was heaven come to earth, but the heavenly woods and meadows had sprouted legs and marched.

And marched. And danced.

Such was my emotion and hope that I saw, but tended to ignore, how the men, when they cut their bloom, had to cut carefully to avoid the tents of hundreds and hundreds of caterpillars. The last time I'd seen the feeding of such a multitude of little mouths had been in the presence of England's king Henry, six, seven years before. The sight then had been part of what convinced me that the Plantagenet could neither rule nor enrich this land of France with his blood. Shortly thereafter, the Gods had led him to drink of the pond I'd poisoned, and so it had been.

That late April morning, I tended not to see the webbed destruction. Or if I did, it was to think only of the way Earth cycles herself, even in the quantity of Her gnawing worms. Perhaps that was a certain blindness in me, blinded, like everyone else, by the Maid in silver armor, the Maid who had slept that night on the ground like her followers, in that armor.

The Scots pumped their pipes for sheer joy, Gilles' Bretons skirled theirs in harmony. The French drums and fifes took up the tunes of the fairy rounds. Everyone sang *Veni Creator Spiritus*, welcoming the Creator Spirit, the pulsing in all green things. More would have sensed the true, pre-Christian meaning of the hymn if it had been in their native tongues.

And then the ancient songs of Maying found the *Te Deum* their counterpoint:

Follow me, love, to the greenwood,

in perfect harmony with:

You, to save the world's impending doom,
Did not abhor the lowly Virgin's womb.

In the person of Jehannette of Domrémy, there was no conflict between either words or theology. All stood at once in our present Virgin-May Day whore.

"Ah, Père Jean," she commented to me as we rode. "Just think of those poor folk of Orléans, besieged these seven months, trapped in the dark, narrow streets of their town without a breath of this beautiful, living world, no sprig of green between the grey stones." Tears flashed like sword blades in her eyes. "Ah, I cannot bear the thought of it."

She turned smartly in her saddle then, swung the banner

with its spray of blossoms at the top and shouted, "Come, men, forward. We bring May to Orléans."

The men loved that. As quickly as her words could be passed from one to the next, they sent the call back to her in waves, "*To Orléans! May to Orléans! Noël, La Pucelle.*"

I saw some of the commanders roll their eyes at this, looking elsewhere for a heaven that in fact stood before them. La Trémoïlle and his seconds smirked in thin-lipped superiority. I could read their thoughts. "Poor fools," they said. "May Day's upon us. The day after tomorrow, no later. No use telling these fools we've weeks of death and misery, months, perhaps, before any of them will go hanging nosegays on any doxy's door within those walls. Those walls have a solid ring of *goddams* to pass through first."

La Pucelle must have read their thoughts as well as I, but she soundly ignored them. I did, too. These were men whose very souls were besieged, trapped away from any contact with the cycle of life, all the things that gave hope and joy, the gifts of our most loving Mother. The siege of Orléans would be nothing to raise compared to the liberation of their hearts.

I had more personal joys to spur me along at La Pucelle's side, to keep La Trémoïlle's skepticism at the edge of my thoughts. The witches had heard my call. Gilles de Rais rode at La Pucelle's right hand, her bodyguard; Roger de Bricqueville led his Bretons among the great lords of the land rallied in their ranks.

Père Michel, my old tutor, must have known before the pigeon ever reached him that the time had come, to arrive all the way from Lorraine on his failing legs. I'd procured a mule for him and he rode a little behind me now, among the priests of the cavalcade.

Madame and Bibu de Sillé rode their palfreys among the baggage wagons. Her maid La Meffraye, like some black carrion bird, flitted here and there, out of sight and then back again, through the woods beside the army's track.

So the rest took their places. I'd see them at the edge of the crowd, in firelight or rising out of the morning mist. Hamish, relishing a chance to speak his native tongue with the Scots as they marched, blind Gwencalon adding the trills of his harp to the marching songs.

We'd acknowledge each other and our mission with a glance, I'd send them a nod of thanks and they'd shrug. Who would miss this, the greatest event of many generations? Who, among those with ancient wisdom?

Best of all was the arrival of my Pieronne. She and Tiphaine of the Mount had come. We'd had several days and nights together in which to celebrate the spring, the young God and Goddess together in it.

We were able to have a convocation of twelve the night before the army marched from where it had gathered at Blois, lacking only Charles the Dauphin. We'd stood in the circle together under the new moon. The cone of power had raised itself and, without any effort on our part, gone out into the whole world. Surely there's never been a Master with such power to wield as I, not for centuries, I thought, not with pride but with awe. Surely a great part of our power came just from La Pucelle, and certainly I must hand it to her to wield. But she had chosen me as her confessor, her Master. I felt fine indeed.

And, of course, there was Pieronne. I kept glancing back among the faceless throng of camp followers as I rode, imagining her crowned with flowers in honor of the ancient Gods. I was just rehearsing our last time together, fancying the next—the beauties of the copulating countryside induced any mind in that direction. And this was perhaps a failing, for in my joy, and my desire to please one woman, I had neglected to pay enough heed to the wishes of another. And that is something a priest should never do.

A voice at the head of the line called out, "There!"

"What's there?" La Pucelle called forward.

"Orléans, Lady."

So it was. We stood on a rise called, biblically, Olivet, where the closeness of forest and undergrowth parted to either side like curtains. Along the far side of the muddy river, broad and rushy, slabbed with flat grassy islands that bisected our view, ran a formidable stone wall. It was over thirty ells tall and a man's height in thickness, grappled by twenty-four massive towers. Wall, towers, roofs and spires stacked against the northern sky. Two or three other heaps of stone squatted on the near side and, around them, the lines of English entrenchments.

"No!" La Pucelle pulled her horse up so sharply he snorted with the bother. "It cannot be. It's the wrong side of the river."

Her anger silenced the entire army. I cursed myself. I'd been so busy congratulating myself on the success I'd achieved so far, I hadn't been looking for possible stumbling blocks to Craft from the outside world. I'd known we were on the south side of the river, of course, the safe side, opposite the beleaguered city. But in my ardor for one woman, I had forgotten to love the other. For the moment, La Pucelle's desire had to take precedence over any other. La Pucelle's first love was danger. As long as she was with us, I had to make it mine. The comfort of Pieronne would have to wait.

Behind me, La Trémoïlle cleared his throat and chinked the trappings of his horse as he urged the beast up closer. A glance at Gilles showed me his hand on his hilt. He had known which side the city would appear on, too. He had not been dreaming of May rites in the meadow. Or perhaps he had—with La Pucelle. And he had gone along with the betrayal knowingly, knowing this was the best way to keep her safe.

Gilles also knew only too well what to expect from his cousin. Would he use that sword against La Trémoïlle? I wondered. Or against himself, now that his deception was revealed?

La Trémoïlle had removed his heavily plumed hat—a velvet concoction, not a *bascinet.* He'd never expected war, not today. He didn't want this confrontation to be too obvious. The bare head and the clutch of plumes at his saddle's ornate, blocky bow gave the air of submission to his approach. But every ear was pricked, even those of the dumb animals, with mistrust.

"Lady, this is the safest way," La Trémoïlle said.

"I—La Pucelle wants the safest way? I told you. My Council said we must travel on the Orléans side of the river."

"The north bank is crawling with *goddams.* Five of their manned bastilles are there. We would have had to fight for weeks before we'd gained such a view of the city as we have here from the safer side."

"You want me just to view the city? I told you, we're to liberate it. My Voices said the north bank. You befuddled me back there where the river passed through many channels. Three channels and you told me we were across."

La Trémoïlle's only answer for several beats was a grin in his hog-thick face. His cronies understood what it meant: Well, if they can't tell you when all the channels of the Loire are crossed, your Voices aren't worth much, are they?

Then he became aware of the restive nature in the slow revival of the men around him. The smile vanished.

La Pucelle's dismay lasted shorter than La Trémoïlle's triumph. It was as if she sniffed the air—and smelled English blood.

"Look," she cried with joy. "There are *goddams* on this side, too." She pointed out the red and blue, rampant lions and fleurs-de-lis, that fluttered from the heaps of grey stone, a pair of fortresses stacked one behind the other, near the water's edge.

She kicked her heels to her horse's side and opened her mouth to cry, "At them, men!"

And she would have been at the feet of the first fortress, by herself if need be, had it not been for Gilles' quick, firm hand on her bridle.

"Lady," he said quietly. "That is the convent of the Augustinians, which the English have captured and fortified."

"Then we take it back."

"But beyond it, see—the twin towers of Les Tourelles. The *goddams* hold that as well, guarding this end of the only bridge across the river and into the town. And seven months of bombardment have left only naked arches standing in the river, with no spanning bridge between."

"Yes, I see very well. If we're to enter Orléans from this side—the side where certain fools have brought us—we must take the convent first, then the fortress. We must take them. Now."

And she shifted again in preparation for a charge.

"Lady, the English have all but encircled Orléans and those are their strongest holdings. A prudent campaign would begin with the weaker forts." There was such love in my milk brother's voice. Such desire to give her anything she wanted, that he almost choked on these words of denial. "Fortresses like those, Lady. They'll be months of siege in the taking. Months for each of them."

"Even you, sire de Rais. Even you have no faith in me."

And she turned from him, like a door shutting. Behind her dark eyes I could see the glint of thoughts, plans about what best to do next, thoughts that did not include the lord of Rais.

Gilles looked as if his heart would break. He crammed his blade back into its sheath with a fierce clatter.

At that moment, a contingent of twenty or so men rode up, bearing the gold and red trappings of the besieged city.

It was obvious which man was the commander. His guard rode respectfully behind, the entire force still damp from having sat out a rain squall in the open under his orders, waiting for La Pucelle's arrival.

The commander did not dismount for this meeting, favoring a left foot still wrapped in bandages rather than a riding boot. It was common knowledge that the late duke's base-born son had been wounded, pierced through the foot by an English arrow, while valiantly trying to win the Battle of the Herrings. By rights he should have won that day, coming at the English with several times their number and fighting as he had. But in the illogic of most French forays—before the arrival of La Pucelle—they had lost ignominiously. And the wound was slow to heal.

I had no doubt of the commander's identity. I even sensed the royal blood in his veins, like warmth in coals that appear to have gone out.

Nonetheless, those who overheard the meeting and La Pucelle's immediate recognition of their leader, without formal introduction, took it as something of a miracle. They passed the tale on to those in the ranks behind them.

"You are the Bastard of Orléans?" she said.

"I am, Lady." It was no miracle that he should have picked her out, the only woman in four thousand men.

"I have the name of Jehanne la Pucelle."

"I am at your service."

When he removed his *bascinet,* the stocky, powerfully built young man revealed a square face, round, slightly bulging eyes arched by dark brows and a small mouth. Helmet lines still crimped the square-cut but curly brown hair. He seemed a man chiseled from stone, rather than grown from flesh, but the effect was handsome enough for one still in his twenties. With his half brother still captive in England, this defense, illegitimate though it was, was all the city had of its own.

And La Pucelle gave nobody time to consider outward appearances. "Are you the one who counseled that we should come on this side of the river?"

"Well—"

"Why not go straight to where Talbot and the English are?"

"I, and others wiser than I, believing it safer and surer ... "

"In God's Name! My Lord's counsel is surer and wiser than yours. You thought to deceive me; it is yourself you deceive. For I bring you better succor than ever came to captain or town."

A grin quivering with amazement stretched the Bastard's thin mouth. "Your reputation goes before you, Lady, and I see it wasn't exaggerated. We're very glad to have you, here at Orléans."

"But I'm not at Orléans yet, as you see. I'm betrayed by those I most trusted."

"I never betrayed you ... " Gilles struggled to justify himself, to get a word in edgewise. But La Pucelle and the Bastard shifted their horses together, effectively sidling him out.

"As you see, we have plenty of provisions for your hungry people," she told the Bastard. "But how to come across?"

"There is a way. We've been using it these seven months. Look across the river and further to the right."

"Barges!" she exclaimed.

"Yes. You see, careful and successful as the English have been, they still do not have the manpower to surround us completely. Especially not since Burgundy has withdrawn his men, fifteen hundred of them, in the last month. A little tiff with

Talbot. So far, we've managed to keep the *goddams* from running a chain across the river, to prohibit our use of the barges."

"The barges must come to this side," La Pucelle declared.

"Of course. Upstream somewhat so we can load out of range of the longbows in Les Tourelles. And set up careful guard around the work to stop any foray, naturally."

"Naturally."

"Assuming such precautions, it's quite an easy matter to get supplies into town."

"Let's do it then. Let's waste no more time."

"The problem is, Lady, that to come across, the barges must sail upstream, against the current, and are therefore dependant on their sails."

"Then let it be done," she said again.

"That's just the problem. It can't be done as long as this easterly wind is blowing, as it has been doing these four or five days and no sign of letting up. No mortal could go upstream against such a blow. Lady, I'm afraid any further action, for all these good men and supplies, must wait on the will of God."

"Bastard, God has arrived."

Before the man could furrow his brow and wonder if he'd heard her aright, La Pucelle turned her horse and eased it past Gilles. Gilles tried to say something, but she ignored him and came up to me.

"Jean," she said. "Père Jean."

I rode up and met her eye. It told me what I had to do.

Fourteenth Antiphon

Sludge and Decay Giving Way to Sweetness and Bloom

Any magician, with his staff and a pool of standing water, can reverse a wind's direction. And there were nine of us.

We circled the little sedge-lined pond in a hollow below where the heads of the army still stood in debate. Their pennants and banners stood at stiff attention towards the west. Banks of willows in young leaf, also tossing to those airy orders, shielded us from their gaze.

With nine of us present, my greatest fear was that the magic would prove too strong, that when the little cloud of power rose off the surface of the water, we should have a gale on our hands rather than a shift of wind. Had a single novice attempted the task, it might well have been so.

But we nine, all so different, yet all working together, were able to tune the magic to a razor's keenness. Just so might Gwencalon, our bard, tune the multiple strings of his harp until, when struck, they all played in beautiful harmony.

Nine staffs struck the pond. The fog, barely visible and with a blue-green cast to it, rose like a single chord. It drifted gently towards the hill where the leaders stood. The pennants sagged under its weight. They stiffened west, then sagged again. The fog continued to rise past such playthings, spreading into the cloud-rippled sky, fusing with the white between the blue. When next the pennants stiffened, it was decidedly to the east. Even the scent was different, the vague smell of sludge and decay giving way to sweetness and bloom.

Down in the hollow, we heard the sharp intake of breath, like the very wind itself, of the men on the hill and indeed, of the whole army behind them. When their breath came out again, it came in a great, triumphant shout. On the next gust of wind, the chords of *Te Deum* rose and came straight down on us from the west.

Beneath the banners, I saw La Pucelle get up from her knees. She'd taken such a posture so that many believed her prayers alone worked the magic. But she herself gave us a wave down in the hollow before she went off with the Bastard, Gilles dogging her heels, to greet the barges the winds now permitted to cross.

I lingered with my coven, congratulating them, discussing our next move. "A priest and oddly assorted camp followers will be among the last to be allowed to use wind and current to make the crossing," I assured them. "There's no rush."

This was not their major concern. "Where is Charles?" they asked, one after the other. "Where's the Dauphin? We kept looking for him on the march. I know they say his poverty makes him dress commonly, but the blood. We would have sensed the blood royal."

"Charles is back in Blois," I admitted.

"But he's coming? Soon? To make our thirteenth? To bring the blood?"

I felt myself hot with shame. Eight pairs of eyes, most of them older and wiser than I, even blind Gwencalon, waited for my answer.

"He is too afraid to march into enemy territory," I explained, but could not meet those eyes.

"Even with his army?" Père Michel asked.

"Even with La Pucelle, more to the point," Anne de Sillé muttered.

The noblewoman, unlike the others, did nothing to hide her scorn. I was the priest of this coven, the first coven to meet on French soil in more than a hundred years, and I couldn't bring all the elements together. I was too young, her scorn told me. Or too common. Or too unlearned in the Craft. Or all at once and more.

"We have La Pucelle—after a thousand years of prophecy—and no Dauphin? Will we get a thirteenth? Some one else? Don't we need the blood royal?" they continued to press.

To all of this I had only the beginning of an answer. "I thought we could do without him, just at first, just for a while. Give him time to see what La Pucelle can do, and that will give him courage. Until then, the Land will provide. Goddess will not let us fail, not now that She's sent us La Pucelle."

This beginning had satisfied, when I had the sight of the gathering magicians to exult me. Now, however, with their input, I, too, began to doubt myself.

I even lashed out at Père Michel, my old, dear tutor. "So why don't you take on the responsibility then?"

His gentle eyes understood that the anger in my voice was at myself for not doing perfectly what no one in living memory had to do before. That made me angrier.

"Or you, madame. Why don't you lead us? You have wealth, nobility and age to get this reticent prince to move better than I was able before the horses were all saddled up and we headed out of Blois."

Madame said nothing, just turned the ripples of her loosened grey hair to me in a gesture that said clearly, "Well, I just might. If you force me to it. If there's no prince, I just might have to take charge."

The sun was hastening towards the west before we made our way up from the pond, then down to the shore where a single barge, half loaded, lay waiting. Where the sun whitened the sky, I noticed a falcon, a merlin, hanging as if pinned to linen sheeting. If our playing with his air currents had confused him, he gave no sign. But perhaps the change had drawn his attention.

La Pucelle and the Bastard were long gone, in the first vessel. The beasts were gone, too, leaving only their smell and their droppings on the muddy shore. The carts' ruts vanished where boat ramps had taken up their store.

More remarkable still was the disappearance of most of the four thousand men and their gear. Aside from the bargemen, growing more impatient by the minute, only one last small corps of men stood about in apparent indecision. The shifting of the four thousand had happened faster than even I had magic for. And quieter, for we'd heard nothing over our low talk down beside the pond.

Lord of the Forest, I thought, bless that Pucelle of Yours. Never had there been such a one for getting things done.

The remaining troop were too many to all fit between the flimsy, rough-hewn slats of the railing on the waiting barge. Certainly we witches couldn't hope to join them. What were we to do, then?

Then I saw that the troop were Gilles', wearing his black and gold livery. My milk brother was the only commander present, and he was in a rare rage, such a rage as might have, in his youth, made rocks fly and tapestries bleed.

Bricqueville was there, too, attempting to calm his comrade and lover. His inability to do so in the old ways had been growing ever since La Pucelle's arrival. I could see the young man's frustration building to a deep and silent hurt. He tried, nonetheless, to keep a step behind Gilles' frantic pacing along the line of pilings that marked this primitive quay.

I hurried towards them, hoping that if I knew little about helping a coven to govern itself, I at least knew my milk brother's temper. I began by trying to give him calmness of my own, with hand signs as well as words, even as I approached.

"There's light enough for another crossing," I told him. "Let us get across, witches and all. Stay here with your men, posting good watch for the English, and we'll send the barge back for you."

I should have known better. From the time we were children, nothing annoyed my milk brother more than that somebody else should tell him his business. His flare of abuse in French sank just as suddenly again, as if under its own weight. With a weary sigh, he switched to Breton, the language of our innocence.

"There will be no more soldiers crossing over after this barge. Not tonight. Not ever."

Naturally many of the witches, coming up and gathering at a distance, could understand him: Gwencalon the bard could, Anne de Sillé and her son Bibu, Tiphaine. My dear Pieronne still understood no more than two French words together. It was his own men from Anjou and Maine, even Bricqueville, Gilles was shielding. I demanded an explanation.

"Ah, Yann. You are naive."

"Naive?" I croaked, offended. "Naive, when I've just changed the direction of the wind?"

"And had La Pucelle nothing to do with that?"

"She played her part," I confessed.

Gilles' shoulders relapsed into a less defensive stance. "Very well, you are wise in magic," he said. "But naive—terribly naive—in the ways of the world."

I said nothing, but waited until he got control of himself enough to say, "Not one of those four thousand men we marched from Blois was ever meant to be thrown at Orléans."

"They weren't?"

"I knew about this, damn it, and kept thinking something would happen to stop it."

"The army hasn't crossed the river?"

"Not a one of them. In such a short time, Yann? You do believe in magic, don't you?"

"Well, yes—"

"Just the supplies crossed—and La Pucelle, with no more than the Bastard and his men to guard her."

"I—I don't understand. Why wouldn't they cross?"

"It's too risky. We aren't strong enough yet to launch a full offensive. And the minute he hears of this resupply mission, the *goddam* commander Fastolf will march from Paris with supplies and troops of his own."

"But—" I must be naive. I couldn't get my mind around it. "All the men? All the men who marched with singing and wreaths for La Pucelle? By the Horned One, I was certain she had them ready to die for her. They aren't across the river?"

"They were meant only as guard for the provisions. Well, and maybe as diversion to get the provisions in once we got them here. Their orders were to march off the moment the last barrel was loaded. And that's just what they've done. La Trémoïlle."

He hissed the name between his teeth, and things began to become clearer to me.

"My cousin hoped to put enough distance between them and the English to get a good night's sleep when they encamp," Gilles went on. "And of course he's convinced the Dauphin cringing back there in Blois that he needs every single man-at-arms he can muster to protect his royal hide."

I looked where Gilles pointed and could just see a plume of dust rising towards us on the wind we'd called. That was indeed where the four thousand men were now, an eighth of the way back to Blois, and not across the Loire. Their haze reached up through the white southwestern sky towards the lowering sun and the falcon who still hung poised, waiting.

Fifteenth Antiphon

Drawing a Circle in Hazy Black

I stole a glance towards the twin English fortresses a league downstream from where we stood. Their bulks blackened as the shadows shifted towards evening and a trick of the light made them seem closer than ever. Watch fires flickered to life on their battlements.

Then I turned back to Gilles and his troop of twenty, no more. This was all that was left to La Pucelle to enter, defend and deliver the besieged city of Orléans.

My milk brother was explaining it to me: "... then we were to see this last barge loaded and follow after—"

"But what of La Pucelle?" I demanded, knowing even as I said it that the same thought was what haunted his dark eyes. "I thought your cousin made you her bodyguard. You've got the whole Loire between you now."

The wide, silent, slow-moving river had caught a brilliant streak of lowering sun on its expanse. Across the glare, it was impossible to tell which shadowy figures now were English and which the supplies, the Bastard—and the girl. Perhaps the one had already swallowed up the other.

"She was growing too difficult," Gilles explained desperately. "If we didn't separate her from the men, they'd never follow our orders again."

It was no use saying, "But that's the idea, Gilles. You know the prophecy. She will command. You sound like your cousin."

Gilles was a commander and, on that level at least, he had seen the logic of La Trémoïlle's argument. He was too used to giving orders of his own to refuse to follow them with an easy conscience.

He was a commander, and I a high priest. I saw a parallel in our dilemmas, and I held my peace for a moment.

"She wanted to go to Orléans. Now she's there," he said.

"Shipped over like one more cow." Or an ox to the slaughter. Even I didn't dare say that last aloud.

"'She's a cowherd,' La Trémoïlle said," Gilles told me then. "'Let's give her work she's used to.'"

I nodded. La Trémoïlle would say that. The wonder was that I hadn't read it in his mind. "So now she's the Bastard's problem, along with everything else in this besieged town."

"Oh, God," Gilles cried, clutching at my hand with a passion he couldn't fling off any other way. "Do you know what she said to me as I handed her up into the barge? Do you know what she said?"

"Tell me."

"Looking across the river, with a touch of what I thought was wistfulness, she said, 'Ah, Orléans. My Voices told me I will be wounded before your walls. Here, my first blood will be shed.' Before I could think what to do or say, the barge shoved off, and her with it. I realized too late, what I took for wistfulness was fear. The first time I've seen her afraid of anything, and I'm not there with her. She'll be wounded there. She may already be. La Trémoïlle hopes for it, of course. She may be dying, and I'm not there.

"Oh, God," Gilles cried once more, and loosed my hand so he could bury his face in his own.

His men were watching our conversation with a mix of scorn and trepidation. They didn't want to leave La Pucelle behind, either. For two full days they'd been under her spell. But if their commander didn't follow orders, why should they? I could almost hear such calculations.

This was my fault as much as his. "Now, see how deluded I've been," I told him. "I assumed she'd got her troops and I didn't stop to consult the Sight or anything."

My attempt to cheer him up only made things worse. "But

you at least were ignorant of what La Trémoïlle had afoot," he said. "I knew this was his plan, to about-face the moment the supplies were safely loaded and La Pucelle out of his hair. I knew it and—and I agreed to it."

"Or pretended to."

In truth, I was myself in something of a panic, thinking as quickly as I could. She was La Pucelle. But she was, after all, only one person. And only a maid. Her magic was to inspire, but for the fight itself ...

"I did think—I did hope *she'd* come up with something before now," my milk brother said. "To keep the troops with her."

Ah, Gilles. He had more faith in the little cowherd than I did.

"Now," he went on, "there she is. Over there. And we're here."

"What an army refuses to do, a full coven might make up for with magic," I said. "But with Charles two days' march away—Goddess, I feel as if my power hand has been crippled as well."

Despair made me lightheaded. Was I going to fall into a spell? No, by the Goddess, I couldn't. Not now.

I took a breath and gathered strength. "Send your men after La Trémoïlle." I met my milk brother's gaze full under the dark brows and spoke with sudden decision. "They won't want to spend the night any closer to the *goddams* than they have to, either. They will prefer to catch up with their comrades if they can."

It took neither the Sight of a magician nor a commander's eyes to know that the men would set on up the hill at a trot the moment they were free to do so. Their glances had been running in that direction ever since I arrived.

"But what about La Pucelle?" Gilles demanded. He could tell I had a plan now, and was ready to try anything, but first concerns first.

"At this point, your mere twenty extra men are not likely to help her much. Nor Orléans."

Gilles turned to give the word to Bricqueville to get the men going.

"But Roger must stay with us, with the coven," I told him. "Give command to your third."

Gilles wrinkled his brow at me with a question.

"It's as I've said. The soldiers that can fit into the last little space on this barge cannot help her. Not nearly as much as a full coven may. And since that is all the room the barge allows, that is what we must send."

"We're still missing one of the coven," Bricqueville said when the men were on their way and everything to this point had been explained to him. Helping to hand the rest up onto the floating boards, his count had made the number twelve obvious to him.

"Charles," Gilles muttered, and looked to me.

"I know," I said. "That's why things were crumbling in my hands now. I'm sure of it."

"We have to wait for you to go back to Blois and convince him, Yann? He won't risk his precious royal blood, not for anything. God forbid, La Pucelle could be dead before then."

I had thought, after I'd tried and failed to get the Dauphin to march with his coven and his troops, that we could do without him. We would have to. Now I saw that I had been wrong, that we could not manage short-handed.

The royal blood was important, but so important? My vision faded in and out, from fully fleshed figures to some that looked as if they were cut of paper, shadows of themselves. I thought: The power of a witch is to work on the whole with nothing more than emblems. A cauldron of water stands for the whole ocean. A single flame burns like love. The mere nail parings or hair clippings of a man could be used to work his whole destruction. It might be possible, it just might, to make a similar emblem stand in for the whole Dauphin, irresolute as that whole was.

Fight it as I might, my sight rolled upward ... Where my gaze fixed upon a falcon.

"Blois is—what?—thirty leagues away?" I asked.

Maybe I should not fight against the falling spell any more. No. Of course not. It was a gift of the power, a gift from our Lady Mother. And when She took me into Her hand, I knew I should go.

"The army was two days marching it," Gilles reminded me.

My mind reeled back over the miles through the wild Sologne.

"Even if you could get him to budge out of his timidity—" Gilles continued, "—and I don't know how you can do it without La Pucelle. She's the only thing able to stir him. Even if you can do it, that's two days to Blois, three days back at a stately royal place."

"And two full weeks of trying to lure his majesty away in between," Bricqueville added, shaking his fair head.

"No time for that," said Gilles.

"No, no time," I agreed. "I must try something else."

Both men seemed to step back from me. Maybe it was just my imagination. Or maybe they could already tell what was about to overcome me.

"Come," I told them. "Give me a hand onto the barge, then pull up the plank. You may have to carry me once we get to the other side. And convince the bargemen they've not taken evil into the vessel. That may be the hardest task."

The two men nodded.

"Gilles." My voice seemed very far away now, even to myself. "The black cherry syrup's with the cauldron."

"*D'accord*, Yann." My milk brother's firm hand had clasped my withered one as we crossed the ramp. I could feel no planking. It was like walking on air.

"Madame Anne is skilled in such things," I offered, and gestured my bundle towards the grey-haired lady. She looked at me with concern from her seat next to her son for whom a barge trip was a cause of squirming delight.

But she nodded reassurance. "Tiphaine also has her skills." Ah, good. The two old witches had already been sharing secrets, though the one had no speech and the other maintained her aloof, noble air.

The bargemen were a little uneasy with the motley crew we offered them. "Orléans is hungry enough without taking on extra, useless mouths," they complained, looking at my state with sidelong glances under their fish-smelling caps.

I saw Bricqueville kindling his charm towards them like candles are kindled when the circle is drawn. If that didn't work, there were the wallets of coin at his side.

Gilles settled me on the barge's bench, and I sighed with relief, closing my eyes and dropping my head back. The rest of the passengers, even the witches, made a ring of respect around me. It was hard to tell whether the motion I felt was the tug of current and the gentle wavelets before my feet. Or the spell.

A magic circle cannot be drawn on water. That's why, in part, it's said a witch cannot cross water.

We'd have to wait until we reached the far shore—and more privacy—before that happened. But for the moment, my mind was drawing its own circle in hazy black.

Flying Straight into the Slanting Sun

In blackness, my mind clung to one word. A name. Charles. In Blois. He must come here. I must bring him. Halfway over the smooth, grey Loire, I opened my eyes. I blinked towards the sun as it sank to a keener angle. Across the blinding brilliance, a shadow cut like the blade of a knife, dropping.

The merlin falcon.

This bird was not escaped from some mews, not he. This was my namesake.

Or I was his.

His brown wings arced, taut with the force of his slowing flight, slowing enough to snatch at the barge's railing beside my left, my power hand. With great dignity, once he'd landed, he mantled his wings over his back, fluffed the feathers of his reddish breast a little, and regarded me with one cold, hard black eye.

I began with that eye, trying to give my own the same opaque, obsidian quality. The transformation came quickly, tiny feathers circling my sight. A rush, as of a great wind, filled my ears.

No matter how many times one has entered the animal kingdom, the irruption never fails to awe, to overwhelm. My vision slammed into a sudden, almost terrifying clarity. What had seemed merely a blur of low rushes and growing weeds upon the far bank was now alive with nesting ducks, a dozing family of weasels, a wading heron.

I breathed the air in that direction with interest, through nostrils set in stiff membrane rather than my normal soft flesh. I opened my mouth and hissed.

Quickly now, I sent my soul in to fill the rest of the offered body, for the falcon knew his world as well as ours was threatened without La Pucelle, without the full coven. I occupied the great, empty orbits of the skull, pushed my way into the hollow bones, lighter than air, where there was always plenty of space. I felt the muffle of feathers overlapping all my flesh.

"Hey, be off now," the bargemen cried, and made threatening gestures in my direction. Calmly as they'd accepted a boatload of motley folk—witches to any one with half a sense—this bird on their craft was an omen with which they could not sit easily.

The moment I felt my feet in horny talons, I spread my wings and let loose the rail. Smooth, grey water shot below me, but by the time I reached the nesting ducks on the Orléans shore, I'd caught a warm updraft and was soaring high. This was not the way to Blois, my human mind told me. But some will—perhaps a vestige of the falcon's—overcame my urgency for the moment.

Some little way upstream from the ducks, I saw the place where the barges, laden with supplies, had landed. A falcon couldn't know, but I guessed it was the closest French stronghold to Orléans, Chécy. Men and animals were still at the quay, busy shifting the supplies.

I studied the land with the magical combination, a falcon's vantage point but a man's values. The distance from Chécy to the walls of the besieged city I judged to be about two leagues.

On this eastern side, unlike north, south or west, the red-split-with-blue of the English flags floated above only a single, small fortress. My keen black eyes caught the glint of men-at-arms standing on the walls of that fortress. They watched the activity at Chécy with interest, perhaps a little unease, but didn't seem inclined to leave the safety of their walls to do anything about it. They tended more to look northward, towards the Paris road. The English would wait, probably even let the supplies pass from Chécy into Orléans. Fastolf's reinforcements from the capital, of which Gilles had spoken, must be large and imminent. Nonetheless, even a falcon's eye picked out no plume of dust to parallel that still seen on the other shore of the French retreating under La Trémoïlle.

Other things I saw Orléans-ward boosted my confidence in the city's defending captain, the absent duke's bastard son. It must have been he who was responsible for pulling down all the suburbs before the English dug in their heels. Any hut or outbuilding the enemy might have used for cover, either for foray or for mining activity, was less than a pile of rubble.

Still, it was probably the English who had destroyed the flour mills on the river, intensifying the siege hunger for those within the walls.

The Orléannais on their parapet were in good order. I even saw the sky glint pale blue off dishes of water they had set here and there along the perimeter. If the English should begin to burrow in an attempt to sap the foundations of the walls, the defenders would know about it almost at once by the vibrations on the water's surface. A quick sortie or two would end the threat.

Orléans, then, looked snug enough—for the time being. It was crowded, all the folk from the flattened suburbs and no doubt beyond, crammed for safety within her walls. With La Pucelle's delivery of food, their hunger would be eased, for a while, at any rate. And the English clung too fearfully to their own walls to be much threat. Their numbers from the sky weren't as great as they appeared from the ground. That made them cautious.

Yes, the greatest lack these Orléannais must feel was, as the girl had said, the lack of spring's bloom within their walls as May Day approached.

The lack of magic. The lack of hope.

And therein lay my task. My task and La Pucelle's.

From down in the English fortress, I heard one man—Norman, by his accented French—say to his mate, "Here, Robinet, I lay you two to one you can't bring down that falcon."

My human mind, which heard and understood, told my wings to flap for speed. I did, just in time to hear the arrow whistle by me without harm.

The tiny, grape-sized heart within my feathered breast, which beat faster than a man's heart even when in an easy soar, took several minutes to calm again. Someone had lost his bet, but I couldn't pause while he upped the ante and wagered again.

Then I recalled that in all my seeing, I'd seen no sign of La Pucelle.

I tilted the front edge of my wings up until I caught another current that swung me around toward the east again, careful to remain out of arrowshot of the English fortress. Here, no further in from the river bank than it would take a quarter hour to ride, I discovered another fortress among the trees. Little more than a tower and its keep, I realized this must be Reuilly. The Bastard meant to keep La Pucelle safe here, there not being enough time now before sunset to make a dash for Orléans itself.

I didn't see the girl, although maybe her horse, one among many in the crowded yard. But a white, swallow-tailed banner floated from the parapet next to the Bastard's own yellow and red. I felt Hamish's magic thick within its seams, so I didn't bother to swing down any closer.

Something did attract my attention, however, yonder in the woods that blackened the northern horizon as far as even a falcon could see.

In the forest's heart, a great, straight oak, taller yet thinner than most, had been felled and its limbs lopped off. A team of oxen was pulling it even now out of the woods and along the dirt track towards the tower of Reuilly.

The English? Had they claimed a battering ram for their attack? Was La Pucelle in immediate danger?

No. The feeling from the wood was all wrong for that.

Yes, I could sense it. Mistletoe had hung in the boughs of that oak. The woodsman had saved those precious tokens of the God's favor. He had picked the tree by just such signs.

I was certain it must be so, for even from my height, this seemed an action of great magic. I could feel the gap of power where the tree had stood, the thrust of it shifting, dragging behind the stolid beasts.

This was no battering ram, then, but a Maypole.

And, of course, such power would be heading towards Reuilly. It was like water flowing downhill. Thus comforted that the Earth, as usual, took Her balance when people did not try to interfere, I could leave Reuilly. Reuilly, blessed for this night with the presence of La Pucelle, where the rest of my coven, even now landing at Chécy, would undoubtedly also find refuge.

All of my coven but Charles the Dauphin. And that thought made me dip my wings to swing round again. I flapped to find some level where the air was stiller between the stiff westerly streams I myself had called up. Then I set off, flying straight into the slanting evening sun.

Seventeenth Antiphon

Ponds of the Sologne Strung Like Beads

I followed the Loire for a way. The setting sun poured the riverbed with liquid gold. I banked slightly. The ground slipping beneath me now was the great, wild, tree-choked lowland of the Sologne.

I soon overtook La Trémoïlle's four thousand, making camp for the night. I found the chamberlain's great round tent by the blue eagles chevroned with red on his pennants. I dropped on the ridge pole, just for a sign: "Power is here, moving in your midst. Look up and see." But nobody in that company read signs.

Somebody did keep hawks, and had taken them out in search of supper. Birds raised in the mews are often as insensitive to the way of the Earth as their masters. A pair of them came at me, giving me the long *keer*, the threat cry, warning me off their stake. I pushed down, up, down, up, feeling the strain across my chest as I let them know they were free to hunt as they would. Other business compelled me.

Charles. I caught a tail wind and flew on.

Innumerable little ponds and patches of wetland broke up the forest that was the Sologne. They were the color of spilled sapphires at first, reflecting the sky. They turned to beads of amber, then coral, then rubies. Finally they faded to turquoise, and I felt myself fading as the world did.

But I couldn't. I couldn't stop to rest, not now, not when this most important member of my coven still cowered in Blois.

I decided to hunt and eat, hoping that might revive me. I spied a rat on his night's first foray into a small meadow. I gave the human prayer for forgiveness before the taking of life. I'm not sure true falcons do that. Before I'd remembered half the words, the hunter had overcome niceties, and I dropped on him like cannon shot.

He was still wriggling and squealing when I'd parted the pale belly fur and reached the heart, but the noise stopped after that. I hooded my kill with my wings, masking him from competing predators. I fed, tearing chunks of still-warm flesh away from bone and bolting them down in coughing gulps.

When I was done, I flew up off the ground to the highest branch in the neighborhood. This was a chestnut with its bloom, scenting the air and still luminescent, like so many glowing tapers in the evening light. A pond, not far away but the only one I could see, was now the color of lapis lazuli and darkening by the moment.

I preened as long as I dared. When even that failed to lift the heavy lethargy from me, I spread my wings, borrowed a little spring from the branch, and took to the air anyway.

I flew low, just missing tree tops and hardly further than across the lapis lazuli pond. Then I simply had to rest again.

How far had I come? Surely not half the distance to Blois, I told myself as I took oil from the gland at the base of my tail to spread between each feather on this shoulder and the other, with my beak. My wearied muscles rebelled at even so little exercise.

I was so tired, I began to lose the grip I had on the bird's body, not to mention on the branch. A vision flashed before my eyes of Gilles and Bricqueville pushing and pulling my inert human body onto horseback for the climb up from the landing site to the fortress of Reuilly. In a moment, I could lose this reality altogether and return to the other, that of a small, crippled man with the falling sickness.

A sudden cry of "Who?" brought me to the darkening wood again. Smugglers signal to one another with the call of the owl. And witches, people of the night.

But this wasn't people.

Squinting my falcon's eyes into the next tree, I could barely make out the figure of another bird from the clumps of leaves that surrounded it. There is an innate hostility between the owl and the falcon. I hissed a threat.

Then my man's mind thought, An owl. Of course.

A falcon, even a merlin, is a bird of the day. His predatory place is taken at night by the owl. No wonder I was so exhausted. I, too, must make the switch.

All the better that this was the large, strong owl called in the French tongue "the grand duke" of birds.

I shifted my talons on the branch and concentrated all my attention towards the owl. I felt my eyes widen and swing full front until they were like the hard rounds of window glass. The light, which suddenly hit the inside of my skull from what was in fact a very dark world, was astounding. So, too, were the sounds that suddenly flooded the dark forest floor below. The flat feathers that now saucered my face caught the sounds and funneled them back to my keen, tufted ears.

This was a bigger body, too, round, less sleek, heavy. But the transfer from bird to bird was less of a shock than from man to bird. I felt a little sick to my stomach at first. Then I coughed up a ball of the owl's last meal, the bones and fur he could swallow but not digest. After that I felt fine.

And when I spread the new, grey wings, although I flew lower, it was with powerful, refreshed strength towards the last light rimming the horizon.

My great eyes picked up silver from the Sologne's ponds now, reflections of starlight. In the heavens over me, the stars seemed stacked, some near, some farther. They pulsed like living things on different crystalline spheres. Below, all was black except for the human habitations, few and far between, but which copied the sky with candles and firelight before sinking behind me into the rest of the world. Nonetheless, it was alive, throbbing with scurrying, creeping night life. I sensed it with every onward beat of my wings.

Eighteenth Antiphon

A Different Night Hunting

In the old tongue, Blois signifies a wolf. I could hear a pack howling to the hunt as I flew over the last stretch of woods before I crossed the Loire and sailed above the town. The town itself rose against the night sky like some great wolf, couchant, and I beat my weary wings towards the head. This was the old château that lay, ears pricked, on the high ground of the steep bluff.

Now, where to find Charles in this dark edifice without raising any suspicions in the watch? The busyness of mice around the kitchen and hen house distracted me to those sections of the castle for a while. But once I'd hunted, gulping the surprisingly long, limp bodies whole, my owl mind relaxed and gave the man space once more.

I recalled that Charles was terrified to sleep anywhere but on the ground floor. The boarding of a second story had collapsed under him once as a boy. He had barely escaped the death that had come to others with whom he'd been speaking and joking just moments before. This remembrance, and a head cleared of the compulsion to follow little scratchings, led me to a golden light that pricked a narrow window out against the blackness of the corner tower.

The window was open to the cool night air. My owl being wanted to flee the glow, but I forced myself closer. My wings took the stress and sound out of the settling of my feather-covered feet upon the stone sill. The wings themselves were more silent than a sigh.

I had imagined the young Dauphin up late with his councilors, burning branches of candles as they sought to sort out the kingdom's innumerable problems. La Trémoïlle was on the road to Blois, but the rest, all in the chamberlain's wallet, might well have been awake. Their plots were elsewhere, however, and I had no desire to rouse them. Charles the son of Charles the son of Charles lay alone in the room.

Ah, Charles. Afraid even of his own shadow, even in his own chamber.

A single candle burned at the bedside. My owl eyes blinked at the brightness and had mistaken the one small flame for candelabra. The light glowing through the flimsy summer hangings about the bed confused my sight. The disorienting tumble of light and shadow would have frightened off any other owl.

With concentration and dependence on my human notions of things, however, I soon picked the pale, sleeping figure out from among the drapery. In this light, and in unguarded sleep, the Dauphin seemed a boy still, though I knew for a fact that he was older than Gilles de Rais. No beard strengthened the weak chin. His hair was also shaved high, to the fashionable bowl-cut which only served to exaggerate the flaring of his large ears. A daily barber certainly earned his keep.

My owl vision caught the movement: the flickering of dreams under bruised-blue eyelids. The twitch of his large, bulbous nose as if he smelled my presence even in his sleep.

Was it just being an owl, or did he always look so much like a skinned rabbit? I wanted to pounce on him and tear out his cowardly heart.

I resisted the impulse, but it set plans in my mind, plans I had not fully worked out when I'd lifted off the Loire late that afternoon. Then, my only thought had been to get to the Dauphin, that thirteenth of our number. I hadn't truly considered the other half of the journey, how I was to bring such a skinned-rabbit sort of creature back with me.

The more so, now that I had only this owl body with which to convince him.

Warning, wheedling him to ride horses with all swiftness to Orléans was out of the question. It would take too long, not to mention exposing him to dangers on the way. The English weren't my greatest fear. He couldn't hope to avoid a meeting with La Trémoïlle that would dishearten him altogether.

But the inkling of plans brought to my brain by the long night's beating of wings began to take on flesh as I stood, shifting my talons back and forth on the window sill. I flew off again, to make more preparations before I woke him.

Belladonna I found in sufficient quantities twining through a hedge just outside the city walls. Aconite was not so easy. I spent considerable time searching the muddy banks of little streams flowing into the Loire without success. Although I was certain that by day, and with human eyes, I would have had no trouble picking out enough of the glossy, tendril leaves to show me where to dig for roots, I couldn't do it as an owl. Even with my night vision as keen as it was, plants meant little to this brain because they had no movement. It was early for the stems to be springing up to their blue, monk's hood blooms as well, so those easiest of tell-tale signs were gone for me.

Instead, in the end, I resorted to the ancient Benedictine house of St. Laumer just a shallow flight of steps below the great rock of the château. Brother Herbalist kept his garden in neat, tight knots. This made it easy to find, although the only thing there of interest to an owl were the mice caught in a wicker trap, squeaking and scrambling, impossible to get at.

The shutters on the nearby infirmary window were ajar. I creaked them apart and flew in.

The first thing I discovered in the darkened room was a basketful of owlets' wings. I squawked and hissed in distress at that discovery, the human ability to see past and present jumbled with the bird's immediate sense of his own kind. Presently, the thought that, in his own way, the herbalist worked the Craft as well as I, helped me attach to his spirit in the room. This returned me to the human task at hand.

One of Brother Herbalist's recent cases must have been a bee sting or venomous bite. (Praise the Horned One, even insects are on my side, I thought.) For he had several of the long, wrinkled, dried roots of aconite laid out by the pestle on his table. I don't know how I should have managed with a stopper, let alone a dozen of them, if I'd been driven to search in a haphazard way. My bird eyes, I discovered, failed to pick letters out from painted vines on the neat rows of jars.

I took care not to carry the root in my mouth. It is very brittle when dried, and one sliver can kill a sparrow in a matter of heartbeats. Even humans have been poisoned by taking too much of the herb through a cut in the hand.

I wasn't going to be able to meld these ingredients into a proper witch's ointment tonight. I was going to have to burn them and rely on the smoke. On my great, silent wings I carried both belladonna and aconite to the not-quite-King to create in him what came naturally to me with the falling sickness.

Once inside the candle-lit tower room again, I set the herbs together in an empty pewter bowl lying on the table at the bedside. I almost blew the candle out with my wings coming and then going again, but twisting my head around on my shoulders assured me that it popped to life once more.

I saved the easiest ingredient for last. In a field of cabbages just beyond the city wall, I spied a hare nibbling on the young leaves. He must have been from one of that year's earlier litters, sent out to fend on his own when the second or third kits came along. He was still small and unwary, and feeding when the rest of his kind had returned to their burrows for the night.

I flew in low and just behind him. An instant before impact, my feet swung forward, my head hoisted above my shoulders, my wings extended fully, my eyes closed in a flinch. I plummeted like a stone, felt fur and the warmth of life beneath. Yet I fought the reflex in my ankles to close the razor talons with a killing grip, fought the instinct to close my beak on the spinal cord. I must bring him alive to the Dauphin's room.

The little creature wriggled wildly in his panic, surprising me with his strength as he twitched his backbone like a whip. Not all creatures, then, had the wisdom, the harmony with Earth, to help this night's magic along.

I clung fiercely, all the time telling myself, with every bit of humanity left to me, Don't kill him. For the love of Our Lady, don't kill him.

I had a terrible time gaining height with all that weight, that thrashing. I had to make two runs at the city wall, circling back, catching an updraft and trying again before I made it. The hare ripped himself free of one talon just as we went through the smoke of the wind-whipped watch fires burning in each crenelation. All I held in one claw for several struggling wing beats was a clump of fur.

Once past those fires, and by letting my line of flight drop dangerously close to the chimney pots and slate roofs, I gripped again. My talon felt wet warmth. I knew I drew blood, but I hoped against hope the wound was not life-threatening. All the while, the effort to flap these great grey wings strained until each beat was like a leap of flame across my chest and shoulders.

But I made it, dropped the creature safe in the tower chamber. How could anything so small to the eyes weigh so much to the talons? Then I flew myself to the back of a chair while I caught my breath and tried to decide which step to take next.

I swivelled my head and great eyes to the dark corner of the room behind me, to rest, and so the sight of easy prey would not distract me as I tried to think. That was what woke up Charles, finally, the soft little sounds as the hare shook himself of his daze and slowly, cautiously, limped about the carpet on the floor. He twitched his nose at his surroundings and tried to find a way out.

Charles sat up in bed with a rustle of sheets and an "Oh!"

I swivelled my head and, without thinking said, "Who?"

That drew his gaze from the hare to me. A big mistake.

The eyes widened on both sides of that great nose until I might have been gazing at my own owl face in a mirror. Charles even took on some of my grey tinge, though he had none of my roundness. Indeed, fear pinched the usual thin angles even more.

His lips moved and the prominent Adam's apple vibrated with the effort of some sort of gurgle. His right hand seemed hardly able to lift itself under the weight of his royal signet. He nonetheless managed to cross himself, slowly. His throat tried some other sound, failed, then came another pious cross.

I don't know which belief crossed his mind, that an owl's cry means a maid is losing her virginity, a daughter being born to a family who'd prefer a son, or a death foretold. Perhaps all three. Perhaps only that owls were the well-known familiars of sorcerers, accompanying them on their night rounds, giving their wings over to magical purposes. Why shouldn't he believe such a thing? My present condition was proof enough that it was true.

That such thoughts should render him speechless with fear was another matter, one that made me shift my feather-cuffed feet slightly along the branched back of the chair. I knew I had to start talking quickly. The moment he regained his voice, he would call for the guards. I would be shooed from the room—if I managed to escape—and the window shut against me.

And the hare? No doubt he'd be served up in a pie by dinnertime tomorrow.

The problem was that with this simple fold of flesh at the base of my windpipe, "Who?" was the only word I could say aloud.

Nineteenth Antiphon

Bubbles of Thought

The hare limped here and there on the artificial garden of the carpet. I worked my talons desperately up and down the branch that formed the back of the chair. I could tell its wood had not been taken from the forest with love, but with thought of profit and courtly honors.

Indoors, and within a forest creature's body, I seemed unable to touch the necessary power to communicate with Charles. The first time I ever saw the prince, long ago on the wren hunt, I saw him crowned with antlers and holly in the wood. Now that vision was hard to recapture, and harder still to transmit.

I could force my thoughts into his mind. Indeed, how else had I thought I could convey to him what had to be done? But I'd never known Charles to pick up mental suggestion very well. I remembered having been a bird before, trying desperately to remind him that he was who he was, that he should not listen to a too-Christian priest who would tell him otherwise.

He might not listen to me in any case. The pulse of fear at my presence must be deafening his mind with panic. The more panicked I let him become, the less open he would be, even to my most forceful thought.

There was no more time to debate. I must try, and at once.

Your majesty, calm.

I formed the words in my brain and pushed them towards him in something like a bubble. Nothing. I tried again, making the shimmering membrane that enclosed the thought stronger, firmer, the better to press to its goal.

Charles, it is I, Père Jean. Jean le Drapier. In the body of this owl. Bubble after bubble. *Charles. Calm and hear me. Charles the son of Charles the son of Charles.*

If any words could bring him to me, it must be this singsong, the deep, prophetic sound of what he was, at his deepest core. Could I not send the pulse of it to the pulse of his royal blood?

Charles the son of Charles ...

The gurgle in his throat suddenly became a little laugh. The laugh grew until he flung himself back on the pillows helplessly.

I knew I was staring. My great yellow eyes would have given that impression in any case, but my astonishment was such that I could do nothing to soften my owlish looks. The sight of the pale young man, sunken back among the pale bolsters and framed by gauzy curtains, played with my eyes. The flicker of candlelight drew forward things which ought to have fallen back into shadow, thus dazzling my sight.

And, for all the Craft at my command, I could not imagine what he found so amusing.

At last he found breath enough to say, "Oh, but this is rare. When I wake up, I won't be able to believe it, either. Père Jean comes to me in a dream in the form of an owl."

My first reaction was to assure him he wasn't dreaming. Then it occurred to me that he might accede to my need more readily if he kept thinking just that. *Yes, think that if you'd like,* I said. *You are dreaming, Charles.*

My reticence to form an actual lie must have made the membrane around that thought weak, for what he received of the message was vague.

"Well, if I'm not dreaming," he said, "then it's finally happened. I'm as mad as ever my father was."

Your father was mad only because he took Kingship while refusing to pay its price. But, in the end, sanity returned and we revere him now as a God.

Charles shrugged and chuckled again.

You were with me there, Charles, I insisted. *In the chamber in the*

Hôtel Saint Pôl in Paris. You helped me come to that point—to do my duty as a priest. You were there when the filth and decay of decades of madness washed away in the shedding of your father's royal blood and when he, Charles the son of Charles, recognized you as his son and heir.

Only I would know this.

The young Dauphin was aware of it. Remembering made him sit up in bed again and rub his eyes, as if against the sting of tears. Then he dropped his arms and hung them limply across his bent knees like one more coverlet. I tried to read his thoughts, though projecting my own onto him was taking most of my magic.

"My father was mad—" Charles looked away, finding the hare. "My father was mad not because he lacked faith but because he had too much."

There, again, was something under his words, though I couldn't read it.

"The idea that a Man in Black could come and demand his life at any time drove him crazy," Charles said.

Not "at any time", I insisted. *At a sacred time, long ago ordained. The King who has accepted this fate is protected and cannot die at any other time.*

Charles chewed his lower lip like a rabbit at work on lettuce. Perhaps he had never considered that promise before. Would he accept it now? I held my shallow owl breath, waiting.

He did not, but chose to consider something completely outside the Craft instead. "If a man—if a King—refused to believe—"

I interrupted him with a squawk.

He grew less pensive at that. He picked at a feather working its way out of a bolster—a goose's, not mine—and said, "Have you come for me, Père Jean? If so, I'll pinch myself quickly and wake from what must be a bad dream ... "

He did scratch his arm then with the pin-like end of the freed feather. He drew blood.

Of course it isn't time for you to die yet, Charles. We've almost two more years until the Sacrifice is due.

"Oh, yes, of course." To himself, he said, "Dream time gets

muddled." Then, to me again, "Go away and let me sleep. Don't turn this into a nightmare. He haunts me often enough, that vision of the Man in Black, coming to demand of me my Kingly blood so the Land may thrive."

Tonight we have other matter in hand, I assured him.

"You try being a King for a while—or half a King—with such a death weighing over you. You never can enjoy life."

But it is when we are in full knowledge and understanding of death that we are most fully alive. Did I have to recite the whole initiation over for him again? *It's Nature's way of telling us that, even on May Day, winter will come. Thus the world cycles, from bounty to restful dark again.*

But I wondered at this terror in one I'd initiated to the Mother's ways. I wondered if this was why Charles continued to drag his feet, even when we had La Pucelle in our midst.

Never mind it tonight, I said again. *Your son is yet too young.*

"Louis? Louis as King? Hasn't France suffered enough? Than to be cast upon the shoulders of that spindly creature who can hardly walk? At six years old, he can hardly walk."

Yes, in two years, he will still be too young to be orphaned.

"Louis orphaned means I'm dead. You're saying I am safe?"

When I didn't answer at once, he said, "Ah, I know. This is just a dream. And promises made in a dream mean nothing."

In two years, France must have a Sacrifice of the royal blood, I said. *And I will do my task as priest and get it. I won't lie to you about that. But you understand that any human with your blood may do the great service. You have many cousins, uncles, sisters ...*

"Women also can be the Sacrifice?"

Of course, I said. Had initiation taught him nothing? *I don't know which of your sisters might volunteer, however, the one a very pious nun, another dowager queen of England, another ...*

"I've far too many relatives. That's why France is torn to pieces before my eyes."

The treacherous Duke of Burgundy shares your blood ...

Charles considered. "Yes, if Burgundy, damn him, were to die, that would go far to restore the balance."

So he hadn't forgotten everything I'd taught him. I didn't

want to get his hopes up in that direction, however. *The Bastard of Orléans, who fights so valiantly in your name, holding out in the city he will never have legitimate right to, his veins also carry royal blood,* I said. *I saw the Bastard this afternoon and he—*

"None of them is initiated. Isn't it true that the Sacrifice must be initiated?"

True, but there's time. Tonight, Your Majesty, we must—

"I wish I'd never been to Chartres! I wish I'd never been initiated there," he cried out with a sudden passion into the bolsters.

Charles! I squawked at the blasphemy.

"See? You won't let me forget for a moment. You won't let me be a King."

I don't let you forget because the memory of your vows towards our Mother Earth are part of what it means to be a true King. Responsibility, not just lording your position over all.

"La Trémoïlle lets me forget," he whined.

Of course he lets you forget. So he'll also let you forget when he snatches the reins of government from you. Which he would hold without a pause to think of returning anything to anybody. Even, my young prince, to you.

"What do I care? I don't want that responsibility. Let him have it. Just so I can have peace."

But you must see the danger there. I sighed. *Christianity does tend to that, to let the mind wander to future goods away from the here and now. Handing us a God who died hundreds of leagues from this land, hundreds of years ago. A faith like that is carried from land to land in a book, so it means nothing real to the soil and plants and animals in some new land. It is written on the skin of dead animals in words that the powerful may change to their own meaning, to bolster their own power whenever they will. Then, oh then, this Land that is my Mother and my Lover, too—as you know Her from initiation—then She is in the most grievous danger of being silenced.*

"At least if I were 'the most Christian king', I would not belong to a faith, as my father did, that wants me to die." The Dauphin chewed his lip again, rising onto one elbow. "I know La Pucelle is—La Pucelle. I saw the angel and the crown in Cabinet.

I know her power. But if I embrace it—and her—I embrace my own death—my own blood sprinkled on the soil of France's fields—don't I?"

I shifted my head on my feathery shoulders in what could pass for a nod. That was what I'd been saying, wasn't it? Only not in so many words. I didn't dare say it in so many words. But he did.

"Well, I don't want that. I think of it sometimes, of how my father just offered his arm for your lancet. I—I couldn't. I see myself shaming myself. I am—I am too afraid. Yes, afraid of my own shadow, if you like. I'm less afraid to tell you this than to think of what must happen two years from now."

He fell back among the bolsters and rolled away from me.

What could I reply? Yes, that was the price of his Kingship. The God came and gave courage when it was needed, the courage to step over into Godhood. Even Christian scripture said such fear as his might be "the beginning of wisdom". Having felt that fear and gone through it was what made a God. But how could I make him see this?

After a moment's thought, I decided to say nothing. What did I know of it, anyway, being only the priest serving the mystery? And a mystery such as the shedding of royal blood was beyond words in any case.

That was the problem with trying to walk the rail between Christianity and the old religion, wasn't it? The rail was so narrow—in many cases, there was none—that someone was bound to fall off. Walking that line too close to one side had made the Knights Templar tumble to the Inquisition the last time there was a coven. The whole coven and many other innocents had gone at that time. Say I only lost one, this one— But no, I couldn't lose Charles the son of Charles the son of Charles. Not now. Not when we were so close.

Charles, I can't let you lie back, give up, give in. Not now, not when the time of La Pucelle is at hand.

"La Pucelle, yes," Charles murmured, and something else I didn't hear. His words came muffled from among the pillows and coverlets. I had to switch my great round face directly toward him. If I hadn't had an owl's hearing, I might have missed the sound altogether. Certainly I must have missed the stifled sobs underneath.

If I'd had arms, I would have thrown them around him. The touch of feathers, I was quite certain, would unnerve him, however. I certainly couldn't preen him, as an owl might do his mate. I could only click my beak in what I hoped were comforting sounds.

You came to this throne, I said gently, *this throne you haven't even really been crowned to yet, with all its responsibilities—when you were very young. Still in need of councilors. Councilors who kept your person safe only to further their own causes. Having been used for others' wills, you still don't trust your own.*

"You will not leave Louis in such a state?"

No, I will not leave your son.

I did not mean to make it quite the promise it sounded. I certainly did not say the words surrounded by the ancient threefold oath calling upon earth and sky and water to witness it. Charles seemed to take it that way, however, and I hastened to add, *I will not abandon him—if you do not. The Gods may visit you with madness, be warned—that is the way your father left you. They will, you know, if you do not embrace your Kingship, the death with the life.*

Charles gave a great sigh, quivering with grief. "Every time I do something, it works out to a bloody mess. On the Bridge at Montereau, when I tried to make peace ... "

Now his voice failed altogether, dissolving into sobs.

I withdrew my mind into itself for a moment, letting him have his cry.

"Now, I don't dare do anything," he began when he could.

A breath of breeze came in through the window. It caught at the bed curtains, made the candle and the shadows it cast dance, ruffled my feathers. And though it was not cold, Charles shivered visibly.

"You see, even thinking about such things as standing up to La Trémoïlle makes my heart beat as if it will burst. My palms sweat. My mouth gets so dry I can hardly speak."

Yes, I've even seen you wet yourself, I mused. *Once, when I was also a bird. And you had only a small bridge to cross, but could not, remembering Montereau.*

I meant to keep the reflection to myself. But I had not made the membrane between thought-speech and simple thought clear enough. He heard, at least some of it. He looked at me, blinking with horror.

Then he shut his mind off from me completely.

The Owl Was Once a Baker's Daughter

Charles, *the son of Charles, the son of Charles*—I chanted. I coaxed. I pleaded. To no avail. Still he kept his back to me, showing me nothing but a tousle of mouse-brown hair. When I tried to pick at that hair gently, he shoved me away, pulled the blanket right over his head, and showed nothing.

In frustration I flew back to the bedpost. There I preened, loosening one feather so it fell down among the bedclothes. Beyond the tall, narrow rectangle of open window, the featureless black of night beckoned me.

And within the room, the hare sniffed over by a buckler and sword propped up against the far wall. Such weapons were only for show. This prince used them to hide behind.

The hare still seemed a bit dazed, certainly confused. A patch of blood glistened on his back, where my talons had struck too deep. Ah, I should just kill the creature, eat him and be off, spreading my swift shadow against the stars. That was where I belonged.

Let the coven manage with twelve for a while. But no, even my owl self knew that could not be. I'd already learned the hard way that twelve was not enough. And of all the members, we needed the royal one most of all. Surely once he saw the deeds of which La Pucelle—and we—were capable, Charles would come around. In time.

But there was no time. "Use me well," the girl had said. "You have me for only a year or a little more."

And so much to accomplish. So much. Too much, for just a year. Even this night must not be wasted.

So I stopped preening. I perched on the Dauphin's bedpost and sang.

At first my words were only "Who? Who? Who-oo-who," interspersed with calls to *Charles the son of Charles the son of Charles*, on the same haunting note.

Then words of other songs came, bubble after bubble, a storm like an otter's wake. I sang folk songs in praise of the owl, then in praise of the King-who-must-die and the blood royal in his veins, blood that will enrich the soil. Even so the owl, if begged in the same tone of awe, will rid the same fields of vermin.

Song wandered into story. *The owl was once the baker's daughter*. I told that old tale, still using the haunting tones of the owl's call. How the bearded stranger had come to the baker's door, begging, because the baker's daughter had failed to set out a portion for the fairy folk that evening. Or rather, she hadn't forgotten, but decided that saving the food for mortals and the morrow would be the wisest, most frugal plan.

The baker's wife set the dough for a whole loaf to rise for the stranger. But the daughter cut the loaf in half, thinking to keep back the rest for the shop.

"For maybe we will starve," she said.

The stranger's lump swelled until it filled the bowl. Again she took half the dough. Again it swelled and filled the pan.

"Hoo, hoo, hoo," the baker's daughter cried in surprise.

And even as she said it, her back sprouted wings, her face a beak, her feet talons. For her stinginess, the stranger had turned the baker's daughter into an owl.

Charles had thrown back the covers now, staring at me with great owl eyes. This tale, known to every common child, must never have been told to this royal one. What was this new theory of tutelage, loose in the world, I wondered, taken up by the nobility first? What was this that calls itself knowledge but fails to include the ancient tales? This would create a class of beings to whom one could not longer say, in a warning tone, "The owl was once the baker's daughter" to remind them. To remind them of the demands of charity, that all the world is connected and each station, from King to fowl, has reciprocal demands upon the others.

Most disturbing of all was to find this forgetting first in royalty. In such minds, an artificial sense of scarcity would grow, making them avoid fear of starvation at the expense of making others starve. In such minds, what impact could even initiation have?

All was not lost to me yet, however. For, from the heap of tumbled bedding came a quiet little voice. "He was Christ? The stranger?"

So some say, I replied. *Others, that he was the Merlin.*

I brought one talon up and used it to comb the white feathers forming a bib on my chest—the closest thing I had to my Merlin beard about me at the moment.

"So if I refuse to give my blood—" Charles began.

You are more stingy than the baker's daughter, for your wealth is far greater than lumps of flour and yeast.

"But the story tells me that turning into an owl is a punishment. Are you being punished, Père Jean?"

No. Transformation is only punishment if you don't go of your own free will, if you spend the rest of your days in feathers wondering how you got that way, asking 'Who? Who?' knowing neither who the visitor was who came to you nor who you yourself are, that you are the man born to be King of France.

"This is chop logic. Regnault of Chartres would tell me so, but I can't understand the fault on my own."

Let him not think of the old archbishop, or all was lost. *It is the logic of a dream.*

"Yes, that's it."

And in a dream, you can come with me, to Orléans, to take your place in the coven.

"Isn't La Pucelle in Orléans?" he said, as if that question would determine once and for all the state of his wakefulness. "Didn't we send her to Orléans, as she asked?"

Yes, but you also sent soldiers under orders to turn back once they'd delivered the girl, Charles. You've left her without the men she needs to work the victory of the God of this land.

"Well, if this is God's work, what does she need soldiers for?"

You must provide the soldiers, God will provide the victory.

"And La Pucelle? What is her part in all of this, except to get me in trouble with my councilors? They think me a fool for believing in her."

And don't you believe her?

Charles shrugged. "When she's around I do. But that may be just a spell she's cast, as La Trémoïlle says."

You mean to tell me we've squandered these two full months, getting priests and prelates to give their blessing to her? A blessing she didn't really need—being La Pucelle—except to get you to feel comfortable in the face of some minor portion of your subjects. We've wasted these months, even after she told you herself you wouldn't have her for much time. "A year or some little more" she said. Well, that "little more" is certainly gone now.

"La Trémoïlle says—"

Monseigneur de La Trémoïlle wouldn't change his mind if the pope himself set a seal to her sanctity.

"You're right. La Trémoïlle believes in no one but La Trémoïlle."

At least he saw that much. *So why do you care what such a man thinks?* I asked.

"Because he has managed to get rid of her, don't you see? He did it, by his cunning. And now he's the power closest to me again, so what does she matter?"

She matters. All I could think of was reiteration. *As much or more than the royal blood.*

Charles rubbed in distraction at his thin neck, as if feeling the blood pulsing so tenuously there. Then, a sudden thought seemed to strike him, to lighten him, in fact.

"Isn't it true," he said, "that I can give this blood to—to someone else? Like I did in the crypt at Angers."

Yes. I joined his involuntary shiver at the memory of the night when Gwencalon, the father of our coven's present bard of the same name, offered himself for the King who would not.

"And the person—the man or woman, say—who dies the death becomes a God?"

True.

"So you say."

You saw it, Charles.

"There must be some out there who would appreciate the chance to—"

Enough of this, I thought. We don't need to worry about the blood yet. *You have thousands of men-at-arms out there right now willing to die for you, Charles,* I said instead. *Not the least of these is La Pucelle, a warrior such as no King of France has ever had given to him before.*

"La Pucelle," he mused. "Yes."

The way he said it made me shiver again, for some reason I couldn't name. I ruffled my feathers and settled them.

So now, you need to get up and deserve this gift of La Pucelle, I told the princely bundle of blankets, *or you're no King at all. There is much you must do to fulfill Merlin's ancient prophecy concerning La Pucelle. I must bring you where she is.*

"Very well. If you must. Come for me in the morning and we can set off then."

Having given this order, he flung himself back into the pillows and pulled the coverlet over his head.

No, you must come now. There isn't a moment to lose. With one swoop on rounded wing, I landed on the bed beside him and began to pick at the coverlet with one talon. Inadvertently, I tore it with a sickening rip, too like tearing animal's flesh.

That made Charles sit up with a start, as if I had indeed cut him and not just the linen. I tumbled backwards, rolling through hills of bedding until I clumsily righted myself again with my stubby wingtips. I hissed and chirred in anger.

The bland brown eyes on either side of the large, lumpy nose stared at me. I stared firmly back. He still wanted to believe he was dreaming, but my performance gave him doubt.

"Part of me is brave enough," the Dauphin said finally.

Perhaps he meant brave enough to die in two years' time, but I took him to mean brave enough to suit the coven's purposes that night. Such commitment was all I asked. *Praise the Goddess,* I sighed.

The eyes peering at me over the edge of the coverlet

blinked against tears. He looked away from my gaze before he continued: "If only you could cut out the part of me that fears and make the brave part large enough to fill a belly—to be a King. For the rest, I might as well be that trembling hare over there as a prince."

But that is just the magic I planned, I said. *For there is no way I can get you to Orléans in this body in time, even if we set you on a horse this instant.*

"What do you mean?"

I mean, it's two days' ride.

With La Trémoïlle and his four thousand men to meet, coming in the other direction. I didn't press the thought towards Charles and worked to keep it from bleeding through. I doubted anyone alive had magic enough to swell the Dauphin's bravery to necessary proportion if once he got talking to his practical chamberlain again. Even now, without La Trémoïlle's interference, my heart was pounding with the danger of dividing a soul so insecure of itself. Charles was more insecure than the baker's daughter of the legend. There was a chance that such division, fragmenting, could lead to a permanent alienation.

I clamped down fiercely on thoughts of such possibility, letting them nowhere near the thought bubbles I kept pushing towards him. I tried to keep them from my own consciousness, too, lest doubts in my own self, added to his, make the deed impossible.

La Pucelle needs you now, I concluded, *Charles the son of Charles the son of Charles.*

"She can't have me now. Not if it's two day's ride."

But it's only half a night's flight. I left Orléans on wing myself not long before the sunset.

"I can't fly."

Charles, there is a way–

"And you can't make me. You can't turn me into an owl. Stingy or generous, I ... I couldn't do that."

I mean to turn you, not into an owl, but into that hare. I swivelled my round head in that direction.

He stared at the hare with new eyes. He was sitting up in

bed again, the sheets crumpled around his thin, flayed-looking chest.

"I can't fit into that hare." He chuckled at the absurdity of the thought.

The brave part can, I assured him. *And the body that betrays you with pounding heart and dry mouth, that body will stay behind, here, safe in this bed.*

He looked at the bed now, in wonder, as if just seeing it for the first time. As if it were the thing with magic.

You will seem in a deep sleep to your servants when they come for you, I told him. *In something of a trance. They will not be able to waken you, but they will know you are not dead. My own body lies thus even now, back near Orléans. I will return you to this flesh again within a night and a day, and no harm done.*

"They will think I am mad, as my father was," Charles considered with a glance towards his door, thinking of the men behind it—the looks they exchanged with one another.

But you will be back ere the sun rises a second time, to disprove them. You will have proven yourself braver than you think. And you will have provided the thirteenth initiated soul—and the only one with the blood of Charlemagne and Charles Martel, Charles the son of Charles the son of Charles—to the coven of La Pucelle.

"If I can stay here—my body, I mean—my body cannot be hurt by coming too close to the *goddam* arrows."

That's true, I said, all the while suppressing from my thoughts the dangers that could befall a bodiless soul lest I pass the fear of them on to him.

"If it's only a dream—"

Exactly.

"And La Pucelle—?"

Yes, do it for her.

"Because of what—" He made a gesture that got broader, as if to contain much more than just tonight. "—because of all she may do for me."

Yes.

Charles nodded, once, firmly. "Very well. Let's do it."

What was this edge of thought coming from him that made

me shiver again? I couldn't catch it, so I turned to the transformation instead.

First, as a man might, I tried to lift the candle to flame the herbs in the pewter bowl. But my talons were too clumsy on the gold handle of the sconce. I tried bringing a branch of twining belladonna from the bowl to the light instead.

"Here, let me do that," Charles said when he understood what I was trying to do.

I hesitated and then, as I skittered out of his way, my wings sent a spark or two popping out onto his skin.

"Ow," he said, and rubbed the place on his arm.

Now he will realize he is not asleep, I thought in dismay. He has felt pain and will realize—

But he did not. The process had begun to interest him so much he forgot to be afraid.

Green and full of sap as it was, the belladonna soon filled the chamber with smoke. The aconite, catching slower but burning deeper, added its own sharp scent.

"Phew," said Charles, waving the smoke away from his face. "If I wasn't already asleep, this would soon put me there."

I hissed and fanned the billows with my wings. I pretended, like him, to clear the air, but in truth I worked the acrid vapors in his direction. My small bird skull was already light enough—but lightness was, in fact, exactly what we needed.

Suddenly, Charles' head rolled as if his thin neck were broken, then he dropped back onto the bolsters. His lids fluttered at half staff, his lips formed a drowsy smile.

"Ah," he sighed, and I caught that bit of his escaping soul and stuffed it, with all the strength of my mind, into the hare.

It was like catching thistle down and trying to fill a basket with it, a task requiring delicacy and patience. Tuft after tuft drifted forth, and I thought I'd gathered quite a bit. But then, pressing them together in the space the skittish hare gave, I time and time again realized I didn't have nearly as much of the princely matter as I had hoped. No more than the fluff of furry tail was full when I compacted the spirit, then the tip of the long ears.

Even once captured, the unschooled soul tended to be swept up by every passing current of power and blow loose, back out into the open air of the room again.

At last, through the drug haze, I saw the princely body lying inert. No more tufts of spirit had the courage to venture forth. Breath rose the coverlets so deeply and so infrequently that the trance seemed closer to death than to sleep.

The hare, however, stopped clinging to the shadows of the walls, stopped searching for a way out, out of my sight. The rear legs gave a kick, found themselves startlingly strong, then loped with more caution, like a sailor trying out solid ground after months at sea. He weaved through the open candlelight to the edge of my chair perch. Here he rose up on his haunches, the little nose wriggling with curiosity, the eyes round and wide with human intelligence.

Let's be gone. Charles' tone made me think human intelligence may be little more than the urge to demand one's own way. But it assured me that the human body was safe to leave like that, as long as the hare stayed well.

The transfer of another's soul had sapped my strength, more than my own practiced metamorphoses. It took me two attempts to get the necessary membrane around a thought of my own to push back at him. *Very well. Let's.* Once I did it, however, I found the feat was easier, animal to animal.

I caught the hare-prince by the scruff of the neck and carried him up to the window sill. The moon was very old, this month and a week after Easter. It had only just risen above Blois castle walls, its thin curve like a fingernail pointing towards the sun coming close behind it now, pointing the direction I must fly. I spread my wings and leapt towards it.

Twenty-First Antiphon

A Soul like Down Tight in its Flower Pod

When I'd considered flying back to Orléans, I'd imagined a body inhabited by Charles' willing soul would be much easier to carry than a terrified, wriggling hare. So he was.

And yet, not so much easier. He still hung like dead weight from my talons until I thought they must rip off at the ankle bones. Before we'd reached even half the distance to the flickering lights of La Trémoïlle's camp, the arc of pain from wing to wing across my chest drove me to ground again. I had to set Charles down—"for a little rest"— before I actually dropped him, with killing effect.

We alit beside one of the thousand little ponds that dot the wilds of the Sologne. I drank, rested on a low limb, drank again and watched the little hare hop here and there, tasting greens tentatively. He liked what he tasted, but the man in him censured the instinct, afraid something might poison him.

I stretched my wings, mantled them, stretched, but every time I thought of picking up that grey weight again, my shoulders cramped unbearably.

I was going to have to put him into another body, one that could fly on its own. But what?

Below me, in a thornbush, my keen owl eyes caught sight of a thrush's nest. The mother slept, her brown body spread and rounded over her nestlings. A true owl would have swept down on her and eaten her in a moment. For my purposes, however, she wouldn't serve. What would it mean, to save

La Pucelle and the Earth and leave a clutch of chicks to chill to death in the night air? To feed with instinct was one thing. To twist nature to the sharp line of a man's thinking was another altogether, something magic must fight against with its circling power.

I listened a moment for the calls of such birds as I might use, the mourning of a nightingale, the whir, like a spinning wheel at this season, of the male nightjar. Such birds would be careful to keep quiet, however, if they knew an owl was by, and so they did.

I hooted, then, to see if these woods were the territory of another of my kind. Before I could hoot again and draw up a rival, who might be in the midst of a hunt just then and unable to answer, my ears caught another sound.

It might have been no more than the echo of my own voice, but I twisted my head quickly in the direction, right and down.

My rapid bird's heart stopped as I saw the barest thread of silver catch on a black spit nosing its way out from under a frond of bracken towards the Dauphin.

I threw my wings out, grabbing for the air, and gave the loudest a squawk of warning I could. As I did so, a streak of tawny red-brown shot from the undergrowth straight towards the prince-hare.

With my warning, Charles was off, a mere nose length ahead of the snapping jaws of a fox. At first, he didn't know where the danger came from and leapt at the predator, just left of his muzzle. That was enough to put Charles elsewhere when the jaws snapped shut and to give him half a panted breath to see his danger.

The long rear legs flashed over a rock, under a fallen tree draped with moss, back through a patch of grass. They pelted here, pelted there, zigged and zagged evasion almost faster than I could see. But they drew the fox like a lodestone. Indeed it seemed, after two quick reels on his haunches, this hunter could read his prey's mind. Knew where he was going before the little rodent brain itself had decided. Back paws hit where front paws had been, once, twice.

I didn't see it for the blur of fur, but I heard the scream that split the night as the salivaed cavern of a fox's mouth closed upon the Dauphin, heir of France.

I was on the scene a moment later, throwing back my wings, landing talons first upon the sleek, red head. As soon as I could throw my body forward, I pecked as well, going for the eyes.

But I also tried to scream in words a fox could hear, *Let go. Let him go. For the love of Our Lady Goddess, for the love of the Land, that is the blood royal. It must be shed, yes, for the good of all, but not now. Not now. Let go. For the love of Our Lady, it's I, the Merlin Yann, who speak*.

The fox loped to a stop and opened his mouth. The hare dropped limply to the litter of the forest floor and lay still. I fluttered off the fox's head to stand beside him, gasping with my beak half open.

Well, how was I to know? the hunter said. *It doesn't smell like the blood royal. And you'd think I'd be able to tell.*

It wouldn't smell that way in a hare's body. And that was when I realized the Dauphin's spirit wouldn't be enough. In order for the Earth, like this fox, Her son, to accept the emblem, some portion of the blood would have to be present. It was, perhaps, even more vital than the spirit I'd worked so hard to bring so far.

At the moment, however, I might have neither. The fox sat on his haunches and looked anxiously from his former quarry to me. Quick, shallow gasps shuddered the hare's small form. He would not live long.

Charles? I cried, hopping nearer. *Charles, can you hear me*?

I got no answer, but I thought—I hoped—I saw a stiff little nod. It might have been no more than a struggle for breath, however, and the last throbs of a ruptured heart.

I'm going to have to transfer you to another body.

But what? What? I looked at the fox, his tongue lolling as he panted for breath. He swished his tail, willing to try ...

It was certain, however, that I could never carry a fox. He could run, but it would be slow, too slow. Maybe just until we found something ... anything else ...

My sharp eyes spotted a flea hopping off the hare, abandoning the dying body.

Quick, into that flea, I cried, and began to work the magic without any more thought.

There isn't room, came a voice, a flea's voice, tight and small, after I'd shoved only two or three thistle tufts of soul into it.

The hare shuddered. Its eyes set.

I'll have to divide you, I said to Charles, *and just take as much as I can carry in the flea. Into that baby thrush*, I commanded.

The spur of death behind him, the rest of Charles' soul shot like down still tight in its flower pod. Being coddled and fed already-digested food would come easily to this prince, I thought.

As he settled under her wing, among the rounded feathers, the mother thrush woke and sensed the change. Worse, she sensed double danger nearby—the fox and me. She leapt off her nestlings and set up a squawking flurry, confused by night and drowsiness.

I finally got the message of who I was over her turmoil, that I was not working with an owl's instincts tonight. She grew calmer.

To repay the disturbance that required the Dauphin to shelter among your chicks, this fox, I said, *will help you guard your nest*.

The mother looked dubious, but the fox yipped his agreement. I finally got the mother to agree, reminding her of the honor it must be to have the Dauphin as one of her chicks, even for but a short time. She allowed the fox to settle down at the base of her tree with his nose on his paws, his watchful eyes alert.

Until I or another of the coven return to reclaim this portion of the Dauphin's soul, I leave him in your hands—or wings and paws.

Thus concluded, I set off, with the flea clinging to the ruff of feathers collaring my neck.

I kept an even flap, flap, the wind the witches had raised blowing steadily at my tail. Yet with every beat the quandary teased at me: Was I going the right direction? I had Charles' soul right enough, at least an emblem of it. But what was I going to do about the blood? Should I not rather bank about and head back to the place where the blood royal lay sleeping in a finely draped bed in Blois?

A line of silver cracked the horizon before me: May Day dawn. I shifted, stiffening my wings to catch the updraft raised by the fires of four thousand camping men and flew over La Trémoïlle's tents.

There wasn't time, there was no time at all.

Chapter Seventeen

Mud and Moss Sucking at Fine Silk Hose

Gilles de Rais had to marvel at the old widow his grandfather had married, Madame Anne de Sillé. He'd considered her as little as he could in the time he'd known her, not least because of her close connection to his own wife. He tended to lump her with his grandfather who, crippled by gout, hadn't budged from Château Champtocé in years.

Madame Anne had a good twenty years on any of the other witches, even Père Michel, who these days wielded his staff more to aid his bad knees than with magic. But with Yann gone, she stepped without question into place as head of the assembled folk of the Craft.

Her long grey hair, unbound, crinkled down her back and mingled with loose, unknotted grey robes, making her look very like an owl. Thus, in ritual garb, she flitted throughout Reuilly keep and roused every witch in her charge while May Day was as yet just the first crisp chirp of birds outside.

Gilles liked nights better than mornings. He liked to sit up late by a fire in his comfortable hall, drinking spiced wine and reading. Or loving. Someone. But he hadn't had the luxury of his own hall for years.

Often, on campaign, he'd had to rise before dawn. To see to the watch. To effect a skirting maneuver under cover of darkness. Never in his life had Gilles de Rais risen early for this reason—to hie to the green wood to go a-Maying.

No matter. Where La Pucelle went, he would follow, and La Pucelle answered Madame Anne's call.

So Gilles found himself shoved from comfortable darkness to the grey light, akin to twilight, magic time, where night met the brilliance of day. On this day, spring met summer, too, met, mingled, kissed, and always the Gods were in such blending. One star, the ancient Goddess, rested over the eastern horizon along with the silver sliver of a moon.

Gilles wished they could be alone, just the two of them, he and La Pucelle, on such a morning, with battle far from them. But the other witches came, too, eleven in all, lacking only Yann and Charles.

Like a general, Madame Anne marshaled her troops, pressing Reuilly's every basket into service for the assault on the wood. She ordered her forces out to fan the countryside, infiltrating not the domain of the enemy, but of Nature. Nature welcomed them with open arms, open sky, open tree limbs, open meadow. Songs and laughter were their battle cries, answered by the wakening birds.

This assault was the reverse of any he'd ever participated in, this begging for the enemy to ravage one's self. This celebrating the World's fertility, this carrying it back like loot to the dwellings where humans, with barriers of wood and stone, tried at other times to cut themselves off from Her. This begging Nature to ravish one's heart, make one as fertile as She was Herself.

Madame sent Roger shinnying up a tree, just as Gilles might have done on a raid of his own, to survey the area. The knife Roger wielded—after a prayer for the blessing of the sacred bush instead of a shout of alarm—cut the highest blooming branches of the hawthorn. Where, in battle, blood might spatter, dew-wet petals rained down on upturned faces, aglow with joy rather than dim with the sight of death.

Gilles heard himself laugh instead of curse. As he brushed petals from his beard, still looking up, his gaze fell on the strangest thing. He saw an owl. A real one, not Madame Anne.

Gilles could attribute his attention to no definable reason, for the creature sat unmoving save for a blink of great yellow eyes. It sat on a broken limb of the tree—an oak? He couldn't tell without acorns to go along with it, but he thought it might be. There the bird sat, round and squat and silent as a keg of verjuice.

Gilles felt a fluttering at his elbow. He looked down quickly, expecting it to be La Pucelle, for he had seen to it that he took his stance there, next to the girl. But she had wandered off. It was, instead, a streak of grey, Madame Anne.

"Gilles," she ordered, pressing a basket in his empty hands—as if he were, indeed, her grandson, and a mere child. "Go after those fraises des bois."

Before complying, Gilles stole another glance up at the owl—and fancied the creature staring wide-eyed at madame's retreating grey back. With intent so fierce, Gilles felt it. Did his grandmother really look so much like an owl, even to owl eyes? Was the bird joining with Nature in Her springtime fecundity? Was it—he—in fact, amorous?

Yann, Gilles thought. Yann would know the habits of such birds. But Yann, of course, was not near.

When the creature did not immediately act upon amorous intention, Gilles had to laugh off the capers of his own imagination. Then he, who would have done his best in battle to stay horsed and armored against all blows, crept on hands and knees, a supplicant's posture. Mud and moss sucking at his fine silk hose, he crawled under a dead tree fallen at a steep angle, to where a pool of the low strawberry plants grew.

His nose close to the ground, he smelled the rich fragrance, not of death alone, but of death turning to new life. It was a wet smell, a dark smell, a moon smell. A woman's smell compared to the men's odor of battle.

Within the hollow, he parted the low leaves, like fairy platters, and found, below rather than above, fairy food. The berries hung like drops of blood amidst their white blooms and green infants. They burst against the roof of his mouth like incendiary shot, the flavor and sweetness a wild, mirror image of flame.

He felt himself astounded. Rather than from smoke or horror, the mirror-shard tears in the corners of his eyes were from beauty. Adding to all that took his breath away, he heard his love's laughter like bird calls on the air that was beginning to glow with promise all around him.

But it was Tiphaine, not La Pucelle, who met him as he crept out of the grove again. This witch-guardian of the Mont-Saint-Michel flashed him her wordless smile. He hoped that meant he'd dashed the effects of womanish tears away. She had a skirt full of other fraises to add to the basket he'd merely lined.

This task done, he looked around for La Pucelle. Had she gathered berries? Could he take them from the short skirt of her doublet? Or even from a white kerchief?

For no reason he could imagine—certainly not because he expected a sight of La Pucelle there—his attention was drawn up among the pale-leafed branches overhead. The owl again.

What on earth did it mean? Gilles had the sense an owl was ill omened. Old wives would throw salt in the fire when they heard the owls' call. Or maybe this presence just meant that a girl was about to lose her virginity. Personally, he took that as a good omen.

"Girls, quick. Ere the sun rises."

Before he found his heart's desire, Madame gave orders again.

"Come, wash your faces in the dew, for beauty's sake."

The dew she'd found clung to the low spikes of white star-studded woodruff. The men turned away in awe, as from before a mystery, as men turn while screaming fellows die on the field.

He heard Pieronne in her Breton tease madame. "What beauty do you look for at your age, madame?"

"The beauty dew gives is ageless," Madame Anne said, getting down to her knees, not without giving weight to her crystal-headed staff.

She wiped her flattened hands over the rising bank of green, brought them to her face, then to the plants again. She waved for others to follow suit.

Now I will go to La Pucelle, Gilles thought. Perhaps even give her the ring. The ruby, the great ornament he'd carried with him all the way from Tours ... now, while the women are occupied here—

For he had found the girl. She stood at the far edge of the great patch of woodruff, the plants drowning her ankle-high riding boots, brushing halfway up her calves, free in their hose. Beneath the sweep of jaunty feathers in her cap, her brow wrinkled for a moment in indecision. The sight kept him from instantly striding through the dew that separated them and offering a berry.

He saw decision came to her, all at once. A nod from her Voices, no doubt. She swept off her cap and fell to her knees alongside the other women.

Gilles stood frozen, unable to tear his gaze away, though he had the distinct impression that he committed blasphemy.

He heard her laugh as the dew splashed into her face, as she slapped it on. Clear and light, unfettered the sound rang, like birdsong. When she lifted her dew-washed face to him, it had taken on the colors the sky was turning, gold and pink.

As if she were some crustacean, dew had cracked the shell of fierce determination she usually wore. She lay open, pink and white and gilded, tremblingly tender, like crab flesh, dripping butter.

Gilles' teeth ran with water. And he had thought that such a sight of female vanity must always turn his stomach.

The next moment, he was on his knees beside her, snatching at the wet plants for his share of that beauty.

La Pucelle sat back on her heels and laughed at him, the sound as pure and bracing as the dew on his face. She scooped up another palmful of moisture and rubbed it into the birthmark shadowing her neck. As mirror to her, Gilles scrubbed a hand, tingling with the chill freshness, into his beard, to his own mark below.

She laughed again. And the other people, who had stopped and stared—horrified into silence at a man about a woman's rite—they couldn't help but forget their concerns and laugh as well. It all came as part of the day's special merriment.

There.

Gilles shoved a sprig of woodruff behind one ear and dropped his hands to his knees. He forced the girl to meet his eyes, to see his beauty, by the intensity of his own gaze.

There! Am I beautiful enough for La Pucelle now?

The force of her dark eyes brought new tears to his own, just as peering into the deep feminine of the strawberry glade had done. He saw something shift in those eyes, some reflection of the dew-drenched woodruff blooms, that told him she saw something of the same in him. The thought made his heart race.

Before more could come of the wordless exchange, Tiphaine, nearby, gave a little grunt of satisfaction. Pieronne scrambled over on her knees to investigate.

"Oh, look," Pieronne said. "My lady Tiphaine has found a slug. More white than black, wouldn't you say, mistress?"

She asked the question with hand signals as well as speech, and the deaf and dumb Tiphaine gave a solemn, though silent, nod.

"That means your true love must be blond. Who? Young sire de Bricqueville?" Pieronne teased, looking around and finding the only fair male head. She pointed, signed, "He's half your age."

Tiphaine gave a wink, as if to say, "Oh, I can handle that. The only question is, can he?"

Roger blushed to the roots of that blond hair and exchanged a glance with Gilles.

But Roger said nothing. It was Yann's voice Gilles heard, sharp in his ear. *Leave La Pucelle alone.*

The order was so compelling, Gilles got to his feet though he'd meant to let the girl at his side move first.

Yann is nowhere near, he told himself, and addressed his attention rather impatiently to Roger instead. I am not embarrassed by such talk, Gilles tried to convey with his return look to Roger, before he hastily withdrew it. I used to be embarrassed by the very thought of congress with a woman. But no more. He was relieved to hear Roger lose his affectation in a hearty laugh.

Someone explained the women's Breton dialect and the slug custom to La Pucelle. "Is it true?" Gilles heard his love asking at the level of his knee. "Then I must find a slug, too, to see what my true love's hair shall be."

Gilles dropped to his knees again and began at once to help, bound and determined to find her a dark grey slug, as close to black as could be, and to squash all competitors.

But Madame Anne interrupted with another project. "No. If you would see your true love's face, more than just the color of his hair, I know what we must do. And just as the sun is rising."

Chapter Eighteen

The Sun Rising in Shifting Silken Ribbons

Madame Anne de Sillé led the group of women down to where a small stream eddied into a quiet pool. Here, she swept her arm over the water, mumbling some incantation, and sprinkled something sandlike pulled from her pouch over the glassy surface.

Then, one by one, as the sun rose in shifting silken ribbons over them, the women knelt while their confidants held back the draping willows.

What did she see? Gilles leaned closer. Perhaps if he leaned close enough, a trick of light would mirror his face into the water when the dark, bristled head bent over.

Gilles, leave La Pucelle alone.

The force of this command pulled Gilles back again. Yann's clear voice? Impossible. Nonetheless, Gilles decided not to join in this rite of women. He had no need of magic to reveal his true love to him while she stood there with the rest, while she strode here and there in her snug hose. While she raked her fingers through her hair, making it stand on end. When some quick smile spread the mole on her lip and sent her dark eyes dancing.

But what did they see?

Did Madame Anne see her husband? Gilles' crusty old grandfather at home nursing his gouty leg. Could a magic pond possibly give back such an image? Did she see the dead husband of her youth? Or did she see the Hermit, dressed as the God in furs and horns, who'd given her that hulking idiot of a son?

Did Pieronne see her Yann? In the same God's guise? Or was that blasphemy, to see the priest who must serve all? Was she forced to see the face of the legal husband she'd left with three stepdaughters so long ago?

What did Tiphaine see? Silent Tiphaine, who loved the stars but whose dumbness would never allow her to tell what else. And La Meffraye? What could the water reflect of her but her own raven black?

Gilles asked these questions of each face as she rose and turned, all smiles, to her companions. But he asked them mostly as a clue to reading La Pucelle.

What had she seen, Jehanne, his Jehanne? Could she narrow down all her wide, wild love to embrace just one man's features?

Strangely, there was that owl again, moved to a different tree now, over their heads. As if it took an interest in what was seen in the pool.

Gilles read nothing but giggles and whispers on the dew-washed faces that eventually climbed up from the hollow to return among the men. They'd seen something, surely. But he, a man, would never know, and the annoyance, rather than making him commune with Nature, made him want to throw stones at the prying bird instead.

Shortly, the baskets were all full, either of strawberries or flowers. There were *muguets* and bluebells, iris and wild carrot, and many other flowers he couldn't name, all crammed haphazardly together into the baskets. Gilles had never been one to pay much attention to the plant world, even in its most brazen bloom.

But he did pay attention when La Pucelle bent and hefted a basket to either hip, carrying them as a peasant woman carries burdens, not as a man does. The burden exaggerated the feminine in her gait. Never would he have thought such a swing attractive. He would have taken the burden from her, if only to ease the attraction, except that he had his own to bring to his shoulder. The fragrances mingled with the full crown of sweet woodruff Tiphaine had made for him.

Why did he seek to ease La Pucelle's burden, to protect her? This was a girl who wore armor, nearly fifty pounds of it, wore it proudly, swaggered in it when she had the chance.

Tiphaine had crowned La Pucelle as well. As he approached, she shoved the *muguets* and bluebells out of her eyes with the shoulder that, her hands full, was all the limb left to her.

She smiled up at him. In those eyes, he could see only himself. Could he see what she had seen in the May Day pond?

"Well?" He decided to make light of it as he fell into step beside her.

"Well what?" she said, looking through blades of *muguet* leaf.

"Did you see him?"

"See whom?"

He remembered their close and private conversation in Poitiers, the word of her Voices. "Did you see the lucky—no, blessed—father of your pope, emperor and King?"

She gave him no answer but a smile that melted her face and his heart into it. If she'd had a hand free, he thought, she'd put a finger to those sturdy, smiling lips to indicate a secret. A secret she'd tell no one.

After that, Gilles had to stop a moment to catch his breath and shift his burden.

Leave the girl alone, I say.

Yann's voice. Yann? But how—?

Gilles looked up sharply. Damn it, if the owl wasn't following them back through the woods.

But Yann's voice?

Gilles shifted his flower basket for a better view. Last time he'd seen Yann—whose twisted human body they'd left in bed, trancing, back at the fortress—he'd taken the body of a hawk. Now—? Was it possible?

"Who?" the owl confirmed. *You know it is part of La Pucelle's power to remain a virgin. Among all witches.*

Yes, so it was possible. Yann in that form. Gilles' eyes widened, then blinked as if he, too, were being drawn into owl world.

"But after her mission," Gilles began—as if one could reason with an owl. "Her mission cannot last forever. After that—"

Yann stopped him. *Let's see her mission to completion first.*

Gilles tried to bring more than the nod of his head into acceding. In doing so, he sensed the exhaustion in the night-flying bird who now faced the morning. "So? Did you get the Dauphin? Where?"

Soon. I'll tell you soon. First tell me. Where's the Bastard?

"The Bastard?"

Messire Jean, Bastard and commander of Orléans. What, surely you've not been thinking so hard of getting bastards of your own that the name confused you?

Gilles grunted. He wouldn't let his milk brother get the better of him like that.

I couldn't find the commander at the fortress, Yann said. *Didn't he stop with the rest of you last night?*

"He did, but he left before light. Same as we did, but he didn't pause to go a-Maying." Gilles suddenly laughed at himself and shrugged apologetically against the burden blooming on his shoulders. It did seem frivolous, all at once. Even for a witch. Orléans, after all, was still under siege not two leagues away.

It is never wrong to take time to observe such old ways, Yann told him.

Gilles shrugged again but kept his attention on business instead of play. "The Bastard left with his men. For Orléans. To skirt the English and prepare the way for the entry of La Pucelle."

The owl nodded into the white beard of feathers on his chest. *Good. I'll find him there.*

"But what do you need the Bastard for? He's no initiate. If it's something to help La Pucelle, let me."

The Bastard is the closest who can serve this turn. Charles is with me.

"Good. You managed. Where?"

I'd rather not show you. Not yet.

Gilles saw nothing on the branch beside the owl. Was the Dauphin invisible?

I have his spirit, Yann's voice went on. *But not his blood. And, as surely you must realize, the blood is the most important part of this member, of all the coven.*

"Of course."

I couldn't bring the blood. Only the spirit. So we need the Bastard.

"Royal blood."

He's Orléans' son. The one closest to us. And the duc d'Orléans is grandson to a King.

"But he's a bastard."

You know the Craft doesn't care. As long as the God and the Goddess were there at his begetting.

Gilles pulled his gaze from the wonder of an owl sending him messages in Yann's voice to watch the group of witches. Roger, he saw, had fallen into step beside the swinging, budding hips of La Pucelle. They were laughing together. A weight on Gilles' heart thrummed in his ears so he didn't hear Yann at all for a moment.

Will you get it for me, Gilles? the owl-priest was saying when his attention returned to him. *It's very important.*

"Get what?"

Some beast for me to send Charles' spirit into for the convocation. And something that can take the blood.

"What? Like a toad?"

Gilles heard a little squeak of protest. It sounded like—it sounded like a flea.

Try for something with a little more dignity, Yann said.

"A horse?"

The flea-squeak seemed to like this better, but the owl twisted its head side to side in a wise negative.

Too big. What I have of the spirit would be lost in a horse. The blood as well.

"So, what? A rat? A rabbit? Tell me."

You'll think of it, Yann assured him over the not-so-certain flea. *I've got to take His Majesty to drink his illegitimate kinsman's blood and come back to my own body again. Before my strength gives out.*

The owl spread its wings and lifted up. It flew low for a while, just over the sun-touched crowns of the trees. The coven on the path, like blooming trees themselves, looked up. At once, they understood and stopped in their tracks at the sheer wonder of it: their high priest and their King, flying over them on great, shadow wings.

Chapter Nineteen

Wild-Carrot Bloom

In the morning, when they'd first returned from the woods, the rising sun had gently kissed the grasses, knee high in places, with a simple sort of innocence. Now, the passion of both sun and earth, answering beneath him, had grown hotter. Wild-carrot bloom chemised the green velvet of the meadow stretching behind Reuilly Castle. Hearts-ease and little daisies laced and embellished it underneath.

Gilles de Rais stood on the verge of the graveled road that skirted the place. Already it felt sacred, though the coven had done no more than choose it and, with guy ropes, carefully erect the Maypole in its center.

This was the place. Here, today, he would present La Pucelle with the ring he'd carried so carefully wrapped in a square of silk in his wallet all the way from Tours. The goldsmith had set the ruby in a great swirl of glittering leaves and flowers, beautiful and heavy and very, very costly. But what mattered the cost? The ring from one related to Du Guesclin to pass on to La Pucelle today. It was perfect. Perfect enough to be magic.

A trio of boys from the castle were swinging by a loose guy rope, spinning around on it from one low hummock to another in the meadow. At any other time, Gilles would have had something else on his mind as he watched them. But now, even in their rowdy play, he felt holiness, an awe of the power of this ancient, joyful rite.

"It looks good. Surely, it looks good." Gilles discovered Gui de Cailly, commander of Reuilly, standing at his elbow, looking in the same direction.

"What a holy thing to have happen in our midst," Cailly continued. "Before I ever saw the girl, the Voices came to me."

"Voices? What Voices?" Gilles felt the fire of jealousy brand his cheeks.

"Saints. Catherine, Marguérite and Michel came to me yesterday. 'Go to the woods,' they told me. 'Go to the woods and cut a Maypole.'"

"Catherine, Marguérite and Michel?"

Gilles remembered the visions dancing on the wall in Jehanne's little cupboard of a room at Poitiers. He hadn't known she'd shared the names with anyone else before this moment.

Somehow, now, putting the appellations of chipped plaster images from a hundred rundown chapels upon her Voices cheapened them. Certainly the notion that she would tell this pear-shaped, pear-complected individual—pear-scented, too, in a brown, overripe way—before she'd tell Gilles de Rais cut him to the quick.

"But of course," Cailly said. "'These saints came to me,' I told her, 'and said I must get you a tall, straight oak.'

"'That's the word of my Voices exactly,' she told me.

"Our Voices must be the same."

And Gilles understood, with a shiver upon the heat of his face, that she had given this man what he was capable of receiving. She had cooked the fruit, mashed it, and served it up in a tiny mouthful on the end of a spoon. Perhaps she had done the same for Gilles de Rais, lying on her bed in Poitiers.

"A tall, straight oak with mistletoe at the top, as is the custom," Cailly went on, oblivious. "'Custom be damned,' I said at first. "'This year our woods are crawling with *goddams*. I have a custom of wearing my skin that takes precedence over Maypoles.'

"But they would not leave me alone, these voices, promising me I could take a team of horses into the woods with no more than a couple men. I could hack away at a tree, have it come crashing down—and English ears would remain deaf to it all.

"I didn't really believe it. I couldn't believe it. But they wouldn't leave me alone, those Voices. So in the end, I took many more men than the job required and went.

"Just as they said, nothing happened. And they led me to the tree, almost as if there were no others in the woods. The task of felling, then hauling, it seemed child's play. Truly wonderful, isn't it? Isn't *she*? I should say, for I know it's all her doing. God working through her and the holy saints."

Gilles tried not to listen to the man's prattle. But he couldn't avoid asking one more time, "Saints. Catherine, Marguérite and Michel, you say?"

"But of course. Doesn't everyone who follows her hear the same? I just assumed."

Gilles nodded. The names, she'd let them stand just to throw the Christians off. Indeed, she'd all but told him that was so. And none of the other witches, to his knowledge, heard anything. Except maybe Yann during his spells. Their powers came in different ways, each to his own. Still, the notion that someone, another man, heard them, whatever their names, made Gilles clench his hands with suppressed rage.

"Here. Let me give you a hand, sire de Bricqueville!" Cailly dropped the subject, shouted and joined Roger in the meadow.

Roger had just arrived with an armful of hawthorn bloom and ribbons the women had fashioned. He had looked to Gilles for aid first, but when Gilles had only scowled and wouldn't budge, he was happy enough to accept Cailly's. The two men shooed the boys away: A Maypole was too serious a matter for mere children. Cailly and Roger loosened the guy ropes, and Roger shinnied up the pole to tie the crown sturdily to the top.

Behind him, Gilles heard the fortress walls ringing with women's laughter and encouragement of the feat. One laugh, one cry of delight he heard above all the rest. He turned to see her, saw instead how the keystone of the arch, every arrow slit and indentation of the crenelation up above now hung with thorn and flowers from the women's activity. No doubt they were trimming themselves in the same manner.

If a *goddam* scout but caught a glimpse of these walls, softened by flowers instead of stiffened by the glint of helmets and lance points, they'd be taken in a minute. Gilles' hand went to his hip at the very thought. But he'd left his weapon indoors when he'd changed, with the greatest care, to this festive garb, this poppy red and deeply worked damask.

He shifted his shoulders into the trim cut of the garment. He had no faith that English eyes would be blinded. He kicked at the gravel with the soft leather of his best boots. What mattered how he stood out if the sound of divine Voices were denied to him? If he could not tell which window her laughter came from now?

Finally, all stood in readiness. A stern, martial plunk of harp strings at the fortress door called attention. The witches, in twos and threes, marched out of the keep and into the open meadow.

Gwencalon the Bard, his harp studded with flowers and streaming with ribbons for the occasion like any man's favorite mistress, led the way. Because his eyesight had gone to the same milky blindness as his father's before him, Gwencalon needed Tiphaine, the silent Tiphaine, at his left elbow, guiding his feet.

To the Bard's stately plunking, Bibu de Sillé, the great idiot God's son followed. He was partnered with a goat. The goat seemed a common enough buck. He was, in fact, the same shaggy, brown-and-black beast Gilles de Rais had rounded up following the owl-Yann's orders. But in the time since Gilles had dragged it to the room where his milk brother's tranced body lay, the baulking, butting creature had been transformed.

Hawthorn and ivy twined his horns. Rather than trying to eat such a crown, the goat waggled his beard sagely to one side then the other like a monarch receiving the adulation of his people. The bright ribbon he wore around his neck seemed more a gold chain of office than a lead. And if Bibu de Sillé at the other end of that lead didn't consider himself the one on a rein, he certainly felt the honor of his position.

For he was paired with the blood royal on this day. A flea's bite to the Bastard's unknowing neck, and the transfer of just so much of Charles' spirit into the goat had worked the magic, under Yann's twisted hand.

Behind the Dauphin and his honor guard came Yann himself, in his own body once more, pale though that body might still be. He wore horns for the occasion, too, a stag's antlers wreathed and tangled with blooms. His Pieronne accompanied him, of course, garbed as the Queen of the May.

Old Père Michel and Anne de Sillé came next, bearing the May wine they'd mulled between them. Her hair was still loosed from its usual severe wimple and lay across her shoulders like a cloak of fine grey bouclé, over a beautifully patterned cloak.

Then came Hamish Power and La Meffraye in equally festive raiment.

Once he saw what followed, however, Gilles had no eyes for them. La Pucelle, astride her white horse draped in floral bardings, rode out into the sunlight.

Roger came panting up from the Maypole then, caught Gilles' elbow and tried to drag him to join the procession abreast of him. But Gilles resisted him until she came alongside. He stepped in then, and caught the bridle to lead the horse, as a humble page might. Roger had no choice but to step around to the other flank.

So they walked out into the meadow where the brilliant sky made love to the springtime earth, their union marked by the beribboned pole. And so the humans processed around the place, every step merrier than the last.

Chapter Twenty

The Binding of the Pole

Tiphaine dumbly helped Gwencalon to the hummock from which the castle boys had earlier been swinging. She did not leave him seated there at once, but gave him a touch which caused him to plunk his strings for attention. The chatter and laughter died in the sunny meadow. As if she could hear their stillness, perhaps through the ground under her bare feet, the witch of Mont-Saint-Michel began.

First she pulled something from the depths of her ceremonial robe's sleeve, which was long and flowing and blue-green, like the sea surrounding the rock of her power. The thing glinted in the sun like bits of sand suspended in the eddy of a wave.

A ring.

The gold and ruby in the wallet against Gilles' hip seemed to suddenly turn to dirty ice. He felt it through silk and leather.

A simple ring of white silver. That's all Tiphaine held.

He wasn't sure how she communicated, this woman of no speech and no sound. He saw her arms move like waves, and the expression of her open, lively face. But somehow she told the tale. How this ring was no ordinary ring. Once it had belonged to Du Guesclin, the Sword of the King, Gilles' ancestor, but Tiphaine's uncle. She had inherited it from him, and he from generations before, back to another Tiphaine who had received it from St. Gildas, a God, before she herself shed Her blood for the Land.

It has the power, Tiphaine said, in her silent way, *to turn black when the wearer is in danger.*

Tiphaine of the Mount had kept it always, knowing that La Pucelle would come. Her uncle, the dead hero, had bequeathed it to the one who would rise up and save France in his stead.

All these years she'd kept it, Tiphaine of the Mount-Saint-Michel. She'd kept it in the underground cavern on her Mount, imbuing it with power, soaking it in the juice of potent herbs, pulling down the strength of her beloved stars to the plain silver.

Then Tiphaine turned a waving hand palm side to the sky and gestured, pulling La Pucelle to her. The girl rose from her seat on the sward and went to the hummock.

And now, it is my pleasure to give my uncle Du Guesclin's ring to its rightful owner, the girl for whom generations without number have waited. May she have his strength, his cunning in battle, but her own magic, her own victory.

The witch said no word, but her meaning could not have been plainer. La Pucelle held out her hand, the one opposite to where she wore the other bit of cheap metal—from her parents, she said. Tiphaine slipped the ring on the finger and the coven cheered.

Only Gilles de Rais felt as if a trickle of melted, dirty ice were running down his leg from his wallet.

Over the cheers, Gwencalon struck a cascade of new, triumphant chords. Tiphaine and La Pucelle left him on his hummock, going arm in arm to sit among the rest of the coven again.

The bard set the pace for the festivities. He took a chord from the cuckoo strumming the psaltery of the nearby stand of trees. He divided the group and led them in a round of the season, in some miraculous way making division an instrument of binding the group closer than ever together.

An ancient carol of simple tune and words, it multiplied in richness when the three parts were sung. The way the music ran, there was always one voice ringing out a simple, clear "*cuckoo*" at the end of each line, echoing the real bird in his invisible woodland haunt, then echoed by a third human voice.

"Cuckoo."

"Cuckoo."

"Cuckoo."

Gilles found himself losing his bitterness. Instead, he was enchanted. Sometimes the bird echoed over here, sometimes there. By the power of his harp and his song, blind Gwencalon had conjured human beings into a forest of rills and whispers, complete with cuckoo call. Gilles was not alone in his enchantment. For the longest time no one cared to let the carol drop, and round and round it went.

"Cuckoo."

"Cuckoo."

"Cuckoo."

Gilles sat in the grass with the others and let the song spin. The bees about the daisies and heartsease hummed along deep in their little throats. And always, always he was most conscious that near him, having let her horse wander off to graze, sat La Pucelle. Her strong, sweet voice, he thought, was echo to his own, what his voice would be if the air caught it and played with it. The sight of her was his own image, reflected in a forest pool.

The May wine went around, and that added its own part to the spell. Floating with the sweet woodruff and wild strawberries they'd plucked at dawn, it smelled and tasted of the dark power of Mother Earth.

Taking this into him, sharing the cup with them all, with *her*, Gilles knew what he sometimes forgot. He knew that by food and drink, breath and pulse, sleeping and waking, birthing and dying, hating and loving—all were, in the end, one. Within the Mother, it was so.

The notion burned him, filled him.

And then they began to dance.

The folk of the fortress had drawn close and joined in the singing. Now they drew back, still using Gwencalon's music and some of their own for dance rounds they made themselves.

The binding of the pole they left to the coven's magic.

To Gwencalon's grand beginning chords, Gilles de Rais and the rest sorted their ribbons from where they hung limp about the pole. They drew back, their stately steps making a red and blue flower bloom in the midst of the love-soaked meadow.

Gilles selected a red ribbon. He'd been watching La Pucelle so closely that, when she picked a blue ribbon, he naturally took its opposite.

Gwencalon played the signal. The women with their red ribbons turned widdershins, the men turned to move like the sun over the spread of meadow.

The stretch of his arm away from their circle, Gilles spied Anne de Sillé's brilliantly patterned cloak, which she'd cast off as the heat of the day rose. He snatched it up as they marked time for a moment, and knotted it around his waist like a skirt. When the music came for each woman to honor the God in the people dancing opposite her, he curtsied as deeply as he could to the divine in La Pucelle. Then, not quite as low, to Roger on the other side. Both greeted the Goddess in him in return, smiling not in derision, but with the pleasure such worship always brings.

Then, in time to the music, he began to dance around the ring to his right, meeting only men as he went. The steps were easy; even old Père Michel had no trouble keeping up. One without a sense of the magic involved might have called them childish, just as the round had been.

Three steps in, Gilles crouched under the approaching ring's blue ribbons. Three steps out, arms high, to give them a loop to pass under.

The long fringe on his cloak-skirt slapped at his boots with every step, first the left and then the right.

Now and again, Gwencalon played the descending trill that meant "reverse". Men must know the counter-circle, the dark and private way. And women need to know the bursting glory of daylight.

Sometimes their movements unwound the pole, spinning dancers out over the daisies further into the meadow. Sometimes their ribbons pulled tighter. The over-under, over-under pattern changed. What had been under and hidden now burst forth, now ran deep below again, twisted in ways their feet, moving here and there, could never guess.

But a record of their movement remained, banded to the pole. Whereas in life a man could ignore the intertwining movement of his mother, wife, daughters, or even the feminine of his own soul, his shadow, here he could not. Especially not while he himself played the woman.

To La Pucelle's man.

All these patterns, these ins and outs, Gwencalon Saw with his sightless eyes, patterned them as if the model spread before him in a grand vision. He directed the dancers flawlessly as if he were some God: His own male playing upon the harp, his beloved mistress.

In and out, in and out, under, over, Gilles went. With the Bard's rhythm, with the steps, his pulse quickened. In, out. They drew closer to the climax, could feel it, then drew back. Closer again— Ah, sweet tantalizing. And so his heart beat. And so, it seemed, did all the world.

A pair of white moths fluttered up around them, set to the same rhythm, yet oblivious in their own ecstasy. The male lark spiraled up after his mate on rising notes that seemed to come from the harp's same throat. The breeze blew, the bees hummed, the sun struck, all to one selfsame time, to one purpose, in one great round.

And when the music ended, leaving the air still throbbing for joy, the tail end of the red ribbon slipped from Gilles' sweating palm, caught up tight against the pole, its wood entirely wound.

Like swaddling bands. Like a shroud. The coming, the going. The mortal heaved up to the skies. The route by which the Gods descend.

In stiff blue, engorged with red, their work thrust there to the delight of Mother Earth so She sang, deep throated and panting all around them.

There was but one more thing human beings could do to better emulate the world, to add their own passion and waves of energy to all the springtime world.

Gwencalon stopped the music on the thought. Gilles saw how, on the same thought, Yann's hand slid from overlaying Pieronne's red ribbon with his own blue one to grasping her wrist. In one quick movement—who would believe it, without magic's strength?—the little priest caught the Queen of May up into his arms and headed towards the closest brake. They didn't even look where they were going, their faces lost in one another, in one long, writhing, wet kiss.

Anne de Sillé and old Michel lingered long enough to bind the dance's magic to the pole with a knot and a little spell at the bottom. But after that, they were no slower than the rest to split up into the couples as Gwencalon had left them, male facing female in the round.

The urge to join in the coupling was overwhelming, like ducks' mating by the streams.

Gilles shook his head, trying to clear it. He felt himself deserted, alone with the thing of ribbon-bound beauty that many hands had erected, hawthorn bloom frothing at its top. Alone, he nonetheless felt himself rigid with passion.

There were sounds, the distant revelry of the castle folk. Gwencalon turned back to his romance with his instrument, plucking out a tuneless sort of afterplay, the nonsense syllables of spent lovers. But for one who was alone, these were the sounds of a foreign tongue, leaving him lonely still.

The pole stood deserted, the stamped grass around it smelling bruised and sweet. Gilles ached in his loneliness. Even Roger was not ...

And then his eyes, as if they, too, were keen enough to see visions in this intense, altered state, glimpsed him just where the forest limned the field, a dark shadow against the low white hawthorn.

Him? Or was it her? At this distance, hazed with May wine and exertion, Gilles couldn't tell. But by the stance, a gesture, a wave in his direction, he knew his object.

Chapter Twenty-One

The Meadow Come to Life

He came upon her in a small, grass-lined clearing, their own private miniature of the greater meadow where communal magic had been drawn. Sun melted its way even here, seemed keener, hotter in contrast to cool, dark shade all around.

She stood turned away from him, her head bent over and her chin buried in the plain grey wool of her old doublet. Suddenly, in one quick movement, she yanked the garment up and over her head, in such haste that she didn't take time to fully loosen all of the lacing. As she did, her linen rucked up, showing him the neat, strong picket of her spine.

He stopped where he was, at the very edge of the clearing, and watched, hardly daring to breathe, as one does who comes upon the startling grace of a doe in the wood. Even if, presently, he reminds himself he is a hunter, and moves into that stance, always before, at first, there is a moment when the beauty knocks the wind from him. For that moment he forgets anything but that he is the lowest of petitioners before the God.

Ere remembrance and shame came, she sensed him. He could tell there was anticipation. Her shoulders raised and lowered a little faster with each breath.

She pulled the doublet sleeve off her left wrist and threw the garment carelessly against a nearby thorn. She turned, her great brown eyes liquid upon him, wild, but unafraid. Her shirt, loosed and open to the waist, released a scoop of breast to its intended shape.

He loosed his belt and slipped it to the ground. Only, as the wallet went with it, did he think to fish out the square of pink silk.

"Here," he said. "I had this made for you."

His gesture was dismissive, and he added words to suit: "I know it's nothing to compare to the ring of Du Guesclin, but it was made by one of his descendants."

It was made with love, he wanted to say. But he did not.

"Very nice," she said. "Thank you."

But she didn't put it on. She seemed to have other plans for it, for him. She swept the silk back over it and tucked it into her discarded doublet.

She was, after all, getting rid of clothes at the moment.

And that was what Gilles wanted. Wasn't it?

Could he do it? Would he, what all nature around him begged for?

"Ah, Gilles, I knew you'd come."

He was certain she said these words. Her Voices had told her and now they spoke to him as well. Or maybe she only thought them, and he, sensing the very pulse at her throat, only caught the thought from the air—finally—as a witch might do.

Thought or speech, it was to this that he replied. "How is it so, my lady, my love? Was it my face, then, that you saw within the forest pond at dawn? Did you find a black slug?"

She didn't answer, but reached out a hand for him and he went to her.

He didn't take the hand, however, but sank to his knees, almost without knowing it. He clasped her legs, aware of the seams of their hose running a little jagged beneath his stroking palms.

"'Twas shadow I saw. Nothing clear. Mere shadow." *But that, I know, is you, Gilles, dark lord of Rais.*

Again, he wasn't sure her lips moved. He heard it only, his face pressed against the spot, the center of her being and her power. He breathed upon it, breathed his own hot, stifled power. It seemed so tiny and hard, La Pucelle's sacred core. He loved it so, his own core ached. He worshiped it.

Shadow, that I must teach to follow me.

He felt her hand upon his hair, twining among the woodruff and ivy there, adding their fragrance to her own gentle sweetness. He lifted his head to that touch and found himself close, too close to the breast just within the shirt. He didn't kiss it. He didn't yet dare. But he breathed the heat of his breath like sunshine and he felt tears upon his cheeks, not as if he were crying, but as if the breath had come back to him and condensed there.

He waited. He didn't move. He wanted her to teach his ignorance, his woeful inadequacy.

Her breasts, both of them now, brushed against him. He felt her quick, strong hands unknotting the cloak from his waist. He heard and felt—for he found himself too lightheaded to trust his vision—her flip the garment out and spread it on the ground. She sat upon it, then reached for him, pulling him to her by one hand. With his other, he fumbled with the laces at his throat, suddenly as helpless as a child with such fastenings.

She pressed him back, onto the ground. Then she rolled and straddled him, helping to unloose the difficult knot. Presently, she pulled her fingers through the liberated cords, right to the end. Then she inclined over him again. He felt her lips on his eyes, his nose, the mark on the point of his chin.

I love you, Gilles.

Did she really say that? Or only think it?

And was this it, then? La Pucelle had prophesied, "I must shed my blood before Orléans." This is what she could have meant, even without knowing it. How wonderful that would be, such an easy, pleasurable shedding. He could certainly do it, he who'd never taken a virgin before, his wife used goods when she'd come to him. He, who'd often doubted his ability to do what other men did. He could just reach up and take her like that.

She felt the magic as well as he, he could tell by looking in her eyes. They were both bewitched. He could take her, even if she struggled. But she wouldn't struggle. She wanted him, as much as he wanted her. That was part of the magic, like their even match in the dust of the lists.

Although, oddly, it was as if he was the void to be filled, hers the wherewithal to fill it.

Even if, at the end, she shook off that afternoon's magic and tried to resist him, he could do it. As other men did, with force.

Then he knew that, by shedding her blood in this way, he would gain more than pleasure, more than unity with the fertility bursting through all the earth around them.

He would save her. From a worse wound. The blood would be his, in a way. And he would save her for himself.

"Cuckoo," cried from the wood, followed instantly by another in the other direction.

"Cuckoo."

And then he knew, much as his every fiber longed for her and she for him, that he could not give her this wound. At least—not now. Even the birds of this land awaited her—what she would do—what she must do—without him.

Without any man.

With all the magic of a coven in May focused in her, he, who had always had his every whim fulfilled, who had always had only the very best of anything, he could not keep this for himself.

He opened his eyes and saw her looking down at him. The light of the sky was brilliant behind her, almost blinding him.

"What is it, my shadow, my love?" she asked.

But she knew. He could tell by her tone. She had offered herself so that he would come to this realization by himself. He had thought to teach her—and she, again, was the teacher.

He had to look away, blotches of fire before his eyes.

He had to look elsewhere, anywhere but towards her. His glance was drawn to a heap of velvet green fabric lying there beside Madame Anne's spread cloak. La Pucelle must have dropped it even before her own grey doublet, before he entered the clearing. He hadn't noticed it sooner, having had eyes only for her and it being almost the color of the emerald sward.

"What's this?" he asked, reaching for it.

Still he felt the need to leave her thighs resting upon either side of his, their warm pressure like the healing heat of a mustard plaster. He could feel, within that pressure, a solid conviction of self replacing the need for union in her firm little body.

"A new doublet," she said, with pleasure.

Still on his back, he picked it up and shook it out, finding the shoulders and holding them apart. So it was.

"Very nice."

"Didn't you see the Bastard bring it? At the end of the dancing. In the meadow."

"I did not." My eyes too full of you, Gilles added to himself.

"Well, he did. He's here. He went to Orléans in the morning and now is back again."

"I see."

"I suppose he didn't want to interrupt our festivities here, so he came and went quietly."

"I suppose."

"The way's prepared," she said. "For me to enter Orléans after nightfall tonight." She tipped her head back and studied the sky. "We can leave anytime now, I guess."

"I guess."

Gilles fingered the green fabric and found his hand met by hers at the same task. Ah, she liked fine things as well as he did. Some day there would be time. There would be time to enjoy such things together.

"Where did the Bastard get it?" he asked.

"The people of Orléans sent it with him to me. Isn't it fine?"

"It is."

Where had they come up with such fabric, a city under siege? Some fine merchant's wife donating her best skirt, perhaps, and half a dozen needlewomen working through the night. All this when they'd heard La Pucelle was here, on their side of the Loire, but two hours away. The hem and false, hanging sleeves of the garment had been deeply dagged, like oak leaves, and there was a matching hat. All in green, the fairy's color.

No, he could not keep her from people who awaited her with such devotion, with such understanding of the source of her power.

Another—later—phase of that power might belong to him. But it couldn't be allowed to take from the people of Orléans—all the world—now.

He asked, "You came here to put it on, didn't you?" Not to make love to me.

She nodded.

"Please do." He allowed himself to draw a finger from her throat to the curve under one breast. "I'd like to see it on you."

He eased her off his lap and sat up. Gathering the garment in his hands, he helped her wriggle into it. I would like to do this forever, he thought. Not only dress her, but provide her, as the folk of Orléans had done, with the finest things to wear. Like the ruby ring.

"I should be finding Roger," he said.

To make love to him instead? It had been a long time. Not once since he'd first seen La Pucelle in the back of the smoky inn. Sometimes Roger would look at him with—with what? Reproach? Longing? No. It seemed, only pain.

But that's not what he told her now. "Our magic is east. Roger and I must hurry back to Blois and bring those troops you need here as soon as possible."

She nodded again. He pulled the shoulder seams straight and bent to lace the garment snugly up over the small sweet breasts. The seamstresses of Orléans had allowed more fabric here than was needed.

"But let me have a look at you before I go," he said. "The memory will speed my steps."

She turned for him, laughing in the bright sunlight. And she did look fine. She looked—like the meadow come to life before him.

"Just a minute." He pulled the lacing tighter and retied it. "There."

Lace her tight against any harm, against any other. If he had power for magic, he put it into the lacing now. Stiffened her for what she must do, a man's office. To thrust her way into a hopelessly besieged town, then—then thrust her way out again.

To him.

Like cuckoos, the love cries of other paired witches echoed one another through the woods. Like cuckoos. He felt the waves of their energy released to the land— released for the girl in dagged green to gather up and take with her. To enfold within her, like the strength of the land of France before men ever laid plow or ax to her lush greenness. Such was the power she brought and returned. Such was her magic.

He pressed energy of his own to her shoulders, kissed her lightly on the forehead. He picked up her old doublet, the ruby ring heavy like a stone among its folds. Then he took her hand and walked her out to the Bastard, the commander of Orléans.

St. Bernard of Clairvaux once told his fellow monks that not to have intercourse with a woman is more difficult than to raise the dead. Gilles had never found it so before. Now he felt himself as ready for sainthood as old Bernard.

He—and she—would have to wait. For another time.

Sainthood—sainthood was now.

Twenty-Second Antiphon

A Nimbus of Light Circling the Rooftops

As he turned his mount's head away from our party, south towards the Sologne, I reminded my milk brother, "Gilles, don't forget. You must wander off the road a little, find the thorn bush."

With all the squires and pages around us, I couldn't reiterate the precise instructions, that he must collect the royal bit of spirit I'd sent into the fledgling thrush.

But, with very human eyes, the eyes of Charles the Dauphin, the gyrfalcon jessed to Gilles' crupper, thanked me for saying as much as I did.

"Greet the fox for me, and thank him," I added.

Gilles laughed, as at fairy tales.

I hoped I didn't have to remind him not to hunt the fox who'd helped us so. I hoped he wouldn't want its tail as a good luck charm on the end of his banner. No, that was more an English practice.

Thus assured, I sent Charles the son of Charles the son of Charles back to his inert body in Blois in a falcon's form, perched on my milk brother's crupper. The Dauphin's recovery coinciding with the appearance of my lords of Rais and Bricqueville at Blois would help give them audience. So I hoped, and would bring their troops to Orléans all the faster, on the crest of our May Day magic.

In the meantime, the rest of my coven dispersed to the countryside, to live as they might until we circled again, for the next great thrust. For my part, I rode with the Bastard's small party, through the rather frayed English lines on this eastern side, escorting La Pucelle to the safety of the city walls.

The Bastard arranged a diversionary skirmish against the English fortress near which we had to pass, that of St. Loup. But more than that, I felt my coven's deep magic over the land, over the *goddams* as well. If they saw our passing, or were tempted by the Bastard's taunts beneath their walls, they did not leave the safety of their battlements.

"It was even so when we brought supplies in this morning," the Bastard said, trying to scratch an insect bite under his gorget.

As an owl, I'd watched Charles the flea creep under that ring of metal to get the tiny droplet of royal blood from his cousin that morning.

"God is surely with her." The Bastard failed in his attempt and resorted to contortions of shrugs instead.

"Surely it is so." I struggled to keep a sober look on my face and kept my hands tightly folded within the sleeves of my black robe, even as I guided my mule. My disguise was holding, then. He thought of me as an Augustinian and didn't hesitate to offer me his confession as we rode.

The denizens of Orléans were not bewitched, as the English seemed to be. Or, their enchantment was of the exact opposite nature.

"I planned for the cover of nightfall for her entry," the Bastard confessed. "Sensing their exuberance this morning when I first brought them word of her approach, I was not so much afraid of the English as of the Orléannais. After dark, at least some of them might have gone to bed."

In spite of the hour, however, he had greater difficulty keeping the townsfolk from rushing out to storm the English under this inspiration than he had keeping the English from pressing in. The entire populace had lined the streets since late afternoon, hanging their balconies and upper windows with tapestries and coverlets that now showed bright like flowers in the torchlight. They looked more like a town rejoicing than one in the seventh month of a siege.

But one could not forget the hostilities. Every once in a while, I had to urge my mount to avoid a great cannon stone that had embedded itself in the street, and no one had the strength to move. Usually the path of its flight could still be traced, through the roof and walls on the English-cannon side of the thoroughfare, deeper black against the sprinkling of stars.

The underlying desperation was part of the passion, of course. I saw it reflected in gaunt, dirty faces and hollow eyes. But this was the desperation of seven overcrowded, hungry, plague-ridden months that finally believes with all its soul it has seen its end.

Now, as she appeared at the narrow gate of Burgundy, they shouted with a single, joyful throat. They pressed so close about her, trying to touch her boot, her horse's tail, anything for a blessing. They lifted their babies high so the tiny eyes would not forget the greatest sight of their lives.

For a moment, I worried. The throng pressed me to the rear, away from her. It was just as it should be, of course. She was La Pucelle and I, only one who had prepared her way. But I worried for her. Gilles wasn't by, to be her guard. She might lose control of the horse in such a press. She, a simple peasant, might lose her own equilibrium.

But this was what she was born for. I'd forgotten. Between her legs, even a dumb beast forgot his skittish nature. And she, she rode holding her banner high but calmly, as if performing some ritual she had undertaken every day of her life.

Her armor caught the torchlight as if it glowed white hot from within. The horse beneath her, too, was an eery, ghostly white. The torches in every bracket roared as gusts caught them, flattened them parallel to the ground. The swallow tails of white silk stiffened and cracked behind her.

The wind we'd called was picking up, even within the sheltered city streets. Now would come the *quid* for our *quo,* the rebound of our magic, as every spell must have its price. Such a barter system teaches the witch caution, that curses, like chickens, come home to roost. The storm had held off while we danced and loved, greeting the May, but now it struck.

The first, fat drops fell, blood warm. A nimbus of light circled the rooftops overhead, flashed upon La Pucelle's upturned face.

But still, no one sought shelter.

"*Noël, Noël.*"

The people sang the ancient words they always use to announce the coming of one who is their salvation. Their voices drowned out the distant thunder.

Then every bell in Orléans took up the shout, the great exaltation that pulls ringers up off the ground with ungovernable exhilaration. The great chimes of the Cathedral of the Holy Cross echoed those of St. Paterne, of St. Aignan. And even, far to the west, I recognized the voice of Our Lady of Recovery, where often our men had prayed upon reaching Orléans' quays with my merchant father's goods when I was a lad.

Another flash of light—and the belfries of heaven responded in kind.

Surely the *goddams* must hear this, if they hear nothing else. Surely they must wake from their bedrolls and listen in dark silence, shiver around their fires and wonder what this meant for them.

This new power loosed upon the Land.

She rode armed, though without a helmet so all Orléans could see her: the wonder of a girl's face beneath a soldier's cut of hair. The wonder of solid steel formed into a white cuirass—with the softness of breasts beneath. All of this caught in the mystical glow of wind-whipped torchlight.

And she did not neglect to wear the gift of this people, her green velvet doublet, slung over her armor like a cape of leaves. So she brought May to them, this shut-away folk. All the power of the dance, of love, of water running to the sea, of sun moving on a blooming meadow, she brought within their narrow walls.

"*Noël, Noël.*"

I sang it myself. I had no choice, and didn't care when, for long stretches of time, I lost sight of her as I worked my weary, outshone mule through the press. She didn't need me, my simple Master's protection.

A strong gust blew the breath back down my throat. Then I did catch a glimpse of her. The same wind flailed her banner. That silk so carefully worked by Hamish Power whipped into the streaming roar of the torch swung by some too-delighted admirer. The fire caught.

Still I could find no breath. Would this be the end? Would all the magic go up in smoke like this? In some degrading accident? Like some housewife shrieking and stomping on a dish rag that has caught upon the cinders?

How could I have doubted? La Pucelle reached up, no rush, no panic, as if she'd been expecting such a thing all along. With one quick squeeze of her gauntleted hand, she put the fire out. There was no more than a shadow of damage.

Just so may any witch extinguish her candles when her spell is done, the power enticed and complete. Now she steps out of the circle she has drawn—and waits for the magic to answer her call.

Chapter Twenty-Two

Battling Wings Against a Cross

"What's toward?" Gilles de Rais shouted to the squire who caught his horse's head. The courtyard of Blois Castle milled with grim-faced courtiers and hangers-on.

"It's monseigneur le Dauphin, my lord," replied the man, who had grey showing in the four days' growth of beard on his chins—all three of them. The time for such a fellow to make knight had come and gone. "God save us, they fear for his life."

Well, Yann had made a blatant mess of things again, hadn't he? Gilles shot that thought to Roger before he left his companion to his own devices and swung out of the saddle.

"I must to the Dauphin, at once," Gilles said.

"They're only letting physicians and priests near him at the moment, my lord," the squire warned.

"They say—" he added, and his voice dropped with fear, "—they say he's bewitched." The squire murmured and crossed himself. "Even as his father was."

Yes, what would become of France's cause without even the poor figure of Charles to rally 'round? His heir was a sickly, six-year-old boy. England's Henry VI was a better candidate. The thought spurred Gilles to even faster action.

"They will let me near," Gilles said. Was it magic that made him so sure?

"My lord?"

"What is it, man?"

Gilles moved quickly to untie the leather jesses that had kept the gyrfalcon on the crupper through the long ride. The neat little rufter trimmed with a spray of dove feathers, which he'd borrowed from Gui de Cailly in Reuilly, still hooded the bird. Gilles ignored the squire's growing unease at his elbow.

"You don't mean to take your hawk with you, my lord? Into monseigneur's sick room? Let me take the bird to the mews for you, my lord."

Gilles elbowed the fellow aside and thrust his gauntleted left hand at the loosed and skittering talons of the gyrfalcon.

"Come, Your Highness," he urged—the bird, not the man. He took the raptor's weight on his wrist. Through thick leather, the grip of its talons was fiercer than the usual clutch of a hunting bird.

Gilles felt the magic in it. And the urgency.

"My lord has a gyrfalcon? The bird reserved by law to the King? And calls him 'Your Highness' after the King, no less?"

Gilles heard no more of the squire's muttering as he strode across the yard and took the low flight of stairs to the Dauphin's ground floor chamber two at a time.

Nobody stopped him. That was magic.

Through a choking cloud of incense, Gilles saw first the concerned faces of his cousin La Trémoïlle and a number of other courtiers. He saw Alençon and all the captains who'd have to be convinced to lead their men back to Orléans. But Gilles would worry about them later.

Now his whole concern was also where the courtiers' lay, in the bed with the thin, skinned-rabbit figure, the hull of Charles the Dauphin. A slow, gasping rise and fall of the coverlet betrayed the fact that the body still lived. There was, besides, an occasional murmur from the thin, parched lips, such things as a mind less than half present might say.

As he stood a moment on the threshold to catch his breath, Gilles heard the words "woods" and "witches". What else might Charles have said, things even more incriminating? Well, there was no time to think of what might already have been said, only to stop him from saying more.

For, closest to the bed, stood a priest in surplice and violet stole with the full panoply of water, oil and salt. His censor was the source of all the stifling smoke, his tongue, the droning chant. The man also held a handful of dead man's bones—some saint's relics, no doubt, but dead man's bones nonetheless—that moved towards the prostrate prince's pale face.

Gilles remembered Père de Boszac who'd tried to exorcise Yann when they were boys. Gilles knew that if their old tutor had succeeded, it would have left his milk brother a lighter hull than Charles was now.

Gilles also remembered the demons their old priest had been unable to get rid of except by throwing a rope over the rafters of the chapel in their home at Blaison and hanging himself there. Gilles at eleven years old had been the first to come upon the body. Something about this present priest moving through incense made him remember. He remembered how he'd taken a switch and thrashed Père de Boszac as he hung there in the red chapel glow. Even as the willow wand had cracked in his hand, the life had still twitched in the old priest's limbs and his throat still gurgled for air.

All of this served little but to help Gilles sense that Charles' spirit had nowhere near the tenacity Yann's had. Especially divided as it now was between falcon and man, it must wither in the face of a similar exorcist's assault. The priest was doing everything by the book, all the right things to cut the Dauphin off from the shadow that haunted him. In this case, as in Yann's, such actions would sever Charles from life completely.

This was not the sort of thing Gilles usually sensed. He left such things to Yann. He liked to leave such things to Yann.

But "this time, the task is up to you," his milk brother had told him as he and Roger had set off a day and a half before. "Once you pick up the bit left in the fledgling thrush, the Dauphin's disembodied soul will be strong enough to know its own mind."

The thrush had been easy enough to find. And, as Yann said, there was a fox keeping watch at the foot of the tree. But that was the point. Animals understood such things better than men.

Yann had also said, "The portion of the Dauphin's soul lingering in his body yearns for the part you carry to him in the gyrfalcon. The two parts know, as an infant knows to suck, just how to remeld, once I have taught them to separate. You must only allow it to happen."

But part of this allowing, Gilles knew, in magic sufficient to the time, required stopping the priest before he touched the relics to the prince's sunken cheeks. The cleric must not be allowed to sever light from darkness in a sorry misinterpretation of what the Gods do when They create.

All this old wisdom he never would have trusted in himself came to Gilles in a flash. As if at the first intuition of prey, he slipped off the gyrfalcon's rufter and flung the bird's weight from his wrist into the censered air. The raptor rose with a jangle of pounce bells and a high, desperate cry.

Gilles caught but a flash of intelligence, sharp as hunger, in the bird's black eyes, a greedy stretch in its long wings. He saw him reach his pitch in the point of the room's arch, then tuck up his wings to stoop.

In this short a time, half a dozen weapons had flashed out of sheaths. Shouts of threat and simple horror flooded over the drone of chant. The bird was beyond human reach for the moment.

Gilles was not. Half a dozen weapons came for him. Cries of "Assassin! Help ho! Save the King," assaulted his ears.

Gilles dodged, going a way they didn't think of, not towards Charles, but towards the closest window where he threw open the latch. Give them air to breathe, if nothing else. Unblind their eyes of the incense smoke.

Then Gilles spun around, dagger drawn, to defend himself. Half a dozen weapons were trained on him, but one was not. This was the priest's golden cross staff. It was long enough, and heavy enough, that the fellow managed, by swinging it above his patient's head, to keep the swooping bird at bay.

The priest caught the falcon a glancing blow. The raptor screamed, then recovered himself with a great batting of wings and jangling of bells against the far bed curtains. Another blow like that, slightly better aimed and landing him against anything harder than damask, would be deadly.

Not only would it kill the King's falcon. It would kill the King, or leave him, for the rest of his days, a soulless shell.

Gilles feinted right, towards his large and slow-moving cousin. He caught Alençon's quicker but still confused and tenuous blade a glancing parry. In these two moves, Gilles found himself beyond the ring of would-be captors. He slowed them with a lash of bed curtain as he flung himself at the exorcist. He knocked the priest to the ground. The staff skittered across the stone floor with a noise as violent as any battlefield.

The falcon stooped again, instantly, dropping onto Charles' limp, pale hair.

For a moment, everything in the room froze. Nobody dared to throw anything at the creature; they'd certainly hurt the prostrate Dauphin as well. In that moment, all men forgot Gilles and turned on the bird instead, to capture him, to pluck him bodily from their prince if need be.

But the deed was done. The gyrfalcon lifted off the man, only avian intelligence in his black-bead eyes now.

Flying straight and low, he beat his way between the dazzled men and towards the window Gilles had opened for him. His sharp, high cries were those of a soul released from purgatory—until he vanished into the air beyond.

Then the courtiers had no enemy left but Gilles.

Charles may live, he thought with a sinking heart, but you'll never get these men to come back to Orléans. You'll never make it there yourself, but rot the rest of your days in Blois' dungeon.

There was certainly much more purpose in Alençon's blade now, even in La Trémoïlle's. Just as Gilles turned his own dagger point towards the ground in surrender, a voice rose from the pillows of the bed.

"Leave him be, my lords," said the voice, weak but lucid, definitely that of Charles the Dauphin. "Monsieur de Rais is not to be blamed for the deeds of a dumb animal. It is a pity, only, that you have lost the creature, Sir Gilles, for I don't doubt you meant to revive me by the gift of such a fine King's bird."

"I did indeed, Your Highness." Gilles made his deepest bow, thereby covering his breath, still ragged with panting.

When he raised his head, he met Charles' eyes. For a moment, the gyrfalcon looked at him, even as the Dauphin daubed tentatively at the raking of bloody scratches the bird's talons had left across his narrow forehead. A doctor moved hastily to tend the wounds.

"And see," Charles said, "it has worked where nothing else, neither relics nor smoke, could do the same."

"God be praised," Gilles said with another bow, hoping his chin upon his linen shirt muffled the article "the" with which he certainly meant to begin the phrase.

Chapter Twenty-Three

A Hawk with His Wings Newly Clipped

With Charles' recovery and good words, it was a simple enough matter to get the captains to agree to bring their men back to Orléans.

Gilles hoped captains and courtiers alike would soon forget that there had been something bordering on sorcery in the business. With all that was required in organizing the troops to set out in the morning, there was a good chance that would be so.

Gilles hadn't counted on the one person in that room who had no pressing distraction—nothing except the thought of how his cure had been outdone by another. And if his cure was from heaven, whence came the other?

Gilles was tossing coins here and there at cartmen to be sure of his supplies. Roger was at his elbow, urging more caution, that there was not such a dearth as all that.

"You could bargain with them a little more," Bricqueville insisted, "and still have powder enough at Orléans for the culverins you had cast for me."

And, "No, they must be wooden shovels, Gilles. Don't pay a higher price for metal shovels. They're for sapping and digging trenches, which we, as the besieged, won't need much at Orléans. Take the cheaper wooden shovels for powder. Metal shovels used with ammunition can throw sparks and ignite the whole lot."

In the midst of all of this, the black-robed figure appeared at the edge of the chaos. Gilles was used to black-robed figures appearing in odd places. They were usually his own kind of priest, his milk brother Yann.

But this was not Yann. Yann was in Orléans. With La Pucelle. And the faster this work went, the faster he could rejoin them.

Even with this realization, he thought little of the matter for a while. There was a priest to shrive his men before they set out to war. That was well enough. At least one person around here did not have his cap in his hands, clamoring for new boots or for hay for his beasts—and therefore, more money.

It wasn't until the priest said, "Good evening, my lord of Rais," followed closely, when Gilles did not reply at once, by, "You lost a fine bird today," that Gilles remembered where he'd seen the man before.

The last posture he remembered the fellow in was sprawled on the floor by the Dauphin's bed. Gilles himself had pushed him away. The cleric's habit had then been above his knobby knees, his cross skittered across the floor. Who had helped this man to his feet? Gilles couldn't remember. Perhaps, in the rejoicing of the moment, to have the Dauphin restored to them, no one had.

Roger gave Gilles a look and, with a sigh, Gilles left his friend to it. He stepped a little aside, towards the dark figure. "Good evening, Father ... er?"

"Malestroit," the priest said.

An evil-sounding name. But, Gilles supposed, the man couldn't help it.

"Think nothing of the gyrfalcon," Gilles said as lightly as he could manage. "He was a haggard, full grown when I took him from the wild. Such birds may be impressive to the eye, but they are always more difficult to train than those bred in captivity. One must expect to lose them."

"Yes. And he was a male, after all, wasn't he? Smaller and less fierce than the females, whom God made to defend the nest and feed the young."

"You are a hawking man, then, Father ... ?"

"Malestroit."

How could he forget a name like that?

"Yes," the priest went on. "I do wear a neat little sparrowhawk on my wrist from time to time."

"Appropriate to your station."

"Yes. But I must say I've often wanted just to look at the royal bird, the gyrfalcon, reserved for royalty."

"Then, for your sake, I am sorry my bird got away."

"Odd that you should have captured such a rare specimen yourself, sire de Rais."

"Just luck."

"And that you should bring it into the room just when His Majesty's life was despaired of. And that such a thing should serve as cure. That seems more than mere luck. It seems closer to magic."

The man's dark eyes grew keener as he said the word. Gilles looked away from them.

"Yes, well," he said, "as you see, I am rather busy at the moment. We march tomorrow, as you may have heard, and I did just finish a hard ride myself this morning, so you'll excuse me—"

"Sire de Rais." Something in the man's voice wouldn't let Gilles complete his turn. "I bring you greetings from your lady wife," Malestroit said.

Ah, that was where he knew the man from, before today. Suddenly the voice, trying so very hard to suppress the Breton mist in it, and the features riveted Gilles' mind to the last place on earth he liked to be: his own lands with his own lady wife. Gilles realized he'd sometimes seen Malestroit among the comte de Richemont's most pious hangers-on. In Catherine's suite, too?

More disturbing than that this man was working at Catherine's bidding, however, was the thought that the hawk nose and glittering black eyes were done without benefit of magic. Gilles shifted his boots uneasily on the unseen gravel at the edge of the riot of torches and rushing men before Blois' gates. It is one thing to be acquisitive for the powers of the Earth, with Her shadow behind you. It is quite another to take on animal features, to be acquisitive, only for oneself.

Gilles asked, "And your connection—?"

"I have the honor to confess your lady, my lord."

Well, that must be a job that required a man to keep a stack of muckendars about, those squares of dainty linen with which fashionable ladies liked to wipe their noses when they wept. More power to him. As for Gilles, he forced himself to say, "Please return the greeting to my lady. And beg her prayers to go with me on this campaign."

Probably, if she did pray for him, it was that he might step in the way of a cannonball. He prayed for the same himself, sometimes. At least he had. Before La Pucelle.

"Your lady is in deep penance at the moment for her sin—"

"Sir," Gilles broke in. "I would not have you break the seal of your confessional."

"My lord, this sin, I'm afraid, concerns you as well."

Gilles shot a glance towards Roger, still busy with his guns and the powder. They hadn't been together—well, since La Pucelle had arrived. He felt wonderfully free of sin in the face of this cleric as a result.

Gilles thought of Yann, of what Yann might think of all of this, and said, "I have my own confessor, thank you."

"Perhaps this is a sin of which you are not yet aware. Or not yet aware of its extent."

"Listen, my man. I have sins enough of which I'm conscious. I don't need to go begging for more."

But Gilles found that the man had backed him to the edge of a bluff. They were at the end of the archbishop's gardens, where the high ground fell away as if making a hollow to protect the cathedral and the houses below. It was growing dark. Gilles could hardly see the pale plaster facades and the blue slate roofs of Blois any more. But there were plenty of torches flaring, as the townsfolk took their opportunities to profit from the army's presence just one more day.

"I am not unfamiliar with human frailty." Malestroit was right at his elbow. Gilles would have backed further if there'd been something besides air to step onto.

"I am a man myself," Malestroit pursued.

Gilles narrowed his eyes at this statement. For the first time in the eight years of their marriage, he wondered what Catherine did with all the space he gave her. Did she take lovers? Could she love—a priest, say?

But there'd been no children, even when she'd wanted them. She'd said she wouldn't cuckold him, even when he told her to. Too damned pious.

That was a sort of unfaithfulness. Torment, anyway. To him.

Gilles didn't feel jealousy as these thoughts niggled him. Not jealousy, exactly. Curiosity, yes. Suddenly, for the first time, he was, just a little, curious about that woman he'd married by force.

"And Lent ..." The priest was babbling on. "Six weeks is a long time for a man—a man in the world, of course I mean, not one dedicated as myself—"

"Get to the point."

"The point is, you may enjoy your connubial bed during the weeks of abstinence, confessing your frailty afterwards or not, as your conscience before God leads you."

Gilles found himself beginning to chuckle. He tried to stifle it, but that made it worse, tickling him deep under his breastbone. It was "enjoy" he found amusing. Linked so closely to "connubial".

Malestroit found nothing amusing. "But when there is a child, that is a very different, a much more public matter."

The chuckle strangled in Gilles' throat. "Child? Did you say 'child'?"

"I did indeed, my lord." Now, finally, Malestroit was smiling. Just a little. "By the Grace of God and by your sin, your lady is at last carrying an heir. She confessed your—your Lenten indulgence, shall we say?—to me as soon as she returned from visiting you at Poitiers. Then, when it became clear that the sin would bear fruit—

"I mean to say, much as the event is desired, still, any man will be able to count back and see just when that child was conceived. 'Expensive children,' I've heard the common folk call these, born as they are during the harvest days when even women's hands are needed in the fields. Then, on top of losing the help of their womenfolk, a priest must, in conscience, charge them at least a pound of wax. Just so no one thinks it's a trivial matter to forget the Passion of Our Lord Jesus and take such pleasure in such a somber season—You understand me?"

Gilles wasn't chuckling now. He was laughing right out loud. Even through the linen padding of his gipon, the flesh of his belly chafed against the heavy plates of his brigandine until it hurt.

"My lord?" Malestroit asked.

When he found breath, all Gilles could say was, "Oh, blessed, blessed girl."

"Yes, well, your wife is deeply concerned about this unseasonable conception."

Gilles didn't mean Catherine was blessed, of course. He meant La Pucelle. He didn't bother to enlighten Malestroit, however, but let him continue.

"Madame seems to think that you, my lord, were born under a curse. Or your parents died under one. Or both, I'm not quite clear. Anyway, she fears, especially because of the time of its conception, that the curse may go on into this child. Well, women in such a condition are prone to fanciful thoughts. But she would rest easier knowing you were doing penance for your part in this sin as well as she."

"Here, here, what do you want?" Gilles gasped out the words as his laughter finally subsided. He'd been lavishing money on carters, why not on Père Malestroit besides?

"What would you take as the ransom of my child's soul from the Rais curse?" he demanded. "One hundred *écus*?"

The black eyes in front of him opened wide and lost much of their keenness. "That's very generous, my lord."

"Here, take one hundred twenty. That's what I have on me. A little extra to buy wax for candles, if that's how the peasantry salves its soul."

Malestroit was simply gasping, like a fish now rather than a hawk. His palm was not enough to take it all. He had to open up his skirt and catch it in there. It delighted Gilles, to give more in penance than this man could take.

"My sin's forgotten?"

"Yes, my lord."

"And the gyrfalcon's, too?"

The answer did not come quite so readily this time, and a keenness returned to Malestroit's eyes. But he said, "Go, my son, and sin no more."

Malestroit was the one who went first, catching his skirts up before him as he ran off with quick, shuffling steps. Like a hawk with his wings newly clipped.

Gilles stood on, watching the dark come over the slow-flowing Loire that only now and then winked back light from a bustling torch. In that direction, she lay. Just two days' march, down the bluff and that way.

And if she could work such miracles upon the sterility of the Rais line, what might she not do for poor, abused France?

It was La Pucelle, of course, that he meant. It mattered not at all whose body he'd gone to in that dark night, whose body, indeed, served as the vessel, as priests like to say in their circumventing way.

A great tenderness welled up from his belly and caught him by the throat at the thought of it.

A child. His child.

His child. And La Pucelle's. As dear to him as all of the new France they would make.

Together.

Chapter Twenty-Four

Goddams Without, La Pucelle Within

Having crossed the Loire at the bridge of Blois, the men-at-arms advanced on the northern, the English side of the river. Halfway to his besieged city, the Bastard of Orléans and an escort of some few of his men met them.

Gilles' first reaction was a sickness in his stomach.

"Where is she?" he demanded. Rather than send a herald, he'd left the vanguard and rode up to the man at a head-long gallop. "You've left her there alone? Don't tell me the city's fallen. Don't tell me she's ... "

His lips couldn't form the word, but for one horrible instant he thought it.

Dead.

"Don't worry." The Bastard laughed out loud in such a fashion that Gilles turned and slowed his horse to fall in beside the commander.

Gilles wouldn't concede to gallop all the way to Orléans without at least first stopping to hear the tale from a face with a grin like that.

"No *goddam's* going to get into that city while I'm gone," the Bastard proceeded. "Not while *she's* there. *She* threw *me* out."

"Did she?"

Gilles found himself already relaxing towards the man's laughter, though he was far from understanding the whole of it. He'd always liked the comte de Dunois, the blatant claim to that name "Bastard" that got men to do whatever he asked. The blocky, granite face seemed battle-worn today, streaked with grime, a bloody cut on his chin to go with the foot he still wore bandaged from the arrow taken at the Battle of the Herrings. The man, too, kept plucking at a rend in what must once have been a new surcoat. He said nothing of it, however, and was, after all, a man who had been commanding a besieged city for as long as a woman carries a child.

"La Pucelle keeps knocking against our walls like a trapped pigeon," the Bastard explained. "'There are *goddams,*' she says. 'I can see them. Why can't we go out after them?'"

Gilles could tell those were her very words. He glowed to hear them, even on this great man's tongue.

"That's not the worst of it," the Bastard went on. "The whole city is knocking at the walls with her. Old clerics with their penknives, housewives with their kettles, little boys with slingshots. 'Let us at them. Let us at them. La Pucelle will lead us to victory.' It was all I could do to keep them from doing just that—and dying by their thousands, you can imagine."

"Yes," Gilles agreed, but more to fodder the tale along.

"'We can only hold the walls,' I try to explain to them. 'We can't sortie with so few men.'

"'First you let the men march back to Blois,' she retorts, 'and then you tell me we haven't got enough men.'"

"I must agree with her logic." Gilles adjusted the reins to keep his horse stepping parallel with the Bastard's big bay, and grinned.

"I got her to promise not to try to fight until your return."

"Ah," said Gilles. He liked the connection, although he was certain the Bastard didn't include just him in the word *votre.*

"And she got the people to keep quiet, too. But, last night, I made the mistake of holding a meeting with my captains."

"What's wrong with that?"

"I—I didn't bother to tell her of it."

"Ah." Gilles saw what was coming—and smiled.

"How she found out, I don't know—unless it was that priest of hers. Such a busybody. He knows anything that goes on.

Find out she did, at any rate, and I got such a dressing down—'My Counsel is surer than yours' and so on. Finally I had to confess what we'd been discussing."

"Which was?"

"The news we'd received that Sir John Fastolf—probably hearing of your recent relief of our fair town—has decided to come to relieve his Englishmen here."

"Ah."

"He set off from Paris, so we hear, with a huge host. It won't take him long to get here. I read it in your face, Rais. You've heard the same thing."

"It confirms the reports we got in Blois, yes. And why, at the last minute, my difficult lord cousin let us have only the men you see here. La Trémoïlle will keep the Dauphin to work as his puppet, whatever becomes of Orléans."

The Bastard grumbled, something incoherently violent, and stared straight ahead, between his horse's ears. A scowl puckered the usual straight line of his blocky brows.

"What did *she* say when you told her the news?" Gilles couldn't leave him alone with his worries.

"'John Fastolf?' she says. 'This is the man who defeated us so badly on the Day of the Herrings at Rouvray? The name French *mamans* use to make their children behave? When "Sir John Talbot will come and eat you" wears out?'"

"I take it the name didn't work with this particular child?"

As he said it—gesturing ahead, towards the Maid and Orléans—Gilles wondered if his wife would use such tactics on their heir. He must take care she didn't. Perhaps he'd even have to spend more time at home. The idea didn't please him. But no, he told himself. Even if the fool woman tried such tactics, they would never work with his child. His child, who was also La Pucelle's.

For one exhilarating moment, he wanted to burst the news to the Bastard. But men on the march didn't discuss such things, so he kept it close, within his heart.

"That's just it," the Bastard replied, never having left the subject. "Instead of shaking in her boots at the name and quickly coming to task at the seriousness of the situation, the girl seemed highly delighted with everything I told her. 'Ah-ha, Fastolf,' she said, and clapped her hands. 'He, too, comes at my conjuring.

"'I tell you, Bastard,' she said, 'If you get sight of this Fastolf and fail to set me on him, I'll have your head.'"

"'Have your head'? Did she truly say that?"

The Bastard nodded grimly, shifting his square head within his gorget as if he could feel it detaching.

Gilles rejoiced at the sound of his own laughter as it pealed through the surrounding woods and back again. He reached a hand far out and plucked a branch of hawthorn from a tree as they passed and stuck it at a jaunty angle in the rim of his hat. The thought of that square, granite head on a pike—in La Pucelle's hand—delighted him. Not that he wanted the Bastard dead, just that he loved the girl's eye for the world and her biting humor.

When he looked back to his companion, he found the Bastard still grim. Jean of Orléans could not take any pleasure in his city's situation, John Talbot and now Sir John Fastolf without, the firebrand of La Pucelle within.

"Oh, come on, man," Gilles told him, reaching across the space between their two horses to clip him on the shoulder. "Buck up. It's a great yarn. 'I'll have your head,' she told you. How many other men are going to be able to say La Pucelle told them that—and then live to talk about it?"

The Bastard passed him a thin, granite smile.

"I promise you," Gilles went on. "The tale will improve with retelling. So, while you practice, the best thing to do is to reinforce your besieged city as best we can—and do everything possible before Fastolf gets here, too."

"Well, that's the next problem."

"What's that?

"These reinforcements you bring." The Bastard twisted back, hand on his horse's crupper, to look at the few score men they could see before the road bent behind them.

"Yes? Don't tell me you don't want them. After all my trouble?" Gilles jested. "Besides, just watch this."

He turned, too and, raising a black, fisted gauntlet in the air, shouted, "*Noël, Noël, La Pucelle*," to the men. The shout that rose, moving like a crashing wave through the ranks to the thousands they couldn't see, tingled Gilles' spine. On and on it came, forward, back then forward again, miraculously strong from throats parched with the pushed march.

"There! You see, my lord count?" Gilles smiled in triumph at his companion as the strains of *Veni Creator Spiritus* continued behind them. "All of France must rise at the girl's call."

To his surprise, the Bastard's face had grown rockier still. "Well, I wish you hadn't done that."

"Why ever not?"

"Morale or no morale, getting these into Orléans is not going to be easy. A little more stealth would not have gone amiss."

"You can't keep nearly three thousand men and a baggage train a secret," Gilles said in his own defense. "What? Does England's sleeping leopard wake?"

"After letting the Maid pass directly under its snoring nose, yes. I lost five men coming out to meet you, and we were few, light and well-horsed." The Bastard crossed himself.

That explained the battle grime Jean of Orléans wore. Gilles imitated the pious gesture as he exclaimed, "What? By that same eastern gate that was like a walk in the park when she and all those cattle entered?"

"The same as we've been doing since the *goddams* set the siege." The commander plucked at the hole in his surcoat again, and Gilles realized it must be a new hole, one made just that morning by an English longbowman. The breastplate underneath, all that had saved the Bastard's life, must sport a new dent.

Gripping his reins grimly, the commander went on: "Last fall, when I first saw what the English were about, I destroyed all Orléans' suburbs. And fine suburbs they were, too, many half-timbered houses, the finest in France. What wouldn't come down with crowbar and pick, we used some of our precious powder for, including, God forgive me, a few dozen churches."

Gilles remembered the wasteland he'd seen running up to Orléans walls as they'd passed along the eastern side to May Day. It seemed so long ago. "Not that I'm the one to shrive you, my lord, but I must say your efforts were admirably successful."

"More so on the east than on the north, south and west. On those three sides—and here's what I fear the good Lord won't forgive me—the *goddams* found enough rubble to dig in. On the east, however, nothing remained for them but the heap of stones of the former Augustinian friary of Saint Loup. A league or so upstream, from whence the brethren oversaw their farms, it was a daughter house to the much larger cloister just across the river from town. Too far away for cannon set there to reach our walls. The English didn't get around to fortifying and garrisoning it until mid-March."

"So you were able to supply your city all winter, as the Maid just did, from the east."

"More or less, yes," the Bastard replied. "And we might still be doing so until the last few days. Until *she* comes along and wakes the sleeping monster up. They were waiting for us this morning, patrols, thick as fleas on an old pit dog."

"On the east?"

The Bastard nodded and touched the spot in his surcoat again before he went on: "Just barely came through with our lives. These men you bring—we'd do better with them manning the walls, but that may not be possible."

"We can fight our way in."

"Not without such a loss of life that I fear must make this new-found morale fade like dew." The Bastard tossed his head back towards the columns marching in their dust.

Gilles doubted it, not with the Maid to fight towards. He did notice, however, that the strains of the hymn were fading out as the march and heat told on the men once more. "It is your siege, my lord."

"We may have to call a halt—not too much farther here—encamp and just do our best from the outside. On top of it, I left only La Hire in command inside."

"La Hire's no fool—"

Gilles stopped as a horse and rider flashed from the trees to their left on the path at the edge of sight in front of them. The figure vanished just as quickly on the other side, but there was time to see the blazon: Talbot's lean, grey hunting hound.

Flinging his arm in that direction, Gilles urged, "Roger, catch the damned spy."

Bricqueville didn't need telling, but had already set off with four or five others to ride after the man.

"If we catch him, we'll soon torture some news out of him." Gilles tried to comfort the commander, although already suspecting Roger's road-weary mount would be no match for the Englishman's, with such a head start on him.

"If Fastolf gets here with reinforcements from Paris before we get in, these men of yours will be surrounded, sire de Rais. It will be a siege within a siege. We'll have to fight back to back."

A wave of horror swept over the dark lord of Rais as the Bastard spelled the configuration out for him. Must they fight separated like this then? It wasn't Roger he thought of, nor the trouble he'd be in, but the girl. She on the inside of the city walls, he on the outside, a solid ring of *goddams* between them. It made him feel like riding onto the next English lance he found.

Roger and his men came riding back then, shaking their heads with disappointment. "Lost him."

Gilles tried to cheer them with a grin and a nod. "Never mind. You'll get a chance to throw cannonballs at the fellow and his friends in a bit."

But once Roger had fallen back in the column behind him and the Bastard, Gilles felt his face lose color again. The spy had seen them; he'd escaped. Talbot would certainly know of their presence by now. The Englishman would do everything in his power to see that the force outside did not join up with that inside Orléans' walls.

"Perhaps, with some sort of diversion from within Orléans—" Gilles knew he was fumbling and stopped before he made a complete fool of himself. Did he think he could send a witch's message inside the city walls to La Pucelle as Yann did?

They rode in silence around the next bend in the road that hawthorn pinched like the pink-stained bandages on the Bastard's foot. The commander daubed at the cut on his chin with one gauntleted finger and gazed at Gilles with hooded, rocky brows. Then the block of a head nodded.

"It might be possible," the Bastard of Orléans mused, "for someone to lead a company out the eastern, the Burgundian gate, and pin down the *goddams* at Saint Loup while we bring these men in. Another, simultaneous sortie should probably be prepared to hold them on the north, in the fortress of Saint Pouair. Sainte-Sévère might be the man for that. Or Graville."

Gilles liked the plan. What was more, La Pucelle would like it. He was so certain she would like it that she might have thought of it. He could easily believe she had sent the idea beyond the walls into their minds with the aid of her confessor Yann. Or, he liked to think, such communication was something they were capable of, just between the two of them.

"The only problem is—how to tell them?"

Gilles was so convinced there was magic behind the inspiration of this plan that it took him a moment to see the Bastard's point: how getting the message around *goddams* and inside city walls was a problem.

"Somebody would have to sneak in to give the orders past all these suddenly vigilant patrols." The Bastard continued to work out the plan in the common mortal fashion. "Someone of a station that will command the necessary respect. And I can't be that someone. I move neither quickly nor very silently on this bad foot."

Gilles met the bulging grey eyes. They knew what his reply would be before he gave it. "I'll go."

"You're a brave man, monsieur de Rais."

Gilles couldn't suppress a chuckle. It would take more bravery on his part to stay on this side of walls and *goddams,* away from La Pucelle, when there was fighting to be done.

"Let's set the time for tomorrow after dinner," the Bastard continued. "The action against Saint Loup is just a diversion, you understand, no more than a simple *vaillance d'armes.* Go out there, hurl a few threats and insults, maybe an arrow or two. Give the English something to think about besides these new troops."

"I understand."

"It will take some regrouping once we're inside before we have the strength to actually try to go against one of these bastilles the *goddams* have thrown up from our rubble."

"Certainly."

Then, as if he were indeed a magician who could read minds, the Bastard said: "What I mean to say is—you don't want that girl to slow you down."

"Oh—No, of course not."

"Perhaps when we have a massive, full-scale battle to be fought, perhaps then we may set her some place off to one side, out of harm's way, a sort of mascot or something."

"Yes," Gilles said.

The Bastard might not have a clear notion of just what La Pucelle was made of, but he was right. A *vaillance d'armes* could be more dangerous, certainly less dignified, than a real battle, with no clear outcome. Besides, hadn't she said that she must shed her blood before Orléans? That mustn't happen before any real fighting got done. It would be better not to tell the girl what was afoot. But surely this would be an action of which she would approve if she heard of it. If she didn't already know in that unearthly way of hers.

The Bastard, riding with his own thoughts during this time, had begun to chuckle.

"What?" Gilles asked.

"Just the word 'mascot'. You know where it comes from?"

"No."

"That word of the French provincial? It means a witch in some of the dialects I've fought amongst."

Gilles bit his lip over any comment. Little did the Bastard know how close to the truth he spoke.

"My point is," the late duc d'Orléans' illegitimate son said, "keep her out of the way until this business is done. And the only way you'll manage that—as I know—is if she—and her confessor—learn nothing about it at all."

"Of course," Gilles said.

"I'll have your head if you keep me ignorant," Gilles remembered La Pucelle had told the Bastard, even as he determined she mustn't know about this particular council at all.

Chapter Twenty-Five

A Golden Icon in the Corner of a Vast Church

And so, from shadow to lengthening shadow, Gilles de Rais made his way to the Burgundian gate of the city of Orléans. He saw the English patrols of which the Bastard had warned him. He saw clear signs of heightened vigilance in the enemy's bastilles of Saint Loup and Saint Pouair as he slipped through the two open leagues between them. But he feared so little that he didn't even get his heart to a delicious race. Because he saw a small figure on Orléans' walls, the angle of the sun catching like a guiding candle on her white armor. He simply made straight for that and knew he couldn't fail. He could feel it in the very dust of the ruined land he crossed.

Gilles went looking for her the instant he'd conveyed the Bastard's plans to La Hire and Sainte-Sévère. Yes, everyone he asked had seen her, and recently. But she moved quickly, leading him a merry chase around the walls' perimeter.

He found her at last where he himself liked best to be, high on the western rampart, facing the setting sun. The sight of her, pink-gold light reflecting off her white armor, blinded him as he approached. This vesper time brought a stiff wind from the same direction. It snapped at her banner as the little page held it faithfully by her side.

He watched her from a distance for a moment. The wind caught the sweat on his face and sent a delicious chill down his back.

From this vantage, they were close enough to see the faces of the *goddams* holding the bastille of La Croix Boissée. The English fortifications were clustered on this side, and close.

Even a mediocre bowman could pick her off if she exposed herself like this. A frisson of fear followed the shiver down his back. She had told him, "I must shed my blood at Orléans." She could watch out for him, allow him to pass thick patrols without a scratch, but she might not always be able to save herself.

The *goddams* did not seem inclined to target practice this evening, even with such temptation. The two sides were, however, also close enough to exchange insults.

He heard her voice, brilliant as the last of the sunlight. "Go home, English. Go home to the land the Gods made for your kind. That is My Lord's will for you. Don't say I didn't warn you. Go home, or by My Lord, I will send you there, those of you who do not claim only enough of this land for us to bury you in."

Gilles doubted the English heard a word of the speech, so wonderful it moved prickles out from his spine to cuff his shoulders and then his forearms. The wind was against her. Maybe Yann and the witches needed to shift the wind again. But to what purpose? He heard a hoarseness in her voice. She'd been shouting this message all day, from every angle, to no avail.

Now the wind carried the English reply back on his ears. "Cowherd! You brought the King of Bourges' cattle here for him. Go back now. Go back to watching patties harden in the fields."

They spoke in French. Those on the English side who hadn't learned the native tongue from their long years of occupation were native-born Norman traitors. La Pucelle, for all the countrified accents on her tongue, the dear cowherd, couldn't fail to understand them, too.

Gilles stepped quietly to her side then and saw, with greater wonder, that tears of frustration were streaming down her smooth cheeks. The light caught them, seemed to make her a golden icon in the corner of some vast church.

"Ah, Lady," he whispered. "Ignore them. Come away to supper. Leave them to their fates this night."

"They have my men, my heralds. I tried to send the warning to them on paper. Twice I sent it, and see? There are my men."

Where she pointed, Gilles saw two men in what had been the royal herald's blue-and-gold fleurs-de-lis, now so ill-used it was hardly recognizable. Both were fiercely trussed and gagged, a dagger held to each throat. Gilles was nearly convinced the next moment would see both of them toppled over the English battlements to their deaths, streaming blood all the way down.

"Why, that's criminal," Gilles said.

If he'd had a bow, he'd have tried to take out one of the captors himself, against the wind and with his bad aim. Then he was glad he didn't, for even with the best of luck, he'd only be able to save one of the men. And that only for a heartbeat or two, before another *goddam* came up and took his fallen comrade's place. "It's against all chivalry to take the bearers of a message from captain to captain like that."

"The *goddams*' meaning is clear, isn't it?" she replied. "They do not consider me a captain."

Something in her voice told him she was fully aware this opinion was something men on both sides of the siege agreed on. And he felt a twinge of guilt that keeping the morrow's sortie from her put him in the same camp of unbelievers.

"Ah, Lady."

He said it a second time as the tears renewed themselves on her face like molten ore oozing from a goldsmith's crucible. In fact, she seemed all afire and, as if a shadow crossed his soul in the brilliance of her presence, he had the feeling he was Seeing prophecy, even as Yann did. He shook the feeling from him. Gilles de Rais never had the Sight. It wasn't his magic.

In his helplessness, in the deep ache of his love, needing the contact as much as he hoped she did, he flung his arm about the little, narrow shoulders.

Then Gilles learned what other names she'd been hearing in his absence.

"Whore, doxy, *catin!*" The ugly cries shimmered across the golden air. Then, "So you're her pimp, are you, sire de Rais? The man I have to pay to get inside her braies along with the rest of your camp?"

Gilles felt the shoulders beneath his arm shudder. He dropped that arm as if the crucible had burned him at the same moment she broke and turned away.

He followed her, but kept his distance now, as if he could feel a dreadful heat.

"Those *goddams* are fools," he assured her. "They would not say such things—if they knew."

What it was the English didn't know, he didn't put into words. But he was certain she understood, better than he.

The tears were coming so rapidly now, she had to mop at them with the back of her hand. She tried to smile at his words and spoke lightly as the barrage of abuse kept coming behind them.

"I didn't know what the words meant. We don't have—I mean, women don't get called such things—don't do such things—at home. Not in sweet Lorraine. I had to ask young Raymond here."

She turned a smile on the boy, twelve or so, who swerved with them. He doggedly tried to do his duty by the banner, though he looked ready to drop, trying to keep up with such a mistress.

"A mere lad," she added. "But he knew. He told me. So you see, Bluebeard." She spun back to him at last. "You see why you must not touch me."

She set her back to him once more. He followed close behind as she began to descend the stairs back to the streets of Orléans.

"At least, not where anyone can see," he heard her say then, so low even Raymond must not hear.

But then they were at street level. Here crowds pressed to her, mothers with their infants, the sick, the scared. After that would be the captains and the soldiers. Candlelight processions were planned, priests carrying the city's relics in a circuit around the walls with their living relic, the Maid, at the head. And after that, a vigil at the cathedral.

A time when no one could see? That would be difficult to find.

Twenty-Third Antiphon

In Wolf's Clothing

"The only thing those late-night devotions seem to have accomplished is to finally wear the Lady out," Gilles concluded to me. He looked with a certain tenderness up at the second-story window of the house of Maître Jacques Boucher, treasurer to the captive duc d'Orléans. La Pucelle had retired to nap there after her midday meal, Boucher's pregnant wife at her side.

A crowd of petitioners, turned away at the door, milled here and there, like Gilles, trying to decide what to do with themselves without the Maid to tell them.

Only that wasn't it in his problem, was it? Every time I looked at my milk brother, I got an impression that set my heart racing with the sense of something about to happen. An image from the shadowy woods, of grey fur and sharp fangs bared. A wolf.

Certainly a wolf was a creature of purpose, deadly purpose to his prey. So what purpose was Gilles hiding so poorly from me? From the Maid?

He was a man, a commander of men, long tried in this war against the English that had been going on since his great-grandfather was a child. Surely I had no need to question what he and his fellow soldiers were about. Yet I knew, without the Maid to lend balance to his actions, how likely my milk brother was to veer to one dark side with no thought of return.

I folded my crippled hand in the deep sleeves of my habit and pretended to consult the few clouds scudding across a narrow slash of sky between close-packed rooftops. The sun stood high; a lazy kite sailed through the gap. There were things about my business, too, I would not tell my milk brother, nor even have him guess. I wouldn't tell him about the sweet woodruff and hops I'd slipped into her midday soup. Not too much, not that she couldn't wake through the spell when she had the desire, but enough to remove that desire from her for a while.

Nor did I mention the invigorating, irritating rosemary I'd slipped in his. Again, not much, just a hint.

"Bless me, Father."

A young soldier trying to buckle on his helmet with one hand while he crossed himself with the other knelt before me. My blessing was a common enough request, whether folk saw through my friar's robes or not. I made the sign in such a way that he could carry it as either the cross or the Stag to whatever engagement lay before him.

And he was anticipating something, as much as ever Gilles was and with much less self control. Through it all the soldier kept up a wide but nervous grin of crooked teeth.

"Augustinian?" he asked, with a nod towards my robes.

I took the safer route and answered, "Yes."

"From Saint Loup?"

I had to take a minute and then recalled all the talk there'd been in town about the Augustinian friary, abandoned by the Orléannais and then garrisoned by the English. "No," I replied. "A friary in Bayeux—under control of the enemy."

"Never you fear, Father. Saint Loup first, then we'll drive the *goddams* past your Bayeux and into the sea—vive La Pucelle."

I saw Gilles toss his long black curls with some impatience in the direction the man should go, to the eastern gate. Yellow canine teeth dripped saliva in my mind as he did.

"Yes, my lord." The man obeyed.

Orléans was a town under siege, full of soldiers on missions, heading to the walls to stand their watch, returning again. This added to the many lumpish bourgeois who thought they were soldiers, and to the expectation, any moment, of the return of the Bastard and reinforcements. I might have thought nothing of this man and the silent order Gilles gave him.

Presently, with a final glance up at La Pucelle's window, Gilles turned to follow his subordinate and four or five others I'd seen heading in the same direction. My milk brother feigned nonchalance in his farewell, as if that direction were as good as any other for an afternoon stroll to walk off dinner.

But the vision I Saw in that turn told me clearly it was not. I saw the grey flag of a wolf's tail. More bizarre, the tail swished out beneath a bishop's dragging robes where were, in actuality, only the clinking spurs and buckled greaves of my milk brother in full armor.

Then I understood. St. Loup had been the bishop of Troyes a thousand years ago, with a hagiography full of the usual miracles and denials of the flesh. But the name—Loup, French for Wolf—made another origin clear. Here was the ancient worship of an earlier, darker spirit, and it was fitting that the Maid's battles should begin at a place of such memory.

Gilles, unaware as usual of all but the surface of things, meant to lead an attack against the ruined friary. But he meant his deeds to have no counterbalance. He meant not to let La Pucelle know.

For a moment, I watched him go, down the narrow, crowded streets of Orléans, as bright as they would ever be that day with the sun almost directly overhead. Should I tell the girl?

Instead, I found an empty corner of a bench across the way to sit heavily upon. I could tell by bubbles and darkness in my vision that the spell was coming fast. It would never do to make a spectacle of myself by passing out, jerking violently, in the middle of the thoroughfare before La Pucelle's lodging. Nor did I think I could make it to the second floor where she slept. I felt myself slump helpless against the plaster wall behind me.

Spells are from the God, when I allow myself to be taken up into His hand, and all must be according to His will. But sometimes, if my will is close enough to His, a spell works one extreme off the other to good purpose.

Or perhaps, at such times, my will simply is the God's.

I've given Gilles rosemary, was the last thought I remember passing through my head. But I hadn't been able to come to

Talbot with some of the same potion. In the journey of my blackness, I might prickle him—somehow.

I never know exactly what happens while my mind is with the God. This time, I did receive a very strong impression of the English captain, however. He stood brave beneath the presumptuous banner of English red spliced into French blue as well as that of his own hunting hound.

"Punish the bastards," was the one clear thought I read in his face.

And then it was all wolves, wolves and lambs, wearing one another's clothing.

I came to myself, the sounds of a great to-do in the treasurer's house across the way. An hour or more must have passed. The shadows had grown longer in the narrow street.

"My horse, my horse."

La Pucelle threw open the door, shouting these words to the milling crowd. Red lines of sleep marked her flushed face.

Others appeared in the opening with her, her squire, Jean d'Aulon, still trying to buckle bits of armor onto her agitated form. Maîtresse Boucher I saw briefly, wringing her hands helplessly over the madwoman she'd sheltered under her roof, even—heaven help us!—shared a bed with.

"Bloody boy," La Pucelle snapped with real violence at the poor young man whose fingers were fumbling. "Why didn't you tell me French blood was being shed?"

Aulon mumbled something too pathetic to hear.

"My Voices tell me so. But they don't tell me where. Where? *Where*?"

There was more helpless muttering, from others besides the squire. People began to listen, to look here, there, and some ran off to see. None of them doubted for a moment that what she'd heard in her sleep must be true.

Her white horse came clopping up the street, led by Raymond, still fussing at the cinch. The beast threw its head and snorted, seeming as anxious as its mistress to be about its business.

"Boy, my banner. We forget my banner. Upstairs. Run."

Aulon vanished. By the time he reappeared, out of breath and flinging wide the second-story window, she was in the saddle and had turned the horse's head east. She knew the direction now, turned by the breath of the God as surely as a weather vane.

Aulon shoved the banner, pole first, through the dark window opening. La Pucelle stood in her stirrups and caught it in both hands while Raymond held the horse's head still. The white silk caught in the wind as it came into the open. For a moment, as it threatened to carry the little silver-clad figure off with it, we in the street were treated to a vision such as only appears to mortal eyes once or twice in a lifetime.

She reached, tension striving in every sinew. Glory, fate, victory stood personified before us, as yet untarnished, better than ever artist captured it in paint or stone. The hair rose on my arms, at the back of my neck, and I forgot all about the after-spell headache and weakness.

In a moment, she'd pulled the banner under control. She took it in one hand, the reins in the other, and gave the horse the spur it hardly waited for.

"France, France, I come!" I heard her cry, and every voice in the street shouted, too, most of them running after her.

The tocsin bells had begun to ring, sending the heart thudding, the ears throbbing.

I followed along with the rest, as far as the first men we met coming the other way, across town, near the Burgundian Gate. These were some of the wounded, being helped to safety by women and friends. Then I saw other directions for my skills besides following in her wake.

"She was weeping," one of them told me as I stanched the horrible gash in his thigh. "She wept to see my wounds. She wept to see French blood fall. Good Lord, how will she ever manage when she sees what's out there, before Saint Loup?"

Chapter Twenty-Six

Boar Bristles of Grey-Fletched Arrows

A goddam patrol was forming outside the gate to Saint Loup when Gilles and his company approached. He kicked his borrowed destrier to a gallop and was gratified to see the enemy scurry back to the safety of their walls like rats to their holes. Mission accomplished: the garrison of Saint Loup pinned down. Now to keep them that way long enough for the Bastard and the reinforcements from Blois to come in from the northwest.

Traces of earlier Orléannais sorties, grey-fletched arrows like boar bristles marked a clear cordon of the enemy archer's farthest reach around the bastille. What a sorry sight no-man's land was. Trying to grow spring green like the rest of the world, it sprouted here and there a daisy or clump of pink clover for the friars' cattle that would not come to eat. Here and there, dried blood matted the abused Earth, broken lance butts and rags of pennant lay among the monks' broken nut trees and fences. Only tufts of dust attained any height.

"For France," Gilles murmured, and pushed to a canter.

Rough, makeshift masonry narrowed the mitered arches—openings that had once graced a cloister—to only bowman's width. Gilles could see his adversaries, or rather, the tips of their arrowheads, twitching. Drawn ready at their loops, they were waiting, waiting for him to make a mistake, to step over the line into the killing field.

Gilles snatched his banner from his borrowed squire's hand, thrust it into the holster on the left of his saddle so he could hold onto his shield and guide his horse as well. He bore the banner's simple, stark contrast of a black cross on a gold ground with a leap directly over the grounded arrows. Then, even as he heard the hum like a roused hornet's nest, he swerved the horse right, back to safety. A pair of arrows hit him, one tearing through his ensign and the other pinging harmlessly aside as he turned his shield to the walls.

"*À moi*, St. Gilles," he cried, though doubting anyone could hear him beyond the cavern of his *bascinet*.

Thus he moved widdershins, the magicians' course of destruction, but only coincidentally. It was the way that kept his better-defended left to the enemy, along the line of spent shafts, daring the *goddams* to come out and fight. With coughs of smoke, a pair of culverines, those small cannon a man could carry on his shoulder and prop against a wall to fire, betrayed their existence at the strongest points. Saint Loup was a modest house by Augustinian standards, but rolled tight and bristling like a hedgehog under the English. Assessing its strengths convinced him it wouldn't fall, not today, and his action must remain in fact as the Bastard envisioned it, purely diversionary.

By the time Gilles had completely circled the fortress, the destrier blowing hard beneath him, the rest of the sortie had caught up. Back in Orléans, he'd thought the thirty-seven men he'd picked—untried to him, but veterans and well enough armed—would suffice for the task. Then some bourgeois had seen them assembling behind the defensive boulevard of suburb rubble just outside the Burgundian Gate. The townsmen, chanting La Pucelle's name, insisted on coming along, on foot, with no more than knives in their hands and their grandmother's kettles on their heads. Now they were getting in the way, singing the Maid's praises, and raising a great deal of dust.

And getting themselves killed. A tanner had stepped over the ring of planted arrows and, playing "dare me", had not stepped back at the first hum of flight. Or perhaps he had, since the bolt was in his back, but not fast enough.

Gilles gave no time to a fallen tanner. From the advantage of his saddle and a little scrub-covered rise, he stole a glance back over the plain to the city walls where, he hoped, the Maid slept safely. He spared no more than a glance, however, because in another direction, out of the northwest, he saw troops riding. This was sooner than he'd expected the Bastard. It made his foray down the Autun road to Saint Loup hardly seem worth the time it took to buckle on armor.

But he'd also expected the reinforcements to make for the Burgundian Gate—not straight towards him—

In confusion, his attention turned back to the tanner. Two of the man's braver comrades had rushed in to pull him, still clinging to his flaying knife as if to his soul, back to safety. Bolts dropped like rain all around the trio, splitting those shafts landed before them. One took off a man's hat, another grazed a cheek, the sort of wound that bled and looked worse than it was. What had the fool tanner thought? That he might flay the skin off the bastille's base like he did in his trade at home?

The walls of Saint Loup cheered roundly, louder than Gilles thought the fall of a tanner was worth. He looked back toward the approaching company. Even from this vantage he could see little. Too little.

And then too much.

He saw what caused the enemy's jubilation: This wasn't the Bastard, these weren't friends of France. The lean grey of the besieging commander's hound ensign stiffened in the riding breeze over helmet crest and plume. Gilles could hear it now as they closed, the battlecry— *"À Talbot!"*—the baying triumph of their beloved leader's name as of so many dogs. The name French mothers used to make their children behave.

Where the hell was Sainte-Sévère? Gilles thought as he urged his frothing mount back down the rise. Saint Pouair wasn't pinned down as it ought to be. Worse, even if Talbot had left that northern fortress just when he'd first seen Gilles' command leave the boulevard, the Saint Pouair garrison couldn't have covered half this distance in the time. Talbot must have guessed the plan beforehand, damn him.

Gilles turned and pulled his horse up, its hooves tripping now on the first of the Saint Loup arrows. He shouted a warning. Then he shouted orders to turn and stand, the words catching on the tightness in his throat. His own men would have known what he wanted without this stupid staring, but his own men were God-knew-where with the Bastard of Orléans.

What was the use? The lord of Rais and his fewer than forty men—and a few bourgeois—were spliced now between the walls of Saint Loup and Talbot's crushing force. Already the ground trembled at their approach, up the legs of Gilles' jittery horse, down his own to the jangling of his spurs. Already he saw the *goddam* he had to take on first. He knew when the man picked him out through the narrow eye slits in his heavy helm.

Gilles had no choice. He snatched his banner up out of its holster. Swallowing his right gauntlet within the guard, he couched the butt under his armpit and caught up the shield to his left. As he leveled the long beam, the horse, reins loose now, skittered back at the wave of fabric before its eyes. Gilles strained to hold his weapon so the clumsy hooves wouldn't trip on the fringe, to grip and hold the beast with his knees and thighs, even to urge it forward. The muscles in his arm, wrist and chest cramped. His abdomen did the same to spare the coming shock to his back. His buttocks tightened within the high frame of the saddle's cantle.

At the last moment, he saw the point driving down on him shift higher, for his eyes. He lifted his shield to counter, having time to but poorly brace it. He howled as his whole body took the impact. Flinching, he heard his opponent's lance first, then looked and saw it snapped cleanly in the middle.

It was only then he realized that when he'd parried with his shield, Gilles had instinctively shifted his own point from eyes to the neck joint. The enemy's shield had failed to follow. Where the oncoming lance had simply snapped, his had splintered. One very large sliver of wood had forced its way between links of mail to the dark life encased within, taking the arms of Rais in with it. The *goddam* reeled, one leg stirruped, the other flailing cantle-level, then toppled.

But it was like the practice field: If he hit the quintain as badly as a novice, Gilles immediately felt assault from behind. The force of the frontal impact had sent his horse stumbling backwards over the line of spent arrows into no-man's land. Before the lord of Rais had time to shake his arm to the chest to rid it of the sensation of burning there, and to draw his sword, thuds were raining on his back. Damned longbowmen could fire so fast that one of them could have two bolts in the air at once. Gilles' horse screamed and leapt forward as metal bit into its rump. The arrow didn't go deep, but the wild, jerking movements of the frightened animal began to work the barb out again, with further pain. Glinting red formed a circle on the dun hair, then up under the saddle.

Which of the screams spinning in his *bascinet* came from beneath him and what from men around, Gilles stopped being able to tell. With his sword finally out, he whacked off the heavy goose-feather fletches quivering behind him with a single blow. More than that a hand weapon could not do against arrows. So he urged the wounded horse on to the next man from Saint Pouair who caught his eye through the narrow slits of a helmet.

Chapter Twenty-Seven

Grey Surrender

The English Lord Talbot, that terror of naughty French children, had not been in Saint Loup to allow Gilles to pin him down after all. In a brilliant counter-move, he brought his men circling out of the next closest of the *goddam* bastilles, Saint Pouair.

Gilles de Rais cursed himself for being stupid, mind-numbingly stupid. Scores of Orléannais bourgeois as well as his battled-hardened men, all of them he had led into this trap. It was worse than the snare the Bastard had feared for the reinforcements from Blois, French crushed between two English detachments. The expectation of miracles had made all of them, but him most of all, stupid—and now impotent, as with a shout, all of Saint Loup's garrison burst back out to meet their friends from Saint Pouair and crush Gilles and his men between them.

Sweat ran between the black steel of Gilles' *bascinet* and his face. He'd been fighting, and fighting hard, for what seemed like days, to no effect except stupefying exhaustion. Exhaustion and confusion. He cut across the unprotected knees of an enemy. The muscles of his sword arm screamed like the hinge, both louder than the falling man. Gilles stumbled, his own knees aching from gripping the horse's belly. Having had the animal finally cut from under him and put out of its misery hardly helped. He was now on a level to fight like the good craftsmen of Orléans who were dropping like flies around him. And what was the difference, after all? It was only work now, bloody, sickening work, and he loathed it to the rising of his gorge.

A blow to the head—he hadn't even seen whence it came—dented his helmet. Red splashed momentarily before his eyes. After that, the whole world went from red to a uniform grey. Foe and friend, he could no longer tell the difference. He no longer cared.

In spite of the padded coif he wore under the helmet, the sweat was running into his eyes. He slammed his visor up, gauntlet metal ringing on the metal, and tried to mop the stinging wet away with the corner of his surcoat. Finding a patch not stiffening with blood wasn't easy. Even then, his vision didn't clear. A shadow lunged for his exposed face. He twisted, up and away, catching the fellow in the groin, under the breastplate and deep into the belly.

When Gilles kicked up to free his sword, the dying hands spasmed on his greave. Another kick detached both blade and boot. Gilles tried to vomit and couldn't, poison the same as wholesomeness. He cleaned his blade on his surcoat, on the spot he'd just used for his face. He wished it were so easy to clear his lungs and his sight. Then he slammed the visor down and moved on to the next grey form.

All color had bled from the magenta ground of his enemy's ensign. In ghostly form, Talbot's silver-grey hunting hound ran on his banners in the haze, its tongue out, panting. Gilles might have been wearing the same colors himself. Covered with grime and other men's hot blood, the black cross on his own surcoat had likewise melted into its bright gold ground in such eerie half light. Trampling men and horses raised a spate of dust. Screams and battle cries seemed no more than the beating of his own blood turned inside out. Struggling shadows of men and horses belonged to another world, a world of only shades, no light to pick out the near points of depth, no meaning.

Like a lone wolf, running without a pack, Gilles saw a rise and staggered towards it. Here, with effort, he made out the lay of the land and the battle all about him. He'd got turned around. The slope was down towards his left.

There, where shades of reed and willow marked the river, there stood the English-held bastille of Saint Loup, the bastille he was meant to taunt. A trick of the light made the stone walls of the former friary have no more depth than parchment. Pitch-thick flames had made an eerie sort of incense and candle glow. Men-at-arms had displaced the men of prayer, screams the stilling drone of mass, pikes the glint of filigreed crosses. The usual sanctuary of church dispensed only death as the world stood on its head. How was one to tell heaven from hell, angels from devils?

The men he'd led were scattering like a flock without their shepherd. Because their way to the safety of the city walls was blocked by Talbot's advancing forces, those who could were fleeing towards the open countryside. Here, one by one, the English would pick them off.

All this Gilles saw, but the view continued to have a dream-like quality to it. It was as if he were sleeping snug in his bed, the whole disaster rolling before him in shades of black and Talbot silver-grey.

"Oh, God," Gilles sighed, as if at no more than the sorry tale of a minstrel's lay.

He'd never surrendered before, for all his years at war. Now he prepared. He hadn't seen the narrow slits over the eyes of the man he was going to surrender to yet, but he was looking. He hoped for some nobility, a knight at least, preferably Talbot himself. In readiness, Gilles slipped his sword into its sheath like slipping off into a drunken sleep. He reached up to take off his *bascinet*, retiring, finished, defeated, his eyes darting, lonely, without focus over the muddled field.

But just as his metal-muffled hands touched the helmet's shell shielding his temples, the action seemed to rivet his sight, his mind and his soul to one single spot.

The spot was, of all things, a butterfly.

Chapter Twenty-Eight

The Contrast in a Butterfly's Wing

The minuscule wings hovered in the air before him. They were black edged with gold, and their sharp contrast suddenly brought contrast and color to everything.

The butterfly vanished as quickly as it had come. But when he looked away, all the world had a gilt edge to it. Knots of men struggling were abruptly friend and foe. The near edge of every breastplate and sword shimmered with light while the depths remained dark on fully rounded, active, vital figures. Even his soul felt etched with the glow. On fire.

Light outlined the form of a horse, black as night, black as the favorite gelding Gilles had left behind with Roger de Bricqueville. This wasn't his horse, but its rider had dropped off in the mêlée. The creature tripped, confused and frightened, straight toward him. Gilles reached out and embraced the familiarity of darkness.

The moment he had hoisted himself into the stirrup, from the other side of Talbot's forces, then, he saw her. Not the butterfly, no. White horse, white armor, white banner trailing behind her.

"No," Gilles groaned. She was meant to stay safe, away from the chaos, tucked in bed in the chamber on Boucher's second floor. "God, no."

She rode at a gallop, her banner's tail flying in the wind with the force of her tilt. She was helmetless, absolutely fearless. Her mouth was open in a yell.

A din assaulted his ears. They'd just burst open, like his eyes. High shrieks gave counterpoint to low groans, heavy clangs set off the rhythm of high arrows' trills, as in some beautiful motet.

He couldn't hear her voice over it all. Except—except he could, in the very rhythm of his heart. It was the belling cry of the she-wolf to her mate, hunting in the brakes.

"My God," Gilles moaned. "My love."

On his next, stronger breath, he gave the answering howl.

Instead of taking off his helmet, Gilles de Rais slammed the visor down and gave his horse the spur, wolf claws sinking deep. From opposite sides of the field, they rode to each other.

By the time Gilles and Jehanne had leapt over enough blood poppies and lance fleurs-de-lis to hear each other, the French had rallied. They seemed to have doubled in size, both the number and each man individually. The troops that were with her began to pinch Talbot.

And they had brought scaling ladders. That was unnecessary, Gilles' thought began—then, "To the fortress," La Pucelle cried. "To Saint Loup!"

They weren't going to just pin down the garrison, which had fled back to their gates. They were going to take the damned thing. It was mad. But there was vivid clarity to that madness.

Those near at hand turned towards the bastille and began to move as a single gesture. Others, farther off, followed, the scaling ladders already swinging up towards the gold-rimmed sky.

They were side by side now. La Pucelle pulled up, the horse blowing and skittish under her, and watched the progress of the men. Gilles watched her.

Awe ached like a hollow in his chest. He wanted to throw himself off his horse to the ground. He wanted to kiss the blood spatters and dust grime on her greaves, like the tokens of some relic.

"Lady," he said instead, trying to draw her attention over her shoulder, away from the immovable stone walls rising before them. "Talbot and a pack of his men are making good their escape, back towards Saint Pouair."

She didn't even look that way. The wind trilled the stubble of her uncovered hair. A fleck of debris shivered there. He wanted to reached up and tenderly brush it away, but his hands were in gauntlets and a wild brightness lustered her eyes, a reflection off Saint Loup's bulwarks.

"To the bastille, men of France!" she shouted. In a contrasting whisper, she shot at him, "Let Talbot go."

"But Talbot is the prize. If some of my men and I could but catch him, there'd be a rich ransom."

His reins twitched with the thought, and the horse beneath him danced a step or two in that direction. Though he pulled the susceptible mouth back parallel, his own limbs struggled to resist the desire to be off.

"Not to mention," his argument ran on, "that we'd chop off the *goddams'* head and brains with Talbot."

"Talbot will be for another day. For today, ride with me, Bluebeard. Spur by spur."

And he obeyed.

By the time they reached Saint Loup, spur by spur, the men had already scaled the walls, then backed down. The interior was ablaze, and to save themselves, the English garrison had thrown open the gates to surrender. The French were taking no prisoners that day. One by one, as the English came out with their hands up, their armor smoke-blackened, their crests on fire, they were hacked to pieces. Only when a group of forty or so in Augustinian robes and vestments came out together did the Maid's shrill voice cry "Quarter!" and the slaughter stopped.

"They're not religious," Gilles protested.

"Of course they are," she snapped. "Monks kept prisoner when the *goddams* took over the friary. Just look at them."

He did. Where she saw only good; he saw deception. None of the robes looked made for the man who had it on. Beneath one, a breastplate glinted.

"Think of Père Jean, my confessor," she insisted. "He's an Augustinian, like these."

Gilles knew what that disguise hid. "Lady, all the true monks fled to the safety of Orléans long before the English took the place. These are the enemy who found habits and albs in the ruined cellars of Saint Loup and helped themselves."

She was still disinclined to believe, but then one uttered their tell-tale, namesake curse, "God damn," as a spur caught in the black sack cloth. Finally, she was content to have them rounded up as prisoners to be led back to the city where they would be paraded and jeered like masquerading fools at Mardi Gras.

When the fire shrank to mere smoldering heaps, they rode abreast into the fortress, his dark armor and plumes a shadow to the brightness of hers and of the banner. She held it still aloft, though how her arm must ache, a mate to the ache in his own sword arm. The English toll was mounting quickly around them as French forces moved through the former priory of St. Loup. Gilles looked anxiously towards La Pucelle. Tears cast a sheen on her face, but the features beneath them were firmly set. A man might think she'd seen such things every butchering day in her father's yard.

The sheen fell on Gilles like spring's warm light on the damp, dark mold in a forest's heart.

"There he is," she said to him at last.

"Who?"

"St. Loup, of course."

In the midst of the bloody courtyard, echoing with the prayers of the dying more fervent than ever the monks had uttered in life, and reeking of smoke, stood an old statue on a plinth. The grey stone had been carved into the form of a wolf with strangely human features: a halo circling his pointed ears, a shepherd's crozier held in two fierce paws. St. Loup, St. Wolf, of course.

Two Frenchmen backed a *goddam* up against the image and cut his throat. The blood spurted into the stone beast's jaws. Gilles flinched at the sight, but the girl beside him did not.

She handed her banner to a passing fellow who'd run out of throats to cut, gave him her reins and swung out of the saddle. She walked to the statue and knelt before it, crossing herself in the old way, with the sign of the Stag's horns. She seemed totally oblivious to the *goddam* expiring at the other side of the base.

Gilles dismounted and went to stand by her side. Such an old, barbaric icon could have very little to do with the fourth-century bishop of Troyes. The figure had, in fact, been too much for the monks who, after centuries of a rougher faith, had made this site their own. They'd refused to bring St. Loup in under the roof of their chapel and probably hoped a score or so years of weather would erase the pagan features. Erased they were, to some degree, the old chisel marks pitted, the details smoothed. But rain and sun had been unable to erase the figure from the mind and devotions of the local folk.

La Pucelle reached out and touched a collection of their gifts laid at the saint's feet, undisturbed by monks before or the garrison after. Little as he was familiar with such things, Gilles thought he recognized the bobbed tails of a couple of lambs, a whole fleece crumbling with exposure, a curly ram's horn, a slingshot.

"The wolf is as important to the shepherd as the sheep," La Pucelle mused, almost to herself, comfort in her tones. This was old wisdom she'd suckled like mother's milk in her peasant life.

She went on: "He brings balance to the flock, else they'd eat themselves out of house and home. The Earth created the world in the same way She brought forth humans, with the same love, and a place for each if there's proper humility. The folk only ask, with these gifts, that when the grey hunter thinks of his children, he'll remember theirs as well. Humans are so slow to return the favor."

Her prayer finished, La Pucelle rose and stepped around to the *goddam*. His eyes were already set, his blood sinking into the porous stone of St. Loup. But she knelt and made the sign of the Stag over him as well.

After that, Gilles himself could look at the ravaged body with more equanimity than he usually mustered, even as a man-at-arms. It seemed, indeed, holy to him. And the thought occurred to him that it was the lone wolf who became the mankiller, the one who didn't run with his pack, who had no she-wolf and pups to care for. As nature intended him.

The lord of Rais' thoughts ran once to Catherine, to the child she carried. His child. No, the time to tell La Pucelle was not yet.

She left the saint's statue and began to go among the fallen of both sides in the liberated Saint Loup, weeping. And thus was the wolf-saint prepared to return to his community of brethren—and to the people who feared and worshiped him.

Chapter Twenty-Nine

The Scapegoat

The next day, Thursday, the fifth of May, 1429, Feast of the Ascension, La Pucelle would not fight. She went to church early. Gilles de Rais went with her, and every other soul in Orléans, to hear mass and watch the ancient ritual. An image of Christ was raised through slates removed in the cathedral roof and a burning-straw satan was cast down.

"Balancing the world," Yann commented at Gilles' side, thinking, no doubt, of the part he would play later in the day, for the rites were only just beginning.

A prisoner was released, one of the *goddams* taken in monk's robes at Saint Loup the day before. He was a Parisian who publicly repented of the sin of following a foreign King. He knelt before La Pucelle, placed his hands between hers as a sign of fealty, and took on her colors.

Then folk brought her the first fruits to bless in her maiden purity. Somehow, the besieged had found broad beans, still with blue-black sprays of blossom above the riper pods. And there were tiny grapes, not big enough yet even for the verjuice vats, but smelling, twined with their leaves, of great promise.

Then it was Yann's turn. In his full regalia as the Horned God—or scapegoat or devil as some were pleased to call him—he ran through the streets with all the people of Orléans behind him. Four of the witches, the haler, not-so-noble ones in frightful costume, ran beside him in the lead. The Orléannais threw their offal at him, the contents of their chamber pots and rags and bones they'd clung to, for what poor use they could get of them during a siege. Now they let them fly at the running goat, receiving in exchange the firm confidence that soon they would not need to scrimp any more.

Thus they drove Yann out the Burgundian Gate, where some of the rougher, braver souls plunged him in the muck until everyone felt satisfied and cleansed.

Everyone except, perhaps, Yann.

"He will certainly need new horns and a pelt for Midsummer," Gilles said to Roger de Bricqueville, new come to Orléans with all the Bastard's reinforcements.

They saw Yann laughing, though, as he took the abuse good-naturedly, as it was important for the scapegoat to do.

"This will unify the people even more," he told Gilles later. "If they have anger festering against their neighbor after these hard months, they've put it now on me. But, by the Horned One, a besieged city is a filthy place. Let us break these *goddams*' backs in a hurry, my brother, so the folk may spread their fields with it and turn the cycle. This time of year, one expects the country lanes where the manure carts have passed, and the fields where the manure has been spread to smell like me. I can't wait for a hot bath myself."

The next morning, early, they were on the battlefield again. Saint-Jean-le-Blanc, the bastille they had planned in their councils to take next, cheated them. Across the river and to the east, they discovered the nervous *goddams* had evacuated during the night. The Bastard set men to occupy it and then seemed at a loss as to what to do with the rest of his day.

Fortunately, the English answered that dilemma for him. They came pouring out of the bastille of Les Augustins, yet another monastery, the mother house, which the English had taken and fortified. This host, braced by the fugitives from Saint-Jean, met the French with a great crash of arms and squeal of men and horses while barges of soldiers were still ferrying over from Orléans. They fought on level ground, relieved here and there only by low shrubbery. They surged, first to one side, then to the other, with neither side gaining advantage all day.

Pairs of carapaced knights charged, footmen strove for his horse's belly, stones from the fortress shattered into deadly splinters, bolts from longbows whizzed. No matter what the *goddams* threw at Gilles, he always kept one eye on the struggling, careening, glowing, glorious figure in blinding white armor.

And this diversion of his attention only made him more efficient in his deadly business of swing, parry, cut, swing and parry yet again. His passion was completely renewed. In fact, he'd never known it so fierce before.

"I must shed my blood at Orléans," she'd said. This must be the day.

At a point very early in the fighting, he saw the high bows of her saddle empty, like the gap in a jaw of a missing tooth. It was a man's saddle, and so didn't hold her as snugly as his own held him. He saw her banner dip below the shallow layer of smoke and plumes and lurching casques around the horse.

Four *goddams* died in the fury of his rush.

Then he saw her, alive and well. She'd merely slipped to the ground, on purpose, to catch up an abandoned sword which she handed to what looked like an unarmed plowboy. Gilles saw her knock the *goddam*—who thought he spied his chance to cleanse the world of the French witch—into that plowboy's arms before swinging herself back up into the saddle and riding on. Her exhilaration infected him, a full spear's throw away. After that, he turned back to enemies of his own.

She was like that all day, up and down, to and fro, here, then there. If he saw her once, she was never in the same place when next he looked, for that place had grown less dangerous and she'd moved on. But he always felt a sixth sense of where to find her, the same sense that always told him where the fighting was fiercest. It was always his practice to force his horse and his sword in that direction. Now, she was before him, herding *goddams* his way—or did he, for all his best efforts, herd them towards her? What sort of bodyguard was he? He never saw her stop to eat or drink. He hardly saw her pause for breath.

At last, as the shadows lengthened, the Bastard waved retreat with his banner. Horns gave speech to the gesture.

Gilles' brain wanted to feel disappointment that they'd made no better progress for a day of effort. But his body was too exhausted for anything save relief. He gave the signal to Roger, saw the Rais arms dip, then dip again.

"What is it, Bluebeard?"

Ah, that voice was reward enough for a dozen such grinding, halting days. He turned and lifted his visor. For the first time since the glow on the dust that now marked west had been in the east, she'd brought her horse close enough to his for speech. No struggling *goddams* writhed between them.

"Well fought, Lady." His voice was hoarse. He'd gone without water because she went without. Words burned and croaked in his throat. He turned for his waterskin, but it must have been cut from his saddle in the battle. Where was the boy—?

She ignored his compliment. "Well?"

"The Bastard gave the signal to retire." Amazing, she could fight like that and not know the signal. "I had Roger give it, too."

"I have given no such signal."

Indeed, her banner, held firmly in the leather brace on her left side and in her left hand, caught the high golden rays of the sun. It seemed to pant above her; it hadn't dipped at all.

"We will retire in good order," he assured her. "See, the *goddams* are as tired as we are."

"No."

"It's not a retreat, Lady."

"Never."

"We'll come back and finish them off on the morrow."

"Never," she shouted.

At her urging, the horse beneath her leaped away and towards Les Augustins as if he were fresh from the stable. The banner caught the wind and went rigid with a snap.

"Lady—" But he heard his own words drowned out by hers.

"Now, men! Now we take the fortress. She is ours!"

Chapter Thirty

Brown Blood Swirling with Yarrow and Sweet Woodruff

The wave of miraculously revitalized men flooding in La Pucelle's wake snatched Gilles up and carried him along. They caught the English—in the midst of blessing the Bastard of Orléans for the first time that day—completely off guard.

The chivalry of the attack was debatable, but the next time he was aware, Gilles de Rais stood with others on the abbey wall. The fortress of Les Augustins behind them settled into a calm and quiet that rang on battle-deafened ears. It was theirs.

The Bastard, Alençon and others were gesturing beside him. They spoke plans for the morrow in low tones laved by goblets of wine captured from the English. Personally, Gilles de Rais was drinking hard, causing the little lads to run up and down the stairs for ewer after ewer. Gilles de Rais was making up for what he'd denied himself most of the day.

La Pucelle was not there. He didn't think it mattered, except for the quantities of drink he let slip past his still-parched throat. Surely she'd arrive soon enough from whatever act of charity before altar or wounded soldier was keeping her. She wouldn't let the commanders council alone if she could help it.

They'd taken the fortress. In one day. In one sharp, final charge, truth be told. They'd seen a miracle—another one, the second in three days. His head reeled, not from wine, he thought. His fellow commanders were fools if they didn't realize what they'd seen—and plan the next day's action accordingly.

From the top of the monastery's wall, they had an excellent view of the greying world. Before them, before the city's roofs, flowed the silent, grey river between its sandbars and the broken arches of the bridge.

But also, on this bank, blocking at least half of the river from view, the double towers of Les Tourelles stood firm. These towers had been built as military posts, guarding the bridgehead. They were not roughly refashioned religious houses, with all the weaknesses that implied.

Nonetheless, with the capture of Les Augustins, the French had Les Tourelles effectively surrounded. The besiegers had become the besieged, in two short days in the field.

"No, I say we just sit tight," Gilles overheard the Bastard arguing. "Les Tourelles are crammed with new men who fled from Les Augustins and Saint-Jean. How many supplies can they have? How long can they hold out before suing for peace? It's safer if we just sit and wait."

"But they—we—expect their relief from Fastolf and Paris any day," Alençon protested. "And Talbot is holding the bastilles on the northern bank. He can always come to their assistance."

"Not if our guns on Orléans' walls and our chains across the water stop any attempt at a crossing."

Gilles took another deep swallow. The wine was warm and dark as the night air and stuffed his ears with its cloying softness.

Let the Bastard and the rest bicker all they wanted. The only way was straight forward. A child would know the strategy now.

And she would show it to them.

The belfries of Orléans rang a vespers more full of promise than any he'd ever heard. They draped his ears in sable.

" ... gone back to town to have her wound seen to."

The sable whipped from his ears, and Gilles lashed after it as he caught the tail end of Alençon's last words. There could be only one person he meant by "her".

"Wounded? She's wounded? How badly?"

"So I heard." Alençon seemed more startled by the violence in Gilles' voice than by anything else on that long, violent day. "I didn't see her. I only heard. Gone to have her confessor tend it, I think."

Without another word or backward glance, Gilles slammed his goblet and then himself down from the parapet. The day's alarms, then, were only just beginning.

He found her at last in Boucher's kitchen, before a low fire. The light from the embers caught the curves of the breastplate she still wore, the dust-covered spikes of her hair, the dirt-streaked tan of her cheeks. His impulse was to cross the room to her in two strides, scoop her out of the chair where she sat and— And clang metal to metal in such a clumsy embrace?

Then he saw Yann. His milk brother stood up from the fire with a bowl of water newly warmed to the smoking point. He nodded to Gilles in greeting and carried the bowl within the drape of his black sleeves to kneel and set it on the floor before the Maid.

"What is it?" Gilles asked, still panting from his haste. "Is she hurt bad?"

He crossed quickly and knelt with Yann on the stone floor.

Gilles watched Yann roll the heavy wool hose down over her thigh, knee and calf, revealing bare skin to the fire's glow. Gilles could smell its warmth, its life, the battle still in every pore.

The fabric stuck on something just past the narrow ankle. Yann looked up questioningly. The girl nodded, "Go ahead." Then she drew her breath in sharply and caught at the seat of the chair beside her hips until the knuckles went white as he gave one sharp tug and set the limb free.

Was it in contrast to the white flesh that the ring on her finger went darker? The ring was supposed to warn when she went into danger. Why hadn't she paid attention to her ring? Worthless hocus-pocus, no doubt, even from Bertrand Du Guesclin the hero.

"It's nothing." Her reply to Gilles came on the exhale of breath. "I stepped on something sharp, that's all."

Yann eased the thin, white-skinned foot with its delicate framework of bones into the herb-strewn water. The girl drew in another breath that came out as a sigh. Gilles saw re-enlivened brown blood and dirt swirl up and mingle with the floating leaves of yarrow and sweet woodruff.

He compared that limb with its shod partner, then examined the boot and *sabaton* that Yann had discarded under the chair.

Both were ruined, the boot punctured and soaked with blood, the *sabaton*'s metal crumpled between the interlocking plates.

"I knew that amorer's work wasn't heavy enough," Gilles complained. Then he asked, "You stepped on something sharp enough to go through metal and thick leather?"

"In the ditch before the fortress, there were all these star-shaped things made of metal."

"Caltrops?" Gilles hissed. "You stepped on a caltrop, Lady?"

"I was in such haste to answer my Voice's call to the walls, I didn't look where I was going." She was laughing at herself.

Gilles did not laugh. She'd stepped on a thing like that—and kept fighting? Sanctifying the ground with her blood with every step.

"The English strew sacks of those things wherever they might do damage. They're made with four points, evenly spaced, so no matter what way they fall, one vicious spike sticks up."

"Yes, that's what I stepped on."

"Do you know what one of those things can do to the soft part of a horse's foot?"

He wanted to order her to stay on her horse from now on—but stopped himself in time. Could it be any safer, high and exposed in a saddle, taunting the enemy with her waving white silk, than down in ditches with such quiet, stationary weapons?

"Is that what they're for?" she asked. "Against horses?"

"Mostly."

"Ah, who would do that to a noble animal?"

An animal? As if the girl, this girl, were not infinitely more valuable. Then his anger rose. Soldiers, he wanted to tell her, usually had the sense not to step on such things. They kept their eyes wary on the ground, not up at heavenly messengers.

With great restraint, he kept his comment to, "Usually the beast is ruined. We have to put them down."

"Is that what you plan to do to me, my lord Bluebeard?" Her dark eyes crinkled. She was laughing at him again.

"Never!" he protested.

"And I assure you, it won't be necessary, Gilles," Yann said, balming the confrontation as, in a minute, he would balm the foot. He lifted the foot out of the water now to examine the white, loose edges of flesh around the puncture. "The wound is clean. At least the *goddams* didn't soak their caltrops in poison before they sowed the ground with them this time."

"Thank God," Gilles said, thinking of the trouble the Bastard still had with a similar wound. Then he added, with an earnest glance into the girl's eyes, "You'll stay off it for a day or two."

La Pucelle smiled at him, but she vouchsafed no answer.

Before he could press her, Yann said, "Why don't you hand our Pucelle her supper, Gilles? Mistress Boucher left a warrior's feast warming in the corner of the chimney piece there."

Gilles found the food, meatless because the day was Friday, but hearty fare nonetheless and not easily come by in a city under siege: trout in a thick cream and almond sauce, stewed fresh broad beans, crisp spring greens with oil and vinegar, an omelet of herbs and mushrooms, a wheel of cheese, its rind sinking with ripeness, a compote of dried apples and strawberries, a loaf of crusty bread to eat with lots of butter, salt and young radishes.

Now that his head had cleared a little from all the wine he'd foolishly taken at Les Augustins, Gilles was famished enough to eat most of it himself. He resisted, however. He chose the best bits to begin with and carried them to La Pucelle.

"I'll just have some of that bread," she said, breaking off the smallest fistful. "And a bit of wine to dip it in, perhaps?"

Gilles got her the wine and held the cup while she dipped birdlike pieces for herself and popped no more than half a dozen of them into her mouth.

"But you must eat more," he insisted. "Shall I spoon up some of the trout for you?"

"No more. I couldn't."

"But you fought like ... like a man all day. And lost blood."

He was ready to eat the whole himself now, to spite her. But he would not, for fear the portion he chose might be the very one she fancied.

What was this girl? Trying to prove herself above the common needs of humankind? Too good even to eat? As if she were refusing to bind herself to this world by even such a simple act. Gilles shivered under his armor's casing in spite of himself.

"I can't," she said. "Too tired."

Gilles looked desperately to Yann, trying to tell him, magician to magician, Do something. Bring her down among us. How can she be mine if she won't even eat?

His milk brother met the look with sympathy, but did nothing except continue to dress the wound with a salve and then to bind it with strips of clean, well-worn linen.

A new thought occurred to Gilles, and he let all the others go then with a sigh of relief.

"Well, Lady," he said. "Your Voices told you your blood must be shed at Orléans. Now it has been. By a caltrop, and a wound my sorcerer milk brother assures me will not fester. I am glad of that. Now I can rest—and fight, too—much easier."

There was another exchange of glances, this time between Yann and the Maid. Gilles couldn't fathom what it meant, but she let him help her out of her armor and then carry her up the stairs to Mistress Boucher's bed on the second floor.

Twenty-Fourth Antiphon

Talisman Enough

I scratched at the door of Maître Boucher's house as she had asked me to, early, the light so dim that I could hardly tell the dark framing from the pale plaster between. Orléans' cocks, those few that hadn't yet found their way into the stew pot during the siege, had begun to challenge one another.

A host of other birds knocked and chirped and chucked and jangled and screamed and crooned and quavered, each according to its own species. They tempted my ear to hear out each squabble and joy, each choir chant and cooed exchange, species relaying species over the dew-slick rooftops of the town. Otherwise, my senses, all of them, found the air sweet and silent with anticipation.

I heard the bolt pulled softly back, behind the heavy oaken panels. The door swung inward on hinges I'd greased and spelled carefully to silence as I left the night before. La Pucelle's thin face appeared in the darkness within and nodded that all was clear.

I gestured behind my back and, from nearby recesses and alleyways, the rest of the witches appeared—each like a different species of bird, yet silent. They slipped through the door behind me.

We crowded into Maîtresse Boucher's kitchen where the banked fire was little more than white ash. Tiphaine set about coaxing it to life with more than her usual silence. There were coughs of flame within the grate by the time I returned from setting a spell at the foot of the stairs, to keep the rest of the household asleep just a while longer.

Also, by that time, Gilles had detected the slight limp in La Pucelle's linen-wrapped foot. He was forcing her into the room's single chair over the claim of his grandmother, the noble lady of Sillé.

"It's nothing," the girl protested. "Truly much better. Père Jean's herbs are magical."

Gilles' jealousy begrudged me even her slight and simply truthful praise. I saw him glancing again and again at Du Guesclin's ring on her finger. It was, perhaps, a little darker than usual.

"Let me have a look at the foot," I said, hoping to keep their voices down. I had magicked the rest of the house, but that would only work to a point. It would certainly not work if those two insisted on setting their own magic pouring between them like a flood.

"Ah, young flesh," I could exclaim as I unwrapped the linen and looked at the foot. "It has magic of its own."

It was more than just youth, more than my herbs, though I didn't like to say that aloud. Her very flesh had power. After the more common wounds in common men I'd been up the night tending to, it was as though it contained the force of a talisman within itself. I could see the puncture still, but it was clean and white and smooth, showing not the first hint of infection, and many of the lower layers must already have darned themselves together again.

I made a show of salving the foot and binding it up, but the linen needed no more bulk than a stocking. Now she wouldn't even limp.

"Well, if I can beg my Lady to stay on her horse in the battle today ... "

So Gilles conceded to her his permission to enter the field, though he got no promise from her. I was glad he believed that La Pucelle, the Maid inviolate, needed to fear the invasion of her body no more than her soul and will.

With that, we all circled her. Each gave of his own Craft.

That ritual completed, Gilles and Bricqueville did more mundane magic, helping her into her metal harness. Bricqueville had the punctured *sabaton*. He'd seen that an armorer spent the night repairing it. Gilles had found an exquisite new pair of boots. I could see that her pleasure at the suppleness and dashing red stain to the leather pleased my milk brother more than if the footwear had been his own.

Before they began with the breastplate, Gilles met my eye. I knew what he meant.

"Lady," I told her. "I have something for you, too. Something to offer a protection that works on a level different from that of cuirass and helmet."

From the deep sleeves of my black robe, I withdrew the stag-skin pouch full of herbs on its leather thong. I held it towards the girl, but she didn't immediately take it up.

"Take it," Gilles said. "My milk brother's amulets work on the battlefield. I know."

And I knew he was remembering the failed storming of Saint-James-de-Beuvron, a tower's explosion and a poisoned wound. My magic had brought both him and Bricqueville through, though many—so many—had been destined to die.

"I only hesitate because I have seen other soldiers wear such things," she said.

"Of course they do," Gilles said. "But Yann's Craft works much better at turning swords and arrows than their pebbles and weeds."

"Every man has his magic," I reminded my milk brother. "His own act of desire may do more for a soldier than ever I could."

Gilles shrugged, full of doubt.

I went on, "But this Hamish and I made with none but you, Maid, in mind."

Still she hesitated to take it. "The matter is, I've overheard some—His Grace the Bishop of Rheims among them—complain that such talismans are mere superstition. Or—worse—devices of the devil."

"And so this one is," I assured her, giving my head a toss, as though the tonsure even then wore its horns.

"I worry that I must be La Pucelle not only of the witches, but of all of France. I don't want to turn any man away because of something outside myself."

I nodded, understanding. "Such rejection comes from their hearts, child, not yours."

"Nonetheless, there is talisman enough in my body for all, including myself."

"I know it."

I set the pouch aside, upon the kitchen table.

Gilles wouldn't let it lie. He snatched it up and held it out to her. "Take it, Lady. For my sake, if not for your own. I know you have already lived the prophecy your council gave you, to shed your blood before Orléans. But that may be because Yann failed to give you such a talisman yesterday. You may be sure I chided him severely for it."

Gilles' ferocity must have broken my spell, for the family Boucher awoke, and we heard footsteps on the stairs. Turning towards the sound, I failed to see just what happened, but when I turned back, Gilles was smoothing the cord of the talisman around the girl's thin neck. The pouch itself lay hidden between her breasts.

Maître Boucher came fussing into the room like a hen scratching, though I was certain this was not a room of his house with which he had much familiarity himself. The rest of my coven knew enough to instantly take on the parts of those come to seek La Pucelle's help, not to give it. Madame Anne begged that her idiot son be touched, Gwencalon that his milky eyes might see.

Boucher shooed them all out, and they went like birds—to fan out, I knew, over the battlefield.

"I must be off," La Pucelle told her host as Gilles and Roger finished clamping her into her armor.

I saw her shift her limbs a moment within the case, feeling where the joints had bruised and chafed her on the previous day, but she made no complaint.

"I'll need my page and squire," she continued. "Please wake them, maître, at once. Have them bring my horse and banner."

"But Lady." The treasurer's wife had arrived now, protesting at her husband's side. "You haven't yet broken your fast. And you ate nothing last night that I could see. There's still the trout in Mariette's special almond sauce—and it is the best trout in Orléans, I promise you. The fisherman brought it as an offering to you himself. He told me that when he found it on his line, he knew this trout was too good for his family. This was the trout a saint and God had put on his line for just such a purpose. And now I see the skin's not even been pricked. Lady, won't you have some of it now?"

La Pucelle laughed merrily. "Save it for my supper, hostess. I'll be hungry then, for I will work hard today, harder than any day yet in my life. And I'll even bring a *goddam* prisoner back to share it with me. We'll march over the bridge together."

Then the girl turned, Gilles and Bricqueville flanking her either side, and left the room with a skip in her step.

"Poor girl," the hostess shook her head in dismay.

"She must be mad," the husband agreed, "just a little, like any saint, with God's madness. For anyone who's been in Orléans even a day must know the bridge is a ruin. We blew up the final two arches ourselves when first the *goddams* came, so they shouldn't have the use of it."

"Peace remain with you," I bowed to the couple and let myself out of their house.

I found the trio of young warriors paused on the threshold as they waited for the sleepy page to bring her horse around. La Pucelle turned when she sensed me and grasped my hand. I saw a very strange thing in the depths of her eyes. A shadow of fear.

"Stick close to me throughout the day, Father," she said.

"I?" I stole a glance towards Gilles and saw his blue-streaked chin twitch with jealousy. She'd taken my hand and did not say such things to him.

"I will work hard today and I—"

I could tell her Voices were with her. Warning? Urging? What? They seemed to have come to her with her first breath of morning air. The grey light had a yellow cast to it now, and it polished her face as it turned up to me.

She touched the place where my talisman lay beneath her armor and said, “I will have need of you.”

“I will be as close as that talisman,” I promised her.

But I already knew I wouldn’t be able to keep that promise, except with magic, for all my best will. I knew I was going to fall under a spell very, very soon.

The Braying of a Donkey Hoof

The eight witches awaited me across the river on the rim of the rise upon which crumbled the ruins of Saint Marceau. English soldiers had sheltered in the chapel during the winter and sights and smells of them, all unpleasant, lingered about the roofless walls like ghosts.

But there were ghosts older than that, much older in this old place. St. Marceau was one who, in ages past, died the Sacrifice and became a God. While his blood was scattered over all the land, his mortal remains were buried here. I could feel them with my bare feet as I walked through the dew-slick grass.

Present cycling demanded most of my attention now, the restoring of life to this plain from which even the bees had perished during the long months of siege. My cronies drew on the power of the old bones beneath us as they made their preparations, of course. They had the fire going, the cauldron full of pure rain water. Deftly keeping the hem of her long grey robes from the sparks, Anne de Sillé raked fresh, live coals from the fire to sit under the great brass belly. She kept the brew just below the boiling point.

The circle shifted and made room for me. I took the southern apex. The field of battle spread before me, rimmed at the north by the walls and spires of Orléans herself, catching the brassy colors of sunrise. Beneath that brim flowed the Loire, nearly four hundred ells wide at this point. It also glinted gold and *coquelicot,* molten metal in a crucible.

As yet unmolten and stark in their matrix, the piers of the ruined bridge punctuated the stream to the final pier, the double-towered fortress of Les Tourelles. This was what the English still held, much stronger than either of the bastilles La Pucelle had taken so far. It had been built originally and at leisure as a fortress, no hastily mortared-up abbey like the previous days' victories.

Les Tourelles formed the center of the bowl of my vision, towards which the slightest jarring of Madame Anne's staff runneled ripples until they collided. From this point, the ripples spilled back over the surface again, ring within ring.

An arm of the Loire looped Les Tourelles on the close, the south side. It was narrow and not very deep; a man could probably stand at its deepest point. He'd have his chin above the grass that drifted slowly westward with the current, among the brassy reeds and tarnished willows. A drawbridge crossed the water here, connecting the fortress with the lip of a dry earthwork barbican. Also choked with brush during peacetime, the blasts of war and foraging soldiers had pretty well denuded it by this time.

On the other side of this barbican stood Les Augustins, the stronghold La Pucelle and her men had taken just the evening before. Many of the French troops had spent the night there. Bricqueville and others had dug in, shifting the captured English guns towards Les Tourelles and bringing in others of their own until the aimed muzzles stood, axle abutting axle, along the parapet. Kegs of fresh powder and arrows had also been rolled in, as well as food and drink for a fighting army.

In spite of the guns and the best preparation a night of laboring by torchlight allowed, the terrain to Les Tourelles was too rough for siege machines. What with the ditches, the dry and the wet, every step would have to be won hand-to-hand.

This was the scene revealed by rising mists, by the wisps of steam skidding across the cauldron's face.

Then, there she was, standing alone on the rim of the dry barbican below Les Augustins. The white armor acted like a lodestone, catching all the golden light in the cauldron, in the whole battlefield. The banner snapped in her left hand. Slowly she raised her right towards the rising sun.

"Gwencalon," I whispered a warning to the blind Bard.

But he knew already, without sight. By sound, perhaps, by the silence of a breath of steam caught in the throat, of all the world quelled, waiting. Waiting for magic to happen.

Gwencalon, seated directly across from me, reached one bony hand over the cauldron. Something brown and heavy dropped into the hot water, an ass's hoof. At the same moment, down on the field, La Pucelle dropped her right arm. Trumpets up and down the French line answered, braying the charge.

As soon as he brought his hand back to his harp, Gwencalon matched the tone. These were not the lilting notes of the banquet hall, but the heavy, driving plunk, plunk, plunk, plunk, marching rhythm of the ancient war harp. In a moment, he began an accompanying chant. It was deep and gravelly in his throat, a song of heroes and of fabled feats of battle, from Arthur to Roland to Charles Martel whose sword La Pucelle bore. Mixed with these images swarmed a curse towards the enemy, blackness swirling with light upon the ear.

Below, in the greater world, both facing forts rocked with cannon fire. We saw billows of smoke and tongues of flame a heartbeat before we heard the thunder, Bricqueville and his comrades working their own magic. Like locusts flew the first volley of arrows. All along the barbican, along the horseshoe which was all the encirclement they could manage before they hit the riverbank on either end, the French surged forward. They met the English who'd dashed across the drawbridge, whose intersecting horseshoe bent in upon itself. Until the moment of that clang, that collision, the French were all but fighting each other in their frenzy to answer La Pucelle's call.

Madame Anne raked more coals to the cauldron. They winked red eyes in the wind as she did. I lost sight of the tiny figure in white armor for a moment or two, for smoke and dust on the field, and for smoke and steam in the water. The smells of fire, blood and discharged powder drifted up to our hill along with the clamor, the regular booms, clashes and screams of man and beast. This was the sulphuric odor, the tortures Christian preachers liked to ascribe to hell, the realm of devils.

They blamed it on our cauldrons.

I rediscovered Gilles first, the black of his armor and the cross of his arms stark against the pale grey of steam and smoke. For a moment I saw him on the cauldron's surface, shoving back his visor, looking for her. We both found her at the same instant. Then, down went the visor and all was right with the world once more.

Indeed, the two of them moved across the field shouting, encouraging, slashing, stabbing, mirror images, she with her banner, he with his sword. Always they were keenly conscious of one another, as if the rest of writhing, struggling, dying humanity about them did not exist. Or rather, as if everything else were mere inanimate objects to be tossed and folded and shifted only at their combined wills. La Pucelle and the dark lord of Rais moved, indeed, as lovers. Or rather, as lovers reflected in some great, dark glass, for this dance was life leading to death as the usual copulation is a little death leading to life. Each desperately sought his own pleasure, and gained it by helping the other to hers.

That was the way of it as we sat on our hill and watched, as all life around seemed to do the same. First the French surged up the English rim of the barbican. Then came a well-aimed cannonball or flight of arrows from Les Tourelles' walls. There was chaos and the surge went up the other side until the French were fighting with their own backs right against the walls of Les Augustins.

The sun rose higher and higher until it reached its zenith, reflected directly into the face of the water of our carefully watched cauldron, and neither side gained any advantage.

Within the beating heart of the cauldron, the donkey's hoof simmered alone until the last of the hair boiled away. The flesh shrank off the bone and into broth. From time to time, Madame Anne added more rain water, but allowed the broth itself to stew down, to grow thick and gluey.

Then, according to a rhythm she alone knew by silently

watching the progress of the sun, Tiphaine of the Mount-Saint-Michel reached out and added a pinch.

Her ingredient was only chopped leeks.

But every time the curls of white and green swirled out of the way before Madame Anne's staff, I Saw in the cauldron.

And what I Saw was neither witch nor warlock. Under a simple helmet with a pointed crown, I Saw the dark but pink-cheeked face of a man, a stranger. He wore no body armor but a simple brigandine snug to his chest from which a number of metal scales had been knocked off by the rigors of the past few days. He stood on the parapet of Les Tourelles. He was an Englishman. Or rather, more precisely, a fellow Celt, though he fought on the other side. He was a longbowman from the dark Welsh hills of Snowdonia.

He was far from home.

Twenty-Sixth Antiphon

Leek Juice

His bowstring was warm with use. Over the choking stench of black powder and burning pitch, he could smell the boiled-hoof glue in which the linen cord had been soaked to strengthen it. He clung to that smell; it had meant security to him, even from his childhood. It had meant advancement, escape from the dark, overcrowded and violent hovel of his childhood. It had meant the camaraderie of his fellows, adventure, triumph, some little looted wealth, everything it was to be an archer in Henry's army.

Now, on the parapet of Les Tourelles, he gave that scent to his nostrils over and over, five or six times a minute. He'd been doing it since sunup, the same movements, over and over.

The leather bracer tied to his left forearm was warm, too. He could feel it through several layers of cloth, the effect of tearing friction, over and over. It was almost as if the beast were coming alive again in this one scrap of its hide.

Even though he carefully used his whole body in the pull as he'd been taught, "not just the arms, not like a prissy nobleman", the archer's muscles were beginning to rebel. Six times a minute, reach back to the barrel of arrows the lads rolled up behind him and opened, one after another as they emptied. Six times a minute, pull an arrow out of the straw protecting its iron tip and fletches.

By weight alone, he would judge whether this was a lighter, aspen-flight arrow to gall the enemy at a longer distance. Mostly, however, these were ashwood, heavy arrows on blocky, square bolts. Thick, to give "greater stripe", as the phrase was. To pierce armor. Back-flanged in the head to stick in flesh and cause more damage coming out than they did going in. The heavier ones were for closer range, but the two were packed together and came to his hand by chance. No, not by chance. He never liked to think that. By the will of God and of St. George, to whom he had offered the best gold goblet of his last looting.

Six times a minute, he nocked an arrow, light or heavy, to this string, just at the point where it was warmest, at the center, well whipped with extra, strengthening thread.

Six times a minute, his whole body swung the bow up and pulled, in one smooth movement, yet with an effort that was equal to lifting eight or nine stone.

Six times a minute, he gave himself that glued linen smell, caught a glimpse of green striping white near his right eye. This green was the verdigris used in fletching glue. The white feathers were army issue, for which the lamented King Harry taxed one goose out of every twenty in the kingdom. At practice, the archer always marked his own arrows, with red and black on the feathers and a distinctive notch in one vane so as to retrieve them quickly.

This was not practice. He wouldn't see these bolts again.

Six times a minute, he aimed, with instinct more than brain.

Six times a minute the two fingers of his right hand, with which he gave the V of the archer's victory salute, gave the slightest twitch.

Six times a minute, the humming twang echoed within the hollow of his *sallet*.

Six times a minute, he felt the sting in his drawing fingers, cracked and bleeding.

Six times a minute he worked his left hand on the wax that seemed to be melting with the heat on the center of the belly of the bow as he reached behind him for the next arrow.

For hours of these six pulls a minute now, his boots had hardly shifted on the stone beneath them. The left foot remained a pace ahead of the right, a foot under each shoulder.

There was never any lack of targets. Light arrow or heavy, there was always some Frenchman or beast in clear range to receive it. Save for that, the action was much as he'd known in all the five years since he'd left his Snowdonia home.

And yet—it wasn't.

The targets were there. But they weren't turning and fleeing as he was used to.

Even more unnerving—always, it seemed, they moved before the arrow got there. And never, ever the way he expected.

At first he'd thought it was only a trick of the mist. He'd moved slower then, not wanting to waste arrows, expecting the mist to burn off. It had done so, but now there was no way to expect the dust and smoke of battle to vanish.

The more arrows he let fly, the less he mistrusted his vision. He saw clearly enough, clearly as one ever saw in battle. And he knew even misplaced arrows served a purpose, cowing the enemy, giving him no peace to think which way to jump.

The problem was, the things he saw were not what he expected, not what they ought to be. The only thing he could liken them to were the wraiths and spirits from the tales he'd heard around the turf fires of his childhood. The firedrake that could mislead wayfarers in a bog, the White Lady, *Dynes Wen*, of uneasy souls around graveyards, the fairy folk who could catch a man and lead him to fairyland forever and ever.

Once he'd got a bow in his hand, a little one, first at age seven, he'd thought such creatures only fable.

Today, he'd begun to believe.

It was the girl, of course. La Pizzle they called her, derisively.

She'd been a joke at first. A girl in battle? A milkmaid to drive England's great army out of France?

Like all his mates, he'd laughed at the idea. A great hero like Owain Glyn Dŵr hadn't been able to keep the English out of Wales. The archer, like the rest of them, had spent the evening hours calling her "cowherd", bragging about what nasty things he'd do when they got their hands on her.

When, in Les Augustins, he'd heard of the fall of Saint Loup, well, things had gone uncomfortably quiet. Then, last night, after seeing her fight, after escaping with their lives to Les Tourelles, they'd begun to talk again. But they talked in whispers. And every tale was closer to the tales of unnatural, devilish things he'd heard around his childhood's flickering flames than the soldiers' usual boasts of seduction and debauch.

They'd all had a good look at her now, that slight though unmistakable little figure in white armor. Why, she didn't even bother with a helmet most of the time. Certainly she rode like a demon, astride, like a man. But that wasn't the worst of it. He'd shot horse from rider before, rider from horse more times than he could remember.

The first few times she'd come into range, he'd chosen a particularly heavy bolt and aimed carefully. Then, with his own eyes, he'd seen it. The arrows sailed right through her and shivered harmlessly in the ground beyond. Or just to the side. Or vanished into thin air.

After that, once he'd calmed himself with a few deep breaths, he aimed at other things. But even those—especially if they stood in the sulphuric glow that seemed to surround her—even they, as often as not, seemed to move just half a step this way or that and escape unharmed.

He'd tried again to remedy this by slowing down, by taking more careful aim with each shot. When that had worked no better—certainly the foe was not as intimidated by arrows whizzing just past their ears as once they'd been—he'd begun to shoot faster instead. Five shots a minute, now six, hour after hour, over and over, in a frenzy of desperation.

In ten years in France, no engagement he'd ever been in had been like this. Always he'd been able to trust to the deadly power of his arm and his aim. There were rules to battle; there were rules to God's earth. As long as a man knew these rules and worked with them, that man came away with his life and a full belly.

And sometimes, after victory, a little bit more.

But this girl, this Pucelle as they called her, broke all rules. She rode like a man. She dressed like one. By St. Winifred, she fought like one against all nature, instead of keeping a soldier's supper warm behind the lines, and spreading her legs for him afterwards.

La Pizzle? There was more than just a derisive meaning to the word. Pizzle also meant the driving leather whip men made from the fiercest bull's privates.

Now at last the archer began to see clearly. She was unnatural. She was a witch. The figures he shot at and missed were fiends she'd conjured out of hell.

The thought made him pause after his last shot. He crossed himself. He touched the scrap of parchment he wore on a thread 'round his neck, roughly drawn with the pendragon of Wales and what they told him was a protective prayer.

Mindlessly, he drew another arrow, a light one this time. As light as his head felt.

Mindlessly, he pulled and let fly.

Even as he did, he wondered, What's the use? When demons walk the earth in the shape of human girls, what use were the efforts, even the prayers, of a hundred sinful men such as himself?

He saw her again, almost where she'd begun the day, standing on the lip of the barbican, arms outstretched, banner limp in the left. An easy shot. An easy, easy—*impossible* shot. The bow sank in his hands as if it had suddenly grown to a giant's size and weight.

At her signal again, the French trumpets brayed, calling for a midday respite. She hadn't gained a pace of ground, but that was illusion. She was the one calling the shots. On both sides.

Unable to will his limbs to move, the archer stood at the parapet and watched the sides separate and pull back. Safely out of range, he saw swarms of French women and children, half of Orléans, no doubt, as well as the very doxies he and his mates had been forced to leave behind in their flight. They came in waves, bearing baskets and platters of warm food, jugs of cool water, and lengths of clean linen to bind up the wounds of the French dogs.

The archer saw the girl still standing where she was, staring at the walls of Les Tourelles. Willing them to fall. Staring—

he felt it—at him. He thought he felt the solid stone beneath his feet shift. His bowels lurched like water within him.

A man, some great lord in black armor, approached her, an offering of victuals in his hands. This was the world stood on its head, indeed. A man waiting on a woman, a lord on a cowherd.

The girl took a drink from him, a few gulps of wine from a flagon. Or perhaps it was only water. But the rest she brushed aside, the lord, the victuals, all, to continue staring up—at him.

In all the morning's fighting, she hadn't advanced a step. But still, she was the one who told the trumpets when to blow, told them all, even great lords, when they could break.

Sir William Glasdale, English commander of the garrison, came by then and finally drew the archer's attention from the witch. Glasdale had been down there in the barbican all morning, leading the men-at-arms on the ground against her. Now, with the bridge drawn up and the lazy arm of the river between them, he was making the circuit of the walls behind him, seeing how these defenses were holding up.

The commander had a kind word for him and the archer tried to answer bravely. All the while he was conscious that, to do so, he had to turn his back—on her.

Glasdale was very English, tall so the archer had to bend his neck to look into his face, and very blond, though it was difficult to tell dust from hair at this point. Glasdale hadn't started as commander at Orléans. Months ago, at the start of the siege, so the story ran, he'd been standing with the earl of Salisbury surveying the position from a window during just such a midday break. A French cannon went off, sending the stone smashing into the window where they stood. A metal bar flying from the embrasure removed half of the earl's face and embedded in his skull. It took him days to die, and Glasdale, with this image in his mind, had been in charge ever since.

Rumor said it was no sharpshooter that had set the cannon off that October day, but a gunner's brat, playing among the already aimed guns while his elders sat down to meat. The gun had been stationed in the Tower of Notre Dame as well, and so must have had Our Lady's blessing behind it. Maybe that had been the start of it, the opening of the maw of hell. The start of women and children fouling up the neat man's world of battle. But nobody had seen it that way at the time.

Nobody'd heard of La Pucelle then.

As he stood there now, memories of that day of tragedy seemed to pass across Glasdale's face, his untended whiskers like trampled straw in a farmyard. What was it that could take this man and spare the one standing next to him for the fortune of command? Glasdale stepped aside a bit, putting the solid crenelation between himself and the French he'd been facing hand-to-hand all morning. Then, as if to hide what he'd just done, he let a smile crack the baked stubble batting of his chin and said some other carefree thing. He moved on, then, to cheer other men.

The lad came to the archer next, the lad who'd been rolling him kegs of arrows all day. The boy brought dinner, some salt herring and dried bread. That's all they had in the siege conditions of Les Tourelles. They. Englishmen who'd had the run of the countryside all these months before Orléans. Was it only yesterday that he and the boy had sat down to eat together and women had waited on them both? It seemed like lifetimes ago, yet the boy was still as young, as painfully young, as ever.

"Is there no water?" the archer asked, more sharply than he meant to, but the dryness in his throat was keen.

"In a moment," the boy called over his shoulder. "But I hadn't hands to carry it all."

The archer nodded, swallowed for patience, then, hating to be alone, looked along the parapet for Griffith, his mate, to break the bread with.

"Where's Griffith?" he shouted.

The boy stopped, turned, went pale. "Didn't you see?"

"I didn't."

"Cannonball from Les Augustins. Piece of stone in the eye. They're tending him below."

The archer crossed himself, closing his own eyes as if to spare them a similar fate. Shutting off sight brought smells more powerfully to his nostrils. Now he could smell things beyond the glue of his weapon. He could smell that, in his terror, Griffith must have shat himself. Close enough for the stench, and the archer had taken no notice of the disaster while it was happening. There was no use asking if Griffith would live. With a shard of stone in the eye, he'd never draw a bow again.

When the archer reopened his eyes, the lad still stood there, his face pale and puckered with grief. The archer pulled himself together and tousled the curly dark hair.

"Why don't you run and fetch your own dinner, lad?" he said. "And water for us both. We'll eat here together, safe behind the battlement."

The boy's face brightened into a grin. He couldn't trust himself to words, but ran off with a lighter foot.

As soon as the lad was gone, the archer looked down at the food in his hand. It was all of a color, a dull grey, both fish and bread. The fish smell was strong, and very like the smell of dying—wounded—Griffith.

The archer's belly growled for it, but between hand and belly was his dust-dry throat. He was certain he couldn't get a single bite of the heavy, salty fare past that obstacle without something to drink first. He set the food aside, spreading a grimy kerchief directly on the stone at his feet, fish atop bread.

This action revealed a single spray of green amidst the grey, a young leek as garnish. The sight refreshed him. He caught the root up, teased his nose with the end of its stalks. He sighed and closed his eyes again, seeing for a moment the whole green, leek-smelling world of his home. He took a quick snap at the white root end. His mouth filled with the juicy, pungent taste, he turned to his bow instead.

The archer considered releasing the string from the horn tip at one end, to give the wood a rest. The yew had a backwards curve when it had first been handed to him, years ago. He'd used it so much since that the wood followed the string now, bent the other way. Releasing the tension for an hour or so would give it more spring ...

Then he rejected the idea. Who knew but what he'd need it again without an instant's notice?

He checked the string, the whipping, the bowyer's knot, the grip. All looked good for many shots more. If not, he had two spare strings, ready cut to length and knotted, at his belt. One and a half kegs of arrows stood to one side. Taking one final whiff of hoof glue, he carefully set his weapon within the sheltering angle of the stone wall.

He meant to avoid the sight, but he couldn't help himself. He put his head around the crenelation and stole one more glance.

She still stood where she'd been, plainer now in the quiet and settling dust. She was a little silver figure, the shimmering color of a spirit, feet apart, right arm akimbo, staring up at him.

"Yes, by my dark minions. You."

He thought he could actually hear her.

The archer bit desperately at the tail end of his leek. He dropped his back against the safety of the parapet and slid down until his haunches fit snugly between the hard stone of the wall and floor.

He tossed the last green curls of leek from him, then looked where they landed, over the bread and fish. Before he could pick any of it up again, a shudder of dread ran through him, shoulders to groin. Every muscle ached with use. They began to twitch uncontrollably.

The shuddering came again. Again. It worked at his thirsty lower lip. Then it came to a place behind his eyes, a place where the leek had risen, a place that had always seemed his own, safe, confident, unassailable. The very place that always told him, without thought, when the aim was right.

That place shuddered. Then crumpled.

The archer laid his face down between his bent knees. He wept for sheer terror.

Twenty-Seventh Antiphon

In the Cauldron

Up in our circle on the hill before Saint Marceau, Madame Anne had her great, slow son breaking up more hawthorn and furze for her fire.

Before us, the pause for the soldiers' dinner was breaking up. I saw a few of the French captains—the Bastard, Alençon, Gilles, of course—draw close to La Pucelle for consultation. The captains kept glancing anxiously towards the walls of Les Tourelles towering above them. They knew this place where she stood was too close, too open to be safe.

Something of an argument was going on, La Pucelle pointing towards the walls again and again, the men pointing this way, that way, any way but the way she wanted.

Then the wind shifted, blowing smoke more to the east, in the quadrant Pieronne held within our circle. Pieronne, my Pieronne, moved for the first time that morning. She seemed only to be moving out of the fumes. But in the same moment, she began to chant, quiet words in the old tongue. Words about opening.

Pieronne took a nugget of what looked like gold out of her wallet and dropped it into the hot ashes at the fire's edge. Almost at once, the metal began to swelter and give off a foul odor.

It was pyrite, of course, fool's gold.

Having proofed the metal this way, Pieronne scooped the nugget up with the flattened end of her staff and tossed it, still smoking, into the hoof-thick broth. It gave off more foul odor, a burst, and hissed as it sank—with the sound of great chains running out.

Even as the stone sank, the bridge to Les Tourelles began to sink. Glasdale and a crowd of his men appeared, ready to cross it, the instant it fell level. They were unwilling to let the French commanders come to any unity before they kept them busy again.

I saw Gilles bring up the Maid's horse and try to get her to remount. She refused, of course, and sent the beast back out of harm's way.

Seeing the bridge come down, a mob of Frenchmen abandoned the tail end of their meals and naps and ran to join La Pucelle, weapons drawn and ready. Among them, I recognized those who'd come with her from Vaucouleurs, many others of similar devotion.

The girl handed off her banner to her page and gestured half of the men down into the barbican at once, to meet Glasdale and his forces the moment the bridge was down.

A wing of black shadowed the surface of our cauldron, and then a sprinkling of white fell on it.

"Wheat. For height," La Meffraye croaked.

Madame Anne, her mistress, raked ashes from the Maypole now to set the simmer.

The rest of La Pucelle's men handed scaling ladders forward from the rear of the lines, three in all. A man to every rung and scores more followed the phalanx with La Pucelle at its fulcrum.

Perhaps it was only the burp of bubble in the brew, but I

heard her young, shrill voice cry: "Go, go, go, for our Mother France." The men roared like an elemental surge deep in the Earth's heart.

"By the Stag," I muttered, suddenly realizing, but finding my body too ensnared by the spell to do more than murmur. "She still has the amulet."

Quick as a flash in the cauldron, Père Michel's old liver-spotted hands added holy thistle.

Ridding her of dross.

"To gain higher aspirations," he intoned.

Even as he did, we saw her yank the thong around her neck to pull out the amulet she'd taken at Gilles' insistence that morning. "Snap," Bibu de Sillé cried, snapping furze with a great shower of sweet-smelling, golden bloom and needlelike leaves.

The amulet's thong snapped from her neck. La Pucelle kept on running, down through the empty barbican, tossing the amulet away from her as she reached the upward berm on the other side.

"Sweet Mary, Mother of God," the young Welsh archer choked aloud, crossing himself with a hand almost too heavy to lift. "They're going to storm us."

She's going to storm *me* was what he felt.

He'd been dozing against the wall in the warm sun, the little lad's head on his shoulder, when he'd heard the chains groaning as they let down the bridge.

Stupid with exhaustion and with crying, he'd taken a breath to realize what this meant. Another couple breaths to rouse the lad and scramble to his feet. Now he saw, and the sight flung him back behind the safety of the crenelation with pure horror.

He thought he was going to be sick. Without the wall at his back, his knees never would have held him upright.

"Come on, come on," he heard the little lad cry. "They're coming, right up the redoubt, right up to this section. Pick up your bow."

When the archer did not respond, the lad snatched the bow, tried the pull. It was too much for him. He shoved it into the archer's hand. He even had to press his elder's fingers close around the smooth, waxed yew, there between the aiming notches.

The lad chose an arrow from the barrel, one of the heavy ones, and closed it in the archer's other hand.

The archer heard the thunk of ladder legs against the pounded earth below him, two similar thunks to either side. He heard the roar of charging voices with them, thirsty voices, it seemed to him. Thirsty for blood. Like dogs baying at the foot of a tree.

Inside Les Tourelles, the message was getting 'round to his comrades. Every spare man was running towards him, converging on this spot to hold them off. He alone stood frozen.

"Come on," the lad cried, trying to turn him bodily around to face the narrow opening between solid masonry.

"Sweet Jesus God," the archer murmured. Crossed himself. Touched his amulet.

Turned.

He looked down, almost straight down, into her face. She was coming up, as if from the smoky pit of hell. The sight made him dizzy. The height bothered him, as it never had in his life before.

She was first up the ladder, though scores of others pressed so close there was hardly room for her to move her heels from rung to rung. She did move them, however, quickly as climbing to the loft in her father's barn. Both hands on the rails, her short hair bobbing with the movements. She wore no helmet. She hadn't even unsheathed her sword for such a climb up sheer pounded dirt—the enemy both at the top and on the fortress walls beyond.

The archer saw, off to his right, Glasdale and his force stopped at the end of their bridge. Men teetered from that direction with poles and axes, trying to knock the ladders down. The narrow berm only allowed one or two to scramble along it at a time. Somewhere in Les Tourelles, Englishmen had fired up their guns again. But they weren't on his section of the wall.

That face—open, fearless, so obviously a girl's face, for all the armor and cropped hair—that face rose steadily below him. So very, very young. It turned his stomach. Dark brown eyes didn't flinch from his but held them steady. Smiled at him, or so he thought. As some lover might.

As some ravenous fiend from hell.

Once more the archer crossed himself. He leaned far over to get the bow at the proper angle.

He pulled. With every fiber of his body.

Beside his right ear, his drawing fingers twitched. As if they had a life of their own.

Hard Shaft Within the Softness of Flesh

The force of the bolt in her shoulder knocked La Pucelle backwards off the very top of the ladder. The bodies of the men behind her broke her fall and then swallowed her out of view.

Quickly I pulled the corpse-white mushroom, known commonly as the destroying angel, out of my sleeve. I was careful to keep it upside down until I held it directly over the cauldron. Then I tipped it. A cloud of black spore drifted into the brew. It was the specific I always used for Gilles de Rais, in all my magic.

On the field before me, Gilles pulled his spore-black horse up so fast, the creature reared and screamed.

Gilles screamed, too. It was the wail of a little lost boy, as if he himself had been hit.

"You'd better go," I said, nodding to a third of my remaining coven, the three witches, Pieronne, Tiphaine and La Meffraye.

The women rose and broke the circle. They headed off down the hill like a flock of ravens to the battlefield. Just before she left, Pieronne swirled a handful of fragrant, dried rose petals mixed with *muguet* upon the cauldron's surface.

For one agonizing stretch of time, I found myself inside the body of La Pucelle. I gasped her little whimpers, shallow and quick because the hurt of taking more breath was impossible to bear. The pound of pain let nothing of the English roar of triumph—coming after a moment of silent wonder—into her skull.

It was almost as wide as her little finger, this shaft that had suddenly fused itself to her flesh. It had gone clean through her breastplate, crumpling back the metal as if it were no more than flimsy paper. It was on the left side, just inches from her neck in one direction, from her rapidly fluttering heart in the other.

Within the softness of her flesh, I could feel it, the hard shaft, the even harder point. The oozing blood quickly brought both to body temperature, but they were still foreign. The backward-flaring tines of the head stabbed at either side of the long groove they'd carved through thew and tissue. The point itself rested against her shoulder blade, scraping it slightly with each breath.

By her own sweet martinets, she prayed to stop breathing altogether, for each gasp jerked the white feathers and green verdigris glue of the arrow's fletches dizzyingly before her eyes. Each breath caught the shaft on the hard rims of her breastplate. Every fiber in her longed to shrink out of the pain, but the heavy steel cuirass bolted it tightly to her.

And, oh, if these men of hers would stop jogging so as they hurried her away from the dangers of Les Tourelles' walls. Two men on each leg, two on her back, one on each shoulder, one on the head. She was in too much pain to add up all their hands and heads, but she knew only too well how, careful and smooth as they tried to make the run, each foot slipped and stumbled over the uneven ground.

Each hand trying to help pulled her in a different direction. And any direction but towards the blackness swirling in around the shaft in her shoulder shot arrows of pain back and forth along every limb.

Overhead, the sky arced. Faces peered down at her from the even, easy blue. Later, she would recognize Jean de Metz and Poulengy, those faithful men who'd been with her since Vaucouleurs. Now, if they weren't her Voices, she had no space in memory for them.

Puffs of cannon smoke were the only clouds. She saw them then, her little black martinets, shooting though that space in the moment's awe, yes, even peace, which her fall had brought to both sides of the field. The birds' high-pitched whistles pierced her ears. Pierced her shoulder. She seemed to hear with her shoulder.

"Daughter-God." Ah, the comfort of her Voices. At last.

Or was it merely the whistle of arrows starting up again?

On the hill, Gwencalon, whose charge had ended with a crashing chord, touched the strings of his harp again. Now he played a dirge.

Chapter Thirty-One

A Scrap of Ste. Aldegundis' Cloak

Gilles de Rais spurred his horse until he broke its skin, and froth from the beast's mouth flew back into his face. All the while, it was himself he wished he were pricking. His own screams of agony that filled his ears. Himself he cursed to the devil and back again.

Why had he ever left her side? Why had he trusted Yann's pathetic magic?

They'd laid her on a heap of cloaks and saddle cloths in the shadow and safety behind the corner of Les Augustins' near wall. He threw the reins to a lad blubbering with tears, and shoved another couple out of the way.

The looks on those faces made him think she must be dead. Gone. Lost to him forever. He wanted to kill. Hundreds. Not just English. All those bodies crammed between himself and her. Corpses enough to stack to heaven to reach her.

He saw her. She looked dead, her eyes closed, her face grey and frozen. He saw no blood. She was past bleeding, even.

Then—he saw her knee twist and jerk. He didn't think that was caused by any jostling man nearby. Though it seemed a mindless, pain-racked movement, it spoke of life.

Someone had the sense to cut the fletches off the shaft so they wouldn't get knocked with every movement. Now, two men lifted her gently to unbuckle the breastplate. He wanted to shove these heavy-handed fellows out of the way and do it himself, do it all himself, even take on the pain. But he saw her wince and grow paler still. He heard her sharp intake of breath.

A jab in his gut and a weakness in his knees made him doubt his ability.

The men laid her back down, then slowly lifted off the metal shell. Once or twice, for all their care, the ragged edges of the hole caught on the shaft. She gasped and arched her back, as if she wanted to rise and go away with her armor.

Then, it was off. The arrow, however, remained, sticking skyward as if accusing heaven of bad faith.

Even on the padded white jerkin below, there was no more than a spot of blood ringing the shaft. It was easier to see her breathing now, the quick, shallow heave of each gasp, the jerk of the shaft as if it were flesh of her flesh.

One man slashed at the jerkin with his dagger, then cut away the linen shirt beneath that. He peeled the fabric back, baring shoulder and neck, just to the rise of breast. Gilles felt ashamed for noticing. Certainly no one else did.

Still the shaft looked melded to her, skin to skin, with but the tiniest oozing of blood at the joint.

On the second attempt, after a heavy swallow to find his voice, the man wielding the dagger said, "Lady, the bolt's wedged against bone. We can't shove it out the back. It's got to come out the same way it went in."

"I'll hold her feet," said one.

"I, her knees."

"Give her my belt to bite on," said a third, letting his smock go free as he made the offer.

"Here, here. Give her a good swig of wine first," someone else said, producing a skin.

She hardly wet her lips.

"Here, here. I have this amulet. It's supposed to staunch blood."

"A scrap of Ste. Aldegundis' cloak. It'll dull the pain. Just hold it in your hand, Lady, and call upon the saint."

She refused to close her hands around the filthy rags they tried to press on her and, with her right hand, waved them weakly away. Though she rejected them, these offers reminded Gilles. He looked and saw—no little pouch of Yann's handiwork, no leather thong about her neck. Either she'd lost that amulet—the one he knew would have power to save her. Or—or she'd thrown it away herself. On purpose.

All his fear, grief and weakness washed from him in a burst of brilliant anger. He wanted to throttle her himself.

Shoving two men's shoulders apart before him, he squatted down to her head and said, "Jehanne, Jehanne, what did you do with Père Yann's pouch?"

Only the fear that he might actually finish off what the *goddam* had begun helped him stifle his anger to these words and no actions, no touch.

She opened her eyes and met his. The dark pupils were firm and unflinching, as yet unglazed by any fever, almost, it seemed, without pain. "Bluebeard? Is that you?"

"It's I, my heart, my soul." How many endearments did he dare with this crowd of buffoons around? And yet, if she was going to die, he had to let her know.

"I had to toss it, Bluebeard," she said. "It had to be. I am the amulet for France, alone."

Fearless as she seemed, surely she was raving.

"That arrow's got to come out, my lord de Rais," the fellow at his elbow insisted.

Gilles nodded, but never took his gaze from her face. "Jehanne? Will you allow me?"

He dared to set one hand on her bare shoulder. With the other, he reached towards the shaft, though he felt his arm shake more violently than the stick of ash wood holding steady in soft flesh.

Her little hand caught his firmly first, around the wrist, then worked until it nestled within the hollow of his grasp.

"I'll do it," she murmured.

In spite of the pressure of communication he felt in his palm, it was with the circling soldier's faces that Gilles exchanged startled glances. Do it herself? Why, even the strongest man was bound to faint halfway through the task, at the most dangerous point, even with other hands doing the agonizing work for him.

"Lady, that will never do," one brave soul said.

Then it struck Gilles. Even for such a thing, La Pucelle required no man.

He silenced the fellow with a gesture. He gave one final squeeze to her hand then gently let it go.

"Very well, Lady," he said. Then, to the men, "Stand back, messires. Give her air. Give her room."

He obeyed the wordless gesture she made with her head to prop her shoulders a little higher with his own rolled surcoat. Then he drew back with the rest, taking deep breaths. As if he could breathe for her.

Her two little hands converged on the shaft. They flexed once, twice, getting better grip, pressing the rise of her skin down and away. Smearing her fingers with sticky blood.

He saw her lips move in some sort of prayer. Her eyes squeezed shut. She clamped down on her breath.

And pulled.

There was one great, long animal cry of pain. She slumped back upon his surcoat as if dead. But the bolt, bloodied up half its length, fell lose from one limp hand.

Now there was blood, spurts of it from the gaping wound the flanges of the arrow had ripped coming out. Gilles caught the briefest, knee-weakening glimpse of the red, open lips. Then the man next to him, holding a clearer mind, slapped a wad of clean linen on them and rocked forward, putting the full weight of his upper body into the task.

"This may have to be cauterized," the man said, teeth clenched over the effort. "Somebody see if you can get a fire going."

Gilles shifted himself out of the way. He had no such skills, truly useful skills. He only knew how to make the worst of wounds, not heal them.

"The bleeding's slowed," the man reported shortly, not without some hint of amazement in his voice that it should be so.

The men with flint and tinder had yet to strike a spark.

"Who had that wine skin?" the one who'd volunteered as surgeon called. "Here. Bring it here. We'll wash the wound out with that. And oil. Somebody have some oil? Walnut's best, to stay the gangrene. But anything will do. Swine grease, if that's all you have."

Gilles heard a sharp hiss of breath pulled between clenched teeth as the astringent wine splashed onto the jagged edges of the wound. She was conscious again. Or maybe she always had been. He didn't return to meet those clear, dark eyes, however. He let the cluster of caregivers close her out of view and walked away.

Where the hell was Yann in all of this? Lets his damn amulet get tossed and then isn't around to magic away the ill effects afterwards.

In spite of these thoughts, Gilles didn't spare a glance back at the hill where the witches said they'd congregate for this day's battle. He scanned the length of the parapet of Les Tourelles instead. The defenders had shoved the ladders back off the redoubt. The flimsy wood lay abandoned in the bottom of the barbican.

A few Frenchmen were still fighting the sortie of Glasdale and his men, but that was the only skirmishing going on. Even this action seemed to have lost much of its muscle. The *goddams* had pushed the effort almost back to the gates of Les Augustins. From Les Augustins, a desultory crack of guns echoed from time to time—Roger keeping himself busy. But for the rest of it, the Frenchmen had all had the wind kicked out of them with studded boots.

If Glasdale kept making progress like that, La Pucelle wouldn't be safe much longer where she was lying. They'd have to get her into Les Augustins' walls, if not further. But it couldn't possibly be safe to move her yet.

Again he looked at the walls of Les Tourelles, studied the point where the central ladder had fallen. The shadow of an English archer flitted there.

Gilles brought his hand to his lips, chewing a knuckle in concentration. A savor like confectionery filled his mouth.

He looked and saw that he still held the arrow the girl had drawn from her own shoulder. It was sticky with her blood.

Then he licked his lips. It was the sweetest thing he'd ever tasted.

Tasting the beloved's blood, he remembered, was powerful love magic.

When he reached his horse again, he slipped the arrow-relic carefully into his saddle bag.

To hell with Yann and his talismans. If ever Gilles de Rais got his hands on the bastard who'd done this, he would work magic on him, all right. His own, personal, black sort of magic. He would see that the man died slowly. His balls first. Gilles would make him eat them.

Twenty-Ninth Antiphon

The Vineyard

In the hills of St. Marceau, more blossom petals and *muguets* went into the steaming cauldron, cooking over grapevine twigs that had been pruned from vineyards.

In the shelter of the wall of Les Augustins, La Pucelle opened her eyes to a lovely fragrance of flowers. It seemed to be the smell of her own blood, sweet and rich. They'd bound her shoulder with well-worn linen, soft, freshly sun-bleached. Under it, her body throbbed. She could still feel every *pouce* of the path the iron had cut, fiber severed from fiber that had been joined since before her birth.

But there was the fragrance again. Like wild rose. And grape vines shimmering in bloom.

She struggled to sit up. Four arms hurried to help her.

"Some more wine, Lady? Water?"

She drank what the man offered her, acutely aware of every muscle required to swallow. Now that she gave him the chance, a second fellow busied himself readjusting the bolsters at her back. The wadded up black and gold of Rais' surcoat he tossed aside as too blood-soaked for further use. She saw her blood had gone clear through, to the soil of France beneath her.

Good, she thought. That's it then.

"The battle?" she asked as soon as her throat was clear.

No one met her eyes. They didn't want to answer that.

"Let me see."

They tried to forbid her, but when they saw she would

struggle to her feet without them, they helped her. Her slashed clothing threatened to fall off. She held it with her good arm, and walked unsteadily so she could see, a man at each elbow.

The *goddams* had beaten their way close enough to Les Augustins to make themselves targets for scalding pitch and heavy boulders rolled directly off the French-held walls. These defenses were slowing down, now that a friend was as likely to be hit as English. The lord of Rais—she always looked for him. There, she saw him, in the thick of it, fighting like a madman. He always did that. The thought almost made her smile. He seemed to be the only one with any spirit left at all.

She turned away, and got a strong whiff of the fragrance over the smoke and dust of war.

"A vin—a vineyard—?" she stammered.

The men with her couldn't think what she was talking about.

Then she saw for herself, beyond their shoulders, to the east of Les Augustins a hundred paces or so. The friars must have once tended the plot. Stakes and trellises still marked regimented rows. Since the coming of the English, the place had been neglected. The winter pruning never happened, and canes coming to leaf draped the ground as well as their trellises.

"Excuse me," she said, and headed purposefully that way.

Her crowd of attendants took her arms and followed her for a way. Once they passed the spot where they'd doctored her and they began to protest her going any further, she shook them off. To her surprise, they let her go.

They think I need to relieve myself, she thought, as she struggled to put one foot in front of the other, to keep going on her own very unsteady legs. The thought amused her and gave her strength. If I'd been a man, they'd have come with me and stood beside me, holding me up. Since I am who I am ...

After all that wine, yes, she needed that, too. But there was more to the vineyard than that. The moment the draping vines with their wine-in-the-bud fragrance enveloped her and the three witches stepped forward to greet her, she was certain.

"She prays," the young foot soldier reported.

That was what he saw, peeking between the overgrown vine canes. Pieronne, Tiphaine and La Meffraye also prayed, or chanted, circling the kneeling girl in the old, dark way. But my spell over the cauldron and each woman working her own glamour assured that the fellow saw what he hoped to see when sent to investigate what was keeping La Pucelle.

La Meffraye offered an opium cup. La Pucelle refused it but allowed the women to treat her with other herbs and magic. They gave her a new shirt, one Hamish Power had the making of.

"It is well." In half a summer's hour, she was able to say this, and walk out of the vineyard alone.

"Lady—" The soldiers greeted her with concern, moving to her as if they expected to have to carry her back to her nest.

One close look, and they didn't touch her. Like a holy thing. She had that air. They parted and she walked through them.

"Bring my breastplate," she said, not looking at them, surveying the ruined, almost abandoned battlefield from the nearest rise.

"Lady?"

"Your breastplate, Lady?"

"But—but the armorer has it. It will be a good day's work before it's fit to wear again." This man's tone indicated that the armor had actually been set aside. No one thought anyone would ever wear the diminutive shell again.

"Something else, then." She worked her shoulder gingerly. "Something a little lighter."

"Mail would be lighter than plate," someone suggested.

"Good. Mail then. Get me a coat of mail."

"But it won't be nearly as much protection, Lady."

"That doesn't matter."

"But, Lady—"

"I've shed my blood. Now I'm not afraid. I'll go in this shirt if I must. But I must go. I must go and show them—all."

Thirtieth Antiphon

Walking On Air

The surface of our brew took on a silver sheen. There she was. I saw her, a spot of silver, striding to the front again.

Gilles de Rais saw her the same moment, just as he plunged his sword into the weak spot at an Englishman's neck. He never saw the man fall, but blindly yanked his sword back for the next blow. His eyes were too full of tears.

Roger de Bricqueville saw her, too, and the guns on the walls of Les Augustins that had been coughing listlessly suddenly burst to life like laughter.

Englishmen staggered back as if they'd seen a spirit rising from the dead.

Frenchmen appeared everywhere, as if sown on the ground like dragon's teeth.

On the hill by Saint Marceau, Bibu de Sillé stacked his fire with everything near him: old rags, rancid fat, animal bones.

On the city side of the river, the folk of Orléans could hardly contain themselves, so much did they want to be fighting, too. They filled a barge with materials like Bibu de Sillé's, tossed in a lighted torch and cut her lines.

The wind shifted and began to blow the acrid smoke southward, straight into my face. I didn't move, however, but watched in the cauldron with stinging eyes as current and wind caught up the drifting vessel. In the heart of the sooty black clouds of smoke beat violent tongues of flame.

On the field, the Frenchmen quickly pressed the English back, but Glasdale and his men retreated in good order, attaining the safety of their drawbridge.

La Pucelle watched their progress then, suddenly, cried to them from her place upon the rim of the barbican. "Glasidas! Glasidas!" That was as close as her French tongue could ever come to saying the English name "Glasdale". "Yield. Yield to the King of Heaven. Surrender now and save your life and your men."

Above the din of battle, the *goddam* commander heard her even as I did, with magic. He looked that way. Around the corner of Les Tourelles drifted the smoking barge. It came directly towards the drawbridge as if it had a mind of its own.

Père Michel tossed a whisk of sedge within the billows.

There, under the bridge, the barge snagged on a bit of river weed. Furry black smoke drew back, revealing orange fangs. They bit deep into the bridge's wood.

The Frenchmen shrank back from the sight. Glasdale and his men leapt for the safety of the fortress across the burning wood.

"Glasidas!"

Bibu's fire cracked and popped and roared.

The fire-weakened bridge gave way beneath the heavy armored boots of fifty or so men. Glasdale dropped through the fire into neck-high water. He didn't land on his feet, and there was no hope for him. The weight of his armor held him under until he drowned.

The three witches from the vineyard returned to our circle on St. Marceau's hill. Tiphaine tossed another handful of leek rounds into the brew before settling herself down with her skirt gathered tight around her haunches once more.

"They need you over at the north side."

The archer heard the order as his hands shook too much to pull his bow. He'd seen his commander sink to the bottom of the Loire in less than two ells of water. No more bubbles rose, but horror riveted his gaze to the spot. His hand seemed more tired from crossing himself than from pulling his bowstring. He tried to clear his mind, to get it around this new order. Who was his new commander, now that Glasdale was gone? He couldn't think.

But why would anyone order him to the north side of the fortress? Nearly four hundred ells of water, deep water, spanned only by the ruined piers of the old bridge stood between them and the enemy in Orléans.

Ah, God save Glasdale's soul from hell, from the flames of this world and the next. He'd feared attack from the fourth side so little, he'd trained none of the guns there, towards the north.

If a new danger were to come from the city side, it was too late to shift those guns. Only archers could move fast enough. There wasn't enough powder left to make wheeling the guns around worthwhile anyway. They were running out of powder in Les Tourelles. The ration each charge got now was barely enough to send the balls rolling to the end of the barrels, and from there, straight down. A child could throw them further.

The archer picked up his bow and a fistful of arrows and moved to comply with the order. What was on the north? He didn't care. It would be good to be away from the south side, this side where she, the witch, was always in view.

She was a witch. He'd never been more certain of anything in his life. He himself had shot her. He'd been close enough to see the bolt go in, and go in deep. He saw her fall backwards into the arms of her men. Such a fall would have killed many another.

But here it was, not two hours later, and she was back at the head of the attack again. He'd been very close. He knew it was the same girl. She wore a different hauberk, the metal having survived less well than her flesh. Which of course couldn't be human flesh, but must be black spirit.

He hadn't the power to shoot at her again.

Yes, why he'd waited for the suggestion to shove off towards the northern wall was beyond him. A wide river, empty save for a drifting fire barge or two, and the ruined bridge would be a relief.

No armored attacker could come from that side. Any one who tried would sink to the bottom of the river, just as Glasdale had done.

Not unless they could walk across the thin air between the ruined piers of the bridge. And no mortal could do that.

Could he?

On the northern bank, the citizens of Orléans began to rebuild their ruined bridge, span by span, out towards the one side the defenders of Les Tourelles had thought safe. They stretched long benches from pier to pier. They rifled the carpenter's shops. They pulled up planks from the ruined mills that had once ground away at their grain under the bridge. They tore the facing boards off house fronts, broke up old barges. A man who'd barely wielded a hammer before suddenly built like a guild master. A guild master built like God. So they worked their way from pier to pier.

For the last span, they got a long piece of lead gutter. It just reached from the last pier to the crumbling dirt at the threshold of Les Tourelles's barred gate.

La Meffraye's taloned hand tossed in a measure of musty Maltese cumin, Père Michel tossed in a lump of lead.

"Let me try it first," a well-built knight in the splayed black-on-white cross of the Hospitalers told the toiling citizens. "If it will hold me, it will hold anyone."

He set one iron-clad foot in front of the other. A light-weight arrow pinged off his helmet, another off his breast-plate. The gutter sagged under the three-hundred-*livre* weight of man and metal. If he fell, things would go no better for him than they had for Sir William Glasdale. Worse. The current was stronger here, dizzying, and the water deeper.

At the middle, the lowest point, the knight began to trot, the bridge springing him forward with each step.

A cheer went up from the folk of Orléans. The bells of their many towers rang out. A pair of men followed the knight, with a scaling ladder between them. Another pair came at their heels.

After their menfolk, Orléans' women pressed to the bridge, armed with their kitchen knives and cast-off pikes. If La Pucelle could do it, so could they.

From a certain angle, the thinly hammered lead of the gutter looked like nothing at all. The townsfolk of Orléans crossed to reclaim their fortress of Les Tourelles on thin air.

Bibu de Sillé let the black smoke dissipate a bit. My Pieronne tossed in more rose petals and *muguets*.

I saw La Pucelle. I saw her stop a moment, hearing her Voices over the din of battle. Something they said made her smile.

Gwencalon played a light, lilting air, lute-like, with a southern flavor. Michel added a piece of dried hake fish to the pot. Hamish arose for the first time since we'd met in the morning. Slowly, he unraveled a piece of white silk, cut from between the swallow tails of the banner he'd made for La Pucelle. Thread by thread, he dropped it into the pot and conjured an image:

"Here." La Pucelle handed her banner to the closest man. Short and dark he was, with an odd accent and his hose tied in the curious cross-garter fashion of the Basques.

"Carry this for me," she said. "Carry it to the wall." When he hesitated, she assured him, "I will run beside you."

Then, behind her, she called, "When my banner is blown against the wall, go, for the fortress is yours."

The word carried from voice to voice across the field in every direction.

Anne de Sillé raked the last of the coals from the cauldron and concluded our rite with the sacrifice of a white dove. Its blood formed a sheen on the surface of the brew.

La Pucelle and the Basque ran together. As fast as they could weave among the struggling and fallen men of both sides, they carried the banner.

More barges, not burning now, had come and collided against the ruins of the drawbridge. La Pucelle and the Basque scrambled across these. Within the lengthening shadows of Les Tourelles, they crouched behind an abandoned mantelet. Little more than a table turned on its side, its forward face bristled with English arrows.

Rubble clogged the way before them, bodies, and men at the base of a siege ladder struggling to rise. The two with the banner pushed a step or two here, forward there. The banner swayed. Then, floating like a white cloud, it caught in the wind, and the tail blew out to touch the wall.

Many a man said he saw a white dove flying over her that day.

A great shout went up. The ladder arced forward through the sky. Thunk, thunk, thunk, ladder after ladder connected with the wall and stayed there as if glued.

Les Tourelles fell.

On St. Marceau's hill, we released the powers and poured our magic down between two stones into the ruined church's crypt.

Tired, a little stiff but jubilant as evening dimmed to slate around her, La Pucelle crossed into Orléans over the sagging lead gutter and the rest of the makeshift bridge. The carpenters set to making the structure sturdy again parted to let her pass, fell to their knees, cheered and wept as Les Tourelles leaped to fire behind her.

In the bowels of Les Augustins, where the more common prisoners had been taken, a damp smell of destroying angel mushroom lingered.

Gilles, the lord of Rais, sat on a stool beside a rough table, a single torch blackening the wall behind him.

The prisoner was hauled before him in chains.

"You're the man who shot La Pucelle this afternoon?" Gilles demanded.

His words had to be translated for the fellow.

The archer crossed himself and muttered prayers, but didn't try to deny it.

"Show me your archer's fingers," Gilles said, rising to his feet with a grating of old wood on stone. "The two that did the deed."

The man did so, with encouragement from the jailers. The fingers were hard as horn with callus, from much shooting.

With a whisper, Gilles' dagger slipped from its sheath.

"We'll start with them," he said.

And on the battlefield, just ahead of the French pillagers, three witches moved like scavenger birds, gathering body parts of the fallen.

Such things would be useful for their next spell.

Chapter Thirty-Two

The Bodies of Saint-Pierre-des-Corps

"Bluebeard, take me away from all this," La Pucelle pleaded. And Gilles was only too willing to comply. It had been weeks since either of them had swung a sword except against each other in exercise. The day after the fall of Les Tourelles, the eighth of May, John Talbot had lined up what was left of his English forces in full array facing the walls of Orléans. There they had stood, their banners playing in the light, warm breeze the only movement, for two full hours.

It being a Sunday, La Pucelle would not fight. "Except in self defense," she'd assured him.

Though it was the lighter chain mail, she nonetheless had put on armor and gone out to watch the enemy from barely beyond longbow range. She'd stood watching them the full two hours.

Gilles was certain the raw wound in her shoulder from the day before had nothing to do with her reticence. He'd thought, though he hadn't been completely sure, that the blood smell lingering in his nostrils was only from his own late hours spent in Les Tourelles' dungeon with the archer.

Then, Talbot had turned and marched his army off, away from Orléans and out of sight.

With their dust still lingering on the horizon, Orléans erupted with joy. Every clapper swung until the impression stayed in the brain long after the bells themselves had stopped. A great, solemn procession of thanksgiving wound to every church, La Pucelle at the head.

Then—then she'd run into this brick wall. Two weeks wide at this point and no end in sight. The Dauphin had called for her to come to him here at Tours. She'd gone willingly enough, though any man who'd taken a wound such as she had would have an excuse to lie in bed for months. The Dauphin was the key to her Voices' next command.

"Rheims. I must take Your Majesty to be crowned and anointed in Rheims," she said, over and over.

So far, Charles hadn't budged.

"Rheims is over a hundred leagues away."

Charles told her that. Alençon told her that. Gilles himself told her that.

"Such a long trip will never be made," she always replied, pacing those leagues in her anxiety to be covering them, "unless the first step is taken. Today rather than tomorrow, tomorrow rather than the day after."

"At every one of those leagues is an English stronghold like Orléans. Or stronger."

"So we must begin. Now."

But they didn't.

"While we sit and wait, the army gets lazy," La Pucelle said. "They sin, they wander off. We must begin now."

"While we wait," La Trémoïlle said, "messengers ride back and forth to Burgundy. The duke of Burgundy has heard about the raising of the siege of Orléans. He may be willing to turn his back on the English at last and recognize Charles as King. The task of liberation may then be carried out at a much more leisurely, much less costly pace. We must give the negotiations time to happen."

La Pucelle was often set to ride off on her own, and Gilles would have ridden against the next English fortress at her side, alone. But it was no use, without the Dauphin. And the Dauphin was listening to La Trémoïlle.

The Dauphin found peace with Burgundy too attractive. He still carried a great burden of guilt for the death of the present duke of Burgundy's father during the ill-fated negotiations on the bridge at Montereau.

Every move Gilles could think of to help La Pucelle counteract this sabotage was met by a silent tap on his cousin's great hogshead chest, where the condemning parchment lay. If Gilles dared too much rebellion, trying to unseat the chamberlain and lieutenant-general, La Trémoïlle would reveal just how close the connection was.

So Gilles was only too glad to comply with his charge's wish for escape, even if it were for no more than an afternoon.

They'd been to the great, wide new walls of Tours before, many times; every time she'd begged the same thing of him. Gilles remembered the walls from when Père Michel had taken Yann and him there as a very young child. They'd watched the St. Martin's Day procession, earning a hundred years and a day's reprieve from purgatory, so folks said. From that perch they'd first seen the old King, Charles' father, marching in procession in a vain attempt to regain his sanity. No Christian saint, but only offering his royal blood for the Sacrifice, had in fact been able to give him that reprieve.

Gilles had told her all of this, and how, from the walls, Père Michel and Yann had planned the wren hunt. He'd told her how the young prince Charles had caught the wren and how Yann had seen him crowned, there in the forest.

"With the Sight, Yann knew that day, though Charles had two older brothers at the time, he would be King. He is Charles the son of Charles the son of Charles seen in the ancient prophecy. As you are La Pucelle. What you so long for at Rheims, Lady, will come to pass, never fear."

Such words, rather than comforting her, however, only made her more impatient. It was as if her Voices yelled so loudly, she couldn't hear him at all. He truly hated that situation.

So, today, he decided not to take her to the walls. He led the way out the eastern gate, along a track towards Saint-Pierre-des-Corps. Something less martial had been on his mind, and so the track was, running through ripening wheat spattered with blood-red poppies. Here and there great trees in full leaf gave welcome shade; and the Loire, running parallel, appeared calm and silent now and then, a constant source of cooler air.

But it didn't take Gilles long to realize they were not the only couple who chose this way. Saint-Pierre-des-Corps was obviously the way local lovers came, to walk alone, and all the other things that lovers did. Were those the bodies, *les corps*, of the saint's patronage? They never actually came upon anything indecent, but Gilles had the terrible feeling it was only a matter of time.

What would she think when she knew? Would she think he'd brought her here on purpose, trying to seduce her? Much as he wanted to, he knew nothing would push her away from him faster than the thought that this was on his mind.

In spite of himself, Gilles began to walk a little faster. Embarrassment flooded him. He knew he couldn't dike it away from his face. La Pucelle, however, noticed nothing, either about the way or about him. She only refused, for once, to meet his pace, and dawdled—waddled, he almost thought—in the glories of the Earth nearing Her full ripeness.

She plucked the swelling heads off stalks of grain, hulled and ate the insides, still soft and green. She pulled up stalks and chewed their ends. She crowned the dark stubble of her hair with the poppies' richness.

As she was, so was the earth. One could not bloom without the other. Juxtaposed to this, the memory of her ability to deal death on the battlefield took his breath away. It was the darkest of magic, life rising from death.

As he was thinking, and as she bloomed thus beside him, they came upon another couple. Gilles tried his best to ignore them, as he had all the rest. But La Pucelle suddenly exclaimed aloud in recognition and ran to embrace the female of the pair.

It took Gilles a moment to decide he knew the redhead, even longer to place her. She was Héliote Power, Hamish's daughter, from the banner workshop. To La Pucelle, however, she might have been a long-lost sister—or more.

His charge seemed to have no notion as to what the sorcerer's daughter might have been doing with a young man in such a place, that they might want to be left alone. That Gilles might want to be left alone with *her*.

The odd thing was, once she laid eyes on La Pucelle, Héliote Power seemed to sprout the same insensitivity. Consumed in each other, the young women ignored their consorts as studiously as the young man ignored Gilles. No doubt intimidated by Gilles' nobility, after doffing his cap and bowing clumsily, the fellow didn't have a word to say. His clothes placed him as middling bourgeois, with wit on the far side of stupid and not a scrap of magic. They couldn't fall to talking with one another as other men on the same path might, when their ladies met. That was just as well. Gilles found him so unattractive as to repulse.

With such inducement close at hand, Gilles would have been more active in trying to withdraw La Pucelle from her friend. But a messenger rode up just then, on a very winded bay.

"Monseigneur de Rais?"

"Yes," Gilles snapped.

The herald dismounted and bent double. "A letter for you, monseigneur, from my lord."

He wore no distinguishing livery, had no more than a hint of what might have been Breton in his speech. This in itself was odd.

Then he said, "Glad I am that you went this private way, my lord. My master told me explicitly to see if I couldn't get this to you in some private place, away from court."

Gilles took the parchment, fingered its fine quality. He gave the man a coin, watched the bay trot off to a well-earned feed and a stall in Tours. Even then, the sire de Rais would have simply pocketed the thing and turned to the more pressing business of keeping La Pucelle's attention on himself.

At that point, however, he saw the seal. An overall pattern of ermine. He knew it. He opened and read.

He read again.

Then he walked along at the arm-in-arm girls' own pace while he tried to decide what to do.

Chapter Thirty-Three

Light to Conjure Words by

"So, because her father has been away from home, working so hard for Père Jean at Orléans, he has made no money, hardly enough to keep them." La Pucelle's words tumbled over themselves as she sat with Gilles. "It's odd—people who dwell in towns depend on money for their living, so their living takes them away from the Craft. Living conflicts with life. The poor here must also be poor in spirit, because they haven't the luxury of more than a rare and cursory acquaintance with Our Lady. When increase comes, it's not from Her but, as I've learned, only from coin with a man's picture on it. The wonder is Maître Hamish has any power at all."

Hamish's daughter and her gallant had left them and returned towards Tours' walls. Though the sun had set, it was still light, late on this day so close to Midsummer. The maid's thoughts along these lines kept her lingering, sitting on a convenient stump among the reeds by the wide, sleepy river. Blackthorn and wild carrot rioted in white bloom on the sheltering bank behind her. Searching the ground between her hosed legs, she found pebble after pebble and tossed them out to plunk in the water beyond sight.

"It was never like that, ever, at home in Domrémy," she added wistfully.

And Gilles, still mulling over the meaning of his letter, had his thoughts diverted by a moment's panic. Is that what she would do when this was over? Go back to the Bois Chênu from whence she'd come? He'd go with her, of course. He didn't have to debate it for a moment. But somehow he'd always imagined she'd come with him, to his castles.

To Catherine? And, now, the baby?

No. But he owned many castles.

Still, there was no doubt in his mind. Even if it meant selling all he had and living a peasant's life—of which he had no more notion, except to despise what he saw, than if it were the distant Holy Land. He knew only what she told him of such a life. He would believe only that. It filled his mind with images of grey nacre, shimmering magic, like the river before him.

"At home, there are always mushrooms to gather in the woods. Sweet roots, acorns. The poor don't know they are poor, with no coins to count up to tell them so. They can always run a goat or two on the common lands. A pig is happy on the mast that falls freely onto Our Lady's lap in the forest.

"But, see, that's not the way of it here. And working with Craft, unlike working farmer's magic in the fields at home, does not bring Maître Hamish wealth—except in spirit."

"Yann—Père Jean—says that's what La Pucelle is sent among us to restore, that connection," Gilles said to be saying something. "At least, I think that's what he means."

"Oh, no, not me." She laughed aloud. "I only need to see the Dauphin crowned at Rheims. I know it's to this end, too, that Père Jean and Hamish and the rest are working. All of them. Except maybe the Dauphin himself, my gentle, difficult Dauphin. Though he is the one I'd imagine would work the hardest, to see the crown on his own head. So then, when Hamish Power hasn't enough money to provide a dowry for his own daughter so she and her lover can marry ... "

"Ah, so that's what all of this was about," Gilles said. "You want me to provide a dowry for you—for your friend, I mean."

"Oh, no, Bluebeard."

She met his eyes for the first time in quite a while. And, for the first time, she smiled.

"It's the city that's at fault here," she went on. "The city that works as ... as a great bucket to carry life away from some and give it in buckets to others, a few others, more than they need. And more than they are willing to give back. Like my gentle Dauphin, maybe."

"You mean to drill holes in those buckets, my dear?"

She laughed again. Her dark eyes crinkled in her suntanned face and the poppies, withering, bobbed amidst the stubble of her hair as if alive and blowing in the fields once more.

"The buckets—the towns of the English, yes." The words trilled on the peals of her laughter. "I mean to drill great holes in them, all the way to Rheims. But for now, I mean not for you to pay for this girl's dowry, but for the town to do so, the town who benefits from her father's labor—and hers—and yet thinks it owes them nothing because it is not written down in somebody's ledger."

"And you'll get the town to pay?"

"Of course I shall. I am La Pucelle."

"So indeed you are, my dear. I hadn't forgotten."

Speaking of dowries—even that of another girl—was the first step, Gilles supposed, to thinking of one of her own. Of course, there were so many hindrances—Catherine and the baby not the least—that it hardly bore thinking of. And yet, he did think of it. All the time. All the time they weren't on the battlefield, fighting side by side.

Of course, Jehanne La Pucelle needed no dowry for him.

He slid an arm around her shoulders, as gently as the sliding of the river before them, for fear of the healing wound. She didn't pull away.

Her worth was so great, he must pay her for the privilege. As much as he had for as long as he lived. Somebody who'd been to the East—he couldn't, now, remember who—had told him once that's how it was among the heathen. A man paid for his bride there, not the other way 'round. "Just as if she were a cow," the man had said.

But Gilles saw it differently. Even all the lands Catherine had brought with her, even so, the match had come to him too dear. And La Pucelle ...

"So, Bluebeard, you won't tell me?"

"Tell you what, my heart?"

"What the letter you received says. I can see it has distracted you."

Truth to tell, thoughts of weddings and dowries had so distracted him that, for the moment, he had quite forgotten the letter, important, disturbing as it was. The memory made him jump.

"Oh, I'm sorry," she said, having felt the reaction through his arm, and shifting her shoulders now beneath it in a comfortable and comforting way. "And does it have nothing to do with me, this letter?"

"Of course it has to do with you," he replied. "Everything has to do with La Pucelle in France, one body emblematic of the other."

"You do talk nonsense sometimes, Bluebeard," she chuckled. The shift in her shoulders had become a snuggle.

"Do you want to hear about it?"

"Of course. If it has to do with me. If it isn't a love letter from your lady wife."

The thought kept Gilles silent for a moment and, when he could speak again, he had decided the best plan would be to read the letter to her entirely.

"'From Arthur, comte de Richemont, constable of France, to Gilles, sire de—'"

"Who's Richemont?" she interrupted.

"Brother to the duke of Brittany. My liege lord, for some of my lands, anyway. Those I do not owe to the King of France."

"Who must be crowned at Rheims." Her Voices wouldn't let her forget, not for an instant.

"Yes, who must be crowned at Rheims," he assured her.

"Do you know this Richemont?"

"Yes. I fought under him, during the civil war in Brittany and then, later, against the English."

"Is he a good soldier?" she asked with a general's interest.

Gilles hesitated more than he'd meant to before answering, "Yes. Very brave. He was sorely wounded at Agincourt. Scars you can still see on his face, black and red, in the shape of the rings of his mail that was pounded through the flesh.

He was left for dead on the field, then he spent quite a bit of time as a prisoner of the *goddams*."

"Like the handsome duc d'Alençon."

"Yes, like Alençon." Gilles wanted to copy her playful mood, but found he could not, not while Alençon was handsome. "My grandfather was responsible for negotiating Richemont's release. Our families have close and ancient ties."

"This Richemont. Did I hear you aright? He calls himself constable of France?"

"And so he is. The Dauphin made him so—oh, a number of years ago."

"If he is constable, why isn't he here, fighting the *goddams* with you and La Hire and the rest? How is it that I have never met him?"

"He ... he stays at his castle in Parthenay, on the Breton border."

"He doesn't sound like a very brave soldier to me." Her animation rocked her beside him. "He sounds like a coward. I wouldn't have him my constable for a moment."

"It's a long story, my love."

"Well, I must hear it. But I promise you, I don't have time for silly excuses. I have to get the Dauphin to—"

"I know. You have to get the Dauphin to Rheims." Having teased out an end to begin unraveling with, Gilles said, "My lord Richemont and I did a lot of fighting together before you came, as I told you." He certainly didn't want things to go back the way they'd been then. "But the lord chamberlain—"

"La Trémoïlle?"

"No, the chamberlain before my cousin got the post. Giac was his name." Gilles wanted to linger on this subject as little as possible. "Giac was—he was not supporting our fighting on the front as he should have done. So Richemont and I ... "

Plotted, kidnaped, tortured, murdered. All those words crossed Gilles mind as the next to say in connection with Giac. But he couldn't confess them, not to her.

"We managed to rid the Dauphin of Giac, anyway," he decided on at last.

"And what? Gave the Dauphin La Trémoïlle instead?"

"He seemed a better choice at the time."

"What? This brick wall I cannot shift one *pouce* towards Rheims where I must go? The Dauphin must go?"

"Yes, I, too, can see now that we were mistaken."

"So?" she said. "Couldn't you and Richemont get rid of La Trémoïlle, just as you got rid of Giac?"

Gilles had to admit, the thought of his cousin tied in a sack and tossed into a river had its attractions. It would take a very large sack. And many men. But Gilles knew the contract La Trémoïlle carried in his doublet with the horseshoe seal on it meant the present chamberlain wouldn't sink at all. Not without dragging Gilles de Rais down with him.

"It's not as easy as that," he said, then went on quickly. "Anyway, not too long ago, troops faithful to my cousin drove le comte de Richemont out of France and into his own lands in Brittany, where he has been ever since. This lack of leadership—or the abandoning of all leadership to my cousin, rather, who has his bets placed both in Burgundy and with the Dauphin at once—this is what had left us in such grim straits before your arrival, Lady."

"So? What does my lord the count say? I notice he wrote directly to you. And by a messenger without blazon."

Gilles had to give up his arm around her shoulders then in order to spread the parchment with both hands and read it in the gathering darkness. White bloom was losing its distinction from dark leaves among the blackthorn and wild carrot he had seen clearly behind her when first they'd sat in this place. Just so was ink fading into the skin on which it was printed. But he'd read it so many times, the words he couldn't make out came back to him.

"'Word has reached me here in Parthenay of the deliverance of the great city of Orléans. More wondrous still is the means of this deliverance. Can it be so? A Maid, they say, fighting like a man? And does she truly come from God? Or from another, unspeakable source? You, monsieur de Rais, may best answer these questions for me.'"

Gilles stole a glance at the little figure beside him. Her light, he decided, helped him to conjure the words. How did she take this reference to herself, to the news having reached as far as Brittany?

She neither blushed nor giggled, but nodded. She took it easily, as if the miracle of herself was something she took for granted, something expected, that she had always known must be.

Never so complacent himself, he read on: "'If the deliverance is sure, if God has deigned to vouchsafe a miracle and save France, I must be on His side. For better assurance, has Our Lord confounded that devil, Georges de La Trémoïlle? If so, I pray you will write me instantly, for I would not be slow in answering the trumpet of God.

"'One thousand men, many of them tried and true Bretons with whom you are familiar, wait for me to lead them in answer to this call. Indeed, I can hardly keep them in order, so great is their desire to march off. I attend only your reply to this letter.

"'May God keep your every righteous desire. From Parthenay this eve of the feast of Sts. Gregory and Urban Martyr ... ' And so on."

"A thousand proven men," La Pucelle breathed with delight.

Gilles doubted if he could ever give her such delight physically as she'd just received from another man's words on paper. "That's what he says."

"With a thousand, I know I could get the Dauphin to Rheims, whatever La Trémoïlle says or does."

Gilles hesitated to put into words something that might not make an impression on his lady at all. Still, he felt he ought to warn her. "My heart, Richemont is—If you couldn't tell from his letter, the count is—how to say it? —a very pious man."

"All the more reason he should be here."

"When I say pious, I mean—he turns a dark eye where he suspects witchcraft. I must admit, he already suspects it in me."

"Not as much as he suspects La Trémoïlle."

"So it seems."

"This will not keep you from answering him. At once. This night." She was already on her feet, scrambling up the bank. "It matters not what narrow path men must set their feet on, for there are many Gods and many paths. I am to serve them all."

"But, my heart, I must consider ... "

"Don't worry. I'll tell you what to write."

Their little path up from the river bank met the larger lane now, and here La Pucelle stumbled backwards, almost into Gilles' arms. He caught her, righted her, then nearly stumbled himself.

A great horse and rider paced heavily between the steep banks of ripening grain on either side. A woman's litter went with him, torchbearers before and behind. It was the identity of the man that gave Gilles the greatest start, however.

It was Georges de La Trémoïlle. As if their speech had conjured him.

"Good evening, cousin," the unctuous voice said, and the reins pulled up with no hint of surprise.

The chamberlain was a big man, and it took a big horse to carry him. He used both attributes—consciously, Gilles thought—to intimidate.

Gilles clambered quickly to the level of the road, to take as much of that advantage away as he could. And to put himself between La Pucelle and the threat. He also hurried to fold up the letter from Richemont and conceal it within the breast of his doublet as he did so.

"How strange to meet you, cousin. In such a place. At such an hour. In such company." La Trémoïlle wagged his chins in a direction for each of these things.

How dare you? Gilles wanted to shout. I should demand my honor, the lady's honor, for that. It would be a pleasure to topple you, then run your pork's carcass through and through.

Then he noticed that the torchbearers were armed. La Pucelle had her sword about her, and he knew she would fight. But the scandal would be worse than the possibility of injury, whether they won or lost with such close odds.

So Gilles kept his temper, with difficulty, though he couldn't resist one little jab.

"As odd to see me here, I suppose, as yourself, my lord." And he nodded significantly towards the litter.

The notion of La Trémoïlle resorting to ripening grain fields for a liaison was laughable. La Trémoïlle chuckled, as if the image diverted him, too. Himself climbing off his horse and rutting here until there was straw in his hair and in his privates, until the broken stalks gave a sweet grass smell to the entire night.

The figure of whom Gilles caught a glimpse behind the silk curtains did not seem to be his cousin's lady wife. And if this was not the former Madame de Giac, who had been appropriated along with the murdered man's post and estates, who was she? Even in torchlight, sight was bad, and the lady, after a quick peek for herself, obviously did not want to be seen.

Maybe it was no lady at all. Maybe it was another assassin.

The amusement was still in La Trémoïlle gullet, but his tone also turned deadly serious. "I think, cousin, you just received a very interesting missive from a mutual friend of ours."

Richemont's seal seemed to smolder within the confines of Gilles' doublet. La Trémoïlle was bluffing. He didn't know. How could he know? The messenger had been unmarked. Had the poor man been spied on? Already caught? Tortured?

Gilles caught the girl's hand the instant he felt her push in beside him and tried to stop her. He failed.

"If you mean the comte de Richemont, sire de La Trémoïlle, he will fight with me." La Pucelle spoke with verve. "Even if you will not, you coward, you underhanded dealer with the enemy."

La Trémoïlle laughed out loud. "Such a pleasant evening, is it not, young demoiselle?" He turned as if to observe the glitter of the night's first star, as if to conjure by it.

Had he known nothing for certain then, only guessed? And with such duplicity, had he drawn La Pucelle out, to give all away?

"Richemont will fight with me and we shall win. I must take the Dauphin to Rheims. I must!"

It was all Gilles could do to keep her at bay. Like a hound set on, she would have leapt for the horse's bridle, then tried to drag the chamberlain from his saddle by herself if he had not.

"Young lady," La Trémoïlle said, no longer admiring nature, no longer toying, no longer even amused. "It is not the Dauphin's will that the traitor Richemont fight for him."

"No one's will matters but that of My Lord," La Pucelle shrieked, struggling in Gilles' arms. "It's not my Dauphin who says such things. It's you."

"Very possessive. Of all kinds of things, aren't you? For a goatherd."

"I am La Pucelle."

La Trémoïlle laughed again, but it was not pleasant. "If you do accept Richemont, demoiselle, the Dauphin will cast you off."

"He will not. He cannot."

"He will, as easily as a dog rids himself of fleas."

"He can't. I am La Pucelle."

"The Dauphin is the one you have to get to Rheims," La Trémoïlle reminded her. Then he drew the reins to urge his horse around them. "I waste time and dignity, talking to you like a fishwife squabbling. You're a rattling, empty kettle, girl. A blamed fool. Without the Dauphin."

"I am not. I am La Pucelle," she cried, tears streaming down her cheeks, as the torches faded unheeding into the night on the lane towards Tours.

Even the English hadn't dared to call her such things.

Thirty-First Antiphon

Butterflies Like a Garment

"Whose idea was that?" It was a month later when I looked up from a beautiful fairy ring of mushrooms into the ravaged face of Arthur de Richemont. The count, flanked by men-at-arms, leaned over the high bow of his saddle and scrutinized me carefully.

I got to my feet, brushing moss and mud from the skirts of my habit. I didn't think the man recognized me, even when I blatantly used my twisted hand for support. A friar's blazon serves to make him one of many rather than a clear individual, as Richemont's black-on-white ermine made him. Still, I worried for the first time since Chinon that something about my black wool and unusual tonsure might strike this letter-of-the-law man as sacrilege.

"Whose idea was what, my lord?" I asked. "The good Lord gives us mushrooms, of course."

Should I go on about the circling of life that had filled my senses until his approach? How powerful is the soft little white-capped mushroom, that turns dead leaf mold into life before our eyes? How visually the lesson was given to us with the fairy ring, as if fairies—or Gods—did indeed circle there?

"No, there," Richemont said. "On the river."

I was glad I hadn't spoken then, as I saw his attention wasn't on me and my dancing wood sprites at all.

I looked where he pointed, out of the woodland shade and down the cultivated fields towards the town of Beaugency. This was the direction whence the steady booming came, sounding like thunder which, the ancients said, shot the God's fertilizing semen to Earth. We mortals sometimes found it—as mistletoe, in the oak's hair. Or as an areola of mushrooms at the oak's foot in the wood.

This noise, however was cannon fire, down where the English held out against La Pucelle and her faithful French. The English held the almost windowless donjon of Beaugency, a great, grey stone rectangle stood on its end. Gunfire from both sides blued the fortress and hid much of the action from sight. We were too far away for it to add its peculiar sulphuric stifle to the warm, woodsy summer air. The struggling, agonizing, dying mass of men seemed insignificant at this distance, too. No more than the struggles of ants in a hill.

Richemont wore the dust of a hard ride from the west. The rest of his men must be waiting for his reconnaissance, further up the road, out of sight. In spite of haze and distance, his soldier's eye had taken in the important facts of the battle in this, his first glimpse of the stronghold. Reading this banner and that, perhaps, and knowing the strengths of each, he had viewed it all like a chessboard and decided the best play.

"Who thought of that?" he asked again. "Who brilliantly saw that the land lies so that even the best gunner could get but glancing shots off at those walls? Who thought to set the cannon afloat and fire from the riverside? Brilliant. They'll have those walls down before the day's out."

I had to smile. "Ah. That was La Pucelle. She has a great feel for the land, always. They say the fresh vision she brings to the field always turns things around."

"Ah, the Maid." Richemont considered, then looked closer at me. "You've met this Maid, father?"

If I wasn't careful, I would make him wonder why I wasn't down just behind the lines with the rest of the priests—and my witches—tending the wounded and dying. But it would never do to mislead the man, certainly not on things he was bound to learn sooner or later.

"I have the honor to be her confessor," I said. "Jean Pasquerel, at your service, my lord."

"We got word as we marched—scrambled, I had almost said, to keep up with you. Jargeau east of here, taken. Meung, firmly invested, and now Beaugency about to fall. Three strong forts. All, they tell me, within a single week's action."

"That's so, my lord."

"You're her confessor?"

"Yes, my lord."

"Is she of God? Can such wonders be of God?"

"Definitely." I didn't say which God.

Richemont and his men sat, watching the battle in intense silence a while longer. Their harness creaked and jangled. Their horses flicked their ears and their tails against flies and shifted their heavy feet here and there.

A butterfly caught my eye. A beautiful, delicate white thing, it danced in the midst of the fairy ring as if one of the mushrooms had sprouted wings and come to life. There was another, a third. They twisted about each other like my limbs when the spell had hold of me. These were spring's destructive caterpillars, having stripped trees, then gone into a quiet state like death. Now, they burst to life like light, needing no more than air, it seemed, to flutter here and there like the sweet breath of a half-forgotten God. There were six of them, then ten.

I couldn't put off my work now, Richemont or no Richemont. While his attention was elsewhere, I held up a finger of my power hand, the left. Butterflies came to it, swirling up from the fairy ring, the very embodiment of death-to-life work.

Go daughter-God. Go, go, go.

I dropped my hand to the level, pointing towards the battle. The butterflies shot off.

What did Richemont see? A monk in a wood, a few butterflies. No more. The real events, or so it seemed to him, were down in Beaugency.

"There she is, my lord," I said, my hand continuing to point after the insects had abandoned it. "There's La Pucelle."

So she was, the flash of white upon the field, the swish of the white silk banner behind her. The butterflies, swooping like the wind, had coalesced above her. Then they dropped, like a garment, until it seemed she was made of their shimmering, panting, pulsing wings.

Did the men beside me see? I didn't know how they could fail to. But all I heard them say was:

"Look. Upon the battlements."

"The garrison is suing for terms."

"I fear, lads, we've come too late to join this Maid in yet another battle."

Later, after I'd led the count and his men to the shadow of the newly liberated keep of Beaugency, Gilles strode forward to greet Richemont, his liege lord. Battle grime and other men's blood still darkened the baron de Rais. Richemont might forgive that, but his eyes did go up at my milk brother's next breach of decorum.

"And, Lady," he said, turning to La Pucelle with the glow his eyes always caught in her presence. "I'd like to present monseigneur the constable of France to you."

The girl turned and, it seemed, hesitated half a martial drumbeat before stepping forward and helping to soften Gilles' elevation of herself by dropping Richemont a gallant bow.

For my part, I doubt the hesitation was hers. Yes, she had to shake the remnants of butterfly shimmer from herself. But there was the intake of breath among the captains with whom she'd been talking, Alençon, La Hire, Poton de Xantrailles. These men had given their word to the Dauphin that they would not accept "the traitor of Richemont" among their ranks. La Pucelle had been with them at the oath-taking and some considered that she had sworn along with the rest.

"I will obey the word of my King," she'd said.

I, at least, had assumed the King was not Charles, for Charles was always "my Dauphin" and would be until she saw him crowned. "My King" was He Whose Voice she always obeyed before anything else. "The King of Heaven," some might say. Or the King Stag, whichever your allegory was for something truly beyond words.

Then, of course, there was the start and hesitation on the part of Richemont. Her figure always gave such pause to those seeing her for the first time, even with warning, even without butterflies. The wild, magical juxtaposition of male costume and movements with female features, it was like fire mixing with black powder, a flash, a flame suddenly in the face.

"My lord, you and your men are most welcome to our cause."

Richemont crossed himself. "I don't fear you," he said, though the croak in his voice made a liar of one who'd braved Agincourt.

"That's good," she trilled. "Only if you've come to fight on the side of the *goddams* do you need to fear me."

"If you come from God," Richemont said, crossing himself again, "I don't fear you, for I'm a just man. If you come from the devil, I fear you even less, for the same cause."

La Pucelle laughed once more. "We'll get on famously with such courage on your part, my lord."

And then I lost sight of her as other Breton nobles were presented to her. These included, for the second time, the two brothers, very young, Guy and André de Laval, kinsmen to Gilles on his father's side, likewise kin to the great hero Bertrand Du Guesclin. La Pucelle had taken the ruby ring Gilles had given her and sent it back to Brittany via these brothers to the women of this family. It replaced for them the one she now wore counterbalancing her parents' "Jhesu + Maria", that ring Tiphaine had brought her that had belonged to the last great hero to rise to France's need.

I did not lose sight, however, of others in the yard: those men who'd sworn on their swords and their faith that they would not fight alongside Arthur de Richemont.

Chapter Thirty-Four

In the Rearguard

"The rear? They want me to ride in the rearguard? By my martinet, why?"

Feeling his mistress' passion, her short little legs gripping and ungripping his flanks, the great white destrier skittered as if he were still a colt. La Pucelle kept him firmly in hand, however, even as she lost her temper at the orders.

A stiff wind ruffled the spikes of her hair. Gilles couldn't suppress the thought of himself as wind, riffling that hair.

Himself as destrier, too, matching her passion, urging it higher ...

But now, at this moment, he had to urge her to calm. "You know why," he told her.

"Because I greeted Richemont, welcomed him?"

"That's right."

"But he brings a thousand men with him."

"I think we're lucky that La Hire and all the rest who obey La Trémoïlle didn't turn on those thousand men and squabble themselves into grave pits, instead of going after the *goddams* this morning. Richemont is allowed to tag along. And so are you."

"In rearguard. Out of sight."

"The forward is for those who obey orders."

"Not those who give them?"

She had a point there, one he couldn't deny. Why did honor always belong to the most staid? Some things about life always raised his hackles, too.

She went on. "La Pucelle belongs at the forward, where we will meet the *goddams* first."

"The English may attack the rear as well as the front. They like nothing better—sometimes, particularly when they feel cowardly—than to cut off a few lances straggling at the rear, the sort of mouthful they think they can manage."

"And because I am here, that will draw them, too."

"That may well be."

Gilles told her this and it pleased her. He liked the thought much less, that she might indeed be getting such a reputation among the enemy that they would come and search her out, personally.

So they rode out of newly liberated Meung that morning, the eighteenth of June, 1429, in the rearguard. Sometimes she let the horse get away from her, accidentally on purpose, and galloped ahead so she might almost tread on the heels of Alençon's men, forming the main body of the army.

But, for the most part, Gilles managed to keep her beside him. They swung north, following the rest of the French who followed the word of the scouts as to sightings of the retreating English. Whether the trail of French or English, the close-cropped forage and droppings they almost waded through would not let them lose their way.

"Exactly where might we expect to find the English?" Père Yann asked.

Gilles' milk brother had been riding beside them these two hours or more, struggling to keep upright on the half-asleep palfrey he rode, suitable to a priest. Yann seemed to sniff the air of the forest around them for the enemy, like a hunting dog.

As if even a dog could smell anything over the stench of the rest of the French army in whose wake they were obliged to march. This was yet another reason, perhaps the greatest, why riding rearguard lacked all honor. It rankled Gilles more and more with every step. He couldn't imagine how the girl beside him was keeping her temper to a simmer.

"Halfway to the Channel by now," La Pucelle answered her confessor's question merrily. "We have them on the run."

Gilles smiled at her, letting her believe what she would, as long as it made her happy. Idly, he decided to answer Yann's question himself. In fact, he thought a priest had no business sticking his nose into matters he couldn't understand. Exaggerated simplicity entered his reply. Yann would do better to stick to magic.

"We have definite word that Sir John Fastolf—for whom we looked with dread throughout the action at Orléans—has indeed at last left Paris with a large number of men-at-arms. He meant to relieve Jargeau, Beaugency or Meung, one or more of them, but moved too slowly."

"We moved too fast," La Pucelle sang, her legs wriggling with excitement along the great destrier's white flank.

"Anyway, the last firm word we had was that he is at Janville. Talbot from Beaugency and Scales from Meung—"

"We shouldn't have given them terms," La Pucelle burst in. "We should not."

Gilles gave her another indulgent, loving glance before concluding his thought to Yann. "These men with what troops remain to them marched north from their defeats, doubtless to meet up with Fastolf coming south."

"Then they will all turn tail and run for the Channel."

"That would be nice, Lady," Gilles said, "but it's not at all clear that's what they will do. The English have been here in France too long, and won too much to give up quite so easily."

"They only won before I came. Now things are different."

"Things are different," he agreed. "Nevertheless, I think once their forces are augmented, I suspect they will find some field where they can dig their archers in behind those stakes so ruinous to our horses. They will dig in and make a stand."

"But we are ever so many more than they will be, even with Fastolf's new, fresh lances."

"That may well be." Considering the dung and garbage they were obliged to wade through, he was almost certain of it. But again—some of it could be English.

"We have Richemont's fine men," La Pucelle tossed her head behind them, "in spite of La Trémoïlle sulking like a crab. We have, as well, every Frenchman who can walk. They've come from everywhere, men armed with billhooks and kitchen knives. No man wants to be left behind when La Pucelle fights."

"That's true, too," Gilles sighed.

That was, in fact, some of the rubbish left behind, men in such bad shape they could not keep up with the advance parties. They were passing three of them now, having to move their mounts carefully, for the men hadn't the sense to stop at a spot in the road where there was space. They lounged out on the narrow verge, legs splayed in filthy, torn hose and kerchiefs over their drowsing faces. If Gilles were any judge of character, this trio would turn to highway robbery before they ever got to a battlefield. Indeed, Richemont's men must consider themselves lucky if they got by with all their gear intact.

One of the vagabonds, however, caught sight of them from under a corner of his kerchief.

"La Pucelle. It's La Pucelle," he called to his companions.

All progress had to stop for a moment while Gilles' charge gave them her blessing.

After that, they didn't seem quite so despicable.

Nonetheless, Gilles had to say, "If you think such untrained men are a nuisance on the march, imagine what they are in battle. Fastolf, Talbot and Scales may have fewer men among them, but every one of those men is a veteran, tough, well-trained and used to obeying orders."

He said this last with a purposeful glance at the girl who was hardly attending him. She had turned in the saddle and was waving merrily back to the slackers, who had now decided to pick up their gear and come along after all—a pox on them. Gilles meant to suggest she was another for whom a little discipline would not go amiss.

The moral was lost on her, of course.

And Gilles had to admit to himself that, if she ever were to suddenly become complaisant, her spell on him would lose most of its force. He didn't want that to happen at all.

"There is a reason the English have been winning for years," he said.

She wasn't listening to him. And Yann had no comprehension of anything that had passed between them for the last quarter league. Gilles assumed he spoke to himself.

But then Yann asked again, "Where will the English be?" He asked it in such a way that Gilles was forced to look around them with new eyes.

They were passing through a heavily wooded area. Under a curtain fringe of green, normal sight vanished after only a pace or two into uniform black shadow. The cuckoo sang, a woodpecker knocked. Otherwise, under the great clatter of hooves and harness and talking men, a shifting, muffled silence reigned.

Ordinarily, if they were going to make a stand, the English would seek open ground, preferably with a height, to give them advantage. But suppose they decided to lose themselves in the woods instead? To wait until the French were cut off from friends as well as escape towards the south, strung out and exposed along an unfamiliar trail? That strategy would double the effect of their well-trained men. Particularly of their dreaded archers.

Gilles was certain the commanders of the two French armies in front of him would never guess at such a scheme. They were too used to the English being open—and victorious. They didn't consider what might happen when a desperate and wounded beast decided to turn and stand its ground. They'd be mowed down like ripe wheat before they ever saw the scythe coming.

Yann's Sight had never been easy for Gilles to trust. He'd grown up with the fellow, after all, used to having the visions treated as an illness. He placed much more trust in the strength of his own arm with a sword at the end of it.

Now, however, Gilles felt as if he could See as clearly as his milk brother. Or, if he could not, if the black depths of the forest revealed nothing to his eyes, he was certain it was failure on his part, not madness on Yann's.

"I think—" Yann glanced back towards Père Michel, signaling to this witch riding closest among the troop. But the others were there, too, among the camp followers. The message would pass. "I think I have work to do."

La Pucelle got the message with the rest. But she got further instructions as well.

"My Voices say—"

Gilles saw that look in her eyes, the look that left him out, that he couldn't follow. He had to ask, "What, Lady?" to try to bring her back.

"Yes," she said upon her return, her glance darting here and there, her horse picking up a trot in response to some hidden signal. "They are taking hidden positions, the *goddams*."

"Where? What shall we do?"

"You'll need your spurs, Bluebeard," she said.

His heart lurched. Now? Now would come the test of his mettle, his desperate need to protect her? "To run away?" he demanded, setting his horse at the same jerking pace to keep up with hers.

"No, no, to catch them. Ah, were the *goddams* to cling to the clouds, we'd catch them." She laughed aloud.

Then, she slowed again and cocked her head. When her look came back to him, it was clouded. "But it's the vanguard that will take the brunt," she said.

She tried to urge her horse forward, but it was no use. The way was clogged with men and beasts as far as the eye could see. She stood in her stirrups and tried to look over them. That availed nothing, either.

Then she turned frantically away, finding no help in Gilles. Yann was now her solace. "And I'm not there. I'm not there to help them. They will fail, if I'm not there."

Yann finally took his attention from the woods around them and settled it on La Pucelle. Some communication passed between them, secret as Sight, and Gilles grew cold with jealousy to watch it.

"Very well, Lady," Yann said after a moment's consideration. "I thought the task was for me. But I don't have a warrior's sense. Yes, if you're willing, the task should fall to you."

She nodded. "Tell Richemont, Bluebeard."

"To stop here?" he asked as she urged her horse away from him and into a meadow that opened up as if at her beckoning to the left hand side.

"No, to keep going, as fast as the foot soldiers may."

"Keep Richemont away from here for a while," Yann said as his lazy mount grew suddenly lively and trotted out into the meadow after her. "That has to be your task."

But keeping Richemont away from La Pucelle meant Gilles had to be away from her himself.

Chapter Thirty-Five

A Stag with Antlers of Hammered Gold

She rode the dove-colored horse out knee-high among the sun-drenched grasses and umbels of wild carrot, puffs of butterflies spraying behind her.

The sight was so beautiful that Gilles hardly dared to breathe. Suddenly he knew, if he kept very, very still, he would see God. Just as Yann had, who always spoke to him of the Horned One, the King Stag, who called to him when he was a child ...

"What ails the Maid?" Richemont had ridden up behind him and saw La Pucelle swing herself out of her saddle.

"That's the thing with women," the count went on, shaking his head. "Even the most rational is always heir to some weakness or other. Because of Eve, you know. Things deep within the flesh that you and I, sire de Rais, can't even imagine."

"Nothing," Gilles replied in a whisper. "There is nothing at all wrong with her."

He wanted to scream at the man. You're so self-righteous. Can't you even tell the holy when you see it?

Richemont shrugged. "Rather a disreputable bunch, wouldn't you say?" He meant the witches who'd begun to gather around her, circling her like dark kites in the sky.

Gilles had promised to keep Richemont away. He knew he must. Every passing moment emphasized it more. He would always stand between La Pucelle and any threat, physical, or this, more spiritual.

Even if it meant he must miss the chance of seeing divinity.

"Come, my lord," he said, turning his horse regretfully the

moment he managed to break the spell. "Nothing's amiss. She will only ... she will only eat and drink a little before riding on to join us."

"Good. I've noticed she eats little, very little. The wonder is she can keep body and soul together."

Gilles had noticed. He wished that, too, was a secret only he and she had to know. He wished that it was all she was stopping for.

"One thinks of saints, fasting to a miraculous degree—" Richemont began the idle, horse-swayed rhythm of men on the road.

Shouts of "Look—Oh, look!" from the men behind them interrupted.

"No! Don't shoot!" Gilles cried as he heard bows unslung and arrows drawn. "As you love La Pucelle, upon pain of death, no one shoot."

For suddenly, in the midst of the meadow, a stag had appeared. The great, branching antlers, five points to a side, seemed hammered of gold. The soft pelt itself was of purest white. It was as if the innocent spots of a newborn fawn had grown to cover all the beast. Or as if La Pucelle's shining armor had suddenly turned to fur.

The impression hit him harder because, when he first saw the creature, it sprang straight from where the Maid lay prone upon the grass of the meadow. All four tiny, golden hooves leapt off the ground at once, over the heads of the witches, crowding low.

The girl in armor didn't move. She might have been dead.

Or, Gilles thought, under such a spell as Yann had had since they were boys.

And yet, the animal was clearly a stag, not a doe, as he would have expected.

Then he had to laugh at himself. What made him think La Pucelle would ever want to be a doe when she could sport a rack like that on her head?

The stag stood for a moment in the midst of the meadow, staring at the men-at-arms. It (Gilles couldn't think "he") blinked once, twice. The great, dark, so-familiar eyes met his with recognition, with greeting.

"Oh, God, don't shoot," Gilles whispered. He couldn't give orders any more. He could only pray.

Then the stag leapt once, twice, and vanished into the forest at the edge of the meadow before them.

"Well."

Beside him, Richemont let out a breath. Gilles found that he had been refusing his own lungs as well.

Richemont said, "Quite a sight. Almost ... almost unnatural, wouldn't you say?"

"Yes," Gilles agreed. Something in Richemont's tone, and in the way the count scrutinized him, made Gilles want to change the subject.

"Keep moving, men," Gilles shouted behind him. "Pick up the pace. And if you see that stag again, for God's sake, don't shoot."

To Richemont, he said, "I think I'll ride ahead a bit and see if they've had any sign of the English."

"You could send a herald," Richemont suggested.

"No. I'd rather go myself. And, my lord, if you could, get the men moving."

Chapter Thirty-Six

The Zig-Zagged Field of Patay

By pushing his mount hard for two leagues or more, Gilles managed to get to the very front of the French march. He was beyond even La Hire and his standard, with a handful of select scouts that the old dog had set to move quietly at the head.

"No, my lord," they told him. "No sign of any *goddams*."

They had passed the sizeable village of Lignarolles. The wood smoke of a smaller place one of the scouts, familiar with the area, called Patay appeared before them on the left side. The thick beech and oak wood they'd been passing through was about to break off for Patay's fields of white grain.

Nobody was in the fields reaping, not even any boys with their sling shots to keep the rooks away. Gilles didn't think too much of that, however. Peasants had their own ways.

He saw how the road, once free of the wood, was thickly hedged with bramble and wild rose blooming. He saw how it took them down to a shallow where a second road would intersect them. This second road was probably never used by more than hay carts, but it did seem to be set here and there with broken stone beneath the overgrowth of moss and grass. The old Roman road, then.

Such sights always swamped his heart with meditations about the transitory nature of existence. How things that were so full of life around him now would some day likewise be ruins, empty—but not soulless, no. Yann would instruct him to see cycle there, to rejoice in the growth of moss as much as of city, to see the regenerative power of mold as well as of the momentary pleasure of the release of his own loins.

A few hundred ells beyond the road ran a ridge. Gilles was so occupied with the thoughts of mortality brought on him by the Roman road that it took him several minutes to send his gaze there. It was empty, save for waving grain and the smell of baked straw, blood-red poppies and a shimmer of heat.

The moment his sight did land there, however, his heart leapt free of its meditations and into his throat. He thought he could see—though truly he could not—English banners waving there, over the ridge of waving wheat.

The God.

That thought seared through his brain half a breath before he saw her—it. He moved to signal the men to pull up.

The great white stag leapt from the wood just on his right, crossed the road in a single, heart-stopping bound. Then it cleared the hedge, and began a wild zig-zag through the grain.

Gilles never finished his gesture. The men had already halted of their own accord, just at the point where they would have left the cover of woodland shadows with their next step.

At the same time, the hedge along the road before them sprang to life. It sprouted arms and legs and lungs. Several hundred English archers had concealed themselves there.

The moment they saw the white stag, however, they couldn't resist. They set up the hunt "halloo!", turned the points of their arrows from the road—from Gilles' heart—or waved the deadly stakes instead of hurrying to plant them against French cavalry. A score of them set after the quarry.

Several hundred more answered the call and dashed out of cover of the woods across the field. On the ridge, banners rose, waving and hallooing. Some men took to horse in pursuit.

The bounding of the stag seemed the erratic moves of an animal about to burst with terror. It sprang here, found its way hedged by shouting, shooting, grinning men, it sprang there.

Gilles found his own heart throbbing as the beast's must, his breath coming in shallow, gasping pants, as if his mind, too, throbbed with a blind urge to flee.

All the while, he knew a human mind, if not a God's, activated the chase. With that reflection, anger pushed all fear from him.

Brave, foolish, *stupid* girl, he thought.

He was so angry, he felt ready to kill her himself. To make her stop giving such pain to his own heart.

To keep anyone else from entering history as the man who killed La Pucelle. No one, or no one else, must take such privilege, such blasphemy. And there were many, so many, scrambling, yelling for the honor.

But the English arrows missed. Some of them sailed through the very tangle of her antlers, some between the spring of her leaps, but they all passed harmlessly on.

Only when it had revealed and distracted every ambush of English troops did the beautiful bundle of white energy flash off the field and into the dark safety of the woods to his left.

Even before Gilles had drawn normal breath again, the men with him had turned their mounts and were spurring them as fast as they could back the way they'd come. Gilles would have feared the English heard their thud and clatter, but that the *goddams* were making so much noise themselves, still hallooing after the vanished stag.

One more step, by any of the French, and they would have been seen by the hidden English instead of being the observers themselves. Five more steps, and four arrows would have found each of their hearts before they knew what hit them, as they would every other Frenchman who carelessly entered that field of ambush from the wood. Now it was the English who would not have time to dig in as they'd planned, not after this little diversion.

"You will need your spurs," she'd told him.

And so they did.

Gilles' poor mount. Though a better animal than the others', it had already been pushed far that day and couldn't keep up. The scouts had already reached La Hire and his men, then spurred on to carry the message back to Alençon and the Bastard, to La Pucelle and Richemont behind them.

The scouts drew a picture of the site in the dust for La Hire, showing him every blind where the English secreted themselves. Now the old dog knew just how to deploy his men and was giving the orders to have them march double time towards Patay.

So near the Solstice, light lingered very late, washing the golden field, the heaps of armor, even the pools of blood with a fine peach glow. The French needed the light, to finish up the looting, the slaughter of the wounded, the collection of the few captives.

Only Fastolf, who'd been set to hold the distant ridge, had time to escape with about sixty of his men. Sixty out of an army of three thousand. The French had lost only three dead.

Sir John Talbot, the best English hope left in France, had been dealt a stunning blow to the head while turning to mount his horse. Even he'd had only so much warning before the attack had been upon him. A priest had been sent to him; he was not expected to live. If he did, by God, the French would set the ransom so high, he'd never see daylight save through dungeon bars again.

"We've repaid Agincourt—with interest!" more than one fellow exulted in Gilles' hearing.

It was true, he supposed, though even heaps of English corpses could never return his Amaury to him. The repair to his heart, he found, was not in the revenge, but in the sight of La Pucelle.

Richemont had ridden in late to Patay, almost too late to claim any booty or captives himself and thus repay his men their long march from Brittany. La Pucelle had come even later, the witches having had to hunt her soul back from the stag and into her own form again.

Now he saw her, riding slowly here and there on her great white horse, speaking to this group of men and that. She seemed tired, weighted. But maybe that was just the way he felt.

She pulled up her reins near the crossroads and watched as a line of ten or so English prisoners was led, hobbled and bound, to their night's rough and open prison. One of them, sorely wounded in the leg and still oozing blood, could not keep up with the rest.

The captor, a man of lower nobility, had the patience of a child who's had too many sweets. With the butt of his sword, he smashed in the *goddam*'s head.

A great cry pierced the field that had gone the color of thick cream. It wasn't the *goddam*. He had slumped, unconscious and dying where he fell.

It was La Pucelle.

In a moment, she slithered off her horse. With one phrase she berated the captor and sent him for a priest. He went, stupefied.

With the next phrase, she was soothing the fallen Englishman. He couldn't have understood her French, even if there'd been life left in him to fill his ears. But there he died, where Gilles thought he must die himself, his smashed skull bloodying La Pucelle's breastplate while she promised him a better hereafter.

Yann was the priest who arrived at the scene even before Gilles himself did. La Pucelle's eyes, when they met his, were those of a deer, hunted, frightened, brimming with tears.

When the magic left her, she was only a simple peasant girl after all.

Thirty-Second Antiphon

Banner Grasped Like a Parent's Hand

Four days after Patay, on a hillside overlooking Châteauneuf and the Loire, we celebrated the liberation of yet another town—and the Solstice. I burned the sacrifice of dogs and cats in the wicker cage, as has ever been the custom. And La Pucelle dared Gilles to jump over the fire with her—the dark one, handclasped with the light—while the flames were yet knee high.

Elsewhere, with the army, most of the commanders, even Gilles, felt that the next logical step would be to march on Paris. As news of La Pucelle's victories spread, English garrisons all the way north to the capital's walls abandoned their fortresses like birds their nests at the approach of winter. The Parisians themselves expected the attack daily, so it was rumored, burning their watch fires and scurrying to repair their defenses.

But "Rheims first," La Pucelle insisted. "It is the will of My Lord that the Dauphin be anointed first."

In the end, all France, from the Dauphin down, obeyed her.

Three short weeks after Midsummer and Châteauneuf, we were in Rheims. With Jehanne and her banner at their head, we had covered over seventy-five leagues of English-invested land. We covered it with the ease and pleasure, Gilles liked to say, of a summer's stroll through one's own park.

Charles made his triumphal entry into the city of his ancestors Clovis, Louis the Lion and Louis the Saint on Saturday, July 16, 1429. He kept vigil that night in the archbishop's T-shaped residence, the Tau Palace. And on the next day, in a ceremony lasting five hours, he would be crowned by the Grace of God, most Christian—and most Craftly—King of France.

Much of the needed paraphernalia for the rite remained in English hands, at the abbey of St. Denis near Paris. The treasury of Rheims cathedral did its best to provide substitutes: their best chalice for the royal one, a curtain rod, albeit set with precious stones, for the scepter, a hand-shaped reliquary for the ivory that traditionally held the King's baton. La Pucelle's sword, that of Charles Martel, stood in for the sword of Charlemagne.

But it was the chrism that was most important to the metamorphosis into a monarch of a man who just happened to be born with royal blood in his veins. By a miracle close to transubstantiation, his body would from that day forward be sacrosanct, moving under a canopy like the Host itself, able to cure the King's Ill, scrofula, with a touch.

And more than ever would his flesh be dedicated to the Land, as Her Sacrifice.

The moon had been full that night, the most powerful of nights. Most of the witches had gathered to celebrate in the fields outside the town.

Lauds had not yet begun when I returned to town. The lesser canons were still unwinding banners to hang from the stone ribs of the cathedral that Sunday morning. The weather promised to be bright, and it was already warm beneath the linden trees in the courtyard of the Tau Palace. So early, having never been to bed, I saw my milk brother off. He rode out the palace gate and towards the south, for he had been chosen, of all the lords of France, for a singular honor.

Not far beyond the eastern wall of the city was the abbey that treasured the bones of the Christians' saint who had also once died the Craft Sacrifice. St. Rémy had given his name not only to the city where he was buried, Rheims, but also to La Pucelle's birthplace, Domrémy, as well. Here, again, was pattern and cycle.

Within the chapel of St. Rémy abbey was kept a vial containing the heavenly oil. For just short of a thousand years, the

Kings of France had been anointed with this chrism upon their ascension. The miracle dated back to St. Rémy again. Christians believed he had received the vial on the wings of a dove directly from heaven when the necessary unguent had failed during his baptism of Clovis, the first Frankish King to accept Christ.

For the people of the Craft, there was no less power in Our Lady's messenger of a dove, in the emblem of anointing. And in Sacrifice.

For one thousand years, the oil had not failed.

Gilles, the lord of Rais and three other highly honored peers of the realm, the marshal de Boussac, sire de Graville and admiral de Culan, rode out of Rheims in full and polished armor, pennants flying. They were to serve as honor guard for the abbot of St. Rémy and his holy oil.

The lindens in the archbishop's courtyard were past their peak, but still heavy with humming bees. The sweet yellow pollen fell like rain, and clung unfading to the rough black wool of my robe. Their fragrance was sweet and golden, sticky in the nostrils.

There was a fountain in the yard as well, older than the cathedral that shadowed it, older than the archbishopric that tried to claim it with walls and with hard cobbles. Usually, water ran in a sluggish trickle from the ancient bronze statue of a Stag.

Workmen busied themselves about the source now, their clanking muffled by the early hour and deafening birdsong. By afternoon, the men would have the thing spouting red wine for all citizens to help themselves. These were the archbishop's men. The imagery was lost on them, no doubt: the King Stag making His people jolly, shedding His blood that they might know abundant life. Or, if the men did see something, it was the one-time Sacrifice of Christ, not that the shedding comes with every King.

I stood under the shedding lindens and watched Gilles and his companions leave. Their pennants caught the first of the sun. Shadows appeared suddenly, long and sharp, as the daystar made His first show over the palace roof.

There was no further place for me here. Christianity, meaning La Trémoïlle and the archbishop, had charge of Charles. They'd had him fasting, watching the night. But I hoped Christianity was so little different at this point from what I would have done, and since I'd had the first initiation of him, I let it be so. I went and found La Pucelle instead.

She stood before the cathedral, that grand edifice not quite completed, showing just how young this faith was here. A great, golden fleur-de-lis flag had been unfurled on each of the twin towers, over the scaffolding. The adjoining wall of the archbishop's palace ran up in small gray stones like a continuation of the cobbled square. The pigeons had settled themselves again after the passage of Gilles and the rest of the escort and seemed yet more cobbles. La Pucelle herself remained a flurry of indignation.

Within the last week or so, many souls had augmented her entourage. Deep in Burgundian lands as we had now pushed, news of her victories had reached even into the marches of Lorraine, to her home. Both her parents and two brothers, as well as a number of friends and neighbors had appeared seeking— What, who can say? They stood to the side of everything in one solid and unspeaking cluster. Wonder confused them, made them stupid.

La Pucelle had greeted them happily enough on their arrival. But she had little time or care to spare for these shadows from a time and place so far removed from her present concerns. It must have been a different girl, in a different life, who knew them.

And they, in their turn, could only stand and stare at her in her full armor, polished for a festival, the banner at her side. If she had died and come back to them an angel, they could not have been more amazed.

La Pucelle's present concern had nothing to do with her past, with Domrémy. Once I had nodded to these figures, I found little to say to them, either. Her concern held mine as well.

"Do you know where that absurd man in canon's robes wants me to stand for the ceremony?"

Her words came in a flood and to me alone. It was as if she suspected the relatives watching her in dumb wonder would not be able to understand her speech.

I looked in the direction she thrust her banner, used to finding English at the other end of such a violent gesture, although never for long. A quartet of men-at-arms in the Dauphin's blue and gold stood before the great cathedral doors. Their pikes saw to it that none of the crowd, already thronging at the steps, got to enter but those allowed by a small man in formal black at their center.

"He will not let you in?" I asked.

"Oh, he'll let me in all right, with a smile like pan drippings. But I have to sit where he tells me."

"And where does he tell you?"

"Not in any place of honor. Not even among the second rank."

I sought to calm her. A figure in full armor was frightening, even such a slight figure, pacing with the slam and crash of joint on metal joint. Some of the gathering throng pointed her out to one another, their whispers like the cooing of the pigeons. Some, no doubt, wanted to have her touch their rosaries for a blessing, wanted to kneel and touch the fringe of the banner.

At the one brave burgher who approached, she snapped, "Touch those beads yourself. That would give you as much blessing."

Nobody else dared.

Her family, to whom she might have appealed had her pride allowed her, continued to stare at her blankly. Having them see her thus only reinforced her anger. And, for their part, they would be lucky, crowding with the rest of the common folk, to squeeze into a place on the porch for the great pageant.

"Let me see what I can do," I said. I went to talk to the man myself.

She was right, of course. La Trémoïlle and the archbishop had charge of this rite, as I'd already decided. They had charge of the order of ceremony. This girl, her armor, her banner and the power of Craft it represented, would take no greater part than they could help. There was nothing I could do about it, either.

My "Outward shows are not important," only infuriated her more, as did my urging to come and take the place assigned to her with a good grace.

"My banner had part of this victory," she complained, magic's regard more to her than her own. "It is right that it should have a part of the honor."

It was right, but it wasn't politically expedient.

"Come," I said, taking her arm. "Come and take the place they've assigned you before the crowds are let in and you lose dignity shuffling with them."

She bowed her head under the gold-fringe tail of the standard, caught by a gentle breeze, and came.

"This wouldn't happen," she said in an undertone as we walked together, "if Gilles were here."

She was probably right. All the honor Gilles and Jehanne might have divided between them, the chamberlain chose to give to Gilles alone. Gilles was La Trémoïlle's kinsman, after all. His kinsman's honor was his own. And Gilles' soul, at least the part of it that fit on paper, La Trémoïlle carried, signed and sealed, within the broad expanse of his pelisse. Jehanne's he could not contain and he knew it. So she must be given all the less honor with which to play.

Nonetheless, La Pucelle meant more by her plaint than the simple expression of frustration with the Christian powers. I suddenly understood that her grief was not for the loss of honor, but for how it would reflect on the Craft. And on Gilles in particular.

Had my milk brother not been sent off to St. Rémy, he would have raised his own particular brand of havoc until he had divided the honor evenly between himself and the girl. Or given her more. But he had been sent away. And she felt herself unable to match such gallantry.

Sidelong, I studied the determined little chin, fighting to stop its own quivering, the ruffle of the spiky hair with the briskness of her step through the morning air. She missed Gilles more, perhaps, than she despised his cousin. She would not have missed her own shadow as much were she to find it suddenly not preceeding her in a long sooty streak across the cathedral square.

Hers was the cry of a child for her family in a time of deep disappointment. The only family she could truly love, because Gilles de Rais was the only family that understood her any more.

But because she was who she was, La Pucelle of the prophecy, she grasped the banner like one parent's hand. She let me take the other elbow and in we went to the great hollow of Our Lady of Rheims.

Thirty-Third Antiphon

Weight the Baton Doesn't Truly Have

I watched the four mounted noblemen holding a cloth-of-gold canopy. They carried it to snap smartly in the breeze, one at each corner, as they flanked and covered the abbot and his burden. The old man rode a horse as stolid and grey as himself and had donned his best robes for the occasion. Pictures of saints embroidered in threads of gold and scarlet ran down either open side of his cope. Sundering these bands, however, was something more precious still.

Mid-chest, from a silver chain nestled among the deep folds of his cowl, hung the holy relic. A frame the size of a dinner plate, seeded all over with gems, enclosed a platter of gold, likewise seeded. Within that nestled the silver and ivory figure of a diminutive dove, grasping in its talons a tiny vial of milky glass no bigger than a man's thumb, shaped much the same.

The abbot bent his bald and white-fringed head with the weight of his burden. The chain assured that his hands, mortal and palsied as they were, would not drop the relic. His care and humility were no less than mine would have been, charged with this heavenly balm.

The rising sunlight was blinding on the tissue over them as they ushered the chrism back along the route they had come. Monks of the house of St. Rémy streamed before and after them, chanting and smoking the way with tapers and incense. With a flight of pigeons came the heavy tolling of many bells.

At the cathedral square, the procession streamed straight up the wide, shallow stone steps, and through the great portals.

They moved beneath the unfinished spires, between the carvings of the Mother of God and the smiling angels. Gargoyles of cows, sheep and long-beaked birds peered down on the square, and the great rose window glittered inside like sunlight on living water.

By now, people of all estates thronged the church. They filled it even to the rafters and the gallery along which stained glass images portrayed a coronation, reflections of the present to shimmering eternity.

Gilles, his accompanying guard and the abbot did not dismount at the doors, but rode straight through and into the nave. Crowded as the space was, an awe-filled silence reigned, then aggrandized in the presence of beasts tempered to human mystery. Even muffled by carpets on the floor, every horse's footfall was heard. The warm wax of flickering candelabra, the heat radiating off the crowd and my own sweating skin found contrast in the vastness of the interior, where cool and darkness still prevailed.

The five horsemen rode straight to the high, Marian altar where, beyond the rail, Charles and the archbishop waited. Here, at last, noble youths in silken array stepped forward to take the canopy and the reins. They held the mounts, stifling their snorts and nervous shifting for the sake of heaven which oversees man and animal alike.

All dismounted, then knelt while the abbot progressed alone to the sanctum with measured steps. Gilles and the others of the escort stood again, at the spot where the floor remained bare of carpet and set with the ancient, magic, spiraling maze of mosaic.

I could tell he'd been looking for her from the moment he'd entered the portal. At first, he'd been blinded by coming from bright light to this darkness. Then, he'd had to set most of his concentration upon controlling his mount in the press of people and keeping his corner of the canopy upright at the same time. Rheims cathedral, packed with people, seemed small and close. Gilles would have had to look up in order to be reminded of just how insignificant humanity is.

She wasn't where he'd expected her, not as close to the sacred, not within the altar rail. I saw his moment of panic, when all Dauphins could go to hell but not his lady. At last he found her by her banner, rising up while the rest of the draperies hung down. She had managed to make it to the front row by her own determination, and I'd gone with her, though we'd faced the archbishop's scowl to do it. Gilles stabilized, as if he'd found his footing.

I knew the moment he caught her eye. Streaks of tears that had been pulsing down her cheeks in golden candlelight surged with renewed emotion. Then she looked away, back towards the pomp at the altar.

The smell of incense and of lilies on the altar cloyed my nostrils. It caught at the back of my throat and made me think I, too, must weep. For I remembered well the time when all this day was only longing, no more than the words of a forgotten prophet and a green-clad boy, blue lipped in the woods of a St. Stephen's Day. Charles the son of Charles the son of Charles came at last to the fullness of his time, claiming the throne that men and events had conspired to keep from him since the day of his birth. Against all the odds, he had done it. We had done it. Craft and coven still had force in the world of Christ and cathedral. My life that had begun commonly and in a swirl of agony and fire in the lonely wood had not been in vain.

Charles the Dauphin, seeming more tired and nervous than triumphant, made the oath to uphold the faith of his ancestors. As a Craftsman I thought of the cycles of pagans as well as the more recent line of Christians.

The duc d'Alençon knighted him, then Charles stood in nothing but a short silken tunic, his feet bare on stone. Slits in the tunic closed by silver cords marked the five places he must be anointed. When the archbishop had received the ampulla from the abbot, he unstoppered it. Within the cathedral space, the fragrance of lilies and incense intensified.

The archbishop took a golden needle and dipped it into the vial. A miracle: there was still oil renewed yet again after a thousand years. All along the aisles stretching now to the end of sight, people crossed themselves and prayed.

The archbishop mixed the tiny drop with other oil, newly consecrated, upon a palette. Then, with his thumb, he dabbed Charles on the head, chest, back, shoulders and finally elbows. From that day forth, Charles should always keep his head covered, for it was dedicated "as a pure Nazarite". The congregation chanted the anthem "They Are Anointing King Solomon" as of old.

After that, the silver cords were retied and a violet tunic placed over the white. Boots and the golden spurs went to his feet, to his narrow shoulders, a cope trimmed with ermine, the back an ocean of blue swimming with fleurs-de-lis. The scepter was placed in Charles' right hand, the baton in his left.

And then, at last, the crowning. They used a simple circlet of gold, lent by the cathedral canons for the occasion, not the more lavish emblem that rested still in English hands in St. Denis. And it slid loosely down upon Charles' small, close and newly cropped, insufficient head, caught only by his jutting ears.

Memories should have kept such shifts from the ideal from bothering me. My vision in the forest near Tours reflashed before my eyes, a vision of that little boy dressed in green, that same pale head crowned like the Stag with holly and ivy. As in everything to that point, I was ready to be taken out of myself and my personal struggle by the eternity of ritual—

Until, that is, I saw, of the twelve peers readjusting the crown there, each with a single finger, the prominence of Georges de La Trémoïlle and his lackeys.

Charles had sulked that he would rather not be crowned at all than have to endure the attendance of Arthur de Richemont, his own constable. So while Richemont lingered elsewhere, the constable's part was played by Charles d'Albret. La Trémoïlle himself stood in for the comte de Toulouse, Alençon for the treasonous duke of Burgundy.

I let my gaze drift back to the shaft of light that caught La Pucelle from a clerestory window. Only that way did I keep from choking on lilies and incense, grown suddenly too thick to breathe. As if they only stood to cover up the stench of death underneath.

To my surprise, and Gilles' as well, I think, after the coronation itself, my milk brother was among those called forward for further honors.

His young cousin Guy de Laval was knighted, then a baton was pressed into his own hand as he knelt.

"Gilles, sire de Rais." Charles' voice cracked with weariness as he read someone else's words from a crinkling paper. "We name you Marshal of France."

I saw the baton slipped into Gilles' hand. The metal was light and base, a cheap trinket from the bottom of the treasury's coffer. Perhaps it was also slick with sweat, with grease. It came straight from La Trémoïlle's hand into his own. For a moment, Gilles had to meet this cousin's piggy eyes. I saw him almost thrust the emblem back, there in all the gathered throng. He must feel himself unclean, as if he'd sunk his hands into a tub of rancid lard.

But then he managed to look ever so slightly back, towards me. Or rather, towards the gleam of white armor at my side, the limp dangle of La Pucelle's banner over my head. His face smoothed, as if he felt clean again.

As Marshal of France, he would have far more opportunity to help her, to help our cause. His access to supplies would be more direct, his orders would get through. La Trémoïlle could be more readily circumvented. Gilles could invite Richemont to the fore himself, for Marshal and Constable traditionally worked closely side by side. As if an emblem of this, the King added a gift of one thousand *livres* to the appointment on the spot, a thousand *livres* Gilles could afford better than the royal coffers.

Gilles bowed his thanks, down to the knees in his full black armor, both to Charles and to his cousin. Gilles grasped the baton firmly. But I saw it wobble in his hands as they failed to give it weight it didn't truly have. Triumphant trumpet blasts filled the airy vaults overhead.

Chapter Thirty-Seven

The End

When all the public honors had been handed out, the feasting began. Whole oxen roasted in the streets. There were hares poached in wine, puddings, sweetmeats and, of course, flowing blood-red wine, for every citizen and visitor to Rheims that day. With only the pretense at greater decorum, the upper echelons of nobility retired to the banquet hall for the coronation feast.

As newly anointed King, Charles had to sit alone on the dais against a fireplace, empty for the season, but plastered with elaborate renditions of the archbishop's arms. Great, dark beams stretched over the rest of the hall, halfway up a high, arching wood ceiling. Tapestries portraying the dormition of the Virgin and the nativity hung against floods of royal fleur-de-lis clothing the walls.

But Gilles sat beside La Pucelle at the table just below the King's, and that was enough Blessed Virgin to fill his senses.

She had changed out of her armor and into the green doublet that suited her so well. He could hardly take his eyes off her. Yet, dazzled though he was, he noticed that she was picking at her food like Charles, whose every lonely mouthful was dictated by ritual.

Gilles tried to press more food on her, the tastiest tidbits: fresh summer figs, some of the grilled lamb kidneys and liver wonderfully flavored with garlic and rosemary. She smiled and thanked him, but would not.

He thought he detected the reason: inactivity. It always

preyed upon her. Even celebration of what had been done to this point, a Craftsman's balance, had no place for her.

"Don't fret, my Lady," he said. "Charles must only spend a day or two in the neighborhood here doing his Kingly duty, showing himself off and touching the sick for scrofula. Then we'll be riding off again."

Her smile broadened a moment, but she showed no teeth, and when she spoke, it was with a stifled sigh.

"I have done all my Voices instructed me. They tell me nothing more. Perhaps ... perhaps this is the end."

He said something rallying. Of course it couldn't be the end. It was, in fact, only the beginning.

The thought that distressed her brought in contrast a brightness to him he had to work hard to conceal and so keep in rhythm with her mood.

Perhaps, indeed, it was an end, as she sensed. Perhaps it was the end of one form of life, a hard, disciplined life that had allowed her no glance either left or right. A very linear, Christian life, actually, needed to pull the off-kilter world into balance again.

But the end of one sort of life, the Craftsman knew, was the beginning of another.

Perhaps now the Maid could move on to something different, a little less hectic, a little less driven.

Perhaps she could leave her virginity behind.

Gilles was careful not to hint at such thoughts, even in the raise of a brow. Such change, necessary as it was, never came without grief, and the ancient wisdom let a person grieve, to turn the world to joy once more, like day following night.

For lack of a better disguise, Gilles gestured to a passing serving man to fill his goblet once again. But the man didn't have a napkin and ewer after all. He approached with a message instead.

"His Majesty's pleasure, if you, La Pucelle, and monseigneur de Rais would be so good as to wait on him."

Gilles looked to the dais. Charles had vanished. La Pucelle, at least, seemed relieved to be doing something. She shoved back her chair, and Gilles followed her and the messenger from the table. They made their way among feasting guests, through a door to the side of the great fireplace behind the King's table.

The door led to a small anteroom where Charles awaited them. While the servant left them, closing the door behind him, La Pucelle fell to her knees. She lifted the ermine of Charles' pooling train to her lips, releasing incense and the smell of lilies trapped within its folds to the close air.

Gilles followed her example, all the while struck by how, even crowned, this man had the air of a skinned rabbit. The lord of Rais remembered that this man's soul had fit into the body of a goat. And a flea.

"It is our desire," Charles said, "to give you, Jehanne La Pucelle, more sure token of our appreciation for all you've done on our behalf. Therefore, I elevate you, and all your family after you, to the nobility. More, I allow you to bear, within your escutcheon, the fleur-de-lis of a prince of the blood."

La Pucelle said nothing. She remained kneeling, her face buried in her clasped hands.

Great honor indeed, Gilles thought, surprised himself to silence. Had the chrism truly the power to alter a man so?

Or—did Charles have ulterior, more self-serving motives?

The instant he asked himself the question, Gilles understood. For a dark figure—the Man in Black—stepped out of the shadows at the far corner of the little room where the mass of Charles' robes had kept him hidden.

It was Yann.

And in his hand was the ritual knife.

With no further explanation, and as if pressed by other matters, Charles loosed his laces. He pulled back first the violet tunic, then the white silk underneath, baring his left arm.

"Lady, do you agree?" Yann asked gently.

"Yes," she replied. "I am honored." And the priest helped her with her green sleeve.

Suddenly, Gilles was tearing at the tight gold lacings of his own black velvet cuff as well.

"Where she goes, I go," he declared, and thrust his arm towards his milk brother over hers.

Charles and Yann exchanged glances. Both then looked at La Pucelle.

"No, dear Bluebeard, you don't need to—" La Pucelle began.

Was everybody in on this but him? It meant nothing that, for once, she had endeared him. He thrust his arm more firmly under Yann's nose and cut her off.

"Of course, I do."

"Very well," Yann said.

"Very well, Marshal," Charles repeated, a slight smile playing about his thin, pale lips as if he were in the process of being flayed alive. "I don't see why you shouldn't set your black cross against fleurs-de-lis. Royal blood is grown so thin these days."

Three pairs of knees sank to the stone floor. Thrice Yann, muttered the ancient words. Thrice, his knife flashed. The first prick of pain grew as blood flowed and raw flesh met the air.

Twice, the flanges of wounds met, exchanged blood.

Yes, here was more than metaphor. Gilles did, in fact, feel something tingling through his veins. Something like molten rubies curled up his arm to his neck and flushed his face. He heard it throbbing, ringing in his ears, a different heartbeat, faster, lighter. He smelled it, acrid in his nose and flooding down the back of his throat as a syrupy taste.

Yann handed Charles a napkin first and helped him to bind it carefully. Gilles saw that the gash had been made on the same pale scar marking the last time blood had flowed from that royal body, in the crypt beneath Angers' chapel.

"We'll leave you," Charles said, quickly slipping silk and violet back into place. "Burgundy's envoy awaits us in the next room. Hearing of our success, we suppose he comes to sue for peace."

"Your Majesty." The three remaining witches bowed and Yann held the door for him to leave.

Yes, bind him first, Gilles thought, watching the King go. Charles won't suffer many more wounds like that in his shallow, narrow span of being.

Peace is it, then? Gilles looked down at La Pucelle. That

meant a new life, a very different life indeed. It would have come, then, even without the exchange of royal blood.

"I only brought one extra napkin," Yann said. "Excuse me a moment and I'll go for another."

Gilles and La Pucelle stood alone, together. She'd been trying to stop the flow of blood from her arm with the fingers of her other hand. She licked at those fingers now, like a child cleaning her hands of honeyed sweetmeats.

Gilles saw the rosy smear on the surprising smooth pallor of her inner arm. He found saliva running over his teeth.

On his own arm, the trickle of blood wicked from hair to dark hair. Like some beast, ravenous but methodical.

Then, at the same moment, the two of them had the same idea. Her open hand came towards him and he sent his to her. The grasp of her strong little calloused fingers on his elbow was like iron bands. He shifted his own hand, jostling his grip for better, tighter purchase, on the magic of her joint.

The lips of their wounds met, and the wonderful shock of it nearly sent sense from his head.

The dark of her eyes widened even as he met her gaze, and threatened to swallow him whole. He saw her lips twitch, as if at a joke, as if she wanted to whisper something in his ear. He bent a little to hear it—and found the pressure of her mouth hard against the stubble of his cheek, partly on his beard where the blue mark burned, partly on his lower lip.

Then Yann was back in the room and they separated. The moment was past, save for a brief shortness of breath Gilles heard in both of their throats.

Yann didn't meet their eyes, but busied himself binding linen to flesh. Nonetheless, Gilles could read his thoughts as if he spoke them aloud.

Now the two of them, Gilles de Rais and Jehanne La Pucelle, had the blood royal in their veins.

Either one—or both—could die the Sacrifice.

AFTERWORD

Margaret A. Murray's books *The Witch Cult in Western Europe* and *The God of the Witches* were the immediate inspirations for The Joan of Arc Tapestries. I am perfectly aware that no respectable scholar since the 1970s has taken her thesis seriously, but this didn't stop me from setting off on my quest. I write fiction, after all.

The longer I live in Joan's world, however, the more convinced I become that it did not hold to the uniform faith the Catholics who sainted her in 1920 would have us believe. In the European farm village where I lived as a child, there was more to do with hawthorne on the cow byre than with any biblical apostles and tongues of fire at Whitsun. I am certain this was even more the case six hundred years before, in the priest-neglected farm village of Domrémy where Joan grew up. Once I'd begun to look for it, sometimes the events of her well-recorded life ring through the Christian gloss with such paganism that I get chills.

The greatest shift I've had to make to fit magic to reality in this volume is Joan's entry into Orléans: I'll confess to moving it by some forty-eight hours from the April 29th celebrated in Orléans even today, in order to allow her to keep May Day outside the city.

I am indebted to hundreds of authors besides Dr. Murray for my research. Not counting general works on magic, folk belief and medieval life, there is more written particularly on Joan than on any other person between Jesus Christ and Napoleon Bonaparte. Interested readers should have no trouble finding plenty to occupy them, but I should mention in particular W. S. Scott's *Jeanne d'Arc* with his excellent maps, *Joan of Arc: A Military Leader,* by Kelly Devries, and *Joan of Arc: Heretic, Mystic, Shaman*, by Anne Llewellyn Barstow. The Osprey Publishing account of *Orléans 1429*, by David Nicolle, is also useful with its wonderful illustrations and its suggestion—with which few other accounts, "clouded by pious legend," agree—that the attack on Saint Loup may have been a diversion to allow the troops from Blois to enter the town.

Please note that I have dated the events as the Christian calendar did in the fifteenth century. The new year began with April rather than the Gregorian calendar's January, so that the first three months of every year are counted with what we consider to be the previous year.